WINDSWEPT

DANCE OF THE ELEMENTS

BOOK III

A.M. DEESE

This is a work of fiction. All characters and events portrayed in this novel are either products of the author's imagination or are used fictitiously.

WINDSWEPT
DANCE OF THE ELEMENTS, #3

Maps by Tiphaine Leard
Cover design by Little Forest Cat Designs
Formatting by Kingsman Editing Services

Printed in the United States of America
First Edition May 2022
ISBN: 978 1 957 412 03 0

www.amdeese.com

This book is for anyone trapped in a beautiful prison.

Sing free.

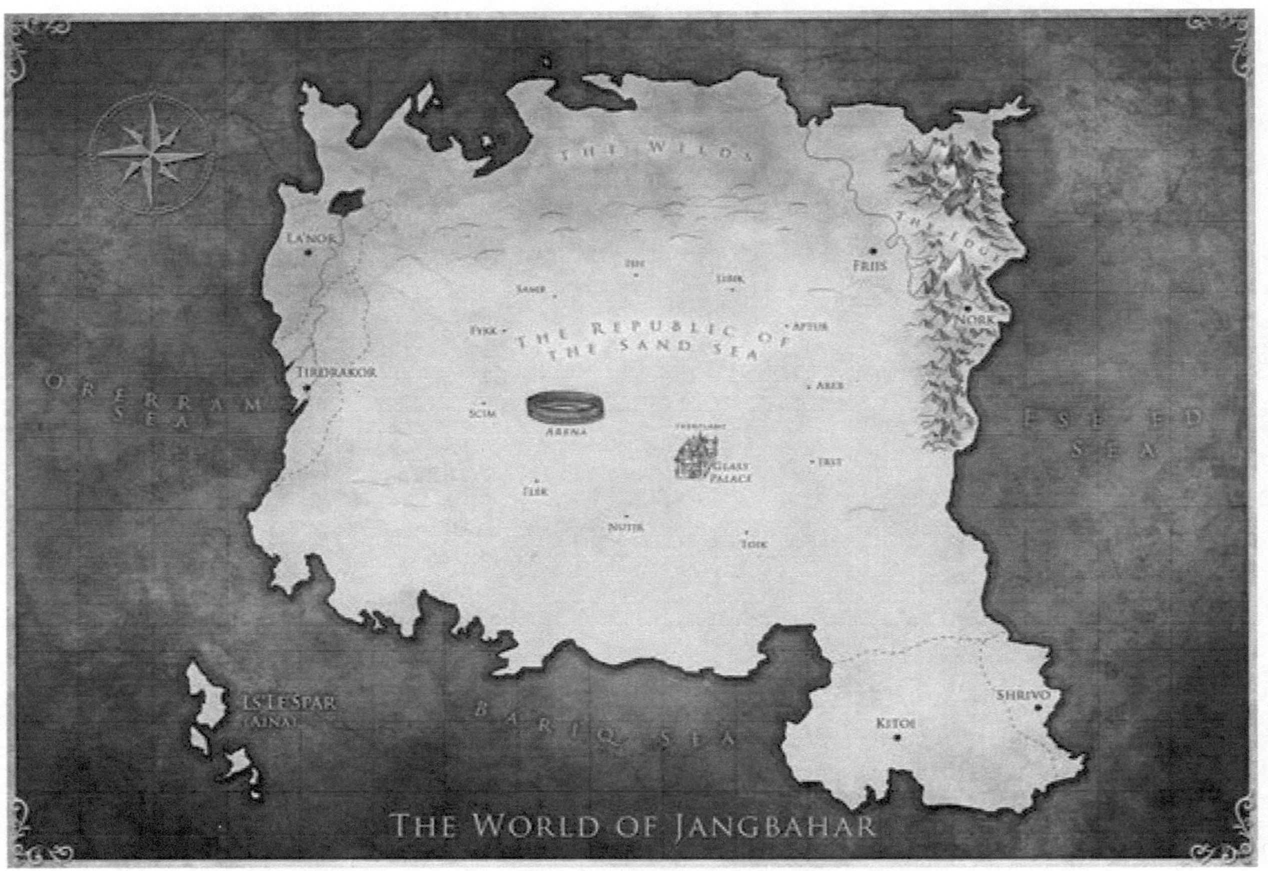

THE WILDS
THE REPUBLIC OF THE SAND SEA
ORERRAM SEA
ESE ED SEA
BARIQ SEA
LA'NOK
TIREDRAKOR
IS'LE SPAR (AINA)
FRIIS
NORK
SHRIVO
KITOI
SAMR
PYKK
SCIM
TILK
NUTIR
TOEK
APTIR
ABER
TRET
ARENA
GLASS PALACE
THE WORLD OF JANGBAHAR

KAY

Chapter One

*K*ay *remembered that smell. No* matter how many times she tried to forget, she remembered the smell. Of the North barn. Of Mama.

She could still smell smoke even though nothing was burning now, not up so high anyways. Not up in the sky from the back of the dragon. The dragon who had killed Ash. The dragon who changed everything.

Kay screamed, releasing a huge ball of flame. Inferno roared too. The sound vibrated throughout her entire body and she trembled, the realization truly sinking in.

She was riding a dragon.

She was finally free.

Kay had always wanted to ride a dragon. She had dreamed she would one day ride Rumble. She had spent hours scheming just how to convince Daddy to let her give it a try with the old family dragon. But Daddy was gone, gone forever—so were Mama and Rumble—and now that her dream was finally happening, it was all wrong.

The wind made her eyes water, or maybe she was crying. It was hard to see anything through the tears, so Kay dipped her head toward Inferno's neck and squeezed him tighter, pretending the thick coil of his neck was Daddy's chest. But Inferno wasn't her father; he was a mean beast who had killed her friends and many others. She felt bad at the thought. It wasn't fair to be mad at Inferno, not truly. He was just a dragon, trapped the same as she had been. She couldn't blame him for hurting people. Hadn't she done the same thing to escape those bad people?

The great fire still boiled within her, mixing with her own sense of heat. Kay was still a bit too frightened to reach for it again. It wasn't easy thinking about what had happened at the arena. She didn't like to think about how Ash had tried to save her, that he had shown her a way to get them out and she had failed. She had failed *him*. Because after he was gone, Kay could barely remember anything. She remembered feeling angry and scared and then she'd Breathed in the giant flame and she'd felt . . . super strong. Stronger than she had ever thought possible, even stronger than Daddy. The feeling had abated slightly, but she still felt prickles along her skin, still felt a new power coursing in her veins. It had felt good to scream. And good now to cry. So she didn't stop.

Kay hoped Inferno knew which way he was going. She felt him, not just underneath her, but she felt a part of him inside her mind, in her heart, an odd connection that hadn't existed before. It was a familiar feeling and yet hard to explain—like when she would notice her father or mother had walked into a room simply by feeling their presence. She felt Inferno now and wondered if she always would.

Kay was confused about many things. She didn't understand why it was so important for the scary people at the arena to watch Fire Dancers battle dragons. It was so mean to the dragons who were usually very nice. Rumble had been so nice that he had died protecting her. He had been her best friend.

Kay had felt a connection to many dragons during her young life but never like this. Not like what she felt to Inferno. She felt tied to him as if an invisible string pulled on her gut and her heart. Kay frowned. Did her connection to Inferno have anything to do with her Breathing in the Everflame? She trembled at the thought. She felt different the moment she'd Breathed in the giant fire.

What did I do?

If she really thought about it, Kay liked the way she felt with the power inside her. Stronger, faster, somehow *even more* special. She could feel it; she just *knew* it. In fact, Kay knew a lot of things she couldn't explain. She knew exactly how many people scurried in the streets far below them. She could sense the tiny spark in each of them, the spark of everything.

It was stronger in Inferno, of course, his spark a massive beating thing that called to her.

She felt him turning and realized he must have circled the city and still did as if looking for something. Suddenly, she felt desperately lost and alone, and it occurred to her that maybe Inferno didn't know where to go either.

Kay squinted, trying to see where they were from her aerial view. It was silly because she was unfamiliar with the streets of the Republic, and everything was pitch black anyway. Inferno dipped lower, gliding closer to the ground so they could get a better look. She wondered if Inferno could feel her thoughts, if that was why he seemed to follow her silent directions.

It was really dark with all the pits extinguished. *I must have Breathed all the fire in the city*, Kay thought with some awe. She glared into the void, barely making out the tiny scurrying forms. The arena should have been a giant shining beacon, but it was reduced to a pile of molten stone and smoldering glass. She swallowed. Were people still screaming or was she remembering their sound?

She had done a very bad thing.

The dragon left the arena behind them with a final indignant roar, flames erupting out of his mouth as he did so, and for one moment, Kay gasped at the destruction illuminated in rich orange light.

She would never forget it.

"I have to get out of here!" Kay screamed. She squeezed her eyes shut and clung to the dragon's neck. "I want to go home. I want to go home. I just want to go home." She would repeat the words as long as it took, if only they'd come true.

The city was behind them now. Kay didn't feel the spark of anyone else for some time and noticed that she had stopped crying a while back. Good. Tears were for babies, and Kay wasn't a little kid, not anymore.

Inferno flew toward home now. *Home.* And then she could make a plan. Mama and Daddy had always said they would be with her no matter what. Kay knew they hadn't meant to, but the promises were broken all the same. And what now? Even if she did somehow make it all the way back home, there was nothing for her there. She missed Mama terribly. She gave the best hugs. They always meant things would be better soon.

What would Mama want her to do?

Mama would want her to stay strong and find some good to do in the world. Mama was always saying things like that. Whenever Kay complained of boredom, Mama would tell her to go find something good to do for someone else. Well, she had done many bad things, and that could be the first thing she changed.

From now on, Kay vowed to be good. That meant no lying and

no stealing and definitely no burning down cities. She pushed the thought away again and focused on the present. Even if she didn't stay there, she needed to go home, Kay reasoned. All her things were there, and it would be nice to have some memories of her home before she once again left it behind forever.

And the dragon? She had sort of done a nice thing when she released him from the arena. Come to think of it, she'd probably managed to release all the arena dragons. At the very least she gave them the chance to escape, and that felt like a good thing too. She sat up a bit taller, once again enjoying the rushing wind on her face.

Inferno climbed higher in the sky, parting clouds, which surprised Kay when they felt wet. This . . . this was freedom. It felt better than she ever imagined. She let herself forget everything, and for just a moment, it was just Kay and Inferno in the wind and sky.

As dread often did, it sank its claws into her as she remembered the red-robes. The arena council had more than a passing interest in her activities. Kay remembered things differently now. Conversations and details from the past were more vivid. Before, she had heard things muffled and fuzzy, but now it was clear. The red-robes and that woman, her new "owner"—they would never allow Kay to live a simple life at home. They were probably on their way after her, even now. They couldn't beat a dragon though. And Kay was confident that no matter what other paths she chose to take, home was her first stop.

She was a little afraid if she thought about it. Home would be so different without Mama and Daddy there to greet her. The same accomplishment that she had worked so hard to achieve was the one that terrified her. How was she supposed to find peace in a home that was now empty? How could she be strong enough to live on her own?

It will be okay. And the voice in her head was Mama's.

She must have dozed off because when Kay opened her eyes, the sky was awash with hues of pink, orange, and golden yellow. Kay squinted, rubbing at her eyes. She'd fallen asleep, she realized, then flung her arms back around Inferno's neck. She'd fallen asleep while flying. What if she had fallen off? She shook her head, clearing away the horrific thought, and noticed that Inferno had started to make his descent. The slow fall caused a fluttering sensation deep in the center of her belly, and Kay suddenly became aware of how bad her thighs ached.

She wondered how much farther they were from home when she spotted a familiar stone well in a field of grass below them. Inferno landed with a gentle rumble, and Kay slid from his neck and pressed her face and hands into the field. The grass was prickly and wet, but Kay didn't care. Nothing else mattered in that moment, not her fears or her guilt or her worries for tomorrow. She had finally made it.

Home.

BESHAR

CHAPTER TWO

It had to be close to dawn by the time they finally emerged from the sewage tunnels and outside the capital city. One night. Albeit the worst night of his life, but in the span of a few short hours, his life was irrevocably changed. No longer Ninth of the Thirteen—no longer anything more than a desperate fugitive, truly—his entire life had been destroyed in the blink of an eye.

Beshar drew in his first ragged breath of fresh air and braced his hand on the metal grate for support. The Shadow Dancer had kept them at a fearsome pace, and he needed to catch his breath now that he could finally breathe without gagging. They had been in that sewer for *hours,* forced to double back and around after an inexplicable earthquake caved in one of the tunnels. An earthquake. In the Sand Sea. It was a bad omen. As if the night needed any more of them.

Doubling back had done more than cost them extra time in the sewers. Beshar knew that every second spent in the Republic brought him closer to his death. And after watching the horrific murder of the alttaw'am earlier that evening, Beshar would rather keep any more gruesome acts far away from him.

If only he'd had the time to go back to his apartments, if only for a moment. Just long enough to speak with Kenjiro and pack a change of clothing . . . perhaps grab a bottle or two of red from his cellar. Flames, but what he wouldn't give for some clarity on what the Everflame had in store for him. Would Kenjiro even be able to find him? Had he left the palace in time, or would he be detained once his disappearance was discovered? Would they manage an escape of their own?

Beshar's torch had extinguished at the same moment as the Shadow Dancer's. As if an invisible breeze had blown out both.

Beshar blinked.

He did not believe in coincidences. Neither did the Shadow Dancer, apparently, and he had forced them to run the rest of the way out through the sewer tunnels.

It was impossibly dark even outside of the tunnels, and if it wasn't for the sweet-smelling air, Beshar would have guessed them still inside. Why were all the pits extinguished? He had a nagging feeling deep in his gut that the cold pits were somehow connected to their extinguished torches. Sandstorms, this couldn't be good.

"We need to hurry."

"Go on without me." Beshar waved a hand in the direction of the man's voice. When would the flaming sun rise? "I need a moment, and I can find my man on my own." He reached for a scented handkerchief that wasn't there. Sandstorms, he needed a glass of wine.

"Abandoning you here would compromise my orders. You get ninety more seconds."

Beshar wondered idly if the man was really counting along in his head but took another deep breath, inhaling slowly and breathing out through clenched teeth. He hadn't given himself time to think of the horrific implications of his situation. He had been ousted by his fellow councilmen, only to be rescued from one ill fate and delivered to another. What did the Queen of Shadows want with him? Denir had hinted that there was a new game afoot, but he had done little to heed her warning, and now look where it had left him. He had thought the key players in this game all involved the arena council—so then how did the Shadow Dancers fit in? And why would the Queen of Shadows need him, of all people, to retrieve information on Jura? Somehow the queen was behind everything. Beshar just had to figure out what she was up to.

"Is this part of her plan too? The earthquake? The blackout?" Beshar couldn't help but ask his questions out loud.

"If you can talk, you can run."

The sun was beginning to turn the color of the sky from a deep purple to a muted gray. Beshar could barely make out the impatient thump of the Shadow Dancer's fingers against his leg. "Can't we walk for a bit?"

The Shadow Dancer sighed and pushed Beshar forward. "Just for a bit. We need to get you outside of Toik before nightfall."

Beshar allowed himself to fall into step beside the man. At least they were walking. He could just make out the silhouette of the Glass Palace behind him, and Beshar wondered if this would be the last time he saw his home. It seemed optimistic to expect they'd reach the borders of Toik within a few hours, but the Shadow Dancer did seem determined to keep them at a harried pace.

"So you're taking me to her then. To Kitoi," Beshar asked sometime later, mind still reeling. If the Queen of Shadows was sending him on a personal mission he couldn't refuse, that would be suicide. But going on this quest to retrieve Jura . . . just what did the queen hope to accomplish?

If she could send someone to retrieve Beshar, couldn't she just do the same for Jura? He voiced the question out loud, and the Shadow Dancer shook his head.

"It is not my place to question the motives of my queen. She has ordered me to retrieve you and see that you make it alive to the southern border of Toik. I will see my duty done and then I doubt we'll ever cross paths again."

"And Kenjiro, my man . . . he will meet us there?"

Was it his imagination or did the man just smirk at him? It was hard to read his expression behind the mask. At least the sun was finally rising.

"Your man was notified of the plans."

Beshar nodded. The Shadow Dancer picked up speed but kept the pace at a slow jog. Despite this, Beshar was soaked in sweat within seconds. Flames, he could smell himself. He needed a fresh steam and a glass of wine. How long would he have to wait before he could indulge in both?

"And what are the plans?" The words were rasped out between desperate gasping gulps of air. Flames, he would drink cictuss juice if it would sate this growing thirst. "I know, I know. I'm to find Jura and then wait for further instruction, but surely you can tell me what your queen's expectations may be?" Another desperate gasp for air. "I haven't got any influence over the daughter of the First or her father so I can't imagine how I can be of any help to a woman capable of blacking out an entire city." Beshar mentally begged the man to give him something to work with, but the Shadow Dancer remained stubbornly silent.

"Unless . . . she's not responsible for the blackout?" It was a gamble, but this time at least Beshar was able to read the man's expression. He watched the slight widening of the eyes, the subtle twitch to the Shadow Dancer's lips before he pulled them into a thin line.

"As I've said before, it is not for one such as me to question my queen's motives. If it were, believe that I would question why my queen sees any value in the likes of you." The Shadow Dancer sneered at him. "Now try to keep up."

Beshar blinked. He was unaccustomed to people speaking to him in such a manner. He wiped at his face, feeling grains of sand cut into his skin, and wondered if he had left a streak of dirt on his face. Not that it mattered at this point when he so desperately needed to wash himself. Not when he had already been reduced to nothing. No longer Ninth of the Thirteen, what was he now? Other than a sweaty, stinking mess?

AMIRA

CHAPTER THREE

The stone was heavy in her pocket, warmed from her hand. Amira's fingertip traced the smooth edges, trailing around and down before she realized she was fidgeting. She slid her hand out of her pocket and intertwined her fingers.

Somehow, she had been elected to wait for the sea peoples. She had been waiting for days. Ten of them to be exact. She couldn't blame Tylak for rushing off like he had—she had wanted to go after Jura too—but Tylak had insisted that Amira needed to stay behind and make further arrangements with the sea princess. He said that she was the only one who could do it, that Jura was counting on her.

Tylak didn't say it out loud, but he didn't have to; Amira *owed* it to Jura. Or at least, Tylak had certainly made her feel that way. And maybe he was right. Jura wouldn't have gone to Kitoi if it weren't for her. And Amira never would have been taken if she hadn't been such a brat and insisted that Father take her along. She shook her head. She didn't want to think about the loss of her family. When she did, she felt herself spiraling back down a deep well of darkness and depression. She worried if she gave into it, she would never leave.

Her life would never be the same. Her family was gone. Tylak had filled her in on that bit too.

He'd barked out a few other random orders—he was terribly bossy for someone with a slave name—but Amira had done little other than nod her acceptance. Besides, she didn't feel much up to giving out any orders.

I am the first daughter of the Third of the Thirteen, she reminded herself. She would do whatever it took. But then the memory of Tylak's awkward apology rushed forward once again, and she swallowed against the push of bile. Her father had been the head of the household, and he and Antar were both gone. What did that make her now, other than a lost daughter of the Republic?

It was nearly dawn. Tylak and his companions had likely made it out of the capital by now and were probably well on their way north. That's where Tylak said he was headed. North and then east, toward the great mountain range known as the Edge. It was the logical place to look for her considering Jura had quite literally been carried away.

Amira had heard of the aliferous, of course, the way children believed stories of distant magic lands and of creatures from other worlds . . . but that didn't mean that she believed in their existence. No one did. These creatures weren't like the elusive Shadow Dancers; this was an entire race of people who left no evidence of their disappearance. History had credited stories of the aliferous to old folk tales and legend. There was no actual evidence of a race of flying bird people and yet, well it was hard to argue against facts. Jura had been taken into the sky.

Markhim had gone with her, so she wasn't alone. There hadn't been enough time for the girls to properly catch up, and Amira hated that. She had so many questions. She had noticed Jura's flirtation with the Light Guard, if one could call it that. Her friend's shyness had always been painful to watch, but that was before. It had been nearly three months since Amira was first taken, and in that time, Jura had seemed to change into a completely new person. She was more confident, and she seemed stronger, taller even. Amira's mouth quirked up at the thought. Jura would get a laugh out of that; she was never seen as tall. She was just awkward and shy and . . . sandstorms, but Jura had *two* boyfriends. She hadn't even had one when Amira last left her. Although her choice of suitors was odd, a Shadow Dancer and a Light Guard, it was clear both men were in love with her.

Jealousy, sharp and swift, stabbed into her gut before it was replaced by self-loathing. Imagine being jealous of Jura who had done nothing but fight for Amira and their friendship. Who, even now, was kidnapped and taken who knew where, experiencing terrors known only to the Everflame.

The disappearance of the eternal flame was another matter altogether. It was terrifying.

An invisible pressure pushed into her temples, and a slight buzzing noise tapped against her eardrums. The stone, which seconds before had felt as cool as a winter night, turned hot, nearly burning her hand. She released it with a short gasp, and the buzzing stopped.

Amira shivered despite the lack of chill. She had taken to squeezing the stolen stone whenever she felt anxious, which, if she admitted it to herself, was more and more often these days. She still wasn't quite sure why she had taken the thing, but she couldn't deny that she had felt drawn to it that night and every night since.

She often held it, wondering about its significance. Tonight was the first night she'd felt any change in the stone. She couldn't have imagined its warmth. She reached for the stone again, fingers hesitant as they stretched toward the smooth surface. But the stone was unassuming and cool to the touch. Just a pretty stone, nothing more.

She sighed. Maybe she was going mad. That would explain everything and made a sandstorm's worth more sense than she had somehow stolen a magical rock. But . . . was the idea so crazy?

There was magic in this world, more than she had ever imagined. Why shouldn't this stone be as special as she felt it to be?

The sun peeked over the horizon. It wouldn't be much longer then. Amira should be exhausted but she wasn't, adrenaline still coursing through her veins from her earlier adventures and the anticipation of what lay ahead.

Not that she thought of them as adventures. No, the last few months had all been an extended nightmare. For weeks, Amira had cried herself to sleep, believing she would never see her home and family again. Sandstorms, she was thinking of home again. What had truly happened to her family? Her home? Amira had been able to learn little. Tylak had confirmed her father's death and that of Antar, though the reasons were all a bit fuzzy. Her family hadn't been killed so someone else could move in Rank. No, her family had been murdered so that the other Amira could gain Rank.

Her stomach rolled at the thought, and she wrapped her arms around her middle in an effort to stop the nausea.

There was no ignoring it. Not anymore. The horrible truth Amira didn't like to think about. Not only was there someone out there who was responsible for the death of her family, but this person was out there, living her life and wearing her face.

Alttaw'am. A doppelgänger of its victim. The alttaw'am used dark magic to steal the looks of its prey by digesting their blood. The old wound on her shoulder burned with a sudden intensity, the pain just as sharp as it had been all those weeks ago at the market.

Don't think about it, she told herself. *Don't think about the alttaw'am living your life, wearing your face. Don't think about it. Don't. They will arrive soon.*

She was tired of waiting, lost in her thoughts and doing nothing. It was too dangerous for her to remain in the city proper, and Tylak had suggested she rent a room in Opyak, the tiny port city on the Bariq Sea. He'd probably given her every water chip he had, and in months past, Amira would have laughed at such a pitiful amount. But that Amira was gone now. So much had happened that she doubted that girl would ever come back. Instead, Amira had taken the chips with a solemn thank you and promptly spent it all just by booking a private room for ten nights. The room was tiny and smelled of rotting fish, but Amira had been grateful for the sleepless nights. Despite everything, she was still free.

If they don't arrive at dawn or dusk by the tenth day, they aren't arriving at all.

That's what the old man, Peppik, had said to her before leaving. He had an accent that should have been familiar to her, but she had trouble placing it. The man had seemed a strange choice for Tylak's companion. He was an odd fellow, fidgety and sneaky. Amira didn't trust him. But then, she didn't trust many people. She was glad Tylak had insisted he follow him because for a moment it had appeared as though the man had meant to stay behind with Amira, and she couldn't have handled that. In any case, it gave her something to do, and she had spent the last few days sneaking out to the beach to scan the horizon.

She wasn't sure what she would do after this morning when the sea people didn't arrive. Tylak had been emphatic that Amira convince them to their side, the side of the Republic. He said Jura's plan counted on the aid of the sea princess. He'd called her those words exactly. Was she truly waiting to meet a princess whose realm was the sea? And how was Amira supposed to convince such a person to their cause? Amira didn't even know what their cause *was* — only that her home and the lives of everyone still in the Republic relied on her. Those had been Tylak's final words to her, delivered just after his friend's ominous prediction.

Convince them to follow you to the Republic. Jura and I will meet you there. Everyone's life is at stake.

No pressure though, right?

Now it seemed she'd spent the last week and a half waiting in vain. She sighed. She had no water chips and less than a skein of water left. Certainly not enough to travel back to the Republic on foot, but perhaps she could barter it for transportation . . . wait. What was that?

There. In the distance, two tall figures approached. Amira lifted her chin. So the old man had been right. They arrived with the dawn on the tenth day.

Even if she hadn't had a previous, albeit brief, encounter with them before, Amira would have marked the couple as outsiders. They were far too tall to be people of the Republic, and once they grew closer, Amira was struck by the startling shade of the women's eyes. She had never seen a color so light a shade of green before.

She was staring, she realized, so she lifted her chin in greeting.

"Greetings . . . Your Majesty? Is that how I address you?" Amira's fingers signed the traditional greeting, twirling on instinct despite the fact that she hadn't needed to be so formal in months.

The sea princess raised an eyebrow.

"You may call her Mistr—"

"Coral will do, thanks," she interrupted her man. He stood just a step behind and to her right. His back was so straight that, if she didn't know any better, Amira could be convinced the man was a statue. He was certainly beautiful enough to be one. The man's chest was bare, and she could see every line on his stomach. Amira shook her head. Were all of the sea people perfect-looking?

Amira realized Coral studied her as well so she gave the woman her full attention.

"Well?" Coral asked. There was an air of expectation about her expression.

"Well, what?" Sandstorms, but she really did have the most extraordinary eyes. They were prettier than Jura's.

"Well, I assume you're here to escort me to her?" Coral blinked. "To Jura? Am I saying the words correctly? I haven't spoken your language in years but—"

"No!" Amira took a deep breath. "I mean, I understand you. It's just that . . . Jura is gone."

Coral exchanged glances with her companion before she took a menacing step forward. "What do you mean, gone? And my parents' murderer?" She narrowed her eyes. "What of him?"

Also gone. Amira swallowed hard to stop herself from saying the words out loud. "Let me explain. Please, just listen." She hurried on when it appeared Coral wanted to say something. "Something happened after you left. Almost right after you left." She glanced at Coral. Her gaze was thunderous.

Amira frowned at the ground before blurting out, "A person with giant wings swooped down and took her away, into the sky. Markhim tried to stop them—he grabbed her leg . . . they took him too."

"Taken by a person with giant wings?" Coral laughed. It was shrill and wild. And apparently not very genuine.

She raised a hand to push back her curls, but Amira saw the hand and fell to the floor, flinching at the upcoming blow.

"Get up. I'm not going to hurt you for such a wild lie."

But Amira couldn't get up. She couldn't move. She remembered Kuru's fists. She remembered tender strokes from the icy metal blade of his knife. Amira trembled and didn't respond when Coral asked her if she was okay. The pressure had returned to her temples. A phantom headache, or perhaps memories of Kuru's violence toward her. The crushing blows to the back of her head. The buzzing sound. It had returned in full force, rattling her eardrums, shaking her to her core. Someone was speaking to her, the sea princess, but the thought was dull against the frenzied whispers tapping in Amira's skull.

Amira couldn't hear anything but the sound.

Soft, cool hands cupped her face.

"You're safe. Shh." The buzzing stopped, replaced by the gentle sound. "Shh, you're safe. I won't hurt you, and I'll be damned if I let anyone hurt you like that again. You're safe."

Amira believed her. The memories quieted. She accepted the young woman's hands and allowed herself to be pulled up to her feet. She wriggled her fingers, willing away the ache that had come over them, likely from clutching the stone too hard during her fit.

"I'm sorry," Amira mumbled.

"Are you okay?" Coral's companion had moved when his mistress did, and he now stood within arm's distance of Amira. She hadn't even noticed he was there.

Amira nodded, but his attention was directed at the scars around her wrists. She wondered what she must look like to them, half-starved with wounded eyes and hacked hair.

"There's nothing to apologize for. I find her scary, too, sometimes." He winked. "My name is Kale."

She took another deep breath. Her heartbeat was almost back to normal.

"I meant what I said. No one is going to hurt you." Coral took a few steps back, gesturing for Kale to do the same. "But we do need you to trust us enough with the truth."

Amira lifted her chin and folded her arms across her chest. The motion was familiar, something the old Amira would do. She felt like two people, riven by the trauma and stress. She would never be the same—she knew that—but in the quiet hidey-hole of her rented room these last ten days, Amira had almost convinced herself that she could be herself again.

"It wasn't a lie." She forced herself to keep her shoulders back and met Coral's eyes. "I know that it sounds outrageous, and I know that you've only come here so that you might seek revenge, but I'm asking you to trust me."

Her arms fell to her side as she began to pace.

"I know that I haven't earned your trust, that my people haven't earned your trust, but please, look into my eyes and see the sincerity there. Jura is a good person, and she didn't leave of her own accord. She was terrified. I could hear it in her screams, and yes, I *know* it sounds unbelievable, but the person who took her had wings. There were two of them, and they both had wings, and they carried her into the sky. I don't even know if she's still alive or . . ." Amira trailed off, still not willing to say the words out loud. Jura was fine. She had to be.

"Jura wanted us to work together. She told me that you want revenge against the Queen of Shadows. I do too. She also told me about what happened at the party, how you were taken prisoner and sold as a slave. I know how that feels. I know what it's like to watch helplessly, to have your freedom stripped away by another. I know what it's like to lose family, to have everything taken from me, everything! I know what it's like to thirst for revenge." Amira stopped pacing. Coral and Kale stood close together, watching her.

"So the aliferous are back," Coral finally said.

Amira's shoulders sagged in relief. "They are, and I think their arrival means it's time to agree that something is happening in our world. Somehow Jura, your family, and I are all connected."

Kale nodded. "It makes sense. Why would the aliferous come back now? After all these years? And to come back simply to retrieve a person. It definitely means something."

Coral rolled her eyes. "Of course it means something. The question is *what*?" She made a sound in the back of her throat that was very similar to a growl. "How are we all connected? We will of course exchange information should any news occur, but I think this means I should return to my people immediately."

"What? You can't leave! We need to stick to Jura's plan. We need to get to the Republic and draft a new peace treaty. We need to get ahead of this war before it starts."

Coral smiled, but her eyes were sad. "I admire your passion, I do. But I agreed to stay and work with Jura, First of the Republic. Now that she's gone with no known time of a return . . . it's just too risky. I need to think of my people."

"Then think of them! Think of what it was like to be forced into a tiny aquarium because that's what's in store for your people if we don't do something about it!"

"Careful. That almost sounded like a threat, and I would hate to regret my promise to never see you hurt." Coral's green eyes seemed to darken as they stared into her own. Amira unclenched her fists.

"It wasn't a threat. These are just the awful facts. There is so much going on in the Republic, and we can do something about it. Now, together. I know I'm not Jura, but that doesn't mean we can't still stick to her plan. The Queen of Shadows is invested in the

Republic. She has to be—otherwise why start this war in our name? You think the kidnappings of your people will stop just because you're aware of their source? That's not true, and if you ask yourself, you can admit you knew that too. Please, I'll beg if I have to because I know that what I'm saying is right." She took a step forward, resisting the urge to take Coral's hands in her own. "*Please.* I need you. Help me change the world."

Her impassioned speech surprised even herself, and in that moment, Amira once again felt her old confidence.

Coral narrowed her eyes at her. "You're just full of surprises, aren't you?"

"Does that mean you'll help?"

Coral spit into her hand and thrust it out toward Amira. Amira stared at the hand before slowly lifting her own. Should she spit too? It seemed a waste of water. Before she could decide, Coral slapped her hand, the grip slick with sweat and spittle.

"I'll help," Coral answered.

It was done.

TYLAK

CHAPTER FOUR

Jura had wind magic. She was as fast as the wind, and those bird people had taken her into the sky . . . It was the only logical explanation. Peppik still seemed to need convincing. The man had balked at the distance they would need to travel, had even suggested they wait for Jura's imminent return. While Tylak appreciated the confidence the older man held, he couldn't stay and wait for her. Not when he could be doing something to get her back.

He had left as quickly as he could, practically dragging Peppik along with him. The man could speak Friisan, and he would need the interpretations, assuming they made it that far. He also assumed Ichiro and Jiro would separate once they returned to the Republic but was at least happy they intended to guide them back. Not that Tylak needed guides, exactly, but he had given all his water chips to Amira, and Peppik could turn stingy when it came to sharing. The Samur were excellent desert hunters, finding food as though their people were made to hunt this land, which Tylak supposed was entirely true.

They made good time, sticking to the trade route and traveling by night to stay away from any who might recognize Tylak as a wanted man. Tylak had a sneaking suspicion Peppik might have more than one wanted sign of his own. The foursome nearly made it to Toik before they had to trade for more supplies. Tylak was keen to get water for the group before they reached the inner perimeters of the Republic where the cost of water tripled.

Aside from the much-needed water supply, Tylak was eager to see what sort of information he could gather about recent events. He didn't care for the sudden disappearance of all that fire or for the fact that Jura seemed to have manifested yet another power. If only they'd had a chance to talk before she'd been carried away.

News of the Republic was grim. It was said the arena was in ruins, burned and destroyed. Frenzied dragons had burned entire city blocks to the ground during their escape, and the city was in shambles, the previous week spent entirely in repairs. The arena would take years to rebuild to its former glory, such was its destruction.

An explosion of some sort—there were few details as most of those attending the event had been destroyed with the arena.

His brother...Tylak didn't like to think of his brother. He pictured himself sifting through the decimated arena proper, looking for a familiar pointy chin, for steely gray eyes that mirrored his own. No, he couldn't think of that.

Some of the Fire Dancers had escaped, they said, or were missing—the body count didn't match the census. Tylak wondered if his brother was among those who had fled for the Wilds and freedom when they could. He wondered if Sykk also journeyed north or if he had died years ago. It seemed now he would never know.

It was easy to leave the trading post after that. The arena was gone, truly gone, and with it was any chance he had of ever finding Sykk. The only ties he had left in this world were to his doddering follower, Peppik, and Jura, the woman he . . . loved? What did he feel for her? The emotions were conflicted, but Tylak knew he would journey to the Edge and back for her. Was that love then? Burn it all, he didn't know. But he would be a flaming fool if he didn't go after her and bring her back.

It was almost as if he'd summoned her to him. He heard it then, barely a whisper in the breeze. Her voice. Flames, he even smelled jasmine. It was her, somehow speaking to him in the wind.

I'm safe. I will come back to you.

He had stopped so abruptly, the man behind him smashed into his back.

Tylak snorted, though he had barely felt it. He continued forward with a decidedly new pep to his step. He would swear he could still smell her, impossible as the thought was. Had he done that somehow by thinking of her? Had she been able to use her wind magic to reach him? Could she do it again? He stopped, tilting his head to the side, listening for a whisper, straining to feel the slightest breeze.

Peppik smashed into him again.

Tylak let out a frustrated sigh that bordered on a growl. "I'm not invisible."

"You're not many things," Peppik grumbled in response. Tylak would have flinched at the almost insult if he hadn't just heard her voice.

"Jura is safe. She just spoke to me." The man's grip on his arm was sudden and vice-like. Tylak yelped in pain, but Peppik didn't seem to notice.

"What did you just say?"

"Jura. I just heard her voice. I think she spoke to me with the wind somehow. I know that sounds crazy, but I've got this theory that—"

"The winds carry truths from beyond where the eye can see," Peppik interrupted. He released his hold on Tylak's arm.

"So you agree then? Jura has wind magic?" Tylak rolled his shoulder, resisting the urge to shake his arm as well. Peppik had a deadly grip for one who appeared so old. How old was Peppik anyway? He was balding, but despite the wrinkles, his face held an ageless quality, untouched by time. He had asked him once, but of course Peppik had managed to answer the question without really giving an answer at all. He was good at that.

"Well, what do you think?" Tylak asked again when the man remained silent.

Peppik blinked. "This . . . I do not . . . she has her stone, as do you. They gather."

"You've said that before. What does it mean?" Tylak looked around. They were alone on a dusty road just north of the Kitoian border. They needed to procure some bactrian before they tried to travel the expanse of the Sand Sea, but the trading post had little to offer other than fresh water and rumors of home.

"Old words." The man stared at Tylak, his deep-set eyes unblinking against the leathery skin of his face.

"Yes, so why say them again?"

Burn it all, the old man shrugged in response. Tylak gritted his teeth, though it was a wonder the odd comment drew any reaction from him at all. Peppik and his nonsense.

He turned his thoughts back to Jura and her voice, which had seemed so close just moments ago. Tylak's mother had told stories about the aliferous. She'd liked fantasy and stories of adventure. Tylak had always thought the stories were simply the way of a tired mother entertaining two young boys, but now he wondered how much truth her tales held. They lived high in the mountains. They were responsible for the rising of the sun every day. Wild winds were tamed by their song. Sometimes the people were described as massive birds—other times simply as humans who could fly. People with wings. He thought of Jura and how she was ripped up into the sky. They definitely had wings. He smoothed his palms flat against his sides, his knuckles aching from being clenched.

"We need to trade for some Bactrian. Cheaper to do it here before we enter the Republic. Especially if even half of those rumors are true." He pushed away dark thoughts of his brother and the destroyed arena. They needed to leave the Republic as quickly as possible. Tylak wished they had some other means of travel. The giant camels were the fastest means in the Republic, but how could they compare to creatures of air? Perhaps if he'd even bothered to meet with the sea princess again, he could have convinced her to help. He'd heard tales of how quickly the sea peoples were able to travel back and forth between Jangbahar and their Is'Le'Spar islands. Burn it all, but he'd been in such a hurry to get to Jura, the thought hadn't even occurred to him until now.

"She'll be there by now," Peppik said by way of response. The man quickened his pace, shoulders stiff with resolve. "Bactrian will be too slow."

It was as if the man were pulling his thoughts from his head. But how could they travel any faster? Unless they doubled back around and traveled up the coast with the help of the sea people. Assuming the sea princess would even help them.

He wouldn't feel so pressed for time if there had been any information as to why Jura had been taken. What did these people want? Was this a political move, or was there a more sinister reason for her capture? She had urged him not to worry, but how could he not worry about the unknown? Sandstorms. Bactrian *would* be too slow. And with every second, they lost more time.

He wouldn't turn back, not now. They just had to stick to the plan: find Bactrian and trade them out often. Travel through the night if they had to. He could do this. He *had* to do this. Flames, but the sun had already crawled high into the sky. They should reach another outpost in the next hour if memory served correctly, the final one before Toik.

Peppik had enough funds on him to cover the cost of the beasts at least. Tylak was unsure how much more the man had hidden on him. The secretive man was constantly pulling out some pouch, vial, or book. The thought jogged his memory, and Tylak reached for the extra pack on his back. Jura had been taken so abruptly, she hadn't even been carrying her pack. When he found her, Jura would want her books. But burn them all, he could resent her love for the heavy things just a bit now. Once again, he perused her small treasure of books, thinking of her and wishing all the answers to their problems could be found between those weathered pages. Jura had certainly seemed to believe in them. He pulled out the smallest of the bunch, *The Five Elements and Properties of Blood*. Tylak had yet to discover why, but this book was important. He'd seen a copy of it once, weeks before in the hands of the Third, just before the man was murdered by an alttaw'am masquerading as the man's daughter. That's why it was so important to return to the Republic. With Jura. Things had taken a dangerous turn there. They were beyond the brink of war. The empire bordered on destruction.

Now was not the time to find out if this book truly held answers. Jura might be capable of reading and walking, but he certainly couldn't. In fact, he should probably work at hiding himself and his companions from sight. He shoved the book back into the bag and shouldered it with his own. He ignored his screaming shoulders and concentrated on finding the heat around him. Pulling it toward himself. Flames, but he was exhausted. This had been much easier with the added power of the Everflame. Without it Tylak had to work twice as hard. He fought back a yawn and blinked a few times in rapid succession in an effort to focus.

There, in the distance, a lone figure stumbled toward them. If Tylak didn't bend the light around them now, they would be spotted, but there was a familiarity in the way the figure moved, something in his wobbling gait that made Tylak hesitate. He held up a hand, asking the others to wait behind him until he could be sure.

It had only been a few weeks since he'd last seen the man, but the change was remarkable. Gone was the self-assured nobleman. In his place was a broken man filled with hopeless despair.

Beshar. Ninth of the Thirteen. But what he was doing out here on the Toiken border, Tylak couldn't fathom. He'd never seen the man without his full guard.

The two Samur traveling with Tylak rushed forward, flanking the man on either side. The man's jowls quivered, and he drew deep, raspy breaths.

"Kenjiro . . ." The voice was barely above a whisper, but somehow the scratchy tone reached Tylak's ears. He exchanged a worried glance with Peppik. What had befallen the man to leave him in such a state? What did this mean about the state of the rest of the Thirteen? "Where is Kenjiro?" Beshar looked around wildly.

Ichiro made quiet soothing noises and offered the councilman his waterskin. The Ninth grasped at the skin, drinking desperately. This was a man who had known thirst. The bewildering sight sent chills down Tylak's spine.

Beshar blinked up at Tylak, recognition coming slowly. "Jura. Is she . . ."

"Gone." Tylak realized the error of what he'd said when the man paled. "Taken," he quickly added. "Literally carried away into the sky."

Beshar's forehead wrinkled in concern, or perhaps disbelief.

"I'm going after her," Tylak told him, giving the man a steely glare. "Whatever it takes, I'm bringing her back."

JURA

CHAPTER FIVE

The moonlight cut a wide path across the width of her room, and Jura blinked at it, her senses returning slowly. The cavernous room was carved into the mountainside. The walls were blown smooth by some sort of wind magic, the door to her room connected by the same. The door was nothing but a series of tubes and cogs intricately carved into the wood, a simple lock with a complicated pattern. It didn't take much to open the door. She'd witnessed it happen: a specific movement of wind through wood. It even made a pretty sound. But Jura had no wind magic, and no matter how hard she blew at the tiny holes, her door wouldn't budge.

She was stuck. And had been for ten days.

She had given in to tears on the third day after she'd screamed her throat raw and bruises appeared on her palms and knuckles from banging on the door. She'd been ignored even after she reduced herself to begging. Jura didn't like to cry. Children of the Republic were taught never to waste water on something so frivolous. But she had given herself the day to feel bad about it. Then she had gotten angry. What right did they have to keep her locked away? Without answers? Without any communication at all?

She had attempted to strike up conversation the first night. Food arrived, along with a pitcher of fresh water and a bundle of fabric Jura could only assume was a change of clothing. She had rushed forward, intent on bullying her way through the door or—at the very least—demanding answers, but just as quickly as her door had opened, it was slammed shut, leaving only the hint of a breeze and its music behind.

Jura grew to hate that sound.

Now she was awake and alone and locked in her room, just as she had been the day before. And the day before that. There were still so many unanswered questions. As much as her captors had stated otherwise, she was a prisoner. She had been given a wealth of water to "freshen up" with and a modest sleeping gown that was several sizes too large. The nightgown pooled at her feet and hung rakishly off one shoulder, but it was soft against her skin and smelled of citrus and summer breezes.

Her room was a far cry from a prison cell. The large four-post bed was more comfortable than her own, and she was always provided with an assortment of fruits and nuts for an evening snack. There were only three walls to her room. Where there should have been a fourth wall were instead five marble pillars. Jura would have thought there would be more of a chill to the air because they were so high up, but there was never more than a gentle breeze.

She had crawled to the ledge again only yesterday, grabbing the nearest pillar to steady herself as she peered over the edge. The forest and desert were mere swatches of brown and green. There was no escape from her open wall, not unless she grew wings like her captors.

No, her exit was through that door. The intriguing, beautifully crafted, wondrously magical, stupid door.

She crawled out of her comfortable bed and investigated the door further. She didn't bother blowing on it again. She felt well-rested so she must have slept for a few hours at least. Time seemed to pass differently here, so there was no saying how long it would be before the sun chose to make its appearance.

In the morning they would bring Markhim. That's what Danos had said to her before leaving her the offering of fruits and nuts. For days now she had been kept in seclusion with only the occasional visit from the Speaker of the Winds. Or Danos. She still didn't know what he preferred to be called, and he didn't seem inclined to share any information with her. Each visit he asked about her health and reminded her that they were at the mercy of the path of Dreams. She had asked what that meant, but he ignored her. He ignored everything she said, even her request to see Markhim. She had been assured of his safety that first day, but as her captors did not bring him to her and since she was locked away, she could only assume he was locked away in a room similar to her own. Every time she asked of him, she was informed that he was safe but could not be seen at the moment.

The moonlight *did* seem to grow paler, and was the sky starting to brighten? She stared at her open wall but made no move toward it. She wasn't afraid of heights, not exactly, but something about the edge left her uneasy. There was something wild and dangerous about the open space.

But then, Jura thought wryly, it was probably less to do with the open space and more to do with the fact that she was imprisoned on the edge of a cliff. She would definitely feel better once she saw Markhim and witnessed his safety with her own eyes. Jura had no reason to doubt her captors, but she didn't have much reason to place faith in them either. How could she truly be assured of his safety? She had no way of knowing if his room was as comfortable as hers. What if he was locked up, enchained in the pits of some dungeon? No, Jura couldn't trust Markhim was safe until she saw him.

And then there was the mystery of the man without wings. Well, more of a boy, really. He couldn't have been much more than Jura's own seventeen years. He'd promised that her whispered words would reach Tylak, but she had never heard of such magic, and there was no way of knowing if the magic had worked or not. Had Tylak heard her whispered promise to get back to him? Would she even be able to keep her promise?

The sun started to brighten the night sky. Morning would come with the sweet promise of answers. And Markhim. She hadn't seen him since their capture. Was he injured? Had they been treating him well? She didn't like to concentrate on how important those answers were to her.

She didn't want to allow it, but her thoughts turned unbidden to Amira and Coral, Commander of the Three Oceans and her would-be ally . . . if the woman still accepted the alliance. Coral would be furious once she returned to find her missing, and Jura doubted Tylak would be able to coerce the young woman to remain on their cause after her disappearance. Which meant Tylak and Amira were all alone to face the nightmares in the Republic. Her country was divided, the government crawling with puppets from foreign enemies. There was literally no one Jura could trust outside her immediate circle of friends, and even that was constantly being ripped apart.

A gentle tap at her door caused Jura to stop pacing. The Speaker of the Winds was punctual if nothing else. Seconds later she heard the melodic sound of her door as it swung open with a gentle gush of wind.

Danos was a short man with a sharp gaze that seemed to see

everything. His gray wings were short, and he kept them tucked close, stubby daggers of silver flanking his sides. He kept his hair closely shaven, but feathers hung from his eyebrows. His pale blue eyes caught hers before Danos looked up at her ceiling. He held a pile of fabric in outstretched arms, and she snatched the clothing from him, eager to wear something aside from the daily nightgown change.

"Please take your time freshening up," Danos said in that beautiful voice of his. The acoustics of the room echoed the soothing sound, reverberating in her ears. "I'll be waiting outside once you are ready for me to escort you to your companion."

He left the room, and the door was firmly shut within seconds.

Jura sighed. She was once again locked away. But perhaps, just for a moment this time? She brought the pile of cloth to her bed and unfolded it. She nibbled on her bottom lip as the length of fabric continued to unroll. At the center of the long length of fabric was another rolled garment that she recognized. Pants!

She pulled on the pants, delighted to find them high-waisted and snug, yet still breathable and flexible enough to give her legs full motion. She tried a few test squats, pulling at the waistband and delighting when the soft material snapped back into place. She allowed herself an indulgent smile before studying the other length of fabric. Like the pants, it was made of the same soft, stretchy material and was dyed to match the same pale yellow. Logic and deduction suggested the material was meant to cover her top half, but how? The fabric was narrow, mere inches wide and meters long. It made no sense.

She brought the image of Danos to mind and struggled to remember his clothing. His chest and shoulders had been completely covered, but his wings . . . of course. Jura sighed. This fabric must be meant to be wrapped around one's top half, and the length allowed the flexibility of altering for one's wings—preventing the necessity of giant holes ripped out the backs of their tops. It was ingenious if one had wings; without them, it was unnecessarily tedious and difficult. It took several attempts and many minutes before Jura decided she was suitably covered.

She was still panting lightly from the effort of dressing herself when she reached her door. Feeling silly, she knocked.

That first day she had pounded on the door and been ignored. Now, the door immediately began its song. Danos stood on the other side, still as a statue except for the slight cursory once-over he gave her outfit. Why did he seem to detest the very sight of her? Or was he just shy? Either way, the man's eyes were directed behind her right shoulder as he instructed her to follow him.

Well, just because he didn't prefer to talk to her, that wouldn't stop her from talking to him.

"Where are we going?" she asked, moving with tiny, measured steps despite the mobility of the pants. She wanted to take in every detail of her surroundings. This was her first time out of her room after all. She had expected the outer hall to be teeming with aliferous, but the open space was devoid of anyone except for her and Danos. Jura tensed, prepared to make a run for it if given the opportunity. Although where she would run was yet to be decided.

The hallway outside her bedroom wasn't a hallway at all but an open atrium. Sunlight streamed in through heavy curtains of ivy. Fat, purple flowers hung from the vines, the enchanting smell carrying on a soft breeze. Jura closed her eyes for a moment and inhaled deeply.

"I am taking you to your companion," Danos answered.

Jura flinched at his voice. She'd been so engrossed in the scenery, she hadn't even remembered she had posed the question. Danos gave her a knowing smile.

"I do apologize for your isolation thus far. There are important formalities to observe. The Dreams offer many passageways, but there is only one true path."

Jura frowned, trying to puzzle out his words. This was not the first time he had chosen to refer to following "the dreams."

"This path," Jura started. She was unsure what she wanted to ask and trailed off as they crossed the width of the open area, stopping in front of a darkened hallway.

The Speaker of the Winds gestured for Jura to go ahead, and she let out an unladylike snort. First he gave her cryptic warnings, and now he expected her to prance in of her own free will?

"It is the way of your people not to trust others. This, you are not faulted for." He said nothing else and simply waited in silence.

Jura sighed. "All right then. I'll go down your creepy tunnel of doom."

JURA

CHAPTER SIX

It was impossibly dark, no torches on the wall or glowing rocks on the stone path, and it was some time before Jura's eyes adjusted to the darkness. She could hear the quiet rhythm of Danos breathing beside her and chose to concentrate on that sound and nothing else, allowing her mind to wander. Hopefully Tylak had received her message by now. She had no idea how long it took for the wind to travel. Was it instant? Would he need a translator? She had been unable to get answers to these questions before the mysterious helper had left, and she hadn't seen him since.

Did Danos truly lead her to Markhim? Was this all an elaborate trap? Danos had said it was the nature of her people to mistrust others, but what had he done to gain her trust? Wasn't she captive? She had been at the complete mercy of Danos ever since her arrival here. He hadn't provided her with any answers except for this moment, and he scoffed at her ability to trust.

Jura's anger grew and she quickened her pace, scowling as she did so. She simmered in silence for a moment before she noticed the light emanating from the end of the tunnel.

"What's down there?"

"Not what, *who*."

"Markhim." Her heart fluttered at the thought. Finally. If she asked her legs to move any quicker, she would be running.

In the distance, she could hear the steady drip of water. It was a strangely familiar sound, like an odd melody one had heard but couldn't place. A strangely sweet smell pervaded the air, and the temperature felt inexplicably cooler.

Jura felt something shift inside her, a realization, a *knowing* that things would never be the same. The tiny hairs on her arms prickled up at the thought, and she shivered despite herself.

"You are fearful," Danos murmured, and though the words were whispered, she felt them in her soul.

Jura lifted her chin, determined to lie. "I fear nothing."

Moments later, she blinked against the sudden attack of light. It was the sun, blinding in its radiance. The long tunnel had opened up to an amphitheater, not unlike the glass arena back home. Although there were hundreds, perhaps thousands of seats, they were all empty. Unlike the arena, there was no glass to temper the radiance of the sun, and green ivy crept up the seats and into the arena proper. There were no battles fought here, not in this overgrown jungle, and Jura wondered why he had brought her here.

"It's beautiful," she whispered. And it truly was. Jura had never seen so much green in her life, astounding in its otherworldly quality. It was all around her, a thick carpet beneath her feet and swinging above her in the breeze. Creeping vines and large leaves covered every surface and tumbled over the dilapidated seating. So similar to the Republic arena, almost an exact replica, but now it was wild and overgrown. The ruins reminded Jura of a venomous snake she'd once viewed at the market.

"It must be a bit shocking to you, I would imagine? So much color? Your world was like this once." Danos said all this while sweeping his arm out in a grand gesture. "Before the Everflame walked the earth, scorching everything in its path. Did you know, your ancestors were directly responsible for its capture?"

It was a mark of pride for the Republic. It was what made them such a strong nation. Her ancestors were gifted powers from the Everflame so that they might tame it.

"And for its release," Danos continued before Jura could respond.

"Its release?" Jura whirled away from the interesting cluster of star-shaped flowers and gave Danos her full attention. "What do you mean we were responsible for its release? What do you know?"

"My people and yours once lived together. Harmoniously. Until your kind grew jealous of our abilities and strengths."

"Is that what all this is? Some sort of revenge plot?" Jura's fingers itched for a whip that wasn't there. Why had Danos brought her all the way out here, alone? Markhim wasn't even here. She gave the arena ruins another quick examination, looking for a weapon of some sort. Jura cursed herself for being such an idiot.

"Of course not." If Danos noticed her defensive stance, he said nothing about it, his tone deferential. "My people have always been and will continue to be at the mercy of the Dreams."

"The dreams . . . you keep saying that. What are the dreams, and what do they mean? Where is Markhim? Why have you brought me here?" It was hard to keep from shouting, and the last bit came out as a shrill squeak.

"The answers you seek, you will find once you learn to look inside."

"No." Jura shook her head, her heavy braid falling over her

shoulder as she placed a fist on either hip. "No. I'm tired of all these cryptic half answers and partial truths. Speak plainly, or take me back to my cell."

The familiar chuckle surprised her, and she turned toward the sound with wide eyes. "Markhim!" she cried out, running toward him.

She threw herself into his arms, and he crushed her against him, nearly cracking her spine in his embrace. For a moment it was difficult to breathe, but she didn't care. It just felt good to feel completely safe, even if only for a moment.

"They haven't hurt you, have they?" she asked, pushing away from him. He looked good, better than good, she realized as she became aware of how close they were. His hair was unusually long, a far cry from the standard cut of the Light Guard. He appeared well-rested, and he smelled fresh and clean as though he'd just finished a steam.

"That should be my line." He chuckled. "But seeing how you've been berating the Speaker like he's a misbehaving child makes me think you must be doing just fine." Markhim raised his eyebrows and took a step back from her, but he kept his hands around her waist. "Have they truly been keeping you in a cell? They had assured me you were quite comfortable."

"It's fine," she answered with a dismissive gesture. "And your timing couldn't be better. Danos was just about to explain everything."

At the mention of his name, the Speaker stepped forward, closing the gap between them. "I will answer you as plainly as I can."

He tilted his head to the side, as if listening to some invisible presence beside him. Perhaps he was, Jura thought, and wished she had the abilities of the Samur, who could tell when people were using magic.

"Be warned, sometimes the answers are not what you seek, and the truth found can break worlds."

Jura rolled her eyes. Getting a straight answer from Danos was more difficult than reading without candlelight. "These dreams you keep mentioning. What do they have to do with anything?"

"The Dreams are our way. They lead our path, give us purpose."

She narrowed her eyes. "Sounds godlike."

Danos shrugged in response. "They are like a god, yes. We follow their way."

"And these dreams . . . they told you to capture me?"

The Speaker's attention was diverted behind Jura, and she turned to see what had captured his attention. A winged guard flanked her on either side but stayed just out of arm's reach, as silent as any Arbe. Markhim shifted beside her, and she noticed the tension spread the wrinkle on his forehead.

"What do you want with me?" she demanded when Danos failed to answer her.

He was silent for several moments, and Jura was about to repeat herself when a strong breeze stirred around them. Danos closed his eyes and let out a low humming sound, not quite a song.

"You must be trained in your magic," he said. His intense gaze angled toward her. "I am told you are strong, but you are like a child in your knowledge. You have much to learn."

Jura exchanged a worried glance with Markhim. She hadn't even had a chance to catch him up on everything. Did he know what she was capable of? Did *she*? Markhim's hand found hers, and he gave it a gentle squeeze.

Jura knew something had awakened in her, but she couldn't explain it. Was Danos finally offering the answers she so desperately needed?

"You'll train me then?"

"If you prove yourself worthy, you will begin your studies tomorrow. Until then you may enjoy some leisure time with your companion." He gestured to the guard on her right side. "Matteus will escort you back to your chambers when you are ready to retire."

"A guard?" Jura spared a glance in his direction.

"An escort." Danos smiled, revealing sharp canines. "I will see you tomorrow for testing."

"Testing? But wait, what do I—"

"Tomorrow. In the morning we will discover if you are worthy."

Jura blinked after him, still amazed at having seen him take flight right before her eyes. Her new guard, Matteus, gave Markhim an appraising look before his expression changed to one of boredom. Like Danos, Matteus seemed inclined to keep his facial hair closely shaved. His eyebrow feathers were a brilliant blue against his tan skin. Jura noticed his wings were the same vivid color, though they were tipped so dark a purple, they appeared black.

"So." Markhim cleared his throat, and Jura realized they were still holding hands. His gaze followed hers to where their hands met, and he raised them until he could place a kiss on the back of her palm.

"Markhim . . ." she began, unsure what she intended to say.

"Tell me about your room." He pulled her after him, escorting her to a seat on the nearest stone bench.

Matteus kept a wary eye on them, but Markhim seemed intent to ignore his presence. He didn't release her hand as he sat beside her.

"My room has an incredible view," Markhim said when she didn't answer.

His tenacity brought her out of her stupor and encouraged her to be present in the moment. Or maybe it was the fact that Markhim's thumb now made small circles on the palm of her hand. Their fingers were still interlaced so she couldn't pull away, not that she wanted to.

"Does yours?"

"Huh?" She tried to swallow, but her mouth had gone incredibly dry.

"Does your room also have a nice view?" A slow smile stretched over his lips. He knew how his hand was affecting her.

"It does. The room is great. The magical door, not so much."

"Magical door?" His thumb stopped, and with it, the spell seemed to be broken. Jura pressed to her feet, planting her fists on her hips with a deep sigh.

"It's been ten days, Markhim! We don't know anything. We don't know what's happening in the Republic, or why they're keeping us here."

"We don't know anything *yet*. The Speaker said answers will come tomorrow."

"And you believe him?" Jura found his easy acceptance of the Speaker's words more than a bit discomforting.

"I know that we don't have a choice."

She groaned, or grunted might be a more accurate depiction of the sound. Either way it caused Markhim to rise to his feet, startling Matteus.

"What do you want me to do?" Markhim whispered. "I think I can steal a weapon, but I don't know how we'd make it down the mountain." His lips barely moved as he spoke the words, his attention riveted on Matteus.

"No. No, we can't do that. They haven't been violent. Yet. I need to learn more. There has to be a library here." She raised her voice back to a normal volume before her escort noticed them whispering.

"I've done a bit of exploring during my free time and haven't come across one yet but . . . what is it? Why are you looking at me like that?"

"Exploring? You've been given free access to this place?" Jura had a difficult time keeping her voice at a normal level. She wanted to shout. Instead, she took a deep breath, slowly releasing it through clenched teeth.

"I wouldn't say I've had free access." Markhim had the decency to look embarrassed. "I asked for you—every morning I asked if I could see you—but they said it wasn't time yet. Jura, you have to believe me. I would have never stayed away so easily if I had known you were being so mistreated."

"I wouldn't exactly say I've been mistreated." She frowned. "But of course, it's hard to come to any mistreatment when one is confined to a single room for ten days. I've been worried for your safety and well-being, for the well-being of the Republic, and you've been 'exploring during your free time.'" She giggled, the sound a bit hysterical. "And you couldn't even find me a library or at least a book to pass the time."

Jura caught her bottom lip between her teeth before she said something she didn't mean. It wasn't Markhim's fault she was here. He hadn't been responsible for locking her away, and yet, for some reason, she couldn't shake away her misdirected anger.

"I can have someone bring a selection of reading to your room if you would like, young Speaker."

Jura blinked, surprised to hear Matteus speak. His voice was even deeper than she imagined, somehow still a contrast to his large frame. His bright blue feathers ruffled under her inspection.

"Thank you, Matteus. I should like that very much. You can take me to my room now, please."

"Jura, wait. Can we talk?" Markhim reached for her, but she stepped away.

"I'm sorry. It will have to wait until tomorrow. I'm exhausted, and I have tests to prepare for." She turned away from him and marched toward the hallway, determined not to look back.

For a moment she thought he followed her, but it was only Matteus, who flew close behind her back.

KAY

CHAPTER SEVEN

Inferno brought her dinner. A good thing, too, because she was starving. And she was tired of potatoes. Mama's garden had been a wreck, overrun with weeds and rot or stripped bare from bugs and critters. But the potatoes had survived. Mama would mash them sometimes with sweetened butter and cheese, but Kay didn't know how to do that. Mama must have used some sort of special magic because potatoes were *hard,* and no amount of squishing or stomping had seemed to make any difference. It wasn't until the next day that she remembered Mama would boil the potatoes first. She discovered she could cook them simply by Breathing heat into the potato, and that was just as well considering she didn't have any sweetened butter or cheese.

Kay was so very tired of plain potato.

But today Inferno brought her dinner. It was most certainly burned, and she didn't know what sort of bird it had come from, but Kay told herself it tasted like chicken and shared feelings of gratitude to the dragon. He grunted in response before curling up in a ball for a nap.

It was natural now, as easy as when she Breathed. She shared most of her feelings with Inferno. Sending wave after wave of emotion the dragon's way had helped her to cope, and it seemed to have a calming effect on the dragon. A part of her knew that their time back at her home was limited, but she didn't allow herself to focus on that. Instead, she watched the day melt into night and morning again, and if it wasn't for Inferno, she felt she might melt away too.

The dragon was her friend. She could feel that whenever Inferno chose to share his feelings with her. His feelings were . . . different. Angry, mostly. And scared. If his feelings were words, they would be shouted. As it was, they seemed to fill Kay up and boil the heat within her.

Kay wasn't exactly sure when she realized they could share what the other was feeling. She knew if she were to tell Daddy or Mama about their connection, they would think she was fibbing. People couldn't talk to dragons. But she could. It had started slowly at first. Kay didn't notice it immediately. But as the days passed, Kay came to realize that Inferno seemed to understand, truly understand, everything she told him. And possibly more than that, because he'd known to bring her here. She had come to discover how to understand him back. At least how he was feeling.

Kay couldn't explain the why of it, but she knew it was because of the Everflame. She was changed somehow, forever different after Breathing in the giant flame.

She Breathed more frequently now. It just felt easier—with so much power wanting to escape every moment. She hadn't taken the time to understand the giant fire before she Breathed it all in. She hadn't really been thinking about the consequences at the time. But what did that mean now? She still hadn't given it much thought other than to acknowledge that Breathing in that flame had made her even more special than she was before.

Kay hadn't tried to get rid of the flame. She wasn't entirely sure if she could, and she worried what would happen if she did. Would the flame once again wander the earth scorching everything in its path? The Everflame belonged back in its glass cage, but that was all the way back in the Republic, and Kay was NEVER going back there. *Ever*.

She must have sent those feelings to Inferno because he lifted his head and looked around, his tongue darting out to taste the air. She hummed an old lullaby that Mama would sing to her whenever she had nightmares. It seemed to calm the dragon down because he curled back in on himself, asleep within moments.

Rumble was the only other dragon Kay had ever known so intimately, and Inferno was his opposite in nearly every way. While Rumble had been a deep, glistening red, Inferno was a dappled blue, the color of the sky after dawn. Rumble was lazy and always napping, but Inferno seemed to rest only when she did. Rumble's skin was smooth and leathery while Inferno had tiny scales down the length of his neck to the base of his wings. Hundreds of scars marred the shimmer of his scales, giving him the dappled color. She knew how Inferno had gotten those scars. She had helped to give him his newest. As usual, thoughts of the other night caused shame to ripple in her belly. She didn't like to think of the bad things she had done, but she couldn't help it. If Mama had been here to see her, she would most certainly have given Kay a good scolding and maybe even a whooping too. But Mama wasn't here. It was just her and Inferno, and she supposed remembering the bad things and all she'd done was sort of a punishment in its own way. Plus, she'd already decided she was going to start trying extra hard to be good, so she should be able to cancel out all that bad in no time.

She sent feelings of home and preparedness to Inferno, but he didn't respond except to open one eye and watch her walk across the yard.

The house still smelled funny. Kay had tried her hardest to clean it, pulling out piles of refuse and burning them in the back. She'd even washed the sheets, or tried to. She had hung them out to dry while the garbage pile was still burning so they were even more stinky than they had been, but they still felt like home. As always, she ran past her parents' room, still too frightened to look in there. Her own room, however, was the safe haven it had always been.

It was exactly as she'd left it. Her chest was still open wide, articles of clothing strewn about, and cookie crumbs had grown stale on her nightstand. Evaline, her doll, lay on her bed. She picked up the tiny replica of herself and scrutinized it with a scowl. She'd been delighted when Daddy had brought her home the year before. Now she couldn't ever imagine wanting to play with a doll again. She reverently placed Evaline on her pillow. Her personal satchel had gone missing during her kidnapping, and she needed another if she was going to pack up her things. Mama had a nice large one that would be perfect. Kay took a deep breath.

You can do this. It's just a room.

But, somehow, she was terrified. More frightened of that dumb room than she had been of anything else in her entire life. She knew Mama and Daddy were gone. Of course, she did. It was just that in the past, anytime Kay had gone into her parents' room, one or both of her parents had been waiting inside.

Every time.

She didn't know what it would do to her to open the door and find that empty room.

She decided to wait a bit longer, going through all her items once more. Each item underwent careful scrutiny before it was placed in the pack pile. This time she would have everything she needed and nothing else.

She eyed the dragon scale armor in the corner of her room. She'd ripped it off as soon as she had arrived, flinging it as far away from her as she could. There, the armor had waited, staring back at her, reminding her of her past actions and a promise of the danger waiting ahead. Kay hated the armor. She hated looking at it, hated knowing that it lay in the corner, waiting for her.

They were valuable, Kay knew, not just for the safety they provided, but people paid a lot for armor like that. Not that she wanted to mess around with the sort of buyer the armor would bring. That was, if a tradesman would even barter with a kid.

If the dragon scale armor alone was worth a fortune, she couldn't imagine the money that would come from trading Inferno. Not that Kay would ever do that! There were many things that Kay didn't know, but she knew with a certainty that she would never harm another dragon. Never again.

Her feet must have moved all on their own because suddenly Kay was standing in front of the armor, the scales glistening in the afternoon sunlight streaming in from her open window. There was a faint breeze from outside, and it smelled of wildflowers and just a hint of Mama's laundry soap. Kay closed her eyes and breathed deeply. This. This smelled of home. But then she opened her eyes and scowled at the dragon armor in front of her.

Mama would say it was foolish to waste something valuable. Kay scooped up the armor, which was surprisingly light in her arms, and placed it on her bed alongside the rest of her belongings. She'd packed a handful of shirts and pants, all the underwear she owned, and her rugged winter boots. She planned on leaving everything else behind.

On a whim, she stuck Evaline on the top of the pile. There. Now she was back to needing a satchel. With a heavy sigh, Kay left her bedroom and trekked down the hall toward her parents' room. It wasn't a far walk, but her heart beat heavy in her chest, and there was a terrible feeling in her tummy. The door was closed, like it always was, but this time Mama and Daddy didn't wait for her inside.

Be brave, little girl, the voice in her head said, the one that sounded like Mama. With a nod, Kay pushed the door open.

The room was as she remembered. The bed was made, with Daddy's pajamas folded neatly on his pillow. Mama hated when Daddy left his clothes on the floor. She threatened to toss all his pajamas in the river once, but she never did. Instead, she would just shake her head and fold them while sending prayers to the Great Mother. "Oh, Mother, may you bless Kay with a partner who has the sense to put away their own bedclothes."

Kay lifted the pajamas now, burying her face in the soft cotton and breathing deeply. It still smelled of Daddy.

She couldn't help the tears then. They came all on their own, but now that they had started again, Kay couldn't stop. She cried until she couldn't see straight—deep, racking sobs until she could cry no more.

When she opened her eyes, Kay realized she must have fallen asleep. Night hadn't fallen, but the sun had moved across the sky, and the night insects had begun to sing their evening tune. She shoved herself off the bed and moved toward her parents' closet. Mama kept her travel satchel on the top shelf, but it was impossible for Kay to reach on her own. She remembered the small sewing stool Mama kept in the linen closet and returned with it. She still had to stretch on her tiptoes, and even then she was reaching blindly, but she managed to pull down the satchel as well as a few other items too.

She ducked from the falling debris, coughing from the unsettled dust and staring at an empty shoe box and a hat box filled with pressed flowers and dusty notebooks. Kay was collecting the note-books when a yellowed envelope fell out of one and to the ground. She bent to retrieve it, frowning at the name scrawled on the front.

That was Mama's handwriting, but the letter was sealed. Mama said it wasn't kind to open letters addressed to other people. Not that Mama could deliver the letter now. And who was to say she'd even wanted to send it? It certainly didn't seem that way, not with the letter hidden away and collecting dust. But did that make it okay to read it now?

She shoved the letter into her pocket and decided she would figure out what to do with it later. In the meantime, she'd gotten Mama's satchel, and it was time to start packing her things. She figured she could stay for another few days before the red-robed bad guys caught up to her. If she was remembering correctly, it had taken her weeks to reach the Republic. She planned to be long gone before they made it here.

She brought the satchel to her room and placed it on the bed beside the armor.

Was this really everything she needed? A small pile of clothing, a stolen letter, and her hated armor. It would have to be enough. She pulled the letter from her pockets and smoothed the envelope against the curve of her dragon breastplate. She really, really wanted to open that letter, but . . .

A strong sense of panic seized her, causing her to draw a desperate gasp of air. Inferno was sending feelings of danger!

She ran to her open window but saw no sign of the dragon. Or anything else. There it was again. Another wild sense of fear. There wasn't much that could frighten a dragon, which only meant one thing.

The red-robed bad guys. They'd come early.

KAY

CHAPTER EIGHT

Run, Kay.

It was her mantra, the only constant in her life since the death of her parents. Run away, run away. This time she didn't think. She rolled everything in her sheet and stuffed it all into Mama's traveling satchel. There was room for Daddy's pajamas so she stuffed those in too. Then she ran after Inferno. The dragon paced along the perimeter of the remains of the North barn. He seemed to prefer to spend his time there, but Kay couldn't say why. Maybe he knew that dragons used to stay there.

Kay hadn't wanted to go back to this section of the farm. She'd never wanted to see it again. Somehow that familiar smell still lingered. The same burning smell from that day of the barn burning, that same smell from her last day in the Republic.

I'm not going back to the arena. The thought gave her the determination she needed to meet Inferno.

"What is it?" she shouted and sent her confusion to the dragon through their new bond. "What's happening?"

But she saw it then. The red-robed bad guys. They were coming in a massive chariot pulled by a team of four dragons.

Inferno's position on the hill allowed him to see them, but he was still obstructed from their view, which meant they still had time to get away. The bad guys didn't know for sure that Kay was at the house, and if she and Inferno could hide, then maybe they would go search somewhere else. But how did Kay go about hiding a dragon? Inferno was far too large to hide anywhere on the property, and there was no place for him to run without being spotted by the red-robes. But that was their only choice. They had to make a run for it.

We'll never be able to go faster than four dragons, Kay worried as she adjusted Mama's satchel to her back. The straps were extra long, but Kay twisted them about until one went over either shoulder and around her waist. There. Now she didn't have to worry about losing it while flying—sometimes Inferno could go a bit too fast. This time, though, she needed him to go fast.

"Thanks for warning me," she said to the dragon. He seemed to understand her words, even if he never responded to them with his own. The strength of his shared emotion was enough. "We have to get out of here."

A rumbling feeling of unease sank into her belly, and she felt the dragon's anxiety mirror hers. "I know, I'm scared too. Do you think you can fly faster than them?"

Twin lines of smoke rose from his nostrils, and Kay rubbed the soft spot between them. "Okay, I'm coming on now."

Inferno lowered himself to the ground so Kay could scramble up and over his neck.

"Go back toward the house and circle up from there. Maybe they won't see us." The dragon began to gallop, and Kay wrapped her hands around one of the raised scales along his neck. He was almost as fast on the ground but not nearly as smooth, and Kay had to squeeze her legs together despite her makeshift handle to stay on. Inferno took to the air with a giant leap that forced Kay's belly to somersault. The rushing wind blew back her hair, and for one shining instant, Kay forgot about the bad guys, about the fact that she was leaving her home again, probably forever. For a moment it was just a girl and her dragon and the sky.

It was beautiful.

Inferno shrieked, and a spike of fear shot through Kay. She squinted through the wind and saw the chariot of dragons below them, galloping along the western pasture, almost as if . . .

"Hurry, Inferno! They're flying after us!" Kay screamed the words and sent them through their connection. She Breathed deep, feeling alive and powerful. Why had she feared this feeling? She needed it. There was an endless well of heat within her. She could Breathe as deeply as she needed without pulling heat from anywhere else. She expelled a rush of flames toward the chariot, hoping to frighten the dragons before they took flight.

But the chariot was in the sky now, the dragons bugling and bucking in the air. The dragons wore enormous harnesses around their necks and shoulders. The carriage hung beneath the dragons, swinging like a great pendulum between the weight of the four beasts.

Even now, they were still determined to stop her. Apparently by any means necessary. She Breathed in deeper, feeling the familiar tingle of her new magic in her veins. *I'm glowing again*, she noticed before she threw her flames at the dragons rushing toward her.

The massive rush of fire bounced off their scales but singed the heavy leather straps of their harnesses. Thick black smoke rolled into the sky, obscuring her vision. Maybe this could work in her favor too? She sent another rush of flames toward the chariot, the surrounding air filled with so much smoke that it was impossible to see anything.

"Let's get out of here!" she shouted to her dragon. She felt him lean away from the wind, banking hard to the right before straightening up and rising above the clouds. Inferno still felt worried. She felt it in the slight tremble beneath her, echoing in her gut.

"It's okay," she murmured, but she didn't know if she believed her words. She stroked the shiny scale, finding comfort in how it felt, like a polished silver spoon warmed by hot stew. "It's okay," she repeated.

Kay looked over her shoulder at the billowing black clouds and waited to see if anything would emerge from the smoke. Nothing did, and soon, the smoke and the last memories of her home were out of sight forever.

BESHAR

Flames, he detested this boy. He was half his age, arrogant, and a smart-ass with a smirk that said he needed to be taught a lesson. A wicked scar that cut across his face said that maybe someone already had. Beshar didn't trust Shadow Dancers. Why should he when all he had ever seen them do was lie and scheme and generally make his life more miserable?

It was difficult to focus on the boy's words. Jura was alive but missing, taken to the sky. It didn't make sense. Except that it made all too much sense.

There was still no sign of Kenjiro. Where his man should have been there was only open desert and this former Shadow Dancer, his aging companion, and the twins, stoic and as stand-offish as before. The queen's man hadn't lingered, despite the brief exchange with Tylak. The Shadow Dancer offered him a terse nod with the ominous warning that his queen would be in touch. Had she truly just wished to see him escorted from the city? And what did she plan to ask of him next?

Beshar sighed, quieting the flurry of thoughts, and concentrated on the present. It didn't matter that he hated the boy. Jura, perhaps all of the Republic, needed his assistance, and he would help the former Shadow Dancer as best he could. If only he had Kenjiro to make things easier.

He held up a hand, halting the fervent begging from the man.

"What do you need? Whatever I can . . ." he said and trailed off, realizing he couldn't finish the sentiment. Asking the boy what he needed as though he were still someone of importance. The old him, the man he was before, Ninth of the Thirteen, powerful and feared — that man could have offered this Shadow Dancer the very world at his feet . . . but what did Beshar have to offer him now? He was nothing without his Rank.

Despite this, his quiet admission seemed to appease the Shadow Dancer as his expression faded into relief. He even smiled before turning to exchange fervent words with his quiet, balding companion.

"What I need the most, is quick transportation."

Fair enough. But again, what could Beshar offer him? He no longer had access to his wealth of gold and water chips. His many Bactrian carriages had likely all been sold. The only thing he had now of any value was his friendship with Kenjiro. And even then, what could his old friend offer except for empathy and his old earth magic?

"And I wouldn't say no to a few answers," Tylak continued.

Such youthful optimism. Beshar sighed. He needed answers of his own. Well, he would answer what he could. "What do you need to know?"

"What do you know about wind magic?"

The question surprised him, as did the boy's earnest expression. Of all things he'd expected asked of him, it wasn't this. And truth be told, he didn't know much on the subject. No one did. He sighed, allowing his frustration to show before giving his answer.

"Not much, only that it allegedly went extinct when the aliferous did. Now you say they're back, or perhaps never left . . . I'm not sure what this all means, but Jura was right. Something big is happening, and it all started with her father." It always went back to Justir. Flames, but Beshar had only known one man with more pride, his own father. At least his father hadn't been a flaming fool. So how did the First family fit into all of this? What did the aliferous, an ancient all-but-forgotten race, want with Jura? And why now?

"Can you think of any reason these . . . aliferous . . . would want to hurt her?" Tylak asked, likely responding to Beshar's concerned expression. Well, there was no sense in hiding things from the boy. He might as well hear it true.

Beshar shrugged, searching his memory for any information stored away on the ancient race of winged humans. How was anyone to believe their existence to be any more than old stories?

Beshar reached into his pocket, his fingers once again searching for a handkerchief that wasn't there. It was flaming hot now in the full sun of midday, and he was beyond thirsty.

All ten toenails. He would rip them off one by one for another flagon of wine. If he ever found himself back in the council of Thirteen, he would lock himself away in his tower forever. Just him and endless crates of wine. He was so tired.

Beshar blinked, bringing the boy back into focus. Tylak stared at him expectantly. Silly lovestruck fool. The world was falling around him, and all he could think of was some girl. Beshar told himself he pitied the boy and shook his head.

"No, I can't think of any. Your queen, however, she has her eye on the daughter of the First." She had plans for him, she'd said. Find Jura and await further command. Beshar wished he could ignore the queen, her plotting, and her command, but the truth was he had nowhere else to go. It seemed the queen controlled more than just his life—they were puppets, all of them.

Tylak grunted by way of response.

"You don't deny it?" The grunt was fitting. Likely the boy knew it was hopeless, if only he would admit it to himself.

"She's not my queen." Tylak's tone was laced with venom. "She's nothing to me. I'm more concerned with that blood-sucking creature parading around as the new Third. She's th—"

"Dead. It's dead. Killed at the hands of my previous escort." Beshar had the pleasure of watching the boy's eyes widen. "That's right. A small pleasure in the midst of the chaos surrounding my departure."

"But then, that means it's safe. If the alttaw'am can no longer do any harm, then it's safe for Jura to return home. And her father must be . . . Why are you shaking your head no? What's happened?"

Beshar explained. The Republic was in chaos, the Thirteen in ruins. The knowledge that the Amira impostor was just the first of any number of alttaw'am. Beshar almost pitied the boy for the sudden onslaught of information heaved upon him.

"You're doing good, boy," he muttered, surprising himself yet again. "She's fortunate to have a man as loyal as you." He sighed. "And I'll help you get back to her as best I can."

The former Shadow Dancer nodded, but Beshar could tell he was having a difficult time coming to grips with everything. He truly cared for her, Beshar realized. Flames, but the boy couldn't have chosen a more difficult conquest. Beshar couldn't fault him, though. He knew all too well the cost of forbidden love.

"It is nearly time for prayer," Ichiro announced.

The twins had been so silent that Beshar had forgotten they

were present. He looked at each now, one man an almost exact copy of the other. Was it odd to be a twin in a land divided and terrorized by alttaw'am? Did the Shrivo even worry about such things, or were they content in their solitude?

"After prayer, then, we'll make camp. And in the morning, we can—" Tylak was cut off by his aging companion. He gasped, clutching at Tylak's arm.

"It's coming!"

Tylak and the man disappeared.

The trembling started slowly. It was several seconds before Beshar could associate Tylak's disappearance with the trembling earth and strange whistling sound. The ground rumbled beneath him, and he cast a desperate glance at his former men. The two Samur appeared equally concerned, and they fell to their knees, muttering or humming under their breath.

Sandstorms. Literal sandstorms. Three whirling vortices of sand and air and death. There was no time to run.

No wonder the boy had disappeared. It was the only defense mechanism he had. No wonder the Samur whispered fervent prayers. The tornadoes ahead were massive, wild tempests of sand and grit. And there were three of them.

Beshar was not a religious man, and he'd heard the rumors from the boy. The Everflame had forsaken them. He closed his eyes and waited for death to come.

The tiny grains of sand sliced his skin along his arms and face as the wind picked up speed. Beshar squeezed his eyes tight, intent on keeping them shut, when a sudden grip on his forearm caused them to snap open. It was impossible to see anything, to know who or what had grabbed him. Was it the Shadow Dancer? Or his odd companion? One of the Samur?

The howling wind stopped. The silence was quick and deafening.

I must have died already, Beshar thought. Taken away by the storm and brought to some silent paradise. But the silence was broken by the groans of nearby men. Not dead then.

A pity.

As the winds ceased, sand fell back to the desert floor in soft sheets, the porous dust cloud rising around him. Beshar coughed into his sleeve and waited for the dust to settle. They didn't seem to be missing anyone. He could just make out three figures to his right and three more to his left . . . That couldn't be right. Beshar shook his head, hoping to clear it. So maybe he wasn't dead, but he couldn't believe what he saw.

"Kenjiro," he whispered.

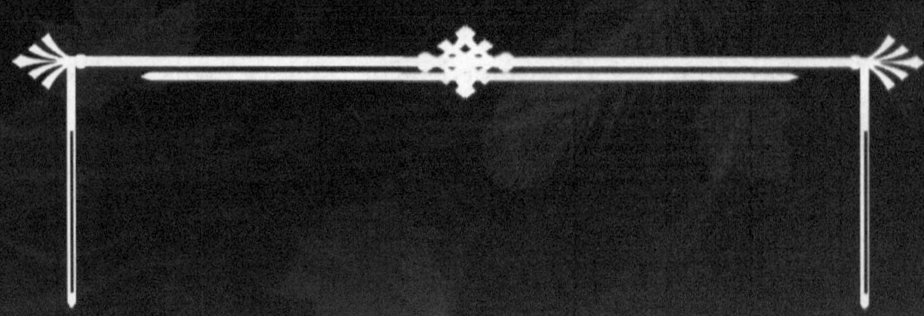

TYLAK

Chapter Ten

Those people just came out of a flaming sandstorm! What kind of magic was this? When Peppik grabbed his arm and screamed at him, Tylak did the only thing he could think of. He'd disappeared. He hadn't been expecting the danger to show up in the form of three tornadoes of sand, and he certainly never anticipated people coming out of them. Was this earth magic then? And how did it work?

He was about to demand an explanation from Beshar, but the man appeared to be just as confused. Peppik also seemed distraught. He stayed behind Tylak, eyeing the newcomers warily. The only people who seemed nonplussed were Jiro and Ichiro. The two calmly shook the dust from their overcoats and began to set up for evening prayer.

Well, best to get this over with. Tylak started forward, hands hovering over his sheathed daggers.

"Who are you, and what do you want?" he demanded, making himself visible as he approached.

"Tylak, this is—"

"You will address His Majesty as King Kutepakenjirotaka," one of the sandstorm men declared, interrupting Beshar's introduction.

Tylak blinked. His Majesty? What in the eternal flames was this all about? Wasn't this man a Samur, like Ichiro and Jiro? Or were they his princes? He shook his head as his outstretched palms fell back to his side. Was the formal greeting enough or was there some small discrepancy because of the nobility? He kept his hands firmly at his side. He already had the sea princess mad at him. Better not piss off any more nobles.

Ichiro and Jiro rushed forward, prostrating themselves even more than they did in prayer. Beshar appeared just as confused. He stared at his man, muttering words that Tylak couldn't hear.

It was up to him to ask the difficult questions. So be it.

"Hello Your Majesty, King Koo-coo—taco," Tylak said loudly, once again starting forward. "I am Tylak, ambassador and personal guard for Jura, daughter of the First Family of the Thirteen." He ignored the glare Beshar sent his way and kept the lie rolling.

"It is King Kutepakenjirotaka," the original speaker corrected Tylak, his gaze raking over him. He sneered at his scar before turning his attention back to his king. "And we have not come to hear such . . . niceties. We have come to declare war."

"Of course you did." Tylak snorted. It took everything he had not to throw his hands up in the air and shout with wild laughter. Could things ever just be easy? His fingertips brushed the hilt of his dagger, and he considered the king now. It would be easy to end his life, to neutralize this new threat before it even started. The sandstorm magic gave him pause, but if he was quick enough . . .

"Kenjiro, it *is* you."

Tylak barely heard the words before Beshar was rushing into the king's arms. The two other guards, or whoever they were, started forward but released their weapons once they realized the men only sought each other's embrace.

Tylak blinked. What was going on?

"The sands are changing," Peppik muttered beside him.

"I'll say."

Beshar and the king were still in their embrace, and the twins began their prayer.

No one seemed concerned or inclined to bring up the fact that mere minutes ago these men had been inside three sandstorms. Flames, maybe they were the sandstorms. Tylak shook his head.

"Danger approaches." Peppik looked up at the fading evening sky, and Tylak followed his gaze. The sky was clear, thank the Everflame, but that didn't mean they were safe from danger. Tylak didn't know if he would ever feel safe again.

"From the sky?" He wasn't sure why he even asked. Peppik rarely responded, and when he did, his answer often came in riddles.

"This danger is closer to the heart."

Well that was grim and to the point. Tylak wanted to question him further, but Peppik could wait. He gave the sky and their surroundings another cursory glance before turning his attention to Beshar and the king.

"I worried you wouldn't come." Beshar's words were hesitant as he finally seemed to notice Tylak at his side. "Tylak, this is—"

"A king come to declare war," Tylak reminded him. "They were extremely clear with their intentions." He took in the king's appearance. He stood like a soldier, dressed in desert darks not unlike his own. The man had an ageless face, but Tylak would guess him to be in his thirties. His hair was closely shaven, and he blinked at Tylak from beneath dark, hooded eyes.

"My men spoke too quickly."

"So you haven't come to declare war?" Tylak asked.

"I . . . it is complicated." The king looked at Beshar, his expression worried. Why was that?

"I think we all could use some answers," Beshar said.

Thank the Everflame, something they agreed on.

"I know you do," the king said. He sent a look of remorse or longing toward the twins as they approached. They ignored Tylak and took up positions with the other two men. So they were part of the Samur. But what sort of secret kingdom was this? He already had enough to deal with between Jura's kidnapping and the Queen of Shadows. He didn't need to add the King of Sandstorms into this mix.

"Tell us then," Tylak said, emboldened by Beshar's familiarity with the man. It hadn't been his imagination. Tylak had seen the gentle way the king regarded Beshar, at the way he had commanded his men to stand down, despite the fact that Tylak's hands still hovered near the hilts of his daggers. It was obvious the king had no desire to hurt any of them. Perhaps he could be turned from perceived foe to future friend. Hadn't Tylak been just as suspicious of Ichiro and Jiro at one time? Now he considered both of them to be fine friends. He tried to catch Jiro's attention, but the man focused on the horizon.

Everything happens as it should, his mother liked to say. She had quoted any number of positive and whimsical things. Silly, nonsensical sayings that were meant to soothe two scared little boys and an anxious young mother. He wanted to believe those words his entire life but how could he? There was so much bad in the world. But this king, this new threat to the Republic and Jura, he'd just given Tylak an idea. He didn't know how it worked yet or how he would convince the man to help him, but Tylak needed him.

He had a way to travel as fast as the wind.

CORAL

Chapter Eleven

She should have considered more carefully before agreeing to help. The trip thus far had been miserable. Amira kept them at a brisk pace—she was a feisty thing for one so slim and broken-looking. But there was nothing broken about her. She was fiercely brave and earning her grudging respect, even if Coral found herself wanting to strangle the girl at times.

In any case, she was no more infuriating than Kale. She still hadn't been able to look at him the same, not since—she shivered. It was difficult even to think about. How could he betray her in that way? They were friends, and he was her soldier. Not to mention the betrayal of Mano. They needed to focus on locating him. Coral needed to see to it that Mano never hurt anyone else, ever again. It would have been too easy to return home and find him waiting there for her. No, Mano was gone and likely planned never to return, not while she was still alive to stop him, in any case. Which meant he probably wanted to find her just as badly.

Coral would bet her right arm he had slithered back to the Queen of Shadows. She was his only protection now. When she had been a child, Coral had loved the wild stories of the Shadow Dancers. They were said to be the only Breathcatchers capable of besting her people. They had a dangerous and secret magic, and they were the best trained assassins on land. There was a rumor that Ailani had met one once, perhaps even loved him. Not that she would tell Coral anything about it. The woman was elusive and had provided her with nothing but more questions during her brief stint back home.

If the Shadow Dancers were the best trained assassins on land, who had trained them all? The Queen of Shadows? The woman was dangerous, obviously so. Coral thought back to their brief encounter. The woman hadn't seemed outright threatening—merely curious. Mostly about Jura.

Why? How did Jura fit in all of this? Thoughts of Jura brought her back to Amira, who marched ahead. She seemed so proud, yet Coral noticed the haunted look in her eyes, the way she flinched at every sudden movement. Coral had seen soldiers returning from battle with the karsh with similar vacant expressions. This girl had known true terror.

"We should consider camping here for the night. We'll reach the last trading post before Toik by tomorrow," Amira said, gesturing to the nothing ahead. It was like the girl had a built-in compass.

"Thank the Mother." Kale grunted at her side as he dropped the two heavy packs at his feet. "She's as strict a drill sergeant as I've ever had."

Coral rolled her eyes in response. He'd insisted on carrying all of their belongings. Not that Amira had anything of her own. Perhaps a trinket or two in her pocket, if the way she kept checking it was any indication. Well, she didn't force him to carry everything. And they did need to hurry. She just wished she had a better idea of what they were hurrying into.

She reached for the pack and began to pull out a bedroll, but Kale stopped her by covering her hands.

"What are you doing?" she hissed, snatching her hands away.

"I was helping you set up your—"

"I can set it up myself. I don't need your help." She could hear how irrational she sounded but didn't care. If he hadn't wanted to make things weird between them, then he should never have done what he did. She shoved the thought aside, determined not to relive the moment, no matter how it danced on the edge of her consciousness.

Fish guts, she didn't want to think of it. Kale and his misdeeds. He was just too willing to help, too *available*. Coral hated it.

"Whatever. You want to set up the beds, set up the beds. I'll ration out our food for the night." She stood up and bumped into Amira, who let out a tiny squeak before she gave Coral a shy smile.

"Umm, I just did that." Amira held out three neatly wrapped packages.

Coral bit her cheek to keep from growling as she snatched her cloth bundle out of Amira's hand. "Great. You two seem like you've got everything under control. Go ahead and rest after you eat. I'll take first watch." She stomped away, ignoring Kale's request to come back and talk. She didn't know why she was so angry, but it seemed that lately any tiny thing was capable of setting her off. Okay, if she admitted it to herself, she knew exactly what was at the root of her problem.

Kale.

Things between them were good, better than good. Especially after Mano's betrayal, Coral trusted Kale. He was her only friend in a sea of subterfuge and lies. And then he went and told her he loved her.

Love! With her? What a load of rotting fish heads. What in the Mother's name did he expect her to do with this information? Did she love him back? Did she even know how to do that anymore? Because for some reason, the idea was only terrifying. And if Coral searched for that secret place inside her heart, she only found more anger, more pain. She didn't want to feel loved. She wanted to feel angry. She wanted to understand why her family had been ripped away from her. She needed answers, not some meaningless words Breathcatchers whispered in each other's ears.

She didn't say it back. She couldn't. And things had been strange ever since. He didn't even say it in a special way. Shouldn't he have made it . . . oh, she didn't know, into a ceremony of sorts?

He asked if she had seen his dagger, and she said she'd put it in his pack and then he'd said he loved her.

Just like that. So now he carried both of their packs and was just so nice, and if he tried to make her smile one more time, she just might strangle him.

She felt the *wei* approach. Not the strong steady pulse of one of her people. Amira then. Hers was light and fluttery like one of those pretty winged insects some Breathcatchers had thought were interesting enough to document in one of her father's books. She'd been fascinated by the mystical bug when she was little, imagining them as large as whales, their wingspan darkening the sky. She was so disappointed when her father brought one home in a glass jar. The tiny thing would barely fill the palm of her hand. It had only lived for a few hours beneath the surface. The Wave Master should never have brought it down.

What an odd memory to have now, Coral thought as Amira settled down beside her.

For a moment the two sat in silence, Coral taking note of their quiet breathing. If she stayed on the surface long enough, would she become like them? Already her connection to the Mother was muted. Her hand played with the ring of salt water around her neck, trying to find peace. When she found the Queen of Shadows, when her enemies were made to taste her blades, would she find peace then?

"I never cared for seafood before," Amira said suddenly.

Coral had nearly forgotten her presence.

Amira had opened a wrapped parcel of cloth to reveal a selection of dried fish and a strip of dehydrated mixed fruit. "Of course, I learned to have a grudging respect for it. Kuru once made me eat . . . well in any case, these things are really good." She bit into the dried fruit strip. "Like, really good. We have tarts at the Republic, and this reminds me of the sweet ones with the candied fig inside. But these are better." She took another bite, closing her eyes and giving in to the simple pleasure of her food.

Coral felt her cheeks redden and was glad Amira was too engrossed with her treat to notice. When was the last time she had enjoyed anything so simple? And why did this girl seem to have a knack for making her feel bad about herself?

"Is that what you're in such a hurry to get back to? The food?" Coral watched Amira flinch at the harsh words and sighed. "I'm sorry. I didn't mean that. I just . . . I have a lot on my mind."

"It's okay. I'm anxious too. Jura likes to eat when she's nervous and I . . . well, I used to talk, and I guess, I'm sorting of talking now. But then again, I'm also pretty nervous."

"It must be frightening. Returning home after so much time away," Coral offered. She felt a tug of empathy for the woman, remembering that she had lost her family, and her homecoming would be that much more difficult for her.

"It is," Amira answered. "Mostly because of the unknown. I just have so many questions, you know? And Jura was taken before we could catch up and . . . there were rumors starting when you returned. I think that there have been some more developments, some very urgent and dangerous developments."

"Like what?" Coral asked, finally relaxing from a squatted position to sit on her bottom. She unwrapped her own food parcel and popped a salted strip of cod in her mouth.

"I'm not entirely sure. Something dangerous with the Everflame for one."

Coral nodded. They'd witnessed that phenomenon firsthand. Jura's scar-faced companion had admitted to releasing the Everflame, and the fire had spread rapidly in the Golden City. Then there had been a streak of light, and the earth had rumbled and the fire had simply disappeared. All of it. As if someone had doused the entire thing with an invisible ocean of water.

She weighed her next words carefully, not sure how much she should share. Amira seemed trustworthy enough, but Coral was still working out how to understand it all herself. Ailani and the other elders had begrudgingly given her the prophecy, an old warning, the triad had called it. Coral had memorized the words: *When the eternal fire once again walks the earth, the stones will be exhumed. The Mistress will bend the knee, and the world will be made new in blood.*

It was as ominous a warning as she'd ever heard. It was safe to assume the eternal fire was a reference to the Everflame, the inextinguishable flame the Breathcatchers had worshipped and kept locked away in a Glass Palace similar to their own. Or so the stories went. Coral had never before been to the Breathcatchers' land, and once she had her revenge, she couldn't see herself coming back. But the Everflame had disappeared, so where did that leave the prophecy now? Was it all over before it even started? The Mistress could only refer to one person, herself. She was the Wave Mistress, Commander of the Three Oceans by birthright, and as such she bent the knee to no one. Then of course, there was that bit about the earth being made new in blood. That part was obviously terrifying. Did that just mean that everyone was going to die? None of it made sense.

"I am scared to go back," Amira admitted. She'd finished her meal and was rubbing her arms, despite the lack of chill in the air.

"My people have an old warning of the Everflame once again walking the earth," Coral whispered. Amira's eyes widened, and Coral remembered another of Ailani's old warnings. *Guard your knowledge for it is power in the Republic.* As much as it galled her to admit it, Ailani was wisest of all her people, and for all her secrecy she never lied. On the contrary, the elder's words almost always had a way of becoming truths.

"What is the warning?" Amira breathed out. "What does it mean if the Everflame escapes?"

"The stones will be exhumed," Coral answered. She pressed her lips together to keep from saying anything more. She would heed Ailani's warnings, all of them, for now. Amira continued to stare at her and Coral shrugged, cutting off her expectant expression. "That's it. When the Everflame walks the earth, the stones will be exhumed."

Amira frowned, gazing off into the distance and dipping her hand back in her pocket in what Coral was coming to believe was a nervous habit. "I wonder what that means."

Coral wondered too. Perhaps it was best Coral kept her secrets. She still had so much to figure out because if she could do anything to keep the bloodbath from starting, she planned on it. And there was no way she was bending the knee to anyone.

JURA

Chapter Twelve

It was easy to wake before dawn when someone told you that your worth would be tested come morning. Jura shoved the thick blanket away from her and sat up, tired of tossing and turning. If she wasn't going to sleep, she may as well get some training done.

If she were back at home, she would have perused her collection of books for some answers. True to his word, Matteus had brought a novel to her room alongside her dinner. It was a short thing, scarcely a novella, with an unoriginal plot and a bit too much kissing. Jura read it three times in a row before sleep claimed her.

After the appearance of the novel, Jura had all the more reason to believe the aliferous had a library. Surely there was one tucked away somewhere. She would have to remember to ask when she was being taken to her studies. Or testing . . . What had Danos said exactly? Jura liked tests; she did well on tests. She had a great memory for things she had read, and she enjoyed reading. As such, academics had always come easily to her. But this test for her worthiness . . . What did it mean? And how could she go about preparing for it? It seemed like she was either worthy or she wasn't.

Jura ceased her useless pacing and forced herself to warm up her muscles. She moved with muscle memory, her body throwing itself into the odd, war-like dance that Akkim, her personal trainer and former bodyguard, had taught her. She had thought it funny when she was a child, delighting in the body movement and various acrobatics. Then her father had caught them at it, and Akkim had been spoken to and then the strange dance was no longer a part of her training. Instead, they began to focus on hand-to-hand combat and her long-distance weaponry.

Respectable weapons for females included things such throwing knives or her whip. Amira was quite adept at throwing daggers; her aim was almost always perfect. Jura felt an unexpected stab of guilt at the thought of her friend, and she stumbled in her steps.

How was poor Amira? Was she heading back to the Republic? Was Tylak with her?

The slightest of breezes entered her room through the open wall. The air caressed her skin, cooling the thin line of sweat she'd worked up against the nape of her neck.

The sun was rising, she realized as the soft morning light began to seep into her room. Last night she'd been given another set of pants and stretch of linen. She began the arduous task of dressing herself, rolling out the length of fabric—today a pale lavender—before wrapping it around herself. Her arms had already begun to tire after her workout, and she marveled at the fact that the one time she desperately wished for a handmaid, she had no access to one. Several minutes later, she was completely dressed and waiting patiently by her door.

She didn't have to wait long before there was a gentle knock from the other side.

"I'm awake!" she called out.

In response, her door whistled musically before swinging open. It was not the Speaker of the Winds, however, but a familiar face from her first night.

"Oh, hello. You helped me the night I was brought here. You said you could get a message to my friends."

"I did and I have. Good morning, daughter of the First. Might I introduce myself to Your Greatness?"

"There's no need to be so formal," Jura mumbled. "Please, just call me Jura. And who do I have the honor of meeting?"

"Priamos. Pri, if I may be so bold. My mother called me Pri." He smiled. He had a handsome face, if it was a bit odd. His cheekbones were high, sharply chiseled against the curved beak of his nose. Feathers tied back his long, dark hair, though he had no feathers elsewhere save for light yellow ones across his eyebrows. He was the first among the aliferous she had seen without wings. His wide-set eyes studied her carefully.

"Pri then." Jura forced a smile to her lips. "It's so good to meet your acquaintance." Her fingers moved on their own, intertwining and wriggling in the formal greeting of the Republic.

"You honor me." Pri dipped his head. "It pains me that I was unable to visit you again until now. My duties—"

"Please, you don't owe me any explanation. Thank you, by the way, for helping me." Jura paused, struggling with how to phrase her next inquiry. "How is it—that is, was that a sort of wind magic you used? Sending that message to my friends?"

Pri looked over his shoulder and studied the empty atrium behind him before answering. "It's probably best not to mention such things again, Greatness. But yes, you could say it was exactly that." He stepped back, his voice once again rising to a normal level. "We can all speak to the wind and it to us, if only you know how to listen."

It sounded like something Peppik or a Shadow Dancer would say, and she smiled wryly at the thought.

His voice dipped down to a whisper and he added, "But your message was well-received. He's coming for you."

Tylak was coming here? How? If it was at all possible for anyone, it was possible for Tylak, but then what did that mean for Amira and the Republic? Had her friend gone back to face the horrors of home alone, or was she also traveling north to rescue Jura?

"They can't. It isn't safe. I need to send them another message," Jura whispered back, allowing her desperation to lace her voice.

"You're right. It isn't safe, but I can't send them another message. Not for a little while anyway. I . . . I'm not as powerful as everyone else." He sighed, pointing a thumb back toward himself and his lack of wings. "It takes me longer to recharge. My connection to the sky is muted or something." He shrugged. "But I'll help you as soon as I can. I promise."

"Why are you being so nice to me?" she asked, worrying what he might possibly want in exchange.

"I'm not sure exactly. You remind me of me, I guess. You don't belong here either."

Jura opened her mouth to respond but snapped it closed as Danos and his two personal guards came into view.

"Priamos? I don't recall seeing your name assigned to the atrium this morning," Danos called out in his beautiful voice. "Perhaps you had best get back to your duties."

"Yes, Speaker," Pri mumbled, shooting Jura another warning glance.

She gave an imperceptible nod back. She agreed to his silence for now. It seemed she might have found herself an ally in all this confusion. She just wished he didn't present so many more questions.

Pri turned sharply on his heel and was out of sight moments later.

"I hope Priamos wasn't disturbing you. He is a curious boy, but we indulge him." He narrowed his eyes. "I trust you would inform me if he, or anyone, were to ever make you feel . . . uncomfortable during your stay here."

"It's fine. He was following up on a wardrobe question I had." She pressed her lips together in a firm line, determined not to catch her bottom lip between her teeth as she lied. Sandstorms, but she shouldn't have to think so much before she'd broken her fast. "It appears my pants were on backward at the time."

Danos gave her a meticulous stare, his gaze roving from her eyes down to her slippered feet. She resisted the urge to curl her toes so he wouldn't look at them. It wasn't fair. She was tired of feeling vulnerable.

She lifted her chin. "If you're quite finished with studying my appearance, I'm ready to be tested."

Danos smiled, revealing his exceptionally long, sharp canines. "It amuses me that you believe yourself ready for what comes next. Follow me."

BESHAR

CHAPTER THIRTEEN

Beshar *prided himself on being* a man who enjoyed puzzles, a man who would, under normal circumstances, be delighted by the living enigma that was Kenjiro. But there was too little time and too much at stake to pontificate on that now.

"This . . . can all wait until morning," Beshar announced. *After I've had time to think.* "Probably best to get some rest until—"

"Burn it all, we haven't come this close to answers only to wait until the morning, have we?" Tylak cut in, his tone wild and bitter.

Well, the boy had every right to be afraid. Beshar darted another glance at Kenjiro, but his man remained steadfast and stoic, his face an impassive mask.

"The young Lord of Shadows is correct. Some answers must be paid." Kenjiro sighed, turning to the men behind him. "Here is as good a place as any to make camp. In the morning we continue our mission, but tonight you will rest and fill up on a peaceful night of sleep."

Beshar blinked at Kenjiro's dismissal of the men, but everyone else seemed to take it in stride. Even Tylak and his doddering follower set about the task of preparing the campsite. Beshar found himself watching Kenjiro, noting the easy way he gave commands. This man was changed from the Samur he had known. This man was a born leader.

"It seems much has changed these last few days," Beshar said out loud.

"Much has," Kenjiro responded. "But in many ways, things are as they have always been."

Beshar thought about this. Kenjiro had always been a natural leader among the Samur. He alone was directly responsible for Beshar's life and had been from the very first moment Beshar had met him. But, the Samur had no kingdom. They were simply a warrior sect of religious followers. So who was this king standing before him now?

"The Samur, th—"

"We are Samur no longer," Kenjiro cut him off. "The sands have been tamed."

Old words. Simple words. They settled over Beshar like a blanket of ice, chilling his skin and causing the hairs to rise on his arms. It was an old saying, one that had lost its original meaning long ago. His father had liked to mutter it under his breath: *I'll take that deal when the sands are tamed.* And then he would laugh because the sands could never be tamed. The sands were wild.

"The Republic no longer speaks for the dunes. I do," Kenjiro continued. His authoritative tone rang out across the quiet desert evening.

"Because you're the King of Sandstorms?" Tylak asked from Beshar's side. He flinched. He hadn't heard the boy approach. In fact, he hadn't even taken his eyes off Kenjiro. He would have to take better stock of his surroundings, it seemed. Especially if he no longer had his Samur to look after him.

Tylak had crossed his arms over his chest, and he scowled at the man he'd just called a king. It should have made Beshar pleased to see the boy treated every noble with the same irreverence, but instead he felt the worry line on his forehead crease with his concern.

Kenjiro was deadly serious about his claim, as serious as Beshar had ever seen him. And to say the sands were tamed . . . what did it all mean?

"I am who I am. No more and no less." Kenjiro had turned his full attention to Tylak and studied him intently.

"A king," Tylak repeated.

"Among other things." Kenjiro looked around him, as though taking stock of where each man stood. His four Samur . . . subjects . . . had finished setting up camp and flanked either side of him, hands ready on their swords.

They were on high alert, Beshar realized, uneasy with the idea. They were just outside of the southern borders of Toik, the distant city no more than a blank dot on the horizon. It was past time for the city pits to be ignited. Another blackout then. This couldn't be good.

"I am King Kutepakenjirotaka, but I was born Samur, as my father was and his father before him."

"Samur, like a special bodyguard, right?" The Shadow Dancer stared at the twins, but they seemed content to ignore him, instead peering into the setting sun as they searched for hidden dangers.

"We are—were—more than that. The mantle of Samur was taken up only after our great betrayal to our celestial Father."

"You betrayed the sun?" Tylak asked.

Beshar blinked at him. What did this boy know of Shrivo beliefs? The Samur had never spoken to Beshar about their religion before.

"In some ways, yes." Kenjiro exchanged a look with Ichiro. "You see, my people have always been gifted with the sun's favor. We are the children of his chosen stars, and as such, he has deemed us with gifts. While our Father has control of the heavens, we have dominion over the earth." As he said this, he snapped his fingers, causing a spray of sand to flourish up behind him. "But while we are the children of his divine spirit, we are also the children of stars—we are selfish and prideful. Ambitious in our need to outshine the others. So it was that we discovered a way to change the magic of our gifts."

Tylak's companion had come to stand beside him. The old man appeared concerned. Well, he had every right to be. Beshar was concerned too. He gave a vigorous nod and gestured for Kenjiro to continue.

"Soon, it wasn't enough that my people could control the earth. We wanted more power. Power to control the gifts of others. Powers of the sun himself."

Beshar swallowed. They sought out ways to harness the powers of the sun? How was such a thing even possible? Normally the hint of such delicious knowledge would leave him salivating at the mouth, but instead Beshar still felt impossibly cold.

"No one can control the power of the sun." Tylak scoffed, but he seemed unsure.

"And no man ever should," Kenjiro agreed. "But my people tried, all the same. We discovered certain stones. Scion stones, we called them. Each stone was capable of harnessing great power. Each stone unique. There were five of them, massive gems embedded in the rock beneath the earth. We should have known then . . . should have seen that even then they hid from our Father's eyes."

"These stones, what did they do?" Beshar asked, dreading the answer.

"They changed the world," Kenjiro whispered. "All these years, we have had to suffer the price of our actions. My people lost more than our kingdom that day. We lost our way of life. We lost . . . everything. We scorched the earth, and in an instant, it was all gone."

"You didn't." Beshar shook his head, unwilling to accept the cold burn of the truth.

"We did. My people created the Everflame and let it loose to destroy the land."

TYLAK

CHAPTER FOURTEEN

It was a lot to process. And yet, it still wasn't enough. Peppik was close again, although for once, Tylak didn't mind. The old man's familiar presence was a comfort. Tylak needed that comfort. It was the only thing that seemed to make any sense these days. He knew that the tiny country of Shrivo was old but couldn't say just how old. Jura would know, probably. Or at the very least she would know which book to dig out for the information. What would she say to all this now? That an entire race of people worshipped the sun. That they would create another god in its image and then release it upon the land.

"But, why?" Tylak voiced the question out loud.

"Pride mostly. Because we could. But it was the ultimate betrayal to our Father, and as such, our sins were punished."

"We must often pay the sins of our fathers," Peppik muttered from beside him, but Tylak shook his head. He had never known his father, and he wasn't about to start taking on the man's sins.

"But what does it all mean? What does any of this have to do with you suddenly becoming a king?"

"He has always been our king," Ichiro snapped.

Tylak frowned at the man's hand resting on his sword. He had thought the twins had come to see him as a friend, but the warning scowl suggested otherwise.

"Please," the new king interrupted, holding out his palm. "I will explain. I have always been the king, but I have not always had a kingdom. Our people did a great disservice to our Father, and we had to be punished. We destroyed our paradise, and it was only through great sacrifice that we were able to survive at all. Entering a life of servitude, banishment from our homeland . . . This is the price of our betrayal. We were happy to pay."

"And now?" Beshar asked. The councilman appeared to have aged ten years overnight. "What has changed?"

"Everything." The new king gestured behind him. "The Everflame once again walks the earth. The sands are tamed. The time has come to reclaim our kingdom."

"War," Tylak muttered. So they were back to this. It was a nice story—he had to give him that. But surely it was just that, a story.

"War is a natural step to reclaiming what was lost."

Fine then, but why did it have to be war against *her*? In any case, Tylak refused to let any of this stop him. He interrupted Beshar's question on the special stones and asked the question that had been burning in his soul since the King of Sandstorms arrived.

"Can you teach me how to ride a sandstorm?"

The king laughed. Tylak didn't fault him for that. It was an outrageous question. Hadn't he laughed at Jura when she'd asked him to teach her to steal fire? But he had to ask because there had to be a way to use this remarkable skill to save her.

"You are serious, young Lord of Shadows?"

Tylak flinched at his new title. It didn't sit well for him to think of himself as the lord of anything. He was just Tylak, nothing more. When he didn't respond to the king's look of scrutiny, the man continued.

"I cannot teach a child of fire how to summon the sands, but I will assist you in this request . . . for a price." The king exchanged a look with Beshar.

The councilman cleared his throat. "Tylak, perhaps it is best if we discuss this privately."

"I'll pay it, whatever it is," Tylak continued, frowning at Beshar. He didn't have time to speak privately. He needed action. Jura had been gone for days already.

The king smiled, the action changing his face. "Then we are in agreement. We leave at dawn."

Tylak slept fitfully, tossing and turning in his bedroll. There was no light from a fire, and each time Tylak opened his eyes, it was to find a dark and ominous campsite. Jura would surely lecture him for agreeing to pay an unknown price, but what choice did he have? When he opened his eyes, and the sky had begun to melt into a muted gray, he rose from his bedroll and began to pack up his belongings.

He was soon joined by the Samur or whatever they liked to be called now as they woke and began morning prayer. Once Beshar awoke and the prayers were completed, the king joined Tylak.

"Are you sure you want to do this? The sands can be . . . unpleasant . . . for those unsuited to that way of travel."

Tylak grunted. "I can handle myself."

"And I'm stronger than these old bones appear," Peppik said from beside him.

"Peppik, I can't ask you to do this." Tylak reached for his old friend, giving his forearm a firm squeeze. "You said yourself these winged people are dangerous."

"All the more reason for me to come and keep you out of harm's way."

Tylak grinned at his friend. "Well there you have it. We're as ready as we'll ever be." He turned to Beshar. "And you, Councilman? Will you come with us?"

Beshar shook his head. "I'm not your councilman, not anymore. I'm . . . not sure what I am. But no, I can't go with you. I'm no warrior, and I'd only slow you down."

"Take this then," Tylak said, struck with a sudden idea. He dug into Jura's sack, rummaging through books and journals until he found what he was looking for. He handed Beshar the dainty lorgnette.

"This is a blood seeker. It can find Jura, wherever she is. I don't know how it works but . . ." he trailed off, acutely aware of the dangerous weapon he'd just handed to Beshar. He wasn't even sure what had made him do it.

Beshar seemed to know the solemnity of the gift and accepted it with a grave nod.

"All right then," he said, turning back to face the King of Sandstorms. "I'm ready."

"Stand between my men, and they will see that no harm comes to you."

Tylak began to move when he realized the king wasn't speaking to him. The King of Sandstorms exchanged an intense look with Beshar before turning his attention back to Tylak.

"You and your companion must step close to me while I call the sands."

"Master, let me take them."

"No," the king interrupted. "This is my agreement with the

Lord of Shadows, and I will see it through. I will return here once the deed is done." He gestured for Tylak to move in closer.

Tylak stepped forward until he was nearly nose to nose with the king.

"Ahh, you will see the importance of the stones," the king whispered before he began to hum.

Tylak glanced down at the tiny blue stone hanging from a leather cord around his neck. "My birthstone?" he asked. "How is that important?"

The king didn't answer, lost in his humming, but Peppik grabbed Tylak's arm, his fingers digging into his bicep. The humming grew louder until it was all Tylak could hear. The sound rumbled through his body and vibrated his soul. His toes tingled, and his legs trembled as the ground seemed to stiffen beneath him, yet it still gave the feeling that he was falling. The humming buzzed in his ears and tingled his spine as Peppik's grip on his arm tightened.

Tiny grains of sand began to slap at his face, stinging his skin. He closed his eyes, overcome with sudden vertigo. His stomach rumbled, and he was thankful they hadn't taken the time to eat anything before he'd undertaken this ordeal. He had to squint so hard now that he clenched his teeth, and still it wasn't enough to keep the sand from bringing forth tears and slicing his skin. He wanted to shout that they had to stop, but he didn't think anything could be heard over that awful humming sound. It was all he heard. It overcame his thoughts.

Then it was over.

Soft dunes replaced the stiff ground under his feet. The stinging sand whirling around him was gone, and there was a blissful silence that Tylak had feared he would never hear again. His stomach hadn't caught up, though, and Tylak found himself on his knees, heaving up whatever contents remained in his belly. Sandstorms, he was never doing that again.

He blinked. For a moment, it didn't appear that he had gone anywhere, but then he saw it. In the east, the jagged outcropping of the famous mountain range known as the Edge.

"Flames, would you look at that." He turned to Peppik. The man was remarkably pale. He probably still hadn't recovered from the ordeal of the trip. Tylak couldn't blame him. He was still a bit dizzy himself.

"I have taken you as far north as I can. The sands will travel no farther," the king said with a solemn bow.

Tylak shrugged, uncomfortable with the gesture. If this man really was a king, then he had no business bowing down to a former slave like himself.

"You've taken me farther than I imagined. You've saved me days, no, weeks of travel. I don't know how I can repay you."

"There is the aforementioned price, of course." Kenjiro gave him a significant look. "Your stone will suffice."

"My birthstone?" Tylak asked, surprised by the request. Of all the things he'd imagined owing this king, his tiny blue birthstone had never made the list.

"Tylak, you can't!" Peppik hissed from beside him.

Tylak ignored him as he pulled the faded leather from around his neck. It was his last memory of his mother, of Sykk and everything from his past. And it was a small price to pay in exchange for the magic done.

The King of Sandstorms snatched the stone from him, enclosing it in his fist. "Your debt is paid, young Lord of Shadows." He dipped into another bow, and Tylak again felt the rumble of the ground beneath his feet.

"Wait," he called out before the king could begin his terrifying hum. "What do you want with it? I didn't think it was valuable to anyone but myself."

The king gave him a chilling look before sliding the leather around his own neck, the stone settling against his skin.

"Everything is valuable if one knows its worth." The king touched the birthstone and disappeared before Tylak's eyes.

AMIRA

CHAPTER FIFTEEN

oik was the southernmost city of the Republic. Amira had once adored the city. She had been enthralled by the busy marketplace with its stunning shopping centers at the city's square. The tiny shops each held an explosion of color, and they had all courted her, or rather her father's money. It was a thriving metropolis known for its fashion trendsetting, and Amira had once believed there was no finer place in all of Jangbahar.

Amira always begged her father to allow her to attend his business trips to the city. Ahmar had often indulged his eldest, and Amira was always gifted a new dress upon his return. Flames, if she was honest, it was always more than just a single dress. She had hundreds of them, and yet, somehow, she had always wanted more. The idea of her wardrobe back home seemed silly now. What was the point of dresses when her family and friends were gone?

It was funny that the city could look the same when everything else was so different. She didn't want to enter the city, but Toik hosted the only road with direct access to the Glass Palace. They had wasted enough time, Coral had argued. It was time for action. The woman was on a mad quest for revenge, and nothing would slow her path. At least it was a path Amira could understand, even if it didn't mirror her own. While Coral thirsted for vengeance, Amira just wanted things to go back to normal. She had a feeling they would both be disappointed.

"Who do we kill to get inside?" Coral asked, poking a finger into her rib cage.

Amira winced. She still wasn't accustomed to Coral's aggressive actions.

"I think what Coral means to say is how do we get past those big glass gates?" Kale said from her other side.

Amira was often sandwiched between the two of them. It seemed better that way as the two were apt to fight whenever left alone. Amira thought that they had feelings for one another, but there were other times when it was hard to tell.

"I'm not sure," Amira sighed in response, wishing she was more help to the group. "I've never had to worry about getting through before. Normally they just see my face and wave me through the gates." It was still difficult remembering her life had been so charmed.

"That's it then! We'll just walk straight through." Coral smiled brilliantly, and Amira was struck by how nice the gesture made her seem, even if only for a moment.

"But didn't you say there was another one of you running around the Glass Palace?" Kale asked. He often argued against Coral's opinions, Amira noted, although it was nice hearing varying thoughts in either direction. Especially when either side argued their case so passionately. Amira tensed, worried they were about to start another argument.

"Yes, but she . . . it's tucked away in the Glass Palace so we shouldn't have to worry about anyone seeing double."

"You can't assume that. We have no way of knowing if that's actually true," Kale argued.

"And you can't assume this plan will fail simply because you're not the one who came up with it. It's going to work," Coral snapped.

"It could, I mean, it *should*," Amira said, desperate to interrupt them before they started shouting. Coral seemed to enjoy shouting. "I can do it," she repeated. "I can play the part of the Third of the Thirteen because, well, I am. I am her, that is." Amira tried for a confident smile but had a difficult time considering that they were discussing her evil doppelgänger.

She tried to ignore the fact that they argued whether or not Amira could successfully play the role of herself. She couldn't blame them for doubting her. She was a far cry from one of the Thirteen now.

"See? She's fine." Coral gave her a hearty slap on the back, and surprisingly Amira didn't flinch.

"There is a problem though," Amira admitted. She stared down at her dirty attire with a frown. "I would never be caught out on the streets of downtown Toik in this."

Coral rolled her eyes. "What are you saying? We need to buy you a new dress first?"

Amira lifted her chin, quoting her mother. "'A woman's armor is worn in silk and her weapons wielded in wordplay.'"

Coral snorted. "A woman's armor is armor and her weapons are sharp and sure. But we'll get you a sodden dress if that's what we need to get in."

After another, albeit brief, argument, it was decided that Kale would circle back to the travel post a few miles back and barter for a dress while the girls remained hidden and formulated their plan. Amira found the arrangement confusing. How could Kale be trusted to purchase a fashionable dress in her size? And what did *she* know of formulating plans to overthrow governments? Perhaps Coral and Kale just liked it better with her under constant guard. She still wasn't free, not truly. Not with Coral and Kale watching her every move. Not with Jura relying on her.

"Tell me again the layout of the palace. We have to be sure I know everything, just in case you . . . we get separated." Coral regarded her with those magnificent eyes of hers. They truly were the most incredible things Amira had ever seen, like green sea foam after a stormy day.

Amira swallowed. She knew that Coral still didn't trust her, but Jura had believed in her so that was something, wasn't it? She repeated the layout, drawing a blueprint in the sand with her finger. She indicated each of the fourteen towers, tracing the lines of each with her finger before coming to a stop over the tower that had housed the Everflame.

"This is where the Everflame was before." She looked up into Coral's sea-green eyes.

"Before it disappeared," Coral murmured. "Do you think . . . do you wonder if Jura is behind it?"

"Behind what?" Amira asked carefully. "The Everflame disappearing? Because no, I don't think she had anything to do with that. Besides, we don't know for certain the Everflame has disappeared."

Coral nodded. "That's true. But, her strange magic. There has to be something to that. What *is* she?"

They had been traveling together for days, and this was the first time Coral had been so direct about Jura. The questions made Amira uncomfortable because she was still trying to make sense of what she'd seen herself. The Jura she'd grown up with didn't have any magic powers. But that didn't change what Amira had seen—what they had all seen Jura do. Somehow, she had shone as bright as the sun and then she'd miraculously healed Kale. Amira had never heard of magic like that before. She didn't think Coral had either.

"She's my friend," Amira answered simply. "She's always been my friend. That's all I need to know."

She wished she felt as confident as she sounded. What was the reason behind the sudden appearance of Jura's new magic? Had she always had it? Held it as a secret from everyone she knew? Or was it something else entirely, a new power only manifested in light of these recent times. If only Amira had the answers. Her hand reached unbidden, fingers stretching for the familiar feeling of the stone held securely in her pocket. As always, she found comfort in its touch.

Coral sighed. "Fine, I get it. I'll ask her myself next time I see her. How much confidence do you have in old scar-face anyway?"

Amira considered this. She hadn't known the man long. He'd appeared in Kuru's home with a letter from Jura and then he'd set fire to the place with a special torch she'd later learned he'd stolen from the Everflame. There hadn't been much opportunity for chatter after they'd been running for their lives. He'd seemed like a capable enough fellow, and if she had been forced to choose a personal hero, she would probably choose a Shadow Dancer too. She said as much out loud.

"He's a Shadow Dancer?" Coral asked, raising her eyebrows. She was impressed, if the low whistle that escaped her pursed lips was any indication. "Well, that explains some things. But what about his queen?" Her green eyes narrowed. "She's responsible for everything, you know. She sent out the orders to massacre my people *and* start this war."

"I know. And Tylak doesn't trust her either. He chose Jura over his queen. I heard him." And she had. Tylak had forsaken his queen just before he'd thrown the Everflame at her. He'd done all this while Amira had stolen the stone.

She still wasn't sure why she'd stolen the item. She'd heard Kuru's father stress the value of the stone, and stealing something that vile man had treasured, hurting him in even the smallest of ways, well, that had seemed motive enough at the time.

Coral grunted by way of response, turning her attention to Amira's blueprint in the sand.

Amira's hand dipped back into her pocket to once again caress the smooth planes of the stone. It was important, wasn't it? Why else would the sea people have a prophecy about it? Assuming the prophecy truly was about her stone. Amira had ceased believing in coincidences. If Coral brought up the stone, it was because it truly was important in some way. Maybe Coral even suspected Amira had it. She should have been more forthcoming with her knowledge of the stone, but old habits were hard to break. How could she trust Coral with her newfound knowledge when it was the only power she still held?

For as much as Kale liked to joke that the trio was becoming quite the team, Amira knew the bitter truth. To them, she was an outsider, and not one to be trusted. She couldn't blame them. The Thirteen were known for their ruthless cruelty. No, it was better to hang on to this new knowledge, to see how it developed, to learn when playing her hand would be most beneficial. Besides, Coral's prophecy called for the *stones* to be exhumed. Stones, as in more than one. How many were there, then? And what did it all mean?

Coral cleared her throat, bringing Amira back to attention.

"I'm sorry?"

"I asked about the prison catacombs? You mentioned they ran

underneath the palace?" Coral stared at her expectantly.

Amira nodded, forcing herself to focus. "Yes, they're an exact replica of the halls above. They can be a bit tricky, but once you mark where the towers are, you can navigate them with ease."

"And the entry and exit? Both above ground and inside the castle walls?"

Good questions. She was thorough, and once again, Amira wondered if she should be so forthcoming with her information about the palace. Could this woman truly be trusted? She hated that it didn't seem to matter. Amira didn't have a choice. Trust her or don't, there would be zero chance of success without their help.

"Yes. All above ground except . . ." She frowned.

"Except what?" Coral prompted when Amira didn't continue.

"Except this exit here. Past the palace proper. Through the city latrine." She indicated the spot with a tiny *x* on her makeshift map.

"So that's our way in, then." Coral grunted as she pushed back to her full height. She wiped her hands on her cloak, frowning at the tiny grains of sand that clung to her palm.

Amira swallowed against the determined look in Coral's eyes as the young woman reached for the weapon strapped to her back.

"The latrine?" Amira kept her attention on the three sharpened points of the long and curved spear, but Coral didn't seem to notice.

"Exactly," Coral said, a wicked grin sliding across her face. "We can sneak into the Glass Palace without anyone even knowing we're there."

KAY

CHAPTER SIXTEEN

I fell asleep flying again.

Kay's eyes snapped open at the thought and she looked around, noting her new surroundings. It was nice, wherever they were. The crisp, cool air reminded her of early mornings in the barn with Daddy. They were in a field that almost looked like home. Green rolling hills and the familiar sound of the morning doover birds were enough to put her at ease.

Inferno was curled into a ball, and she could tell by the steady rumble of his body that he was still asleep. He had probably flown all night.

She Breathed deeply, throwing out her awareness in search of other dragons. It was a trick she'd learned during her time in the arena, but Inferno was the only large presence she felt.

They were safe, for now.

That made her feel better. She slid off Inferno's neck and gave him a careful once-over. The name had suited him once. The dragon's scales were dim compared to others she'd seen, his belly scarred from his many previous battles. He had seemed ferocious at one time; he *was* ferocious. He was responsible for the death of not one, but two of her friends. A part of her would always hate him for that. And yet, he was also the only friend she had in the world. He represented her freedom, her future, and for that reason she also loved him.

That was it then. Inferno no longer suited him, and the name had to go. She wondered who had thought to even name him that. The councilman probably.

Disjointed memories constantly spun in her head. At times the memories brought her to her knees. The memories came more often now, likely another side effect of Breathing in the eternal flame.

Councilman Beshar.

The name suddenly came to her, although Kay couldn't remember learning it. She remembered many things differently. Bits and pieces of previous conversations heard in Jangba floated back to her, now translated, now clear. Entire moments in time that had once been unclear or perhaps lost, memories from her childhood even . . . Kay remembered so much. Too much.

They had named her that final night in the arena too. Her new owner, and the red-robes, and everyone else. Kay had heard them all chanting her new name, Fire Shot. A stupid name.

Kay took a deep breath and unclenched her fist. She didn't have to be Fire Shot, not now, not ever again. And Inferno didn't have to be Inferno anymore. He could just be her friend, like Rumble had been. They could start over together.

She left the sleeping dragon and began to explore their new surroundings. There was an outcropping of trees just to her right, and through them Kay could hear water. Daddy's words tumbled back to her. *If you ever find yourself in unknown surroundings, find water, find shelter.* And then he would promise to find her. Kay didn't like to remember that last part—didn't want to think about a world where her Daddy would never find her. She took a deep Breath and walked toward the trees.

It was as many as Kay had ever seen, an impossible amount. A land of dark limbs and knurled roots as far as she could see. A jungle. It was difficult to pinpoint the sound of water beyond the many singing birds, but Kay stumbled forward, determined to find its source. She continued to reach out for anyone else's Breathing but couldn't feel anything beyond the nearly infinite number of tiny critters around her.

She pushed farther, careful to walk in a straight line so she wouldn't get lost. Just when she thought it might be time to turn around, she found the rushing river ahead. The water ran at a steady pace, tumbling over rocks and cutting the jungle carpet in half. Although it curved around and beyond sight, Kay assumed the river ran for miles in either direction. If someone wanted to cross the river, they would need to be really good swimmers or have a boat or a dragon of their own. That made getting to the other side seem all the more important. If they were on the other side of the river, then maybe she could feel safe.

She turned around to walk back to her dragon, allowing her thoughts to wander as she ambled along. Finding the river and crossing it were just the beginning of things. Next Kay would be expected to find shelter and food. There was a group of boulders on the other side of the river, and Kay thought she might have a chance of making a home among them. The way they had been positioned had almost formed a sort of cave. Things would be so much easier if she could find an adult and ask for help, but Kay didn't trust any of the adults she'd come to meet so far. Everyone seemed to have a secret plan against her. Everyone wanted to hurt her.

She worried the red-robes would never stop searching for her, and it terrified her that she didn't even know why. Even now, after the arena was in ruins and most of the dragons had escaped. Did they really want her to fight so badly? What would that prove?

She realized she was still Breathing and exhaled, feeling instantly deflated.

Perhaps it was time to admit that maybe the red-robes still chased her not because of who she was but because of what she'd done. Maybe they chased her because they felt she needed to be punished. She should have never Breathed in the great flame. She wondered what Daddy would say about her Breathing in so much heat all at once. He probably wouldn't even believe it possible, not at first. And after . . . well, she would definitely get a whooping.

She would take all the whoopings in the world if it meant she could tell Daddy about what it meant to Breathe in the eternal flame. How even when she wasn't Breathing, she could still feel that intense heat searing her from the inside. How the boiling heat, however discomforting, made her feel less alone. Kay knew she was more special than anyone had ever thought possible.

Now when she Breathed, she only had to pull from the immense well of heat within herself. And it seemed that source of power was endless.

She felt a distant tug in her belly, a new awareness that tingled her skin. Inferno was awake. Somewhere in the back of her mind, she was aware that her connection to the dragon was growing even stronger, but she never dwelled on the idea. Things were scary enough already.

Kay quickened her step, eager to discuss a new name with Inferno. She hoped he wouldn't be offended by the name change. She wanted him to see that it meant new beginnings and friendship because she would never make him change his name if he didn't want to. She remembered how much it had hurt to be called Cadet.

She understood now that Ash hadn't done so to hurt her feelings—just the opposite in fact. He had cared for her in his own way. The problem was his way was broken, just like the Republic was. That place had been terribly strange, and she was glad to be away from it, although sometimes she would still think about the people who had lived there. Maybe she always would. She pushed away memories of Ash's gentle words and Kindle's tough smile. Always better not to think about these things.

Like Mama and Daddy. Thinking about them made her feel empty inside, and she didn't have time for that. Not when the red-robes were just behind her.

She could just make out the clearing beyond the trees ahead, and she was about to call out to her dragon friend when she became acutely aware of the fact that she was being watched. Kay cast out her Breath, searching for anyone around her. She found a lone presence, just behind and to her left. Maybe they hadn't seen her dragon yet. She stopped, stooping down and pretending to study a tree stump. Why was this person watching her? Was it one of the red-robes? If not, what did they want?

She had only a few options. She could continue to ignore the person, and maybe they would get bored with watching her and go away. Or she could run to Inferno and fly away, but then she would have to leave the river and the tiny outcrop of rock behind. Or she could find out what this person wanted. The flame inside her boiled at the thought, and Kay pressed her hand to her tummy to quiet it.

Maybe it was time she was finished with running. Maybe it was time she started demanding answers of her own. She Breathed.

"I know you're there. Why are you watching me?" Kay called out in the direction of the spy. She reminded herself of the limitless heat inside and lifted her chin. "Show yourself."

A lady stepped out from behind a tree and started toward her. "I'm sorry. I was trying not to frighten you."

"I wasn't frightened," Kay answered. She studied the woman's approach. She was younger than Mama but not by much, and she had her same easy smile. She had the dark features of one from the Republic, but her dress was more like the sort she had seen Mama wear. Kay suddenly realized she was speaking Jangba and had been this entire time. Probably another weird effect from the flame. Like her new memories and her connection to Inferno.

The woman came to a stop a few meters away, holding out her arms to show Kay there was nothing in her hands. "It is not my purpose to alarm you, but there is a dragon sleeping just ahead, and you must never rouse a sleeping dragon." The woman kept her tone neutral, but her gaze was focused beyond Kay and back to where Inferno lay napping.

"That's *my* dragon." Kay tried to match the woman's tone.

The woman's eyes widened, and her hand flew up to her mouth as if to hide a startled gasp. "Well, I suppose that negates my next question and lecture on the perils of a young girl alone on the border of the Wilds." The woman smiled. The expression made her seem really nice. But Kay had seen a ton of smiles from evil people. "Forgive me. My name is Izel. And you are?"

Kay didn't answer. She couldn't trust her, not yet.

"Did you run away from someone or . . . I can help you, that's all I'm saying. Offering." Izel moved forward but stopped after a few steps. "I'm certain you are more than capable of looking after yourself and your . . . companion. But if you should need anything, I'm just two miles north, after you cross the river. I always welcome a hungry traveler."

She left in the direction she'd come, and Kay bolted back to Inferno. She found the dragon still sleeping where she'd left him. He opened one large orb at her approach.

"I met someone," she told him. Kay sent images of Izel's face along with the discovery of the river and the cozy rocky outcrop. The dragon grunted in reply. "There's room for you, too, just not as cozy." She laughed at his growl. "I've been thinking that maybe Inferno hasn't always been your name and maybe you want to change it?"

The dragon lifted his head. His forked tongue darted out, testing the air beside her. He snorted, a puff of smoke drifting toward the sky.

"Sky. I like it. It sounds like freedom."

Sky bugled in response, a stream of fire billowing up in the clearing. Hundreds of startled birds took flight, and Kay wondered if Izel had noticed and what she thought of her and Sky's commotion.

It really had been nice of Izel to offer help. The idea of a hot dinner, cooked properly and not burned by her or Sky's efforts, sounded divine. Warm blankets and a cozy bed . . . But what if it was all a trap? What if Izel worked for the arena?

No, it was a nice idea. Nothing else. A dream of something that would never be. Kay and her dragon belonged out here on the edge of the Wilds, where the red-robed guys could never find them.

JURA

Chapter Seventeen

Danos *led her through the* atrium and back to the deserted arena grounds. They were as before, quiet and haunted, surreal in their beauty. Early morning light shone through, casting the stone floor in a soft orange glow. And there, almost unnoticed, a small armory on wheels.

She squinted at the discovery of weapons. Was this part of the test then? A challenge of her skill in weaponry? She normally performed very well during written tests involving studies or debate, but if this was a test of strength . . . *I still shouldn't worry*, she thought, lifting her chin. She was a daughter of the Thirteen. She'd learned the basics of nearly every weapon ever forged. She could hold her own in combat. Her father had seen to that, and she'd proven it with her actions over the last few weeks. *Be brave*, she told herself.

"Am I to pick a weapon then?" She crossed her arms over her chest, grateful she'd taken the time to exercise this morning. Her muscles were loose, ready for whatever he chose to throw her way.

Danos smiled. "If it would make you more comfortable. They are at your disposal."

She walked toward the display of weapons, frowning over the various options. She found swords too heavy for her, the assegai much too tall and therefore encumbering. She'd never quite gotten the hang of the bow and arrow, and she didn't think distance weaponry would be of much help against someone who had the power of the wind at their disposal. There was no whip, and hers was abandoned along with the rest of her belongings back in Kitoi. She sighed and gave the collection a more critical stare. Twin daggers in a leather sheath were hooked to the side, and she reached for them, testing their weight in her hands. Tylak would choose these.

She turned back to find Danos still watched her with an amused expression. Why did she feel like the test had already started?

"All right, I've chosen. Now what? Do I just . . . come at you?"

Danos chuckled. "Skies, no. I would prefer that you did not 'come at me' as you so eloquently described it. But if you are at the ready, then we can commence the test."

"Oh," Jura mumbled. She relaxed her shoulders just a bit, rolling her neck. "So, I'm not fighting you?"

"The test is not for you to fight anyone, little warrior. The test is simply to return to your room."

"What? So why did I have to pick a weapon?"

Danos spread out his wings, and Jura couldn't help but gasp at the sight. He lifted his shoulders in a hapless gesture. His silvered wings, which before had seemed so short, cast a shadow over her as they stretched out to their full length.

"You have merely completed the first test. Go forth. Find your way back to your room, and we will know you are worthy to speak with the Dreamer."

Before Jura could ask who Danos was talking about or get any further explanation, he beat his magnificent wings and rose into the sky, disappearing from sight.

She blinked after him. It couldn't be this easy. He hadn't brought her here and given her a display of weapons to choose from simply to tell her the great challenge was to find her way back to her room . . . Had he?

That wasn't difficult—leave the arena, go down the scary hallway into the atrium, and just like that she would be back in her room. She might have some difficulty opening that magical door of hers, but Danos hadn't said she had to enter the room—merely that she had to return to it.

But then, why would she need weapons if all she was being asked to do was walk back to her room? Maybe it was some sort of test of character or wits? Perhaps by choosing the daggers as her weapon of choice, she had already lost. She caught her bottom lip between her teeth, worried she had somehow already doomed herself and all of the Republic.

You can't just stand here all morning. Make a decision.

She took a cautious step forward, half expecting the ground to rip open or the sky to turn dark. When nothing happened, she took another step forward, then another. Maybe the task was to sneak back to her room without anyone seeing her? Sandstorms, she wished Danos had explained things properly before flying off.

She glanced around, but the arena was still empty as far as she could see. She regarded it with another critical eye. It was actually a bit smaller than the arena back home. Aside from missing the glass dome, this dome also lacked a dragon's entry. If there were any battles fought here, it was done with beasts smaller than dragons. Or with beasts that flew in from above. She frowned up at the open ceiling and was greeted by nothing but blue skies.

She looked back around the rafters, noting just how much

greenery had claimed the benches meant for seating or the small trees that blocked some aisles. If this arena wasn't meant for battles, then what was it used for?

Jura frowned, resisting the urge to rub at the fine hairs lifting on the back of her neck. Was she being paranoid or was someone watching her? She turned in a slow circle, again squinting up at the rafters, just to be sure. She didn't see anyone, but perhaps she was being watched from the shadows or from a distance, her every move tested and scrutinized. She quickened her pace, dropping the sheath to the floor and palming a dagger in either hand.

She still felt eyes watching her, but she was already almost to the exit, and Jura didn't care if it made those watching her laugh. She planned on sprinting down the long, dark hallway.

A soft note echoed in the distance, and Jura stilled at its sound. It was odd, familiar, and yet Jura couldn't say if the note was from any instrument she recognized. For all she knew, it could be sung by one of the aliferous, or perhaps several of them. The note grew in volume—two in perfect harmony—and then more joined in. Soon it was a chilling crescendo, and it was all she could hear. Jura wanted to fall to her knees and cover her ears. She might have screamed, but if she did, it was lost in that terrible beautiful song. There was a buzzing as a wild vibration thrummed in her ears and . . . darkness.

When she opened her eyes, she was not alone.

A massive bird stared at her, tilting its head from side to side. She sat up, aware that she still held the daggers. She loosened her grip, wincing at the thin trails of blood left on either palm. Her grip must have tightened after she passed out. Now she was no longer alone and no longer in the jungle-filled arena.

She was on the Edge. The rocky face of the mountain cut a

jagged path against the shoreline, the ocean an infinite expanse of deep gray and tumbling blues. If she had rolled over or moved to the right even a fraction of an inch, she would have fallen off the side.

She swallowed before climbing shakily to her feet.

The bird continued their silent appraisal of her. It was beautiful in a terrifying sort of way. The way there was a dangerous beauty to dragons. Something to admire, but more importantly something to fear. This bird was large enough to give a dragon a run in any arena. The bird's beak was massive and strongly curved. Jura had a difficult time deciding which part had the potential to be more vicious, the beak or the sharp talons of their feet. The feathers were long and brilliantly colored in tones of blue, green, and red more vivid than she had ever seen.

Had the bird carried her up here?

"Where am I?" She hadn't expected an answer, but the bird opened its mouth, and from it poured that beautiful crushing sound.

"No, stop! Please!" Jura yelled, and she was surprised when the bird stopped, once again cocking their head to the side.

"I, I don't understand." She turned back toward the ocean but it was gone, replaced by a sea of sand. Jura blinked at the rolling dunes. Her shoulders sagged at the sight, and a sudden crushing weight pressed on her chest. Was this all a dream then? Some sort of vision quest brought forth by Danos to test her? She turned back to the massive bird but it was gone. Only the bare rocky mountain remained beneath her feet.

Jura looked around her changed surroundings, her gaze wild, frantic. What sort of lesson was she to learn by being dropped off at the top of a magical mountain? She had to find her way back. She started forward, small stones digging into the thin soles of her slippers. She didn't look back toward the ocean that was no longer an ocean, and as she began her descent, she heard voices ahead.

She paused, debating the next careful placement of her foot as much as wariness for what may lie ahead.

Jura adjusted the daggers in either hand and rolled her shoulders to stay loose. May the Everflame keep her safe. The voices grew louder, approaching her despite her indecision to move forward.

"I have the stone." It was whispered by her ear.

She turned sharply toward the whisper, but there was no one there. Her breath quickened. Someone had said that. She knew what she heard. Or was she slowly losing her mind? The mountain path seemed to have steepened, the jungle dense around her. Hadn't she been climbing down? She shook her head to clear the confusion. Nothing made sense.

Once again, voices carried from the distance. Was someone up there? Had she truly heard voices? She had to know.

Jura ignored the wild beating of her heart and started back toward the small clearing. The voices grew louder at her approach and then they were just there. Four of them, sitting around a small wooden table.

"How did you get here?" Jura called out to them. Never mind how they had managed to bring the table and chairs up and start a meeting without her noticing. Or why anyone would choose to host a gathering on the edge of a cliff.

Jura's question was ignored, even after she waved her arms in a final desperate attempt to capture their attention. They couldn't see her. What was this, then? Some strange vision? But of the past or future, she couldn't say.

A large man sat at the head, his presence dominating the narrow table. A thin golden circlet surrounded his shiny bald head, and his beard was sharply shaven down to a tiny point. He gestured to the table, his peers nodding in agreement, though Jura could see nothing of interest on the surface.

"I have the stone." The repeated words came from the man who sat to his right. Like the first man, he was shaved bald, but his beard was thick and full, coming to a stop well past his chin. "Preliminary tests all produced desired results. I don't see any reason we can't proceed immediately."

The first man nodded, stroking the fine point of his beard. "And you, my son? What are the thoughts of our prince on this matter?"

Jura's attention moved to a young man sitting across from the assumed king. He was a younger version of his father, though he lacked the growth of a beard. He was handsome in a boyish way, his features still too round to be considered manly.

"We surge forward. This is the age of a new and glorious empire. One where our people take their rightful place and claim dominion of this land." The young man's eyes shone with fervor, but the father only nodded, seemingly unconvinced.

"And you, Blood Maker? What are your thoughts?" The question was directed to the young woman sitting to his left. She was reading a book, her head bowed as she skimmed over the pages. Jura knew she had seen it somewhere before, perhaps even owned a copy of it herself. She took an involuntary step forward, though whether drawn to the book or the woman, she couldn't say.

The woman had hair the color of molten gold, her skin tanned and glowing. She lifted her chin and her gaze met Jura's. Wide-set amber eyes widened at the connection, and Jura felt inexplicably and completely *seen*.

Jura turned to run, stumbling over a loose pebble and falling backward.

It seemed she fell forever.

The stone was cool beneath her skin. She liked that. For some reason she felt incredibly hot. Jura blinked her eyes slowly, wondering how she had fallen out of bed and how it was that she had come to rest so peacefully on the cold stone. Then she remembered everything. She bolted upright, taking in her surroundings. She was back in the arena. There was no trace of the giant bird or the people at the table. She shivered, remembering the woman's eyes on her. How had she made it back to the arena? Had she even left at all? She pushed herself to her feet, stifling a groan at the strain from her aching muscles. She certainly felt as though she had passed some sort of physical test, though she couldn't say just how. She frowned down at her palms. The skin was irritated and red from the shallow cuts but, like the daggers, all traces of blood had disappeared. The experience had been unlike anything Jura could have prepared for. Danos had said nothing of teleporting to a world of disappearing oceans and strange visions, and his request that she merely return to her room seemed ridiculous now.

She no longer felt that she was being watched, but she drew another slow, cursory glance around the arena before she limped down the dark hallway.

She was quick about it, half jogging down the hall and through the nearly empty atrium. She passed a few of the aliferous, ducking under wings when necessary. This was the most populated she had seen the hall. Jura would have liked to stop and make the acquaintance of a few of them if she hadn't felt so unsettled. Did their presence mark the beginning of a new change? There were always any number of guards, or waiting escorts, as Danos liked to call them, but Jura had seen no indication of families or any women at all. Where was everyone? In another part of the keep? She hoped all her questions were about to be answered. If not, she would demand so. She refused to continue on this blind path.

She found Danos waiting for her outside of her room.

"Jura, you have returned." He smiled, long canines gleaming.

"I have." She allowed her gaze to pass over the length of his body, noting the rippling muscles in his arms and chest. They were shaped like warriors, all of them. Everyone she had met were male and dressed in the garb of royal guard, but she hadn't heard of any titles except for Danos as that of the Speaker. What did it all mean?

"Does this mean I've passed your test?" she asked. "Does this mean I will finally receive answers?"

"That depends on what occurred in the arena." He regarded her carefully, his expression guarded.

What was she missing here? Jura had assumed they watched her the entire time, but apparently, she had been left on her own.

"Well, I assume that after I was taken by that giant bird thing, I had to f—"

"You were taken?" Danos interrupted. She was impressed by the genuine shock he'd managed to inflect in his tone. "You left the arena and returned?"

"Yes, as I'm sure you're well aware." Jura crossed her arms over her chest.

"I was aware of no such thing. The path is different for us all. Where did you go?"

Jura narrowed her eyes. "That's what I was hoping you would tell me. Something happened and I . . ." She cocked her head to the side, regarding him anew. "You truly had no part in any of this?"

"As I said, the path of life is different for us all, and no one can presume to know the outcome of any one decision. But the Dreams can light the path and shed light on the way." Danos bowed low before her, touching a finger to his forehead. "The Dreams have foretold of one who will travel such a lighted path. An outsider who will walk the path of Dreams. One who will remake the world."

The weight of his words was stifling, and Jura suddenly wished she was back on the arena floor. "I don't understand. What are you saying?"

"Come. You will meet the Dreamer now."

TYLAK

Chapter Eighteen

H*e didn't steal my abilities*," Tylak said, flashing in and out of visibility despite his lack of a nearby torch. He needed to prove to himself that the sand king had taken his birthstone and nothing more. He was still the same Tylak he had been this morning.

Peppik grunted by way of response. He had made his approval of Tylak's decision known, and Tylak didn't think he could take any more of the old man's grumbling. He took a deep breath. *What's done is done.* There was no sense in wasting the day overthinking what he might have lost. He had to focus on Jura, on the next step to bringing her home.

"My plan is for us to enter the nearest city. Speak with the locals. There has to be some truth to their old tales." *We'll find where the winged ones live and we'll get her back.*

He took another deep breath and allowed himself to study his surroundings. Burn it all, but he had never seen so much green in all his life. He had thought Jura's gardens were lush but this . . . this was different. This was everywhere. It carpeted the ground he walked upon. Grass, Peppik called it, though he had never heard of such a thing. The trees were different here too. Thick and tall, some stretching so far into the sky that they seemed to reach forever. The air was thick, sticking to his lungs and somehow covering him in a fine, invisible mist. This was how land used to be, hundreds of years ago before the Everflame scorched the earth.

Peppik grunted beside him, gesturing off to the distance. Tylak squinted, seeking out what the old man saw. There was nothing as far as he could see, save for more of the massive trees, but in the distance, Tylak could just make out the rhythmic beating of drums. War drums? It was hard to say. He scanned his memories, trying to remember what he knew of the old countries. It was said they existed in a world separated from his own. A world in which the people were not enslaved under the desert, where water held little value and there was no fear of an all-powerful flame. A place where man worshipped gods Tylak hadn't even known existed. Perhaps if he prayed to one of those gods now, they would provide answers for him. At the very least, these gods didn't seem to abandon their people as the Everflame had. And Tylak still had a worrying suspicion he was in some way responsible for its disappearance.

The drums of war seemed to be everywhere these days. Had the hands of war in the Republic stretched so far? Tylak sent a prayer up hoping that it wasn't so, though he did not know to whom he prayed.

Peppik had started his low shuffle in the direction of the drums. He was typically slow in pace, conserving his energy, but Tylak had seen how nimble the old man could be when he so chose. The man's demeanor darkened under the shade of the trees. A whisper of a breeze caressed the fine hairs on the back of Tylak's neck and he shivered.

He'd decided there would be no escape from war. Tylak had never wanted to be a warrior. He detested the arena and what it represented. Hated that his world was forever carved by violence. But he would do it all. He would do anything just to get back to her.

Despite the proximity gained from his ride on the sandstorm, it was still several days of travel before they reached the border proper. Tylak held little knowledge of Friis. Peppik called it a dark place, although he wouldn't say why. Tylak suspected the man had lived there in his past, or at least very near it.

"Can't you tell me anything? You speak the language." Tylak bit back his frustration. Getting angry at Peppik for being less than forthcoming about his past wasn't fair. They all had their secrets.

"It's a monarchy, right?" Tylak prodded. Starting with the basic government structure seemed an easy approach to the topic. "Queen Veleria?"

"Queen Vaneera Caligulas." Peppik spat out the name as if the words were venom in his mouth.

"Not the most benevolent ruler, I take it?" Tylak asked.

"No."

Tylak waited a beat for Peppik to say more, but when it became apparent he wouldn't, he asked, "Hasn't she been ruling for a hundred years or some nonsense?"

"Seventy. Friisans value stability in the monarchy. That's why the crown is passed on to the youngest daughter, so that the queen's rule be continuous."

"Not at all the setup of the Thirteen."

"Don't let the monarchy fool you. The crown is just as treacherous as any member of the Thirteen."

"Good thing two travelers such as ourselves won't have to

actually *meet* the queen."

Tylak glanced over at Peppik, but he was lost in his thoughts and focused on the ground before him.

"Come now. There has to be something good to say about the country," Tylak prompted, uneasy with the tense silence. They were making far too much of a racket to keep the birds from settling into their songs, and the rest of the jungle creatures seemed to be following suit.

"The food is incredible," Peppik muttered.

Tylak looked at him, nearly tripping over a thick vine. He didn't think he would get the man to crack. "That's something. What was your favorite dish?"

Peppik opened his mouth to respond and grabbed Tylak's bicep, mouth still hanging open.

"What is it?" Tylak asked, looking around. Something nagged at him that the situation wasn't right, and he wondered if he should make Peppik and himself invisible. The canopy of trees afforded little sunlight, and he no longer had access to an eternal torch. Would he even be strong enough to hide the two of them for any length of time? And hide them from what, exactly? Tylak could see nothing but trees, vines, leaves, and moss.

"Shh," Peppik hushed him, his fingers tightening around Tylak's arm.

Tylak still didn't see anything. Didn't notice anything amiss at all save for the eerie silence of the jungle.

Except . . . there. Just ahead, in that tree, a silhouette of something large.

"Get down!" Peppik shoved his body into Tylak's, sending them both into the soft earth.

Peppik was on his feet instantly, planting himself in front of

Tylak. The silhouette moved. It leaped from the tree and landed before them, its body shimmering in the dappled light of the canopy.

Marbled black, dark as midnight, darker than any shadow. It was some sort of cat, or bird, or, Tylak realized, some monstrosity between both. The cat part was massive, sleek, and shiny with tufted hair on its tail and paws. Sharp claws, just as black as its coat, peeked from beneath its paw, and long white canines hung from a growling maw. But the cat had wings, massive, feathered wings sprouting from its back.

"Don't move," Peppik whispered.

Tylak didn't think he could run if he wanted to, despite every instinct in his body screaming at him to escape.

The creature ceased its growling and sat back on its haunches. It tilted its nose upward, sniffing the air while its tail thumped the moss-carpeted ground behind him. Tylak kept every muscle tense, not even daring to breathe.

There was a sound in the distance. A snapping of tree branches and a hooting call that diverted the creature's attention and sent it scurrying off.

It was several moments later that Peppik grunted in satisfaction and turned around to haul Tylak to his feet.

"You stepped in between me and the beast," Tylak acknowledged, dipping his head in respect.

"I was keeping you from doing something foolish."

Tylak hid his grin. "You think there are any more of those out there?" he asked, hoping Peppik would deny it.

"You can be sure of it."

The two traveled for another few hours without incident. If the map in Jura's book was to be believed, they should arrive on the Friisan borders within the next day or so. It was difficult for Tylak to get his bearings after his flight on the sandstorm, but it seemed as though they were just south of the mysterious kingdom. Tylak would have taken Peppik's advice and avoided the border altogether if it hadn't been for their urgent need for supplies. He couldn't be sure, but Tylak assumed it was a fair assumption their desert darks would mark them as clear outsiders. Not to mention they needed food and water. Flames, he could use a hot steam, too, if they could get access to a public steam hall. He said as much out loud, hoping to entice the old man with the promise of a clean backside.

"Don't have steam halls," Peppik grunted. "Baths. Water rich, the entire lot of them."

What a concept, baths! The corner of his lip twitched, amused by the idea.

"I wouldn't take to grinning like a fool just yet. There's danger still afoot."

That sobered him up immediately. Tylak had no business poking fun at Peppik, especially after all he'd done for him. "You're right. Don't worry, we won't stay in the country any longer than we have to. In fact, if we can manage to find a trade post outside the city wall, we can avoid it altogether. No one will give us any trouble, you'll see."

"Friis is nothing but trouble," Peppik said.

"Flames, old man, you've well enough made your point. If you truly hate it out here, why did you even come along?"

"Someone had to keep your scrawny arse out of trouble." Peppik scowled, but his shoulders softened.

"And I'm grateful for the company, but you do know that I can take care of myself, don't you?"

Peppik rolled his eyes, mumbling under his breath.

Tylak had to give him several pokes in the ribs before he could be prompted to speak again.

"Wings on wind can only glide so far," Peppik finally said out loud, and Tylak sighed. He'd lost him again, at least for the moment.

Tylak would have liked to quicken their pace, but their surroundings were making that difficult. For one it was sweltering hot. If these Friisan baths involved cool water, Tylak bet it was refreshing. He was sweating profusely now as they climbed through the dense green terrain. The jungle was everywhere, so much more vibrant than the desert sand and pulsing with life. In the Republic, one was more likely to spot the odd rat or lizard but here there were any number of untold creatures. Tylak found it a wonder that they could all survive, so close in proximity. Were they at peace? There was much to learn from these creatures then. The farther they walked, the less intrusive the jungle seemed to find them. Birds began to call to one another, and monkeys could be heard howling in the distance. Tylak wondered what other sorts of beasts awaited them.

If the jungle welcomed them, Tylak's body rebelled. It grew increasingly difficult to breathe, his hair and clothing was plastered to his skin, and he was losing more water than he had ever drank in a single sitting. He would need new boots soon, but even his footsteps fell differently here, his heels sinking deeper into the earth as they struggled to find purchase in a ground that was unyielding and covered with life. His muscles ached, and he was more tired than he had any right to be.

Perhaps that was how he'd let his guard down. His attention was focused on his screaming muscles and the absurd shrieking call of what he could only assume was some sort of bird when Peppik seized him by his left elbow.

He froze, immediately seeking the light around them. Burn it all, it was difficult under the canopy. A man and woman stood just ahead, carrying weapons similar to the scimitar made popular by the First, only these swords were shorter, wider, with a denser blade. They were made of metal Tylak didn't easily recognize. The pair wore light leather armor over their chests and an odd sigil painted on the front, what looked to be two clasping hands. Guards. They must have been closer to the city than Tylak realized.

He drew another labored breath, weighing his options. He was already dehydrated and weak from overexertion. He wouldn't be able to hang on to his invisibility much longer, now dizzy from the intense concentration needed to maintain his magic.

"We've seen you, Shadow Dancer," the woman crooned. Her ebony hair was cropped as short as any man's. Her dark skin appeared mottled in the cracks of sunlight. Impossibly, her eyes seemed to find his. She smiled, revealing gleaming white teeth. "We've seen you," she repeated.

"Akk," the man spat. "Let 'em hide. It's more fun this way." He swung his weapon in a display that was meant to be menacing. It showed his level of clumsiness with the sword and proved to Tylak it was probably even heavier than he imagined. He had to be careful then. A rightly timed swing and he might lose a limb.

Flames, he was dizzy.

He dropped their invisibility, drawing a deep, rasping breath.

"Akk, he's come back out." The guard dropped his sword into a ready position.

Tylak didn't reach for his daggers, yet. He wanted to try persuasion first. It was what Jura would do. "We're just travelers. Passing through in search of provisions. Then we'll be on our way. We don't mean any trouble for your city."

"Do you even know where you are, Shadow Dancer? This isn't

no city. You've reached the keep of the monarchy herself. You're in Friis now, and you're a long way from home," the woman said in her crooning voice. She had sheathed her weapon and gave Tylak a careful appraisal.

"Exploring all the fine countries this land has to offer. I had hoped to visit Friis, but if we are to be sent on our way, then my companion and I will do so immediately." There. How was that for a performance? Jura would be proud. He made to move forward, but the guards remained where they were, blocking his path.

"We won't be allowing you to pass." The woman's voice had lost its playful tone and held a dangerous edge.

Tylak's fingers twitched over his dagger.

"I know you for what you are, Shadow Dancer, but more than that, I know *who* you are, Tylak of Ish. And you won't be leaving the kingdom. You're placed under arrest by order of Her Majesty, Queen Vaneera Caligulas. You can choose to come peacefully, or I will escort you by more . . . forceful means. It is your choice but either way, Shadow Dancer, you're coming with us."

JURA

CHAPTER NINETEEN

Answers. Finally, she would have some answers. Jura trembled at the imaginary creeping fingers that traced down the length of her spine. The rush of nerves, the anticipation and anxiety . . . it was all a bit too much. She wished Markhim was with her, if only to have a friendly face at her side, but she had been escorted from her room down a twisted path through the mountain. In her previous "outings," Jura had only left her room to visit the arena ruins and atrium. Jura suspected the mountain keep being larger than what she had seen thus far, but nothing could prepare her for the first glance at the outer courtyard.

It was stunning. Jura was at a loss for words. There were so many open walls and so much greenery where the sprawling mountain painted a landscape as far as she could see.

An unfamiliar roaring sound came from ahead. Upon their approach, Jura realized the sound came from water falling off the side of the cliff. *Waterfall.* The foreign word returned to her memory. Jura felt she could stare at the majesty of so much fresh water for an eternity, but the pull to receive answers prompted her along.

"This is a direct path to the Dreamer. All who enter here must be prepared to yield to the truth of the Dreams."

"Is he through there, then? The Dreamer?"

Danos frowned at her. "The Dreamer is beyond the constraints of gender."

"Or a proper name," Jura muttered, but Danos ignored her. His steps were quick and measured, much the walk of a soldier, and Jura once again found herself wondering about his specific role. It seemed he maintained a position of leadership, but he deferred to this Dreamer, whomever they were. At least now she was finally meeting this person. Jura hoped that all her questions would finally have answers.

Danos came to a stop before a large archway carved from the mountain.

After her journey here, Jura had expected the room to be . . . well, not this. It wasn't as stunning as the rest of the mountain keep. There was no greenery, and the only sound was a soft humming that seemed to vibrate from the walls. The room was well lit but sparse, with a large desk dominating its center.

The person sitting at the desk had their head bowed low as they scribbled furiously onto paper. The quill was unique. The large feather was a dark blue with shades of gold, and it shimmered as it swished in the air. Jura was so captivated by the person and their writing that she didn't immediately notice they were surrounded by a tiny handwritten library. One entire wall was filled with nothing but scrolls.

She gasped. She couldn't help it. The person writing looked up, their eyes finding Jura's.

They smiled at her, revealing sharp white canines glowing against their deeply tanned skin. Their hair was closely shaven with colorful eyebrow feathers and more pinned to the back to give the illusion of hair length. High cheekbones framed full red lips and a pointed chin. Their eyes were ageless, knowing, and seemed out of place for one so young.

The Dreamer is no older than I am!

The Dreamer did not get up when they said her name. "Jura."

Jura bit her bottom lip to keep from flinching. The Dreamer addressed her so informally. Apparently her titles had been stripped from her the moment she'd been carried away to this place. She lifted her chin.

"And what am I to call you, Dreamer? As you know me so informally?"

Was it her imagination or did their smile falter?

"The Dreamer is who I am, what I am. All of life is a Dream." Their voice was achingly beautiful. A soft song of notes, caressing each letter before sending them echoing across the sparse room.

Jura crossed her arms over her chest. "Spare me your pretty riddles if you please. I came here for answers." She approached them at their desk. "I'm not going to pretend to understand anything that's been going on around here. Now I assume you sent for me with what you believe to be a good reason, and it's time I heard it because I can assure you my patience is wearing thin."

Jura was unaware of just how close she'd gotten until she felt a razor-sharp talon dig into her shoulder blade.

"The Dreamer will not be threatened," Danos growled into her ear.

Jura froze.

"Please, Speaker. Retract your claws. Jura will not harm me." The Dreamer rose from their chair, and Jura was surprised by their great height. They were tall and willowy, their movements slow and graceful like a young sapling swaying in the wind. "In fact, leave us."

Jura felt Danos stiffen beside her as he shoved her away. "Dreamer, please. Allow me to stay. This one is . . . dangerous."

Jura raised an eyebrow at his words but kept quiet.

"Do you question the wisdom of your Dreamer?" Their voice was quiet, inquisitive.

Danos shuddered. "Never." He bowed low, his wings arching out so quickly, Jura had to nearly prostrate herself to avoid being bashed in the face by his feathers. It was several seconds before he arose, darting another quick, worried glance at Jura before departing.

"He loves you," Jura realized. The exchange that passed between them was more than just that of a loyal servant. And the way the Dreamer's eyes had softened at his departure was not without knowing.

The Dreamer watched her with those wide, knowing eyes that seemed to see right into Jura's thoughts.

"Yes. He loves me. As a loyal servant." The Dreamer continued, "And as a father."

"Your father?" Jura asked.

"Indeed." The Dreamer sounded amused. "It makes him twice as fierce as a Speaker. He loves fiercely, my father. As do you."

"Why am I here?"

"I admire this trait of yours." The Dreamer gestured to something in the corner, and a stool tumbled across the floor and came to a stop beside Jura. "Please sit. You should be comfortable for this, at least."

The stool was awkwardly high, and there was no easy or graceful way but to clamber atop. Jura perched up straight, feeling a bit like an exotic parrot she'd once seen on display at the market.

The Dreamer approached, and even sitting on the stool as she was, they still met her eyes. Now that they were so close, Jura was able to examine the Dreamer more carefully. Their features were certainly more human than bird, but they looked unlike anyone Jura had ever seen before. Their eyes were exceptionally large, dark pools that flashed silver or darkened to the color of spilled ink.

"Those paintings on your skin—"

"Dreams. They're the Dreams of my ancestors. They're permanent, not paintings. Although their visibility wanes with the times." As they spoke those last words, the images swirled, some darkening in color while others faded away. "These are eventful times."

"What is it about your dreams that makes them so special?" Jura thought again of what had occurred in the arena ruins, a chill running along her spine. Surely the event was connected. "I mean no disrespect, but even I have dreams." Jura couldn't help but lean forward, mesmerized by the display of colors shifting and swirling on the Dreamer's skin.

"You are a curious creature. Another trait to be admired. And I would be happy to teach you more of our ways to the path of Dreams. But these are not the answers you seek now. You have asked why you are here. The simple answer is because I have commanded it. If you were aliferous, you wouldn't question further because you would know that I, the Dreamer, only speak truths gained from the knowledge of Dreams."

They were talking in circles, and it was an effort to keep the scowl from playing across her expression. The Dreamer pressed on before Jura could argue.

"But it is not simple for you, you who are ignorant of the path of Dreams. You are a child of the new world, and your nation is built on the power of secrets and lies. Do not take offense." The Dreamer waved a lazy hand, fingers and feathers fluttering. "These are the platforms on which your country has grown strong. You are all warriors in this new world, and it suits you."

Jura shook her head. The Dreamer was finally giving her all the answers and yet still not saying anything at all. "This new world you're referring to? You mean after the Everflame appeared, scorching the land? Danos said my people were responsible . . . Is that what this is all about? Am I brought here to pay for the crimes of my ancestors?"

"History does repeat itself," the Dreamer answered. They shook their head and let out a soft, sad sigh. "But no, you are here because the path of Dreams has diverged and you are the cause."

"Me?" Jura made to rise from the stool, but she forgot she was so high up and her feet didn't reach the ground. For a half second, she scrambled in the air and nearly fell face-first, only to be rescued by the Dreamer's firm grasp around her wrist. The touch sent thrills down her spine, and a million voices thundered in her ears.

The Dreamer gasped, stumbling backward and gaping. All at once the majestic choir was silenced. Jura knew the confused expression they wore must mirror her own.

"If there were any doubts to the path that clears it. It *is* you." The Dreamer narrowed their eyes, noticing Jura's birthstone for the first time.

The stone must have tumbled out from where she'd had it tucked underneath the stretchy fabric. Stupid stool. The thought occurred to her that the aliferous could not have the luxury of a low, comfy chair with a high back because of their wings. She was so lost in her tumbling thoughts, she missed what the Dreamer had asked her.

"I'm sorry. I'm still . . . What did you say? And what were those voices?"

"I asked where you got that stone. How long has it been around your neck!" The Dreamer's voice had lost all melodic quality and was borderline shrill.

"M-my birthstone?" Jura shook her head, still processing. "It was a gift for my sixteenth birthday, so a year and a half or . . . why? What does it matter? Almost everyone in the Republic wears one. What does this have to do with anything?"

The Dreamer wasn't listening. They had moved away to pace the length of the room, and their willowy presence seemed to fill the tiny space. A new burst of colors appeared on their arm, swirling into a dozen patterns before settling into one that looked eerily like that of her birthstone.

"What's happening?" Jura whispered, though her voice carried across the silent room.

"The Dreams . . . Another path emerges." The Dreamer's captivating face fell into an expression of utter hopelessness and despair. "History . . . there is no escaping the mistakes of our past. I want to help you, warrior of the new world, but I am wary to trust you. Tell me, and please answer truthfully. Are you working with your sister?"

JURA

Chapter Twenty

"M-*my sister? I don't have* a sister!" Jura's thoughts tripped over one another. She flipped through dozens, hundreds of memories, searching for a small clue to her existence. A sister. There was nothing.

It was impossible.

"How is this possible? Who is she?" Jura demanded.

The Dreamer shook their head. "I can show you the path, but I cannot lead you along it. Search your heart, and I think you will find the answer."

The answer to a question she hadn't even dreamed of mere moments ago? Amira had always seemed a sister, but that was impossible. Amira had known both of her parents, had mourned the loss of her mother as Jura had mourned her own. There were no other significant women in her life who would fit the Dreamer's idea that she could find the answer. No one in the entire Republic who was the least interested in boring, lost-in-a-book Jura. It certainly wasn't Coral. Or any of the children of the Thirteen. No, the only other female she'd any other interaction with, the only person who had shown any interest in her at all, was . . . Realization hit her in the gut, hard enough to make her gasp. It didn't make any sense, but Jura knew with certainty.

"It's her. The Queen of Shadows. She's . . . but how? I don't understand. She's insane. She's behind everything. Why didn't you just bring *her* here?" Jura tried to take deep, calming breaths, but each breath was more ragged than the last. *Don't panic. Be brave.*

Jura didn't feel brave. She felt lost, drowning in a sea of lies.

"Tell me why I'm here!"

"Because only you can stop her. And only if you follow the path of Dreams. Things are not so simple as you believe." The Dreamer stared at her intently.

"Simple? That's a joke. Nothing has been simple in my life for weeks! Maybe ever. What is this Dream path I'm supposed to travel? Are we destined for some great stand-off of wind, fire, and water? Is that why the sea people were involved? Am I here to learn wind magic? Am I going to grow wings?" Jura squeezed her hands into fists, feeling her nails bite into her palms. The pain reminded her that this moment was real. She was there, even if she felt she was fast sliding out of control.

The Dreamer blinked at her. "I am unsure which of those I am to answer first. I do not know if it is possible for you to sprout wings of your own or not. I have never before studied one of your kind."

"One of my kind? What am I?" Jura managed to leap off the stool without falling. She stopped in front of the Dreamer, hesitant and struggling not to reach out and touch them. If she did, would she once again hear that beautiful choir of voices? *No,* she realized. *Of Dreams.*

"Please, do not touch me," the Dreamer whispered, seemingly pulling the thoughts right from her head. "I could not bear for you to touch me again. They are already so loud. And the pain is . . . they are never-ending."

"The voices?" Jura asked, though she already knew the answer. They nodded.

"But, they hurt you? You can't make them stop?"

"They are my responsibility. My gift and my burden. But knowledge is often both, wouldn't you agree?" The Dreamer pressed on before Jura could answer. "There is a prophecy. The first Dream after the Scorching. A herald of the new world. A prophecy about *you*."

"If it's about me, I'd like to hear it." Jura flattened her arms by her side and took a deep breath. "Please."

"When the eternal fire once again walks the earth, the stones will be exhumed. The Mistress will bend the knee, and the world will be made new in blood."

"Oh." Jura repeated the strange mix of words to herself, struggling to puzzle out their meaning. They were ominous, that much was certain, especially the last part about the world being remade in blood. She swallowed against the lump forming in her throat. "I don't understand," Jura started. "What does that have to do with me?"

"The paths are not certain, but they confirm your involvement in this. If I didn't know before, the appearance of your stone confirms it." The Dreamer looked down to where the image of Jura's birthstone still burned on their forearm. "I do not know yet what road you will choose in the path of Dreams, only this: your choices will alter the course of fate as I know it. We must discover the allegiance of the Mistress, and I have my suspicions that it is you who will remake the earth in blood."

"Me? But . . ." Jura faltered, suddenly wishing she was sitting back on her stool. She struggled for a deep breath meant to calm her, but it was hard to breathe at all. "Please, I don't understand. How could I accomplish what you're implying? What am I?"

The Dreamer moved away from her, the myriad of colors painted on their body shifting and muting as they walked. "Blood Maker. Gifted with the innate ability to alter the course of your blood . . . and of those around you."

Blood Maker. Jura had heard the title before. She was connected to that woman in the vision. But how?

"I don't understand. Controlling the course of blood? What does that mean?" Jura resisted the urge to shake the Dreamer for answers instead of slow wonderings.

The Dreamer waved their arm, feathers fluttering behind them. "Please, I will tell you all that I know to tell. Have you ever performed some task you thought impossible? Perhaps accomplishing something simply because you *wanted* to? That was your gift."

"My gift," Jura repeated, feeling numb. "Blood magic."

"The rarest of magics now. The Creator was a Blood Maker. I know, tiny warrior of the new world, you believe the Everflame to be your entity. I have watched the many paths that have led to this faith. And now the eternal flames have been released from their glass cage, sparking the beginnings of the path most treacherous."

"The Everflame was released?" Jura could barely draw a breath when she saw their imperceptible nod.

She replayed the night of her capture, the sudden burst of power she had felt holding the bleeding warrior of the sea people. The way the city fires that Tylak had ignited had all been extinguished, all at once. Had she done that?

Was the Everflame really and truly gone? Released from its glass cage and missing from the Republic? But how? By her? Or some other strange twist of fate?

Jura sat heavily on the floor. Although nothing but mountain granite was beneath her, some sort of wind magic had polished it smooth. She would have so many more questions if only she could think clearly.

Jura tried to organize her thoughts into tidy little boxes. She had blood magic. She could figure that part out. She had already witnessed all that the Dreamer had described. She had changed the course of someone's blood when she had healed the wounded sea soldier. She had willed his blood back inside him. And when Coral had tried to drown her, she must have altered the level of oxygen intake in her blood. Blood magic didn't have to be evil, did it? Did that mean the Queen of Shadows had blood magic too?

And if that wasn't enough to stuff into her overfilled box of worries, there was the fact that the Everflame was missing. What did that mean for her faith? For her people? How were the people of the Republic lighting the city? Burning their prayers? Was there a destination for a prayer to a missing god?

"How . . . how did it escape?" The words seemed to slip from her mouth with a mind of their own. Jura tried to ignore the intense shame she felt at the question. *You don't know you had anything to do with its disappearance,* she told herself. Although she had no proof against the fact either.

"The eternal flame walks this earth, but it doesn't do so freely." The Dreamer approached her from across the room and kneeled beside her, although they were careful to maintain a cautious distance between them. They made the act of folding in on themselves appear graceful despite their tall frame. Their wings reflected a dozen colors all at once—iridescence—and brought to mind the Justice Dome back home.

"Elaborate, please. What do you mean it doesn't walk freely? Does someone control it?"

"The path is unclear." The Dreamer's voice was a lullaby. "I know only of the bonds forged in flame." Their eyes rolled back, the canvas of their skin swirling and slithering into shape. "The eternal flames have bonded with a young soul that is made of both pure love and pure hate."

"Pure hate and love? Those are opposite things!" Jura sighed, frustrated. "This prophecy, that's the reason you've brought me here? That's what you said, right? And that's the reason the Everflame has disappeared?" Jura narrowed her eyes. "Is your intention to hold me here so that I am unable to play my part? Whatever my part even is? I don't know anything about my magic. Do the Dreams tell you that? I can't control it. I can't do anything with it. How do you even know you've brought the correct sister here?" Jura shoved herself back up to her feet, ignoring the sudden splatter of color on the Dreamer's forearm at her movement. Was she truly so linked to them?

"This . . . is not an admirable trait," the Dreamer admonished lightly. "You ask so many questions at once. It is hard for me to distinguish the truth you seek. Especially with all the other whispers."

"You can still hear them?" Jura watched the swirling patterns on their skin, noting the slight tremble to their body. They had alluded to the pain of hearing them. Was the Dreamer being tortured by the voices even now?

"I always hear them."

"What are they?" Jura asked, afraid of the answer.

"It's everyone. And everything. Every event that happens on this earth, every word ever spoken to existence. All of them are whispered back to me from the many voices of the wind. I know everything that has ever happened, and all that happens now."

"That's it then. You know what's going to happen, and holding me here will somehow stop the prophecy?"

"Skies, no. I see only the various paths for you to take. The Dreams are whispers on the wind, yes, but they are more than that. They are the code by which we live by. I hear the whispers, therefore, I have the knowledge of all that has come to pass. And all that is spoken now. The Dreams are the truths within these whispers, the unspoken foretelling of what may be, but it is the accumulation of all these many voices which allow a dream to be learned. There are infinite Dreams because you still have your free will, warrior of the new world, and you may use it as is your right as a living being. We believe that while there are infinite number of Dreams, there is only one true path of Dreams. We devote our lives to following such a path. I only wish to enlighten you about the various repercussions that will occur from your actions. I know you see the Dreams on my skin, how they swirl and change when I'm near you. That's because you're important. Your actions have the capability of affecting hundreds of lives, thousands. There are dozens of outcomes, but a prophecy . . . this prophecy . . . in all the paths I see you take . . . each path would have you play your role, Blood Maker." They shuddered, looking skyward as if to search for answers. "You will break the world."

"But *how*? How can I change anything if you don't tell me what to do? And why would I ever do anything I don't want to do? Why should I want to break the world? You said there was a new path emerging when you saw my birthstone. Why? What does my birthstone have to do with any of this?"

"The prophecy speaks of stones that will be exhumed. It is my belief that this stone is important to your path. To all paths. I . . . was not aware you had been gifted the stone."

"My father gave it to me on my sixteenth birthday. It was wrapped in a letter from my mother," Jura muttered, lost in the memory. It had been such a treasure to read something new from her mother, a message beyond the grave from a woman taken too early from her. Had she truly birthed another child before her?

The Dreamer nodded. "It was not spoken before, and therefore, the path was unclear." They stared down at their skin, at the swirling colors they interpreted with ease. "The stones will all be exhumed if they haven't already. Next the Mistress will bend the knee." Their words were once again a song, the foretelling a chilling crescendo.

Jura didn't know what that meant or who the Mistress referred to, but she also knew that she didn't plan to give in to any one person's demands. Especially not those of some self-proclaimed prophet or those of her nefarious sibling, the Queen of Shadows.

"Do you know what she wants, then? The Queen of Shadows?" *My sister.* Jura swallowed.

The Dreamer lifted their shoulders, wings expanding in a slight shrug. "Like you, your sister has opened many paths."

"But you have to know *something*. If you can hear every word that's ever been said, then you know something of her plans. What does she want?"

The Dreamer moaned, a low haunting sound made deep in their throat. "She searches for the stones. She has the knowledge to wield them and yet still she searches . . . There is a book."

A breeze pushed into the closed room, rifling papers on the desk. Jura had only a moment to wonder where such a breeze had even come from when the Dreamer gasped, back arching as a single note erupted from their diaphragm. The sound was both beautiful and terrifying all at once. Jura fought the urge to run from such an awful sound.

"She knows you are here. She knows, *she knows* . . . she knows many things about you. She searches for the stones. And for those who can wield them." The Dreamer shuddered. "She has dark plans. Like you, she means to break our world."

"Then what can we do to stop her? You're supposed to be all-knowing and wise, right? Tell me, what am I supposed to do?"

"You are here to learn of your role in destiny. You are here to learn to accept your powers. If it is the path of your sister to destroy our world, then it must be your path to fix it."

TYLAK

CHAPTER TWENTY-ONE

There was a time when, if he had been asked, Tylak would rather die than be confined in another prison cell. He had danced with lunacy then, finding comfort in the steady cries made from his fellow cell mates. He had imagined a different life for himself then. He had less to fight for then. Now, it seemed he had traveled full circle, and instead of the old, familiar madness, Tylak felt a steady calmness brought on by the comfort he found in his thoughts of Jura. This was not the end of his story, not here in this confined space.

He was pacing again, as he often did. There was little to do in his cell, and though he could see Peppik through the narrow bars, the man had been silent and lost in his own thoughts since their capture. *He did warn you not to come here*, Tylak reminded himself. Little good the thought did him. Tylak hadn't had a choice. They needed the supplies. He'd wanted fresh water. At least now they had plenty of it.

They had been escorted directly to their cells, shoved in none too nicely. Moments later a guard appeared with bowls of rice and jugs of water for each. Both times Tylak had found himself in prison, he had more access to water than any other time in his life. What an unfortunate irony.

He drank the water greedily, saving only less than half in case it was a while before they were given water again. He had tried to talk to Peppik a few hours ago, but the man had grumbled a string of incoherent words at him and turned to his cot for a nap.

Full jugs of water and a cot off the ground. Prison life really wasn't so bad.

It wasn't that he intended to stay, of course. He never meant to get captured, but it was nice to relax and get a few hours of uninterrupted sleep without the constant fear of being captured because, well, he already was. After his nap, he was feeling more like himself and was able to bring up his invisibility with enough ease to make him grunt in satisfaction. His powers truly remained then, despite his lack of Everflame and missing birthstone. He had the nagging fear that his power was more connected to the stone than he cared to admit, but he still didn't regret giving it to the sand king. He would do anything to save Jura.

They had saved time with their travel in the sandstorm, but Tylak still worried over what Jura might be experiencing under the care of the bird people. Tylak cringed. No, that wasn't right. What had Peppik called them? The aliferous. In any case, Tylak didn't want Jura to remain in their captivity a second longer than necessary.

Tylak didn't have much concern that he wouldn't be able to escape their jailer. He just had to wait for the right opportunity to make his move. Tylak knew the chance would present itself. He simply had to be patient. The problem was, he didn't have time to wait for the right moment. He needed that moment to be now. Every moment spent wasting away in this cell was another moment Jura was left alone . . . with Markhim. Tylak tightened his fingers into a fist at the thought of the young Light Guard. He hated remembering that Markhim was there with her. If only he'd reached her sooner.

"Peppik, are you awake?" The late afternoon sun had set quickly, and Tylak found himself squinting into the darkness at Peppik's form in the other cell. "You're not still angry with me, are you?"

The man was emotional but never angry. If anything, he had a borderline-docile personality. Tylak had never seen him as upset as he had been at the loss of his birthstone. It wasn't like Peppik had to give away the last memory of his mother.

"I know, you didn't want to come here, I make bad decisions, blah blah blah . . . You can't ignore me forever."

"I'm not ignoring you, you imbecile. The ears are everywhere," Peppik snapped.

Tylak frowned. Peppik liked to give an insult as much as the next person, but he had never talked to Tylak like this before. Well, maybe Tylak *was* talking too much. He assumed they would make an easy escape once he'd rested, no matter their circumstance. He'd given little thought to who had him arrested. Perhaps there *were* spies listening. The Shadow Dancers had certainly used their extensive network to announce Tylak's warrant for arrest. And there had to be a specific reason for Peppik's fear or discomfort of the place. Perhaps he shouldn't have such a cavalier attitude. He was about to beg Peppik to explain his fear when the distant sound of footsteps echoed down their hall. Tylak turned toward the sound, senses made all the more alert by the dark setting.

"Ach! You've got 'em sitting in the dark. Change the battery, then, would you? Don't worry, my pretty prisoners, we've come for you." the voice called out. Once again the Jangba was strangely accented, clipped and foreign to Tylak's ears, even if it probably was spoken for his benefit. It was difficult to make out their words. What was a battery? A weapon of sorts? They had taken his daggers, but Tylak aimed not to give in without a fight.

A low humming sound filled the room, and Tylak found himself blinking against the sudden onslaught of light. He didn't detect any fire or glow stones, and the source of the light seemed to come from above. The light was brightest on the ceiling but illuminated everything. The ceiling flickered and snapped along to the tune of the steady humming noise.

"Ach, you should see 'em. Poor new worlders haven't ever seen electric lights before." The guard chuckled. It was a new face, and Tylak studied it, mind reeling to translate the foreign words.

The man had dusky copper skin and a firm chin framed by a thin mustache and tiny beard. His dark eyes gleamed with amusement. He carried the same short knife-like sword as the other guards, but he was dressed more plainly. No armor. That was a mistake, Tylak thought, clenching his fist and getting ready.

"Ach, now I see you, and I know of your abilities, so I'm just going to say it. You don't want to give me any trouble. I'm here on Her Majesty's business. And before you get any idea of asking me just what Her Majesty's business is, you should know that is something you will have to hear from the lips of Her Majesty herself. Understand me?"

Tylak nodded once, gruffly. "I'll come quietly. And my companion, is he to stay here for the duration of my interrogation?"

The guard smiled. "Your interrogation. I like that. But no, Prince Peppik isn't staying here. Her Majesty is eager to be reacquainted with her son."

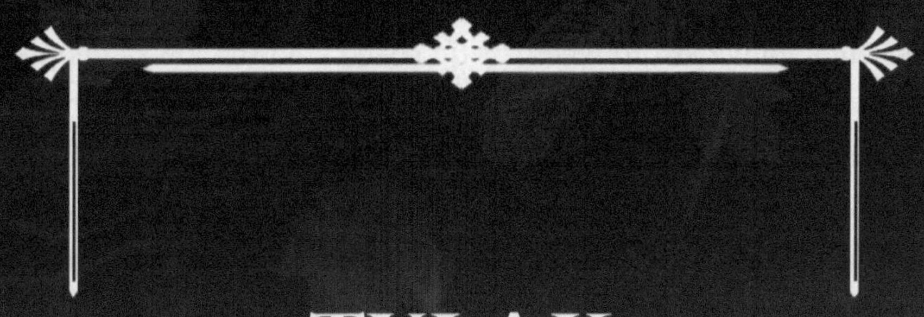

TYLAK

CHAPTER TWENTY-TWO

The expression on his old friend's face was made of stone.

He doesn't deny it. Tylak's mind spun. How was such a thing even possible? Peppik had never given any indication of his birthright before. Tylak hadn't even been entirely sure he wasn't born in the Republic. Now he was faced with the knowledge that not only had his friend allowed him to believe he called the Republic home, but he'd also hid his relation to the monarchy. What would spark him to make such a decision?

Tylak and Peppik followed the guard through a series of steps out of the dungeon and into what Tylak could only assume was the palace proper.

They were crossing into yet another spacious hall when Peppik made a sudden run for freedom. He kicked the guard in the kneecap and raced down the hall, only to be stopped by another pair of guards, both carrying the knife-like sword common among the soldiers. Tylak recognized the female guard from earlier, and she tossed her chin in a friendly greeting.

"You're a squirming one, that's for certain." She peered down the length of her sword where its tip rested at the hollow of Peppik's throat. "Don't worry your pretty little neck. I'll leave it attached to your body just as I've found it." She winked at Tylak. "Imagine my surprise learning I captured not only a wanted Shadow Dancer but also Her Majesty's own son! I imagine the rewards I reap will be sweet, so don't go spilling your own blood before Her Majesty feasts upon you with her own eyes."

Tylak offered Peppik a sympathetic look, but the man ignored it. What about his mother had Peppik so terrified? Tylak wished for his daggers, for any weapon, truthfully.

The female guard had taken to studying Tylak, her knowing eyes gleaming as though she had access to his internal struggle. "Eager to meet your new queen, are you? Well, it's only just through this door. You don't have to travel far." Her voice was almost gleeful as she kicked open the heavy oak doors, which creaked open slowly, the sheer size of them enough to make the endeavor difficult. Tylak found himself leaning onto his toes to catch an early glimpse through.

The room was grand, that was certain. Tylak scowled at the huge ornate tapestries, at the brilliant light flooding from the open doorway, another indication of the mysterious light magic they called electricity. And barely, across the wide expanse of the room, Tylak could make out a gigantic throne.

"Greetings." Her voice carried across the room, clear and distinct and almost girlish. "Welcome to my home, Tylak of Ish." She gestured them toward her, and Tylak started forward. Peppik, too, after a not-so-gentle prod from the guardswoman.

The queen was ancient. Her hair was stark white and wispy thin, piled in a knot atop her head. Most of it was concealed by a gaudy crown that made the cabochons of the Golden City appear poor. Wrinkle after wrinkle marred a face that may have once been beautiful, but now it was impossible to tell. Her cheekbones were hollow, her lips pale.

She smiled at their approach, revealing a surprising mouthful of teeth.

"Welcome home, my prodigal son."

Peppik shivered but continued to stare at the ground. It was clear he meant to avoid eye contact. Tylak pressed on, determined to help his friend and hoping for answers.

"Your Majesty." Tylak gestured grandly with a deep bow. "We thank you for your hospitality."

"Hospitality?" The queen sniffed. "Do my dungeons bring such comfort then?" She tilted her head to the side, her eyes raking over Tylak's form, seeming to memorize his every detail. "This was not my intention," she continued with a frown.

"Be that as it may, I have enjoyed more hours of uninterrupted rest than I could have ever hoped for." Tylak grinned, not entirely lying.

The queen stared at him, her impassive face neither inquisitive nor concerned. There was no joy or anger. Then she lifted her hands and clapped once.

It was more massive than any creature ought to be. Half the size of an arena dragon, the creature emerged from the shadows. It was covered in purple-, blue-, and gold-hued barbed hairs. Its bulbous body, covered in the same hair, had several long legs extending from it. Eight of them. The creature smiled at them, working its red mandibles.

It's a spider, Tylak thought dumbly. Although it was a hundred times larger than any spider he had ever seen.

"Tylak, this is Goliath. She is so much more than a mere pet. She is one of my closest confidants. We have many things in common, but can you guess what the biggest commonality is?"

Tylak heard the queen's words, but his attention remained on the ferocious creature beside her. The huge furry beast began rubbing two of its legs together, emitting a high-pitched noise that had Tylak covering his ears.

"Tylak, I asked you a question." The queen's voice took on a slight warning tone. "You would be wise to answer my questions as I ask them. But no matter. I'll tell you what Goliath and I have in common." Her grin was sinister. "Despite the masculine name, Goliath is a female. The stronger of the species. Did you know, they actually devour the male after copulation?"

Tylak swallowed. "Is that what you have in common, Your Majesty?"

"Hmm." The queen lifted her shoulders in a careless shrug. "Females are often the stronger sex in a species, not that any man wants to see the truth. They're more loyal too. Certainly, more loyal than my son here." Her eyes found Peppik, seemingly seeing him for the first time. "Skies above, boy, you look positively *old*."

Her sudden eruption of laughter sent her into a coughing fit, and it was some time before she could speak again.

"How many years has it been, boy?" Queen Vaneera managed to wheeze out.

"Twenty-three years, Your Majesty, and still too soon by my account," Peppik said. His eyes were filled with such an intense hatred that Tylak had to look away.

The queen pointed a gnarled finger at him, trembling with anger. "You should have stayed away, boy. I am the Queen of Friis, and you will regret this day you've crossed me. Goliath, you may fetch your dinner."

"Goliath, hold." The giant spider stopped at the command, legs trembling.

Tylak was hesitant to take his eyes off the monster, but curiosity had him peering behind him.

"Mother? I thought you were entertaining guests?" a soft voice questioned, her tone cautious, intelligent. "Have our guests turned sour?"

Tylak turned to see a lithe woman dressed in soldier regalia. She was well-armored but in a decorative fashion. As a princess would be, Tylak realized, replaying her words. He reminded himself that he was unarmed while Queen Vaneera had Goliath, and this newcomer sported a short, stubby blade with a wicked curve.

"Ach, Daciana, put away your machete. As Mother said before, these are our guests. And, if rumors are to be true, family." The new voice was huskier, slightly more confident. When she was first brought to focus, Tylak blinked in surprise. The two women appeared to be copies of one another. Identical twins? Alttaw'am? Or some other sort of magic?

The second woman chuckled as she pushed past Tylak, not even caring that her arm brushed his on her way to the high dais holding the gigantic throne. He stumbled, but only slightly, as he was shoved out of her way.

The princess bent to kiss her mother's cheek, mumbling incoherent words, but soon the queen settled back into her throne. The woman tsked at her sister, who still had her weapon pointed in Tylak's direction.

"Come now, Daci, whatever game they were playing is over now." She turned back toward the queen, mumbling something that made them both chuckle.

Daciana lowered her weapon and slowly took her place by her family.

Side by side, it was even more amazing to see the similarities between the two women. They were around his age, with shortly cropped hair and angular faces framed by golden chains. A gold ring pressed through the center of their noses and connected the golden chain to either ear. It brought to mind the mask of the Queen of Shadows, and Tylak frowned at the thought.

"Do you know why my sister stopped Goliath?" the second sister asked. "No? It's because she doesn't like the mess she makes."

The first sister, Daciana, nodded mournfully. "We still haven't gotten the blood stains out of the tapestries from the last time."

"I trust that I am correct in my assumption, Shadow Dancer?" the second sister continued. "You will cease the rude mockery of my mother and queen?" The words were asked lightly, but the woman examined her blade as if mentally gauging its sharpness.

Tylak afforded a terse nod in response.

"Excellent. Allow me to introduce myself. I am Ulfa, and I believe you've met my *younger* sister, Daciana. It isn't often the queen is insulted in her own home. If you do it again, I can promise you it will be your final act. But I think Goliath here should be enough to keep you in line."

Tylak eyed the beast warily, nodding his acceptance. He didn't like it, of course, but he was weaponless and wildly outnumbered. He and Peppik needed time to orchestrate a proper attack. Perhaps once they were back in their cells.

The dagger took flight toward the queen's throat before Tylak could even react. Somehow, the crazy old man had managed to sneak a dagger in his boot. It was the first sister, Daciana, who leaped to action. She somersaulted forward, blade whirling to knock the dagger out of harm's way. She hissed an insult at her brother, but her mother's chuckle ceased her from further attack. The princess settled for a scowl in their direction as she picked up the dagger and sheathed it on her bracer among others.

"Stop it, both of you. Peppik, you will cease trying to kill me this once. I am your queen and your mother, and you are in my home. Daciana, Ulfa. You will treat your brother with the wariness and respect you afford all your siblings. Ulfa, if you'll show Tylak to his new rooms. Nothing grand, mind you. He was impressed by our prison. No sense in wasting the good linen. I'll meet with him in the morning with his assignments, but this afternoon has already exhausted me." She snapped her fingers, and the giant spider scurried forward, lifted her up in its embrace, and cradled the queen as though she were a small child.

"Now just a minute." Tylak started forward. "I'm not just going to stay here and wait for any assignments. I'm in the mid—"

"And I haven't given a question to you. My kingdom, my whims." Queen Vaneera smiled at him from her perch. "You've a handsome face. I'd hate to have Goliath cave it in."

CORAL

CHAPTER TWENTY-THREE

Coral would never think to admit such a thing, but Amira did seem to have donned armor of a sort. The woman held her shoulders straighter, her chin higher now that she wore the dress. Kale had surprised them both with a stunning gown in dark purple and gold. Amira had seemed amused by the colors but had merely explained the color combination was common for the Thirteen families. She didn't seem so nervous anymore either. Amira had taken her arm and nearly dragged the threesome into a narrow alley between two squat buildings made of clay.

"Why did we stop?" Coral asked her. She ignored Kale who was actively wriggling his eyebrows at her, trying to catch her eye. She still felt strange toward him.

"I just needed a moment," Amira muttered. She peered around the corner of the building, frowning at the city square.

Well, of course she needed a moment. Kale had done more than just return with a dress. He came with the news that the Everflame was well and truly gone, disappeared since Jura. Coral feared this was more than just a coincidence but still failed to see how everything fit together. What must it feel like to be abandoned by your own god? The Great Mother was everywhere, and her own connection to the great entity was infallible. But what if she could no longer feel the gentle hum of her *wei* inside her? Already their connection was such that Coral felt physical pain at her separation, such that she had fashioned a necklace of water just to keep the Mother close to her. How would she feel if that comfort was gone?

She patted Amira's shoulder in an awkward attempt to bring her peace. This was outside her range of emotions. Coral liked to solve everything with a swift jab from her trishula, but she couldn't spear emotions away.

A moment later, Kale made a show of clearing his throat, and Amira wore a forced smile.

"I'm ready."

"You sure?" Coral didn't plan to rush this. The way she saw it, they had one chance to use her image to sneak past the glass gates without raising alarm. They had to let people notice her without attracting too much attention. She didn't feel nearly as prepared as she would have liked, but the weight of her father's trishula strapped to her back gave her comfort. This was just another step forward to finding Mano and the Queen of Shadows. A tiny detour on the journey toward vengeance.

"You can take as much time as you need," Kale offered.

"She knows that," Coral sighed.

"Well sometimes it's nice to hear it. Maybe she just needs to be reassured."

"And maybe she is standing right here and she already said she was ready," Amira snapped.

Coral blinked. Weapons of wordplay indeed.

"Apologies, Am—"

"Silence," Amira said loudly, stepping away from the safety of the building alley. "You fools, must I do everything?" She sighed loudly, thrusting both hands toward the sky in a hopeless gesture. "Assistance required!" she shouted. "Attention, please. I require assistance."

She's gone mad. Coral exchanged a wild glance with Kale, mind racing. What should she do now? Tackle the woman? They'd already been exposed. Amira was already causing a scene. Coral lost her train of thought as the crowd of people around Amira began dipping to the ground in low respectful bows.

"One of the Thirteen."

"Third of the Thirteen."

"It's the Third."

"The Second now."

"I can't ever keep track. Did old Velder finally sputter out then?"

"She killed her entire family to come into power."

The frenzied whispers carried across the courtyard, and if Amira heard any of the fearful and wild speculation, she didn't acknowledge it.

"I'm in need of a personal palanquin." She snapped her fingers, though the gesture was unnecessary as a man was already pulling his wife from their curtained vehicle and offering it to her.

Amira nodded, taking his fawning behavior in stride. "And a cart. To transport my slaves. I don't wish for them to tire any more than they have on our journey home." She turned toward the man, her voice dipping several octaves. "Are your feet made of honey? Hurry along, man. Retired Fire Dancers move faster than you."

The man nearly tripped in his effort to get the cart to her in a timely manner. The smile Amira rewarded him with was chilling.

Coral shivered despite the desert heat.

"Get in the cart," Amira said in her general direction. Coral bit the inside of her cheek to keep from giving Amira's backside a firm swat with the flat side of her trishula. Did she have to play the part so well?

Amira snapped her fingers again, and it was only the gentle squeeze on her elbow from Kale that reminded Coral of their mission. She climbed into the cart, sliding across the wooden bench to make room for Kale, but not before shooting a deadly glare in Amira's direction.

"I assume one of you lazy lot has the time to transport us through the palace gates," Amira called out. It wasn't a question, merely a command issued by one of the Thirteen, a command they were all eager to obey.

"Great job," Amira whispered. "Keep your heads down and stay quiet. We should be inside the gates within the hour." Then she climbed delicately aboard her palanquin.

"Advance," she called out. Moments later they were being pulled toward the glass gates.

So much for not making a scene.

There was a small delay at the gates. Amira exchanged several words with the guards, and although her new friend still used the same imperious tone, Coral could not make out her words. A small eternity later, and they were moving again. Still, Coral held her breath and tensed when they once again pulled to a stop.

Amira didn't thank anyone but merely turned on her heel and made for the palace proper, snapping her fingers at them to follow.

"If she snaps those things at me one more time, I'm going to break them off," Coral vowed to Kale, and they exchanged a quick smile. She ignored the rush of nerves his smile brought her and hurried to follow Amira across the northwest side of the palace courtyard.

"We have a bit of a problem," Amira said once her group of doting subjects had departed back through the glass gates and the threesome was well away from prying eyes.

"I'll say," Coral quipped. "Was that attitude really necessary? Is that what it means to be one of the Thirteen? I thought you were a fierce people made of dragon killers and forbidden knowledge. Those were the actions of a bully."

"You should talk," Kale muttered beside her.

She whirled toward him, gaze thunderous. "And just what is that supposed to mean? Do you see me as some sort of bully?"

"I don't know. Tell me what it means when someone's go-to answer for everything is to stab it." Kale jabbed a finger toward her. "I'm sure you'll know what that means because you know everything."

"This isn't helping," Amira said. She pressed her palms together, the knuckles of her fingers going white. "Please stop fighting."

Coral sighed. Now she felt awful for once again stirring up whatever dark memories lay nestled in Amira's mind.

"We're not fighting," Coral started.

"Really? Because I would beg to differ." Kale reached for her arm.

"We're not," Coral answered firmly, stepping out of his grasp. "Not anymore. I'm sorry, Amira. I didn't like seeing you that way." She took a deep breath and shot a glance at Kale. "And I guess I didn't like to think of myself that way either."

"You could never be like that," Amira whispered. Her voice

was so soft, Coral had to lean closer to hear her, and she doubted Kale could hear at all. "I didn't think I could be like that, that I could be her again. I don't even know if I want to." She smiled quickly, pushing away any room for discussion on the matter.

"We almost had a bit of trouble at the gates. It seems I—that is, the fake me, has been missing for a few days. There was an inspection pending, and I was believed dead. There will be an emergency council meeting to declare Rank."

Coral frowned, taking in the new information. "What do you think happened to her? Another mission? Or is it . . ." She trailed off, leaving the obvious unspoken. Was her evil look-alike dead? And if so, what had killed it? Did that mean that someone wanted Amira dead too?

Amira shook her head. "I don't know. But I need to go to that council meeting. I need to show that I'm still here, alive and ready to take my position in the Thirteen. For all we know, the alttaw'am is still alive and plotting their next move. This meeting can set the stage for everything."

"I don't like it. Aren't these council meetings dangerous? My tutors suggested a person's Rank could be seized in an instant with executions carried immediately after."

"Not exactly. Executions are only carried out once a week." Amira studied the sand beneath their feet.

"How tidy," Kale muttered, but both of the girls ignored him.

"What will you do if your alttaw'am is at the meeting too? We don't know they're dead simply because they haven't been seen around the palace for a few days." Coral could still see too many dangerous variables. A council meeting simply wasn't a good idea. Couldn't she see that? *Stubborn Breathcatcher.*

"I know it isn't the best plan, but we need to move quickly and work with the knowledge we have." Amira gave their surroundings another furtive look. "Right now, we still have the element of surprise. If someone did murder my double, then perhaps we can expose their treachery when I arrive alive and well at this meeting."

Despite the strands of logic tugging at her gut, Coral had to shake her head. "I just don't think it's our best move. You said yourself, no one knows we're here. We need to play that to our advantage and stick to the original plan. We need to get to the secret entryway through the latrine. It was a good plan. Infiltrate the Glass Palace, access what intel we can, and plan a perfect strategy of attack. Then we bring the Thirteen down from the inside. We have to be patient. I know I'm right." Coral heard the desperation leaching from her tone but she couldn't stop it. She knew she was making the right decision for everyone involved. The Thirteen were a dangerous lot. Hadn't they all just been reminded of it firsthand with Amira's previous behavior?

Amira stubbornly shook her head, probably ready to begin a new string of reasoning when her eyes suddenly went white, and her skin paled several shades. Coral turned around, reaching for her trishula, prepared to fight whatever creature or person had terrified Amira into such a state. She didn't expect the source of Amira's fear to be such a tiny woman, a slight thing scarcely taller than Jura, although her face was aged, and her body held more womanly curves. She was beautiful in the way Coral found her mom beautiful, but there was something cold and hard behind this woman, a sharp edge of a beautifully crafted sword.

The mere fact that the woman was alone and unarmed stayed Coral's arm. There was no need to unsheathe her trishula, yet.

"Whoever she is, get yourself together. She's nearly here," Kale whispered in warning, getting as close to Amira as he could. He and

Coral towered behind her, watching the woman's approach.

"My, my. You've returned. I was only just telling Ishani we couldn't rid ourselves of you so easily." The woman's voice was a low, soft purr. She seemed as deadly as a hungry shark and her expression just as vacant. "Hmm," the woman continued as her gaze moved between Coral and Kale. "And you've brought friends."

Amira blinked a few times, though her face had yet to return to its normal color. Coral gave her a gentle poke in the back, prompting her to say something. Anything. She was about to open her own loud mouth and let some excuse fall out of it when Amira finally cleared her throat, a smile clawing its way onto her expression.

"Denir," Amira squeaked. "My lady Fourth. How lovely to see you."

AMIRA

Chapter Twenty-Four

Amira could see it in her eyes, a small glimmer of excitement and a tiny inhale of breath from the woman in front of her. Sandstorms, she'd messed up and given the woman power in some way. Had the woman's Rank changed? Had her own? She hadn't even given that a thought, but it was a strong possibility.

"Fourth? Do you care to finish your insult or perhaps you care to explain where you've been?" Denir lifted her chin at the sea people who flanked her. "Who are they?"

"The reason I've been away. Alert the men to drop the golden banners. And if you'll excuse me, I'm exhausted and my guests and I—"

"Just a moment. You've been gone for days! Ishani and I—" She cut herself off and gave the courtyard a furtive glance. "We've covered for you, but Justir has called for a council meeting so your timing could not be better."

Amira studied her carefully. The woman was testing her, probing at what she knew. She cursed the fact that she didn't have a mirror, worried at what a sight she must be. She hadn't had a proper steam in weeks. Her hair was a greasy mess of ragged length around a face decidedly paler and gaunter than the one she'd shown six weeks ago. Had Amira the fraud kept up her appearance? She replayed Denir's words. She said she'd been gone for days. Was it too much to hope that they might stay gone? Perhaps a bit of luck was finally shining her way. She had to remain in control. She straightened her shoulders to exude confidence she didn't have.

"Naturally, I'm on time. She arranged it that way." It was only a small gamble. If Denir was working with the Queen of Shadows, then she would assume Amira's mission to be her business. If Denir was ignorant of the queen's plans, she would still assume Amira was working from someone else's schedule. A puppet master in control of every character on stage.

"Shall I assume this can all be explained . . . under the same arrangement? Guests included?" There was a small catch in her voice when she asked the last question, and Amira wondered what it meant. It had only been a few weeks since she had left the Republic and its intrigue, but only minutes into her first confrontation, and Amira felt as though it had been years.

Coral tensed behind her, likely itching for a fight. It seemed that woman was always up for a confrontation, but now was the time for smooth words, not bloodshed. Amira pushed all thoughts of her ragged appearance and the worry over her evil doppelgänger aside and focused on the moment. It wasn't easy, but somehow, she found the old facade and wrapped it around her tightly.

"You can assume anything you'd like." Amira smiled. "Now if you'll step aside, my guests and I are tired from our journey, and I must change before the council meeting." She didn't wait for a response, stepping forward and shouldering the older woman on her way past her.

"You'll be in attendance then?" Denir called after her.

Amira stopped to look back over her shoulder. Denir wore a polite smile and clasped her hands behind her back as she strolled forward.

Amira sighed. "Why wouldn't I be? Am I not the Th—the head of my household?" *Don't dare say your Rank. It may have changed.*

"Of course you are, dear, you've only mentioned your weariness and—"

"Is this an attempt to keep me from my rooms?" Amira snapped. She allowed her natural frustration to seep through, sharpening her tone. "I've grown tired of this conversation, and I have pressing matters to discuss with my . . . guests before the council meeting."

Kale snorted behind her.

Denir held her gaze for a moment, the look on the brink of a challenge. Then she shrugged and tossed a hand back in the general direction of the First Tower.

"You can cease any subterfuge—the majority of the council will be hidden away before the meeting. I doubt anyone will even notice you and your party on your way into the Second Tower."

The *Second* Tower. Was it a trick or a small nugget of sympathy or faith? What had happened to Velder? Amira forced her expression to remain neutral. "Until the meeting then." She inclined her head in farewell and turned toward the gardens.

There was only a single pair of palace guards at the courtyard entrance, and they allowed Amira and her companions to pass through with no inspection and little expression in their blank stares.

The garden was both exactly how she remembered it and yet different at the same time. The water from the fountain sparkled in the afternoon sunlight, and the heady aroma of citrus and jasmine assailed her nostrils. But Jura should be there, fingers trailing in the fountain as she read one of her silly novels and ignored Amira's story of her latest suitor. Antar should be there, showing off his latest skill with his scimitar. This empty garden . . . this was no indication of home.

"Are you all right?" Coral asked. Her tone was soft. It held a gentleness Amira was beginning to realize was not as foreign to her as she would have others believe. "Who was that woman? One of the Thirteen?"

Amira nodded, forcing the old memories out of her mind. "She's a mean one. But then, so am I. Or I was anyway." She sighed. She didn't even know who she was anymore. "Come on, I think my apartments are just through here." She gestured forward meekly, her feet impossibly heavy. It was a shame she had to change for a council meeting. A nap sounded glorious.

"You think?" Kale asked. "Shouldn't you know?" He scratched at the sleeves of the tunic they had forced on him.

"When I left, my father was in charge and we were the Third family. But Denir acted insulted when I called her the Fourth, and then she referred to the Second Tower as my home. Either she was lying to set me up, which is entirely possible, *or* I'm beginning to suspect the more likely scenario. Something has happened to Velder." She sighed. "And I'm now second-in-command over the entire Republic."

KAY

CHAPTER TWENTY-FIVE

*I*t *was easy to build* a pattern here by the river. Wake up, gather water. Wash up and drink while checking for fish in her homemade line. Daddy had shown her years ago, and she had always enjoyed fishing with her father in the tiny stream near their home. But fishing wasn't as easy here. The river ran a tumultuous course over sharp rocks and narrow banks, and she had yet to catch a single fish. She had been trying for nearly three days.

Sky could be counted on to bring her midday meal at least. He often took to the skies before dawn, returning with some offering of small game.

Kay was *tired* of rabbit.

She missed the garden of vegetables at home. How she and Daddy would pull down the sweet summer corn while Mama made bread in the kitchen. As usual, thoughts of home and Mama brought an overwhelming wave of loneliness, and Kay dug in her satchel for her doll. She had chided herself for bringing the toy, but it was moments like these that she was so happy she had. The doll hosted a strange odor of lilies and ash, but its hair was still soft to the touch, despite the smoky musk. She rubbed the doll's hair against her cheek, remembering how Mama's hair had felt as soft.

The corner of an envelope yellowed with age protruded from the opening of the satchel, worked free when she'd tugged out her doll.

Kay frowned, picking up the sealed envelope and drawing it up to her face. A letter from Mama . . . Mama's writing . . . It called to her as fiercely as freedom once had, even if the letter wasn't meant for her.

William. She frowned at the name. Daddy's name. Why would Mama write a letter to Daddy when she could just tell him in person? Maybe she did and that's why the letter remained unopened. Kay felt her tummy doing tiny flips as she thought it over. She knew she wasn't supposed to read a letter that wasn't meant for her, but the temptation to read Mama's words finally won over.

Kay ripped open the letter before she could give her brain a chance to talk her out of it.

The paper was not as yellowed as the envelope protecting it had been, but it had dozens upon dozens of creases on it, as if someone had balled it up only to smooth it out into the envelope fold.

William, my beloved husband,

This letter is more difficult to write than I had ever imagined. Before anything else, I want to remind you I was (and am still today as I write this, pregnant with our child) very aware of the risks in this world, of the risks and dangers made all the greater by who you are. I know that this child I carry inside me may be threatened by those same risks. Know that I am not afraid. If I had to start my life again . . . I would still choose you. I would choose this life of love.

You might find it silly, my insistence to place these worries on paper, and perhaps I am but indulge me, as I have you, all these years. Please, Will, my beloved, if anything should go wrong, save the child. If this baby is even a fraction as powerful as we believe, then everything depends on their safety.

If you are reading this, I can no longer accompany you on our adventure. Take care of my baby, tell them of my love, deep abiding and endless, just as my love runs for you.

PS

I've had Josep fashion the stones into earrings, they will be ready in a fortnight. I still don't believe the stones will work until all the pieces are gathered.

K

The letter ended there. Kay wanted to crumble it into a ball and burn it into a pile of ash.

Why would Mama write such a letter? And why would she keep it after Kay was born because surely the child mentioned was Kay. What was the meaning of that last part, the bit about her earrings? The letter left only questions and confusion and Kay wanted to scream. The special flame inside her rolled in response, her skin turning hot to the touch. If the flame had an emotion, it would be angry, Kay thought. Which was just as well because Kay was angry too. And why shouldn't she be mad? It wasn't fair. None of this was fair!

It was almost as if she were Breathing, only she wasn't. Normally that would scare her, but her burning skin made her feel alive. It didn't hurt, but when she noticed the edges of the letter start to sizzle, she dropped it to the ground and gave it a few stomps for good measure. The paper was still smoking, but only a little, and Kay stared down at it, chest heaving. She couldn't explain why the letter had made her angry but it had.

It wasn't *fair*. How could those be the last words from Mama? How could Mama have been so okay with leaving her? As if she had known Kay would lose her one day. And why would she talk about the earrings? Kay had always believed Daddy had them made for her, but Mama made them before she was even born!

Kay unballed her fist and reached up to touch her earrings. She wasn't sure what made her do it, maybe just the fact that she wanted answers, but Kay touched the stones and Breathed.

The light was blinding, so bright Kay closed her eyes. *Is that me? Am I glowing?* She dared to open her eyes but then she was falling, sinking into sand, the tiny grains rushing over her until she was buried in the darkness.

Get up. Breathe.

Kay didn't know the voice in her head, but she listened. She reached for the endless supply of heat within her and Breathed deep.

A hundred images rushed through her mind, each lasting for only a second, each bringing forth a new memory. Entire conversations spoken in Jangba, conversations that had once eluded her, came forth with rushing clarity. And past events, things that had seemed a lifetime ago—her time in the arena, her memories of Udo, Wallace, Akil, and Ash. Everything was different.

And suddenly, the startling realization that she wasn't alone hit her hard.

Release me.

Kay released the earring with a gasp. She was back in her cave, but maybe she had never left it? She climbed to her feet, blinking in the semi-darkness. She didn't trust herself to Breathe a flame yet.

"Is anyone there?" she asked, feeling silly.

There was no response. Kay wasn't sure that she had truly expected one anyway.

She left her tiny cave feeling oddly deflated. What had happened just now? Kay knew something special had happened when she touched the stone and Breathed, but she didn't know what that meant.

Kay felt Sky before she saw him. A distant pull in her gut, a sense of knowing that reminded her of summer nights when she would fall asleep in Daddy's arm and wake as he turned up the hill into their home. The sky darkened briefly as Sky's massive body covered the sun and his shadow smothered the surrounding land. Kay looked up with a grin and watched as the dragon landed lightly beside her, the ground rumbling at his descent.

He dropped a burned piece of meat at her foot. Kay's smile fell. More burned rabbit. There must be millions of them out there, and Sky had no problem finding them. She thanked the dragon for her meal and picked at the offering, pushing it back toward Sky once she'd had her fill. He ate her leftovers in one gulp, twin trails of smoke curling from his nostrils in what Kay had learned was a clear indication of his pleasure.

"I read Mama's letter," she told the dragon. He watched her, eyes sparking intelligence. The connection between them felt sad, and she saw a picture of a boy crying in her mind.

"Yeah, it made me sad." He did that sometimes, shared emotions or images that were human. Kay didn't know if the humans were people he'd once known or just images conjured by her mind, but they were a comfort all the same. She reached for his nuzzle, rubbing at the smooth leathery finish between his long canines.

"Haven't you ever wanted to find your family?" She felt a brief pull of desperation but then the dragon snorted and turned away, sniffing at the air.

"I think, if I try really hard, I can find more dragons . . . I can feel them." She watched Sky, carefully trying to gauge his reaction, but he had settled down to curl in on himself, stretching his neck toward his tail, and seemed intent on ignoring her.

A part of her tugged at the idea of further exploring the letter and her earrings. But something else, a larger, stronger part of her, was afraid to think about the past. She didn't think she was ready to explore her new powers with the earrings. They were just too scary.

But the idea of finding more dragons . . . well, that sounded like fun!

Yes, find them.

Kay flinched. Sky poked her with his nose, no doubt sensing her spike of alarm just as she now felt his worry. "It's fine," she said, more than anything trying to convince herself. She waited for a moment, but she didn't hear any strange voices in her head. She Breathed.

She hadn't tried to track dragons with her power before, not really. Usually, she only reached out to see if she could feel anyone else's Breath around her. More like an inventory of her surroundings. But why shouldn't she reach out farther? Search out the Breath of other dragons? It should be possible. With the Everflame inside of her, Kay felt stronger every day.

Why hadn't she tried to find more dragons? It should be easy now. She closed her eyes.

It was different from Breathing. Almost like holding her breath and then blowing out bubbles. The bubbles floated away and popped against other living fires. There. Two large masses off in the distance. That had been easy.

Kay opened her eyes. "I found two dragons. They're not too far away." Now that she'd located them, their fires called out to her, to the giant flame inside her.

Yes.

She shook her head. "We could be there in an hour."

Sky lifted his head and blinked at her.

"Oh, come on! Don't you want to get back up there? Wouldn't it be fun to meet more of your own kind?"

Sky's tongue darted out, the forked ends snapping like tiny whips.

"You didn't say no." Kay grinned, pushing all thoughts of Mama's letter out of her brain. Flying was so much fun. There was nothing else she wanted to do, and going on an adventure to find more dragons? What could be better?

Sky huffed out smoke and growled deep in his throat, but he lowered his neck for Kay to climb on. Once she was perched atop the thick coil of his neck, he shot up, giant wings unfurling and beating fiercely. Kay didn't have to direct him, and she wondered idly if Sky could sense her connection to the dragons or if he had his own.

Soon she was lost in the fierceness of the sky. Kay loved the wide expanse of nothing but the occasional cloud to block their way. The ground was nothing more than swaths of brown, red, and green. Kay loved the swirl of colors they made whenever Sky dipped in flight.

She would have thought the dragons would all be in the Wilds by now, but these two were too far south. Probably escaped from the arena, Kay thought with a sudden twist of guilt. She should be happy that she released the dragons, but the singular good deed did not erase all the bad things she'd done. She tried not to think about those things, but the memories always rushed back to her. More so now that she'd devoured the eternal flame. She didn't know how to explain it, but she remembered everything. Kindle and Ash had both wanted Kay to stay out of the catacombs, but they had never explained why. Had they wanted to keep her from finding more dragons? Had she always had this strange ability to find other dragons, or was this a new power due to the Everflame?

Kay tried to remember her previous powers and their limits, but that particular memory eluded her, as if the final thread to a former life was long forgotten because, surely, she had never been so weak. Now, with the Everflame, her power seemed limitless.

Daddy had always had more power than her. He'd warned her about burning out. He *had* burned out, right in front of her. No, not that memory. Kay tried to block the memory from returning but she was too late.

Ash, trying so hard to befriend her. But then she'd stolen his glass map and later broke it. It shattered when she tried to escape the first time. No, not that memory either.

Meeting Kindle for the first time.

Mama burning. Kindle burning.

Udo's boot.

Kay let out the Breath she'd been holding, determined not to draw more power. She wasn't even holding on to the earring now, so why were these memories rushing back at her?

"Stop it!" she screamed.

Sky sent a spike of alarm to her along with images of their rocky outcrop. Maybe they should head back and wait until she wasn't sad anymore.

"No." Kay rubbed at his neck, blinking back any tears. "We're almost there."

She could feel them now. Two large living fires that called to her and nearly a dozen smaller ones. She frowned. Those other fires were much too large to belong to more rabbits and entirely too small to be more dragons.

Sky began his descent, gliding toward a soft stretch of grass nearly a mile from the dragons ahead. He still seemed concerned, a low growl rolling in his throat.

Kay agreed. Something about those dozen other living fires didn't seem right. They belonged to something much larger and more powerful than any other animal besides dragons.

And then Kay realized what they were.

Humans.

KAY

CHAPTER TWENTY-SIX

Her immediate thought was to run. No one had seen them yet. They were still too far away to have caused any alarm. The last thing Kay wanted to do was run into more red-robes. She and Sky had managed to stay out of their way lately, and Kay wanted to keep it like that. But then, the red-robes didn't usually travel all together like this. Had they sent everyone after her? Doubled their efforts to find her? Or were these small fires simply a band of traveling merchants? Either was possible, and Kay decided she had to find out what was the truth.

Sky circled widely, gliding on an air current before banking right and back toward the dragons. He landed far enough away that they were still out of sight, and Kay jumped to the ground and told herself to ignore her wobbling knees.

There's no reason to be scared, she reminded herself. *You're special.*

Either the people were red-robes or they were not. Somehow, repeating the simple fact made her feel more at ease. She started forward, and Sky followed behind, snout raised to sniff the air surrounding them. Despite the fact that the dragon moved as silently as he could in the forest, there was no masking the snap of twigs and branches as he followed behind her.

"You should probably stay here," she whispered to her gentle giant.

Sky growled in response.

"I know, but I want to sneak up on them, and you are just too noisy. I'll call you when I need you." She fell into the soft fluttery steps of the Blue Form, her feet whispering against the soft grass. Kay remembered all the details of the various Forms. The frantic twists from the Red Form and the many spins and flips found in the Green. The colored Forms were all part of the deadly dances used by the Fire Dancers, and Kay had mastered them all.

They were closer than she thought. Two massive dragons, one nearly double the size of Rumble, and he was the biggest she'd ever seen. The smaller dragon was curled into the ground, barely moving aside from the steady rise and fall of its chest.

Kay swallowed and risked stepping closer, squinting as the rest of the clearing came into view. There were several people here, men mostly, and although none wore the red robes of the arena, there was at least one Fire Dancer present. He wore glittering green scales of dragon armor across his chest and juggled a mediocre flame between two large, awkward hands. The rest of the men circled at a careful distance. Kay Breathed in, stirring the great flame within her. Her original assumption was right. None of the other people present were special aside from their funny clothing.

Kay turned her attention back to the dragons, careful not to make any noise as she crawled in the tall grass. Now that she was closer, she could see why the smaller dragon hadn't moved. He was pinned to the ground by a heavy metal net. The sides of the net were staked into the ground by long steel pins.

Kay clenched her fist.

The other dragon had taken a defensive stance in front of the smaller, more vulnerable one. The massive beast had several assegai protruding from its side and wings. It snarled and bellowed another flame at the crowd of hunters in their strange clothing, but the Fire Dancer caught the flame and tossed it back toward the netted dragon.

Kay decided she had seen enough. She jumped to her feet and started running forward, Breathing deeply as she did so. The crowd of people had their focus on the dragon ahead and didn't notice the tiny girl running toward them from the woods. They didn't notice her until the grass began to burn around them.

"You! Little girl!" A startled woman turned toward Kay, her long arms reaching for her, but Kay ducked under them and ran toward the Fire Dancer.

Another person reached for her, and Kay fell into a side roll, flowing into the rolling motions of the Green Form. She shot a tiny ball of flame at the man, but it barely singed the fabric on his arm, and Kay realized the purpose of their strange clothing. It repelled the flames. No wonder these hunters felt confident enough to take on a dragon!

With a grunt, Kay shoved her body into his, tackling him around the bend of his knees and bringing him to the ground. She leaped over him and Breathed in more, shooting a ribbon of flames out around her.

"Sky!" she screamed as loudly as she could. "I need you."

She sprinted forward, but she was snatched up from behind, her arms pinned to either side as a large man scooped her up in a reverse bear hug. She kicked wildly, but the man's thighs were giant tree trunks and her kicks were puny against him. She Breathed in, satisfied when steam formed against the strange wet fabric covering the man's arms.

"I don't know what you are, but you're coming back with me." The man sneered down at her. The clipped Jangba sent shivers down her spine.

No. Not again. *Never* again.

"Let me go!" She wriggled as hard as she could to slither out of his arms. She expelled flames, but she was unable to aim properly, and they shot out in wild little bursts around her, sizzling out against her captor's fabric.

"Erila, help me!"

The woman approached, giving them both a wary look.

"I don't like the look of that one. Remember the tales we heard from Niko at the pub last..." Her mouth fell open and her face turned pale.

Kay grinned.

Every hair on the back of her neck shot up at the sheer volume of Sky's roar. Kay wished she could have seen her captor's expression, but he dropped her so quickly, she was still clambering to her feet while he began barking orders at the others to assemble their weapons. They scrambled into formation to block Sky from advancing.

Kay took the opportunity as a distraction and she sprinted forward, giving the dragons a wide berth. Poor things were in a frenzy of fear, and Kay wanted to be sure that both dragons could see her approach. Unfortunately, so could the very busy Fire Dancer. They were the only person to remain undistracted by Sky's appearance, and their focus remained on the angry green dragon in front of them.

The dragon was so dark a green that he would have looked

black were it not for the sunlight reflecting off those scales. Dark horns rose from behind its snapping maw. Kay swallowed. *I'm going to help you,* she promised.

The dragon reared on its legs and hissed at the Fire Dancer. Kay scooped up a fallen assegai, which had snapped in half on its shaft, but that made it just the right size. If she could just free the other dragon, the duo might have enough of a chance to escape. Kay just needed to get close enough to unchain him.

She ignored the Fire Dancer and the dragon in their battle and hurried to the trapped juvenile. She was able to reach one of his pins first, and she bent forward, wrapping both hands around the wide metal spike. She pulled as hard as she could, but there was no budging.

The hunters were scrambling about and yelling at one another in confusion. Sky shot a continuous stream of fire between them and the dragons, snapping at anyone who got close.

She was never going to be strong enough to move the spikes on her own, and she didn't know how long Sky could hold off the rest of the hunters.

She gave another wrenching heave on the spike, but it didn't budge. She was running out of time. She Breathed in frustration. What could she do? If she got Sky to help her move the staked net, it would give the hunters and Fire Dancer a chance to make their move. She could attack the Fire Dancer, but that didn't seem wise. Kay had never wanted to battle anyone in the arena and didn't like the idea of doing something so bad. In fact, the idea of doing more bad things terrified her. She Breathed deeper.

She was trying to do something good. She was trying so hard to do good things. Dragons should be free. They were meant to be free, so why was this so hard?

The assegai erupted into flames. Kay blinked down at the burning shaft, dimly aware that she was still Breathing. Then she Breathed more. She had melted stone before. The memory had been hidden, another echo of someone she had once been, a part of her past now unlocked.

If metal was hot enough, it would melt too.

Kay thought of the Everflame and unleashed its heat into the giant metal spike. Bits of metal exploded around her, singeing the ground and leaving a bitter smell in the air. The Fire Dancer sent a flurry of flames in her direction, and Kay Breathed them in lazily, swallowing their heat and adding it to her own. Moments later the second spike melted, and the smaller dragon rose to its feet.

The Fire Dancer faltered, his puny flame sputtering out. There was no flame for him to grab, and for a moment, he appeared helpless. Then Kay remembered how deadly Fire Dancers could be, armed with simply an assegai, and she started forward.

"Leave. Leave them alone and get out of here. And don't come back." Kay Breathed again so that a ball of flame surrounded her fingertips and licked down the length of her arm.

The Fire Dancer gestured for his men to fall back and threw his assegai onto the ground in front of him. "Who . . . what are you?"

Kay was close enough to see his face and was surprised by how young he was. Younger than Kindle had been, certainly. A fuzzy patch of hair shaded his skin, and his dark eyes were wide and frightened.

Sky landed beside her, growling low in his throat. Kay looked at her dragon and then at the other two who still stood quietly behind her as if waiting for a command.

Kay's parents had always told her she was special. She had believed them then, but now . . . what was she now?

"I am Kay," she whispered at first, but her voice grew louder with every word. "I used to be a daughter and a cadet. I used to do bad things. But I've always been special." She Breathed in deeply, aware that her skin seemed to glow every time she scratched the surface of the vast well of heat within her.

"Tell all the hunters, the dragons are meant to be free. That all dragons will be free. My name is Kay. And I am the Rescuer of Dragons."

JURA

CHAPTER TWENTY-SEVEN

Jura was escorted back to her rooms by a surly Danos. He had been waiting outside the door of the Dreamer's alcove and frowned when Jura emerged before entering the room to exchange quiet words with the Dreamer.

When Danos returned, he'd snapped his fingers at her and began striding down the hallway, his footsteps quick enough to give the impression that he was flying. He wasn't. Jura double checked. She guessed he didn't care for the fact that the Dreamer had so easily dismissed him.

"Are you angry with me?" The question tore out of her. She never would have described Danos as friendly, but she also never thought to see this outright disdain. "Have I done something to offend you?"

Danos stopped abruptly. "Your very presence offends."

If the words hadn't been so shocking, she might have gasped at the stinging remark. Instead, she merely gaped at him, mouth falling open slightly.

"I'll assume you can find your way back from here," he

continued, gesturing at her door, which was still several meters away.

"My presence offends? You think I *want* to be here? Miles and miles away from my home and the rest of my friends? You think I like hearing that I'm some . . . some—"

"Blood Maker." Danos spat the words as though they were a curse. Perhaps they were. It certainly seemed that way now.

"I don't even know what that means!"

She wished for his expression to soften, but he only made a low growling sound in his throat. "You'll come to know soon enough." He flicked his wrist in the direction of her door and it swung open, its whistling melody a soft whoosh in the silent atrium. Once again it was nearly empty save for a pair of guards against the western hall that led to the arena ruins. Perhaps this wing of the aliferous keep was reduced to housing prisoners and no one else . . . but that didn't make sense. Not when the alcove of the Dreamer was so near, not when Markhim was given free rein of his quarters.

"Where is everyone?" she asked, gesturing to the open space surrounding them. "Where are the rest of the aliferous?"

Danos clenched his jaw, a thin muscle jerking up and down his jawline as he did so.

"Gone." He pointed at her doorway. "Go, rest. The Dreamer requests that you begin your studies in the morning."

"Gone?" Jura ignored his pointed glare and his resigned sigh after. "What do you mean gone? Where did they all go?"

Danos glared at her. "If I had meant for you to know more, I would have been more forthcoming. Now, if you will excuse me, I have much to prepare before our lesson plan tomorrow."

"But . . . so you're to be my teacher then?"

"It would seem so. Ah, your companion." He nodded beyond, and Jura turned to watch Markhim's approach. Danos took the opportunity to leave, briefly touching fingertip to forehead before taking flight. Jura frowned after him.

"Was it bad news then?"

"Was what bad news?" Jura blinked at his appearance. His dark, unruly hair was in desperate need of a haircut. She resisted the urge to brush the curls out of his eyes. She realized he was referring to her meeting with the Dreamer and nodded.

"It's worse." She repeated everything she'd discovered, leaving her connection to the Queen of Shadows for last.

"You're related to that . . . that creature?" Markhim reeled back, eyes wide. "How?"

"I'm not sure," Jura murmured, thinking of her father. He'd always kept his secrets. Now it seemed he still had a few more. "I don't understand how my parents could do this."

"She's dangerous, Jura."

"I *know* that."

"Do you?" Markhim stepped closer, shoving up the light fabric of his tunic to reveal a chiseled abdomen marred by scars. "I don't even remember how I got these." He gestured toward himself. "And the scars I do remember, I pray to the Everflame I'll someday forget. Jura, the things she made me do . . ." He trailed off, pulling her toward him.

Jura allowed herself to be folded into his embrace. "I don't know what to do next," she mumbled against his chest.

He gave her another squeeze before gently releasing her, taking a step back, and grabbing her hand. "Come on. I have a surprise for you."

He pulled her past the open door of her room and beyond the atrium and its hall to the arena.

"Where are we going?"

"I just told you, it's a surprise." But there was a lightness to his tone, an easiness in the way he held her hand that Jura had missed. It was almost like the way things were before.

"How do you know your way around here so well?" she asked when he pulled her toward a narrow staircase. She wouldn't have even known to look for the structure there if he hadn't led her toward it.

"Well, while you've been meeting Dreamers and hearing life-altering prophecies about yourself, I've been exploring."

"Right." She tried not to let the reminder of their separate situations sting. "Because they aren't keeping you locked away in your room."

"No." Markhim stopped short, frowning down at her. "We should probably talk about that a bit more. They told me that door was for your protection. I truly had no idea you've been so isolated."

Jura snorted. "Protection from what?" She tossed up her hands, breaking the connection between them. "It doesn't matter anyway. I'm . . ." Fine? She was anything but fine! But what could she say to Markhim now that would change anything?

"Hey, you know you can tell me anything, right?" Markhim pushed her braid back over her shoulder and smiled at her. "I'm not going anywhere."

The intense stare he gave her sent shivers down her spine and her heartbeat quickened. Was he about to kiss her? Did she want him to?

"Come on. We're almost there." He grabbed her hand again, and they descended the open staircase to the lower levels of the keep. They traveled in silence for several moments, and Jura realized that as they stepped down that they turned back toward the mountain, a ceiling eventually emerging above from the carved mountainside.

Jura felt they were descending forever before the staircase began to twist back around, leveling out into a large cavern that revealed a cozy library. Shelves were carved out from the rock, and from floor to ceiling was nothing but books. She gasped at the sight.

"How did you find this?"

Markhim grinned, giving her hand a tiny squeeze. "I told you, I've been exploring."

He indulged her by pulling her into a gentle spin, the slow twirl revealing nothing but an endless circle of books.

"Do you like it?" he asked, pulling her toward him.

Jura was instantly aware of just how near the two were. Her hand in his felt electric, and she found herself staring at his lips.

Someone cleared their throat behind her, and Jura jerked out of Markhim's embrace, the moment lost.

"Priamos?" She blinked at the aliferous. He offered a weak smile in return.

"Speaker of the Dunes." He touched his finger to his forehead lightly. "Warrior of the new world." He nodded to Markhim.

"Where have you been?" Jura demanded, stepping away from Markhim and closing the distance between her and Pri. "I thought you would find me again, so that we might talk more."

"My apologies, Speaker."

She felt Markhim's hand fall on her lower back, letting her know that he was near. Or perhaps staking claim.

Pri seemed not to notice. "As I have assured you, your message was received, but there has been no way for me to garner further response."

"Message? What message?" Markhim asked.

Jura ignored him for the moment. "Well, surely you know something. Is there anything you could . . ." She glanced at Markhim, feeling him tense. "Is there any word on the Republic? Of home? I'd like to send another message, if I could."

Pri looked around, but the cavern was empty save for the three of them and the endless hoard of books. "There is not much I can do for you."

"Because you can't, or you won't? Please, Pri, if you know anything."

"You spoke with the Dreamer? Did you not?" Pri gave her a meaningful stare. "What did they reveal to you?"

"I know who my sister is." Pri didn't react so she continued, "They told me what I am." She swallowed hard, the foreign title echoing in her mind. Blood Maker. She closed her eyes and said it out loud.

"Then there is not much more I can reveal to you." Pri cast a sidelong glance in Markhim's direction.

"It's okay, you can trust him," Jura said.

"There are many volumes here," Pri said by way of answer. He gestured widely. "Any topic from ancient histories and geography to original theologies. Many that I feel might interest you."

Jura smiled. "Any specific recommendations?" Her mind was already flipping through her mental inventory of useful titles. Had she envisioned a Dream earlier? Was she somehow able to connect to a Blood Maker from the past? And what had they been discussing at that table?

"I am sorry, Speaker, I must attend to my duties." He bowed in a quick dip, his finger lightly touching his forehead. "Please, make use of the ladder. You might find a title you seek hides just beyond your reach." His gaze was meaningful, and he nodded once more at the both of them before leaving the round amphitheater.

Jura smiled at Markhim. "Well, you heard him. We're looking

for a book on the top shelf."

He sighed, crossing his arms over his chest. "Jura, I don't trust him."

She snorted. "That's fair, because I'm fairly certain he doesn't trust you." She began to walk toward the ladder attached to the far wall.

"What were you two talking about anyway?" Markhim asked, grabbing her bicep to slow her down.

"Nothing. He got a message to Tylak, that's all." She pulled out of his grasp, and his arm fell limply to his side. She snuck a quick glance at his profile and noted his jaw working. "Are you mad?"

"That you talked to Tylak? No, why would I be mad? But that you wasted your contact with the outside world and didn't think to call for help—"

"Contacting Tylak *is* calling for help. Besides, we don't need to be rescued. They'll let me go just as soon as I finish my training. I have to believe that; I have to." She whispered that last bit. She needed to learn how to use her powers. She needed to discover what it meant to be a Blood Maker, to be capable of breaking a world.

"I'm sorry. You're right. You . . . you don't need this from me. Come here." He reached for her again, and this time she leaned into his embrace. "You feel good, you know that?" He mumbled the words against the top of her head, and she almost convinced herself she imagined them.

"Markhim." She pushed back from his chest, looking up to find him staring down at her. "I thi—"

Her words were captured by his kiss. Her breath hitched in her throat, a warm feeling spreading throughout her naval and along the length of her spine. She pressed herself closer, opening her mouth against his. His lips were frantic, roving over hers and stealing her breath away.

She pulled away first, hands trembling. "You interrupted me," she said, clearing her throat against the heat flooding her face. Their first kiss and she was admonishing him for interrupting her. Honestly, she no longer remembered what she had been about to say.

"I'm sorry for the interruption, but not for the kiss. I've wanted to do that for a long time." His gaze was smoldering, his eyes intent on her lips.

Her cheeks burned, and she tried to keep her lips from exploding into a giddy grin. "I . . ." She didn't have words still. At one point in time, a kiss from Markhim was everything she dreamed about. Now, while the reality had been a delightful experience, she didn't have the time to give the kiss the unhealthy amount of overanalyzing that it deserved.

"I need you to hold the ladder," she whispered.

Thankfully, he obliged, guiding her to the ladder and holding on to either side of the railing behind her. "Maybe I should climb up," he murmured against her ear.

Jura swallowed. She didn't dare turn around or she would find them nose to nose with each other. "Don't be silly. You don't know what I'm looking for . . . even I don't know. But also, you'll be better suited to catch me should I tumble."

"I'll always be here to catch you."

She smiled and started up the ladder.

JURA

CHAPTER TWENTY-EIGHT

Jura was, *for once, excited* to be locked back in her room. Markhim had been reluctant to leave her and she him, or at least she thought she *could* feel that way.

She couldn't stop thinking about Tylak and what kissing Markhim meant for the two of them. Maybe she was foolish for holding on to any sort of romantic ideal between her and Tylak. But she had felt something there and he had felt it too . . . hadn't he? She changed into her pajamas despite not having eaten her evening meal, and the sun still illuminated her room in its soft evening glow. She had no business worrying about kisses and romance when the entire continent was on the brink of war.

She threw herself onto her bed and stared up at her stone ceiling. Her training began in the morning, and she still had no idea what that even meant. So far, her experiences up here had been unlike anything she could anticipate. And just when she thought she had a handle on things, another disaster arrived.

Brimming with restless energy, she reached into the folds of fabric that covered her upper half, making a mental note to ask her captors the name of the garment. It had served its purpose well, masking her theft of the book. Not that there had been anyone in the tiny library to prevent her from borrowing it. Was it truly stolen then? Jura liked to think not.

The Five Elements and Properties of Blood.

It was not her first time seeing the title. The book had first appeared in the hands of Ahmar, the deceased Third of the Thirteen and Amira's father, killed by her alttaw'am. And again, in Kitoi, hadn't Peppik found a copy of the book there?

This book meant something, although, she had no idea what. It was too much of a coincidence that it would appear again now. She flipped through its pages, frowning down at the nearly pristine copy until stopping at one of the pages at random.

It is my observation the use of our ancestors' magic should be focused through the use of the scion stones. This might be amplified through the blood of the gifted should it evolve to its purest form.

Hmm. That could be useful. She frowned at the mention of scion stones and blood—those words were significant, although it was hard to interpret their meaning. She blinked at the page, storing it in her memory for later. The book seemed full of information like that. What had the alttaw'am, the Queen of Shadows, and her minions wanted with this information? What did it all mean? The book had to be older than she believed for there to be a copy of it here. Unless the aliferous traveled down more often than they would have her believe. Just how often did they really leave their home? And what further secrets did they hide? She resigned herself to a long night of reading and more unanswered questions.

Hours later and Jura was near ready to give up on the book. She had almost read the entire thing, and while interesting at times, Jura could see no reason the information inside was worth dying over. She yawned loudly, stretching back and delighting in the slight strain against muscles that had cramped after hours of reading. Perhaps best to put the book away and finish it in the morning. But there were only a few pages left, and she bit back another yawn, determined to power through. She turned the page, and her heart flipped.

> *The scion stones must be gathered to work, but there are several fail safes in place before their true power can be accessed. Without the proper keys, the magic will self-destruct. Among these keys and arguably the most important is the book of—*

The bottom of the page was torn. Jura flipped to the next page, frantic for some clue to the mentioned book.

> *. . . alone is responsible for the beginning of the end. It can only be accessed by a Blood Maker and will heed the call of no other.*
>
> *These studies are the intellectual property of Xao Shin. Any attempt to replicate . . .*

Jura stopped reading the acknowledgments and flipped the page. Surely there was more. But no, nothing but blank pages followed. She hated when books did that. She thought she'd had more reading. She thought she would find answers. Instead, she only had more questions. Someone had ripped that page on purpose. It was too great a coincidence that the page with the book's name would be missing. And what did it mean that it could only be accessed by a Blood Maker? That it would somehow heed her call?

These thoughts and others tumbled through her mind, and it was many hours later when Jura finally found sleep.

The following morning, she was awakened by an insistent knocking on her door. "Well come on in then. It's not like I can open it," she muttered, shoving sleep from her eyes. She got up and moved to the corner, relieving herself behind the silk screen and then washing her face and mouth from the endless wealth of water in the basin that was somehow always fresh and full and waiting for her. When she finished, she found Pri waiting for her, fidgeting by her bed.

"Oh." She blinked in surprise. "Good morning, Pri. I assumed you were Danos. I would have given you a warmer greeting." She beamed at him, her eyes darting to her pillow where the corner of her bookish contraband peeked out from under the silk case.

"I apologize for waking you." Pri wrung his hands together, appearing worried.

I shouldn't have spent half the night reading, Jura chided herself as she fought back another yawn. To Pri, she tossed her hand in a dismissive gesture. "Please, don't. I'm sure it will only be a matter of moments before Danos arrives. That is to say, if you had something private you wished to discuss..." She gave him a meaningful stare.

"I have been hoping to catch you alone. I thought I could ask, if you wouldn't mind—" He cut himself off, swallowing hard.

"It's okay, take your time." She squatted beside her bed in search of her slippers. She was still stuck with the delicate satin dance shoes she'd worn her last night in Kitoi, and she thought longingly of her sturdy walking boots left behind. Perhaps Danos could provide her with more footwear.

"Take me with you."

"To training?" Jura furrowed her brow, surprised by the request.

"To the Republic. Anywhere. Just away . . . from here."

"Away? But why? I mean, what is wrong with living here? There's so much water." It was difficult imagining anyone wishing to leave such a paradise. But then again, wasn't her departure back to the Republic foremost on her mind?

Her door began its whistle, effectively silencing any response that would have come to his lips. Pri's eyes caught hers, desperate.

"Behind my screen. Go." Jura jerked her head behind her and rushed forward, meeting Danos at the door. "Good morning, Speaker. I have a small issue I would like to discuss with you before beginning my training."

Danos frowned as she pushed her way through the open door and out into the hall. Luckily, he followed. Pri was safe, for now.

"You said there was an issue?" He cleared his throat, his expression darting back to her closed door.

"My toes," she blurted.

"I beg your pardon?" Danos returned his gaze to her, blinking slowly.

"Yes. My toes need better protection. These slippers are not meant for sparring."

Danos chuckled. "So quick to battle, little warrior. We do not spar today."

"We don't?" Genuine surprise laced her tone. "But I thought—"

"I assume you are more than proficient at hand-to-hand combat and close-range weaponry. Or are the rumors surrounding the children of the Republic false?" They both knew they weren't, so he continued after a beat of silence. "No, your training is not for your body but for your mind and spirit. This training will finally make you whole." His mouth twitched. "But if a new pair of shoes would make your spirits soar, perhaps the war can wait?"

Jura decided not to retort to his sarcasm and instead gestured down the hall toward the atrium. "This way, then? Or am I to go back to the Dreamer's atrium?"

"The Dreamer needs rest after your visitation yesterday. The . . . duties of the Dreamer are more arduous of late, and it pains them to be near one such as you. You will not see them today nor will you seek them out. Now follow me and cease wasting everyone's time."

Sandstorms, she got the point. Jura didn't say that out loud, but she allowed herself the pleasure of shooting a glare at his departing form. She followed him down the hall and beyond the arena to a tiny open courtyard. The square was cut out of the mountainside and framed by quartz so pale a pink, it appeared almost white. There were a few marble benches along its perimeter as well as more ivy around the edge.

He gestured for her to take a seat at the nearest bench and she obliged, sighing with some content at the warmth of the seat bathed in the early morning sunlight. In the distance, she could just make out the steady rush of water roaring from the falls.

Danos came to stand before her, clasping his arms in front of him. "Now then. Show me your current limits within your magic capability."

"Show you . . ." She snorted out a breath that was dangerously close to becoming a wild giggle. "You want me to do a display of my power? Of blood magic?" She did laugh then, the sound wild and off-pitch. "I didn't even know I had blood magic until yesterday. Everflame only knows how you came to be certain of my abilities at all. Don't you get it? I don't know who I am anymore!"

"Breathe, warrior. All of life is not such a battle. There must be times of peace." He reached around and plucked out a single feather, flinching slightly at its departure. "Consider this feather. I can direct it to the ground with my powers or I can release it and assume it will follow the laws of nature and find its way to the ground, but its journey is only truly found upon its release." He flicked the feather, and it caught on a current, dancing before them before rising in the air and beyond her sight. "Release your hold on your magic and allow the magic to flow in its rightful path. You do not need to harness it now."

Jura frowned. "I know that was supposed to sound all inspiring or something, but I just . . . what? What do feathers and wind magic have to do with blood magic? And how come more people don't talk about it? If the Dreamer knows everything, why don't they just tell us what the Queen of Shadows is up to so we can stop her? And why have—"

"You will cease talking."

Jura's mouth snapped shut. She ground her teeth, thinking of just what she'd like to say by way of response.

"The Dreamer warned me of this," Danos continued. "Of your incessant inquiries."

"*Of course* I have questions," Jura said. "You just dumped a ton of information on me, and between that, and meeting the Dreamer, and all this prophecy talk, and these weird dreams about giant birds and lost memories, it's only normal I have more than one inquiry!" She realized she was shouting, and she couldn't remember jumping to her feet. She ceased pacing and crossed her arms over her chest.

"Ah yes, let us discuss these dreams of giant birds. Do they frighten you?"

"All that, and the giant bird dream is what you want to focus on?" She sighed. "Was that some sort of weird magic thing or was it just a weird dream? Because see, that's the thing. I don't really know what to think of as real anymore. You call me a Blood Maker, and that terrifies me. Am I this creature of gore and evil?"

"A Blood Maker is a dangerous thing and certainly one to be feared." Danos pressed on before the weight of his words could sting. "But any creature of great power should be feared. That doesn't make one evil."

If Jura didn't know better, she would think she had seen his gaze soften. But while the Speaker could be categorized as many things, soft was not one of them.

"Now, release your fears. Release the worry that weighs upon your shoulders. Release your thoughts . . . that's it. Concentrate."

Jura sighed. "I am to somehow both release my thoughts *and* concentrate? How?" The two concepts seemed contradictory.

"Think of the other times you've accessed your gift. You did not have thoughts. You were concentrated solely in the moment. Focused on your release. Follow your path." He gestured upward, and Jura fought the urge to repeat her earlier argument.

How did one release all thoughts yet remain focused? How? When all her thoughts tumbled over one another, what was she to make of it all? Pri and his strange request, the return of Markhim, the renewal of her dormant feelings for him, her separation from Amira and Tylak . . . It was difficult to think of Tylak without hearing his sarcastic tone, seeing the hard lines of his face, or remembering the soft touch of—oh.

It seemed she *was* capable of both focusing and losing all

thoughts. A deep well opened within her, a new sensation that was somehow familiar despite it being indescribable to anything she'd ever felt before. A steady thrum of heat and awareness beat deep within her. She opened her eyes to find Danos regarding her with what could almost pass as a smile.

"There. Have you found that part of yourself, little warrior?"

Jura nodded. She was afraid that if she said a word, she would lose whatever fragile hold she had on that deepest part of herself, and there was no time for that now.

QUEEN OF SHADOWS

CHAPTER TWENTY-NINE

The first thing any Shadow Dancer learned upon induction was that the Queen of Shadows was accustomed to getting her way. And Everflame protect any person foolish enough to stand in front of something she wanted. Early on she developed a reputation of violence, where swift and often gory retribution was meted out to any who opposed her. No one opposed her now.

That hadn't always been the case. The early days of her life had been spent in confusion, a time when a young woman wasn't sure of her place in the world much less if she even belonged in it. Back then it certainly didn't feel as though she belonged anywhere. Those days had been dark and desperate. Long nights in gutters with only the frenzied desert rats as her friends.

But she was no longer a small, destroyed child. Now she was a queen, a ruler and commander of men. Soon the world would be hers.

Tsillah smiled as she watched the man approach from her place carved into the stone wall. If she was a true queen, she would be perched on a throne. A true queen ruled over her subjects from the safety and comfort of her castle. But Tsillah had no castle and had lost any chance of a home, any home, more than a decade ago.

The man approaching wasn't her usual type. Not that one needed a type of brainless slave, but these days Tsillah felt she could grant herself a few indulgences. This one was much too large to be marked as one of her favorites. His muscles cut across his skin and brought to mind the stone statues that had once been popular in the Golden City. This was the sort of man who one knew was dangerous with one look.

That did make him a bit more her type. Tsillah enjoyed a man who knew to toe the line of danger. She enjoyed it more when the man brought with him a threat.

She could take care of herself. She had a legion of men and women at her disposal who proved just that.

Tsillah held up a gloved hand, effectively stopping his approach. Today her mask was gold wiring with silver threads and dark onyx polished smooth. The stones hung heavily around her chin and ears, leaving only her mouth and eyes exposed. She wondered if he caught the hint of a smile that still played at her lips.

"That's close enough." Her voice was confident, strong. It always was. "I didn't summon you." She was careful to keep any question out of her tone. A queen did not question her subjects; she commanded them. What was he doing here? "Give your report."

The man dropped to his knee. Despite this, his head was barely shy of her chin. She lifted her head higher and peered down her nose at him.

"My Queen."

She said nothing, waiting for him to continue.

"My apologies for the unexpected visit. I was forced to deliver the news in person when—"

"News . . ." There would be no mistaking the smile under her mask now. She allowed amusement to color her tone. "You seem to be under the impression you have news that has not reached my ears." Her head lilted to the side as she regarded him. The unspoken words drifted between them. As if anything was just allowed to happen in Jangbahar without her knowledge.

"Of course not, my Queen. But then, you know that I had to come. My position has been compromised. I . . . I await further instruction."

He bowed his head. Shame perhaps? She had no way of knowing, although she would wager water and gold on it if she had to. It probably galled him to forsake one mistress only to bend to another. And why? A small promise of power? Wasn't that always the case with men? She watched him for several moments, noted the steady rise and fall of his shoulders with each labored breath. She'd heard it was painful for his kind to be so far from home. She could understand that. She had been ripped from her home when she was just a child, and she remembered it still. The smell of citrus and jasmine in the hot, stale air.

She could almost smell it now.

"You were to neutralize the Wave Mistress, seize power for yourself, and return home for my further instruction."

His head slowly rose until his eyes reached hers. If he could, he might see one arched brow, but it was covered beneath the mask. She was beautiful now, in this moment. And she wondered idly how he would react if she were to remove the mask. Would he see what she wanted, or would he cringe in fear, not seeing but somehow knowing of the monster trapped beneath the skin that was not her own?

She wouldn't give him the chance. Her fingertip stopped its

path down the length of one of her silver chains and she rose to her feet, striding forward until she was close enough to touch him. She did, the hand landing softly on his shoulder.

He flinched.

He knew of the monster then. She lifted his chin with her pointer finger, forcing him to his feet. He kept his eyes downcast, fearful. As one should when they dared to look upon their queen.

"It would seem to me that you have not completed your mission. Therefore, it confuses me just which instructions you wait for. Neutralize the Mistress of the waves, seize control of your people, and return home." She pushed his face away from her, satisfied when he missed his footing and stumbled back.

"Go on." Tsillah smirked. "You have a job to finish."

He turned to leave, nearly tripping in his scramble to exit when she called out to him, effectively halting him in his tracks.

"Mano."

"Yes?" His voice croaked as he turned to face her.

"Yes, what."

"Yes, my Queen." His voice came out breathy and fearful. No, more than that, reverent.

She smiled. "Don't return until the young Wave Mistress is well out of my hair. She's a threat to us both, you understand."

His head bobbed up and down. Yes, he understood. She dismissed him with a flick of her wrist and he scampered off, eager to do her bidding. She sighed, allowing herself to feel the utter exhaustion weighing her down, if only for a moment.

Her hold on him would remain for as long as he wore the chain, but his obsession with her would wane with distance. It was tiring to hold so many, but those she could trust with the full scope of her plans numbered fewer than a handful, and she couldn't be sure of anyone's motives when they were not a mirror of her own.

She closed her eyes for a moment, allowing her emotions to slip away into the night. Allowing herself to feel like herself. Tsillah the woman, nothing more.

"My Queen?"

Her eyes snapped open to find Loga lingering in her doorway. She withheld another sigh and nodded, granting entrance to the man. The Shadow Dancer was young but eager, desperate to prove himself. His impulsive actions had already angered her more than once, but she had a soft spot for him. He reminded her of Adham, yet another flame lost to the gluttonous Thirteen.

"I hope you come with news meant to return you to my favor." She gave him a thorough examination, noting the dust stains on his desert darks, the russet color of dried blood on his neck and arms. There was no saying whose blood stained his skin now. She should still be angry with him for that stunt he'd pulled earlier. Killing Pilar was a tragedy. Not only was the loss of a trained alttaw'am devastating, but with it came the allowance for the return of Amira. Now there was an actual teenager playing second-in-command to the entire Republic. All because Loga couldn't control his temper.

"Apologies, my Queen, I've lost sight of her . . . again." He dropped to a knee and removed his mask. He had a handsome face, or he had at one point as long as he hadn't smiled. Now the eyebrow and cheekbone on the right side of his face were scarred from a severe burn. A face like Adham's. She swallowed hard, ignoring the quick stab of pain.

"She's a child," Tsillah snapped, the volume of her words giving strength to a conviction she didn't feel. That girl was no child. She was so much more. She had Breathed in the Everflame in its entirety. Her actions had complicated things, to say the very least. Loga said nothing.

She had played her hand too early, allowing her impatience to get the best of her, but Tsillah would not make the same mistake twice.

"It won't be much longer now," Tsillah said so softly she might as well have spoken to herself.

"What can I do? I am here but to serve you, my Queen."

Unlike so many others, Loga meant it. He didn't even wear chains.

Tsillah considered his offer. Her current priority remained — she needed to collect all of the stones. They nearly had them all. Not in the physical sense, but Tsillah knew the locations of nearly all of them, including the one that had remained the most elusive all these years. She knew the brat had it. Amira was most likely oblivious to its true power, even if she saw its value. The stones were known as nothing now but old heirlooms and forgotten prophecies.

The world had forgotten, but she hadn't. The stones were her ticket to a free world. A world in which she could be herself, a world free of any restrictions. A world where the Thirteen was made to pay and the Republic burned to the ground.

But the stones were only part of the issue. There was also the problem of her sister, Jura. Jura was nothing like she expected. She had had no mark of power throughout all these years . . . until now. What had changed? Had the girl simply come into maturity? And now that Jura had such power, what was her intention with it?

Tsillah had no plans to wait around to see it play out. No, she was an orchestrator, and up until recent events, she had been in complete control of everything around her. She couldn't lose control now, not when she was so close.

Her destiny was at hand. She could feel it. But then the child had Breathed in the Everflame and disappeared in the Wilds. And Jura had forged an alliance with the aliferous. How had she accomplished that? What did Jura know that she didn't?

For the first time in nearly a decade, Tsillah did not feel she was in total control.

It was time to implement the next phase of her plan.

"Loga, rise. I have a new mission for you."

The man sprang to his feet, lithe as any jungle cat, which was just as well.

"Let the child play for now. The stones are gathering, and I have to intercept certain players before this happens. Tylak and my sister care for one another. I know I've placed him and Jura on my 'do not touch' list, but I've changed my mind. I want you to find Tylak and bring him and his birthstone to me."

Loga nodded, slamming his fist against his chest in an affirming gesture meant to reestablish his duty to her. "I'll see that it is done. Thank you for this chance, my Queen. I won't let you down again." He pulled his mask into place.

"See that you don't. And Loga, Tylak is sure to give you trouble. He's formidable, but it's imperative you get that stone. If you must, kill him."

Foolish boy should have taken the opportunity when she gave him a chance. Now he and Jura were in for nothing but heartache.

AMIRA

CHAPTER THIRTY

The apartments of the Second Tower were much like her old. Amira found the majority of her belongings in the glass foyer being organized or picked over by a handful of servants—none of whom she recognized. Amira dismissed the workers and ushered her companions inside the privacy of her stone bedrooms before they garnered any further attention.

"What is going on?" Coral asked. "Kale! Put your shirt back on." Color flooded to her cheeks, and Coral grabbed Amira's elbow with a low growl.

"It itches," Kale grumbled but pulled the tunic back over his head.

Coral ignored him. "How is any of this possible? I don't understand how you're suddenly second-in-command with an entirely new home and staff. Is this . . . normal?"

Amira shrugged in response, staring at the pile of dresses thrown on the large bed, at the way the swirl of colors stained the soft gold linen of the sheets. The bedding was new. It was one of the last purchases she had made in Kitoi before she was taken. She'd never even had the chance to sleep in it.

Coral asked her another question, but the words were muted, a low rumble, difficult to discern beyond the roaring in her ears. Amira didn't know how, but suddenly Coral's arms were around her own, and she looked down at the tossed clothing and torn sheets, the golden fabric still twisted in her fists.

"Shh," Coral whispered, and the roaring in her ears stopped.

"I'm sorry," Amira mumbled against her embrace.

"There's nothing to apologize for."

"I agree." Kale smiled beside them. "That bed looked extremely uncomfortable. Probably same material as this." He scratched at the sleeve in disgust.

Amira choked back a laugh and took a deep breath, effectively stopping any tears in their tracks. "Thank you. Seriously, I . . . well, just thank you."

Coral regarded her, the sea green color of her eyes burning into hers. "It's all going to work out. You'll see. We will have vengeance." The tender strokes from her fingers were a direct contrast to the vehemence in her tone.

Amira stared down at those fingers and became acutely aware of the fact that she was still twisted in Coral's embrace.

She pulled away, awkwardly wiping at her eyes.

"I should probably get ready for the council meeting. There should be more stone rooms down the hall. Take your pick. I . . ." Amira trailed off, at loss for what to say next. *I hope you enjoy your stay? My home is your home? Try not to stab anyone?* That last one probably needed to be mentioned. "Just remember to keep a low profile until after I figure out what's going on with the Thirteen." She made to give Coral a meaningful look but found herself dropping her gaze once their eyes met.

Coral nodded and pulled Kale out of the room. She seemed to understand Amira craved privacy.

And she had. She truly had. So why did she feel so alone?

Amira had never attended a council meeting before. Only the voting member of the thirteen ranking families was allowed in a closed council meeting. That position had always belonged to Amira's father. But now he was dead, gone forever, and Antar too. She was still processing what that meant for her. Her counterpart had been playing her role well, assuming the role of Third seamlessly. Was that truly how things would have played out had Amira been herself?

She knew enough about voting days to acknowledge the meeting required formal attire. She frowned at the pile of discarded dresses, noting that she hadn't seen any ceremonial robes in the stack. Kale and Coral were exploring the apartments and restoring their connection with the Mother, whatever that meant, so Amira was alone for the moment. She didn't have much time before the meeting, but despite that, she found herself ambling along the length of her room, exploring different objects and reminding herself who she once was. The clothing, the jewelry and trinkets . . . all pieces of a girl she had once been. A girl she felt she could be again, if only she could just remember the way those pieces fit together.

Amira hesitated in front of her large armoire. It was a massive piece of furniture, stunning in its simplicity, and exactly the sort of piece the old Amira would have chosen. And she had never seen it in her life. She opened it, first smiling at the familiar teal of one of her favorite sleeping gowns and then frowning when her gaze fell upon the hanging swaths of purple fabric. The golden stitching represented the strength of the Republic, how each nation was stitched together under the leadership of the Thirteen. She would come to earn her robes, her father had told her. When the time was right, he would commission her first. Now she owned three sets.

She jerked the fabric toward her chest, surprised by how heavy the thick cotton felt. She blinked furiously, swallowing any lingering pain and refusing the tears access to her. With a few steadying breaths, her fingers ceased their trembling, and she was able to dress herself. No one came to look for her, so she called out that she was leaving and her voice echoed back to her in the empty hall. She would have to remember to commission a new Arbe. It seemed something had happened to them—to all of her staff, in fact. It was a skeleton crew, but they were made up of strangers. She'd have to dismiss them all after the meeting. Unfortunately, they couldn't be trusted. She had no way of knowing if they worked for her evil counterpart or not. A distant gong sounded, marking the hour, and Amira hurried to secure her hair into some semblance of a braid. The ragged mess still hung unevenly across her cheeks and eyes, framing her face.

Let me see your eyes.

Amira shivered at the memory of Kuru's knife. She gave herself a physical shake, forcing the mental block away and leaving the privacy of her stone apartments.

The glass halls were just as she remembered them. A lone figure or two darted toward the Justice Dome, but they were too distorted through the layers of glass to identify. From her new home in the Second Tower, Amira had the shortest distance to travel, even less than Justir, who had to cross the length of his courtyard and the gardens of his late wife. Despite this, she was one of the last to arrive for the meeting, and several heads turned at her approach.

Amira swallowed, making her way toward the long stone table. She'd been in the Justice Dome before, but never for an official meeting, and she paused at the table, unsure where she should sit.

There were several open spaces where chairs should belong but not a single spare seat for her. A mistake? Or a power move by one of the remaining Thirteen? She caught Denir's gaze. The woman arched a brow at her, a slight smile of amusement playing at her lips.

Probably getting ready to laugh at you. Amira returned the haughty stare, willing to engage in a blink-less battle of wills, when she was interrupted by Justir clearing his throat.

She turned toward the sound and met the confused expression of the First. "If you would." He gestured to his right, indicating she should come to stand beside the dais. "Call the meeting to begin."

Amira recovered quickly, coming to stand at the place he had indicated. She clapped her hands together once and declared the meeting had commenced.

Was that even how it was to be done? She honestly hadn't a clue, but that seemed to appease everyone and Justir began talking. It was difficult to focus on his words, hard to hear anything beyond the incessant buzzing in her ears. She took a few deep breaths, allowing her fingernails to bite into the meaty flesh of her palms.

Everything is going to be okay, she reminded herself. She brought Justir's words to focus, something about the draining crops of the cictuss harvest and complaints from local growers.

He'd always had such an easy leadership about him. Now . . . blood chains? Something else? Amira had no idea what force controlled the First, but she knew the proud man would never willingly allow someone else control of the Republic. She frowned at the lengthy stone table, noting the six empty spots. Half the council demolished, just like that, and here Justir spoke of cictuss. Well, the plant did provide livelihood for thousands of citizens. It was a meager and distasteful excuse for water, but it kept the civilians hydrated between water rations. And here in this desert wasteland, water was everything.

But still, shouldn't there be more concern for the six seats missing from the council?

Amira ran the mental list of Rank, struggling to make sense of it all.

Justir and then herself—which was still impossible to believe but there it was. Then Denir, it seemed, followed by Fourth, Fifth, and Sixth, and Ishani. Amira didn't know much about her, but she had luncheon with the young woman just before she'd left for Kitoi with her father. Amira had been unimpressed with the woman then. She remembered finding her boring, in fact. How was it that the woman had made it into the Thirteen? She tried to recall more of her background and was concentrated thusly when she felt the sharp thrill of Justir saying her name.

What was wrong with her? She had but one job to do here, pay attention, and she couldn't even manage that. She turned toward the First, biting the inside of her cheek to stop herself from offering him a weak smile. "Greatness? I apologize." She dipped her head, willing him to forgive quickly.

Justir crooked a finger at her. "I asked you if you would like to explain where you've been."

"I—" She swallowed. She most certainly did *not* wish to explain herself. She couldn't, even if she did. Because while she had been gone for weeks upon weeks and this was her first council meeting, the other Amira had been gone for only days, and there was no way of knowing what her nefarious intentions had been. But everyone stared at her now, and she had to say something. The longer she stood there stammering, the quicker it would be before she was caught. Denir already didn't trust her. She caught the gaze of the woman now. Denir wore an open and curious expression.

"I've been away, back to Kitoi on a b-business t-t-trip." *Slow down*, Amira warned herself. A stutter would only alert them more.

"And? What news of home?" Ishani asked. She leaned forward, placing her elbows on the stone table and cradling her chin in her hands.

"Jura is well," Amira started, watching Justir for a reaction. He gave none and merely gestured for her to continue. "The city was in flames but recovered before there could be substantial damage. She . . . continues on the mission you've assigned her, Greatness."

He stared at her for a long moment and Amira braced herself, waiting for him to call her out on the lie. Finally, he nodded. "It pleases me to hear news of my daughter and that she is doing well. But, why the nature of secrecy behind your trip? Why wouldn't you ask for the blessing of your sovereign and the father of your charge?"

"And what did you mean about the fire at Kitoi? Does this have anything to do with the disappearance of the Everflame? Why are we not discussing *that*?" Geedar's voice was a wild panic, and one or two muttered agreements, though they were ignored by the First.

"I asked you a question, Second. Why the secrecy?"

"Not secrecy, an opportunity. A delicious morsel, fallen into my lap." Amira lifted her chin, rushing forth with the lie as false confidence bloomed in her chest. "Secret knowledge." She looked around, meeting and holding the gaze of everyone in the room.

For all the things that had changed in the Republic, with herself, one thing remained constant. Knowledge was power.

She plunged her hand into her pocket, feeling the smooth, polished stone. The stone, as always, was light as air in her hand. It was cool to the touch and fit perfectly into her palm.

"Well go on then. Don't leave us all in suspense," Denir drawled.

"There were many discoveries on my trip. And the secrets are my own to keep. Unless any would challenge me for them?" She dragged her eyes back to the First, surprised to find him watching her, his expression amused.

"I could make you." His soft-spoken words echoed in the domed room. "The meeting is not adjourned, and we have not yet voted."

A gentle reminder that her Rank could be taken from her at any time. That her life was only allowed at the whim of the Thirteen.

They could. They had before. But they wouldn't.

The stone was now ice on her fingers. It nearly burned, but Amira didn't notice. She could only think of Jura, of Coral, and the fate of the Republic resting on her shoulders. Of her ability to bend the truth in her favor, to expose secrets and manipulate lies. The old Amira would never be afraid. She would seize the opportunity presented to her with both hands. It was what her sinister look-alike had done. It was what she must do now. She allowed herself to smile, suddenly feeling more like herself than she had in months.

"You could make me. That is true." She turned to smile at each of the remaining Thirteen, even taking the chance to wink at Denir before returning her gaze to the First. "But you won't. You can't risk allowing such a delicious secret to die with me. You see, I know the identity of the Queen of Shadows."

AMIRA

Chapter Thirty-One

*A*mira *had expected utter pandemonium* to follow her announcement, so the immense silence was somewhat anticlimactic. Justir stared at her, his intense glare calculating. Denir was the first to make a sound, a somewhat strangled gasp silenced by her quick fingers.

It was Ishani who spoke first. She rose to her feet and glanced in Amira's direction before turning toward the First. "Greatness, with your permission, I would like to extract that information. The Queen of Shadows is a wanted fugitive in Kitoi. The proper documents must be drawn up, and we must make a move toward her arrest."

Justir raised his arm, and Ishani fell back to her seat, bowing her head at the breach in decorum.

"I see no reason to extract such information . . . yet." He looked toward Amira with a pointed expression.

Amira stiffened. Her days of listening to others speak for her were over. "Nor did I offer to give any willingly." She reached for the stone in her pocket, squeezing it hard. *Breathe. You're okay.*

The stone, which had moments before felt as light as air, now weighed down her pocket. Whispers flooded in from every direction. Not the disassociated voices of the Thirteen arguing around her. These whispers were different. An incessant overlap of a thousand different voices, all fighting to be heard. A low humming sound emitted from the stone, vibrating in her hand. The frantic whispers increased, the endless buzzing searing her eardrums and rattling her bones. She clenched her jaw to keep her teeth from chattering and struggled to discern the recognizable voice barely drifting above the others.

Jura.

Suddenly it wasn't a bluff, and she *did* know the identity of the Queen of Shadows and more . . . so much more. She released the stone with a sharp intake of breath.

That man wasn't Justir. She knew that with a certainty. And Ishani really didn't know the identity of the Queen of Shadows, but she wanted to, desperately. And Denir had so many secrets.

"Her identity isn't the only secret I've come to know." She interrupted the mumbled voices around her. They weren't speaking any truths she didn't already know. "Would you like me to share them all—perhaps we should discuss Kamal?" She inclined her head toward the alttaw'am masquerading as the First, who stiffened. She resisted the urge to clutch the stone again, although she was intensely aware of it. She threw her shoulders back with false bravado and strode forward, closing the distance between herself and the First's dais. She was aware of every eye in the room following her, but her gaze remained locked on Justir's face.

His face was an anchor. Telling her racing heart to calm itself didn't seem to be working. Each desperate gasp fought to claw its way out of her lungs. And still the faint buzzing, the chill of the many whispers, tumbled over one another and fought to be heard like pinpricks against her skin.

"I am of the opinion that we have wasted enough time on these theatrics and should return to the present matter of the vote. Would anyone speak out against another of the Thirteen?" Justir's voice echoed throughout the Justice Dome.

Amira finally tore her gaze away from their impostor leader and looked at each of the remaining Thirteen. Some refused to catch her gaze, others met it with sympathy, and still others a bit too boldly. Ishani's gaze was almost hungry. She was desperate for the identity of the Queen of Shadows . . . Why? The stone trembled within her pocket, beckoning her to embrace it once again. Perhaps then she could find out why Ishani was so desperate but—no. She needed to get back to Coral and Kale. She needed a plan.

"Moving forward then, would anyone like to nominate?"

Amira squeezed her fingers into a fist, relishing in the feeling of her jagged nails biting into the meaty flesh of her palm. She knew there was more pomp and circumstance to asking for nominations to the Thirteen, but she couldn't remember them despite the hours of labor from past tutors. There was only Amira, the stone, and its buzzing, and the searing sting as her nails slowly sliced into her palm.

Denir leaned forward and mumbled a name that was drowned out by the whispers. Amira closed her eyes to focus, but the stone only called louder. How was it that everyone wasn't on their knees from the sound? Couldn't they hear it too?

Concentrate, Amira.

Her vision blurred, and she dropped her gaze to the stone floor. She blinked at the sudden splatter of red. The drop of color was brilliant against the dove gray flooring. Around her the whispers grew louder. The discussion of the Thirteen around her? The whispers that still called? One, two more drops of red rain. Amira regarded the stark crimson color with dismay.

She unclenched her fist, gaping at the small rivulet of blood that trickled down around her wrist, dripping on the floor. She gasped and shoved her hand into her pocket. Her fingers brushed the stone and she grasped at it, giving in to its call. All at once the whispers stopped. She drew in a ragged breath, then another. The voting continued around her. The buzzing disappeared, and she was left with only the steady hum of her thoughts. She didn't dare let go of the stone. Not yet. Not when she wasn't sure it had stopped the humming.

What's happening to me?

By all appearances the stone was just a stone. But if that was true, then why did Amira feel so drawn to its power? Why had holding the stone given her access to more knowledge than she'd ever thought possible in the mere blink of an eye, only to just as quickly shake her to her core? How could she explain anything that was happening without including the stone?

Don't let go.

Don't. Let. Go. Amira was unsure if the whispered command ringing in her head was her own.

"Councilwoman, if you would." The command snapped her back to attention.

Amira's head turned back to the man playing the part of the First, and she gave him a careful once-over. He was willing to keep her secrets so long as she kept his. It would be so easy to claim his true identity now, before the entire council. But where did that leave the real Justir? And where would that leave Jura upon her return? No, for the moment, Amira would allow him to continue playing his part. Everything about him appeared as it should. His voice, his mannerism, even the imperial tilt of his head as he sneered at the rest of the Thirteen . . . It was all so rehearsed, so perfect that it made Amira's stomach turn. How had she not noticed it immediately? How had no one else?

She nodded, remembering she'd been asked to close the meeting. She jumbled that, too, she was fairly certain, but no one seemed to notice, the six members of the Thirteen each rising to their feet and nodding a terse farewell to the First before leaving the Justice Dome. She was ignored, save for a few casual glances sent her way via Denir. She was the Third now, Amira reminded herself.

And next in Rank. Watch your back around her.

The Third's look lingered, and she seemed inclined to approach when she was cut off by Geedar. The Fourth grabbed her elbow and began rattling off his list of concerns, the highest being the disappearance of the Everflame, and Amira was at least saved from that encounter. Besides, Amira wanted to talk to the impostor. She felt that if she could just get the First alone, she could get proof that he was an alttaw'am. Perhaps the First was even taken by the same villain who had impersonated her.

"My lady Second," Ishani questioned from behind.

Amira turned around, biting back the urge to scowl. She must have done a sorry job because Ishani dipped into a quick curtsy, her fingers awkwardly signing the official ceremonial greeting.

"Apologies, Second, but if I may beg a moment of your time."

Amira shuffled her feet so that her shoe covered the drops of blood. Her opportunity to have a discussion with Justir was lost, and now, more than anything, she wanted to retire to her apartments and figure out her next step. She loosened her grip on the stone, aware that it was now slippery with what was probably a mixture of sweat and blood. "Well, go on then," Amira prompted when it became apparent Ishani wouldn't carry on without permission.

Ishani thrust an envelope forward, and Amira reached for it with her left hand, refusing to release the stone. Ishani's gaze fell to the hidden hand but quickly rose to meet Amira's with her rushed explanation. "It's a request for an address. I'd like to ask for an audience to discuss a matter I hold close to home and heart."

"An address? But you know where I—"

"Please, it is how things are done. If I may, send a request at a time that is convenient? Then we can find a time when we can converse freely."

The stone trembled in her hand. Or her fingers were simply shaking from the stress of the perpetual clenching. "Are we not conversing now?" Amira sighed when Ishani didn't answer. "Yes, fine. Send an audience request or whatever to the Second Tower."

Ishani nodded, her fingers fumbling through a farewell before she hurried away, and Amira was finally alone with the silence of her thoughts.

TYLAK

CHAPTER THIRTY-TWO

Ulfa did not seem keen on waiting around for them to acknowledge her before she started down the long stone hallway. Tylak exchanged a wary glance with Peppik before hurrying after her. She must have assumed they would follow, and Tylak had to jog to catch up. Peppik dawdled behind at an ambling pace.

The woman slanted a glance his way when he arrived at his side.

"Is this your first time meeting him, then? Your brother?"

She darted a quick look over her shoulder before sneering at Tylak. She was a tall woman, nearly eye level with him. "Ach, can't say I'm too impressed."

Tylak remembered her previous display with her machete and nodded. "Still, it must be strange meeting an older brother who has been away for so long . . . How long would you say he's been gone anyway?"

She snorted, the sound a deep chuckle that remained lodged in her throat. "Oh no you don't, new worlder. I'm not about to do your dirty work for you. You'll have to ask my brother yourself."

"Fine then. If I'm not to ask about your brother, I'll assume your mother and your other siblings are off-limits. So, perhaps you can tell me more about yourself?"

"I might," she answered.

"Daciana is your older sister, and yet you look exactly the same."

"You don't have identical twins in the new world?" She allowed the laughter to ripple out then, the rich sound filling the hall.

Tylak thought of Ichiro and Jiro—they had appeared very similar—but there were several differences between the two. Perhaps if he got to know Ulfa and her sister a bit more. As it was, he could honestly answer that no, he had never before seen an exact replica of another person. Unless one counted his encounters with an alttaw'am. His thoughts turned to blood magic and evil doubles, and he shuddered.

"And the new world? Is that how you see the Republic?"

"You're the new world. Ain't no way in seeing that other than the truth." She narrowed her eyes at him and came to a stop. "I assumed the lot of you would be a tad hardier if that same truth be told. Is it true you have powers of your own?" Her expression grew skeptical, and she crossed her arms over her chest, giving him a thorough once-over.

Peppik caught up to them, and Tylak noticed the slight shake to his head, warning him to admit to nothing.

"I haven't any powers aside that of my skill with my daggers." Tylak shrugged.

"Mother seems to be of the opinion you would make a fine thief." She looked from one man to the other. "Do either of you support this claim?"

Peppik scowled by way of response, and Tylak forced another shrug. "It's been a while since I've had to survive off another man's goods, but I've been a wanted man for worse crimes."

Ulfa grinned, the sudden softening to her face transformative. She was still beautiful but now in a more approachable way. "I know of your past discrepancies. You still are a wanted man, after all. Is it true that you stole your own god away from its cage? Tell me, how are you hiding it away?"

Tylak closed his eyes and let out a quick breath through clenched teeth. Denir . . . Would he never escape her lies? "Is it still gone then?"

Peppik began humming, ignoring them.

"Don't you know?" She shook her head and started forward again.

"There hasn't been much word on the road," Tylak said, falling into step beside her.

"Well it's still gone, to answer your question. Ach. New worlders, you all are a funny lot, worshipping the very force responsible for destroying all your lands." She made a tsking sound in the back of her throat. "No wonder you stole the thing. I'd be angry too." She slapped him heartily on the shoulder, laughing at her joke.

"You mentioned your mother—"

"The queen, to you. She's my mother, but you don't have any right to address her so informally. Nor do you," she spat in her brother's direction. Tylak flinched at the waste of water, old habits hard to break. When Peppik ignored her scowl, she turned her gaze back to Tylak. "Go on, new worlder, ask your question."

"You mentioned the queen might have need for the services of a thief? I'm not sure if I'll be able to help, but perhaps if I had a bit more information about the job."

Ulfa was back to smiling, and she shook her head as the same playful smile spread across her lips. "Ach, the business of Her Majesty is no business of mine. She'll tell you when she deems fit."

She came to another stop, gesturing at a simple wooden door. "Your room." She flicked her hand forward lazily, indicating across the hall. "Brother, your room awaits. Good night." She turned back toward Tylak. "Ach. You, new worlder. You best get some rest."

Tylak tried to grab Peppik's attention as Ulfa departed, but his companion seemed to have little interest in sticking around. He continued down the hall in the direction his sister had indicated and eventually disappeared through an open door. Tylak waited in the hall for several seconds, but Peppik seemed to have closed himself up for the night. With a sigh, Tylak pushed open the wooden door to his new quarters.

It was a solid improvement from the dungeons. The room was lit by a soft glow, though there was no presence of any fire. If Tylak listened closely, he could barely make out a gentle humming sound, and he wondered if this meant he was once again in the presence of that strange magic called electricity.

The room was sparsely decorated, a bed dominating most of the space. The floor was covered in thick furs from a variety of animals, some of the striped and spotted pelts unlike anything Tylak had seen before. He grunted at them but had to admit they felt glorious when he dared to remove his boots and experience them on his bare feet. Aside from the bed and the rugs, the room held an empty chest and a narrow bedside table. Tylak placed his boots under the table and longed for his daggers. They weren't exactly prisoners, but he was far from free to take his leave. And what of this revelation with Peppik?

He sighed, falling back on the bed and feeling pleasantly surprised when it was like falling into air. The pillows were light and fluffy, and he sank into the mattress with a moan. Flames, but it had been ages since he had last rested on a proper bed. Ahh, Peppik. Why had his friend kept this secret? It was obvious, now, that Peppik never wanted to return home. Tylak had to force him to travel through Friis, and now he knew why.

But that didn't explain why Peppik would be so ashamed of his heritage. It only hinted at the rift between him and his mother. His mother! And he'd thought Peppik was old. That woman had seen better days, well, better decades. How was it even possible she still lived, and even more so, how did she manage to have daughters nearly as young as Jura? Tylak was still reeling from the mere concept. His thoughts were so consumed by Jura and his previous encounter with the royal family that he almost didn't hear the light tapping at his door.

Assuming it was Peppik come to explain himself, Tylak heaved himself out of bed and padded to the door.

He swung it open to reveal Ulfa. He blinked at her. "You . . . you're back."

She stared down at his bare feet, and for some reason, that realization had heat rushing to his face.

"Shh, no one knows I'm here." She pushed a palm to his chest, effectively shoving him back into his room.

He swallowed hard as she shut the door behind her. "Ulfa." He hesitated, not sure where to start. He definitely didn't want this princess hanging out in his room, and not just because she was dangerous.

"Ach, be quiet."

The princess started forward, and Tylak was further embarrassed by the tiny yelp that escaped his throat as she closed the distance between them. How insulted would the princess be when he turned down her advances? She obviously wanted to kiss him.

"Umm, the thing is, Your Highness, I—"

She slapped firm fingers across his lips and gave him a stern look that warned him to be silent. As if he could talk with her hand clamped over his mouth. She smelled like water left too long in the sun.

Seconds later, the sound of footsteps came from the hall. The footsteps fell in an organized and timed fashion, likely those of the guard, Tylak figured. They came to a stop outside his door, and he and Ulfa both tensed. After a few moments, the footsteps continued on, and Tylak was released.

They both breathed sighs of relief.

"I'm not Ulfa." She wiped her hand against the leather bracer on her opposite arm, and Tylak wondered if she was disgusted by him, or had he simply been a sweating mess? He acknowledged his clammy hands and figured it was probably the latter. "I'm Princess Daciana, heir apparent of Friis. Daci to my friends, which you are not."

Tylak tried not to sigh. Great, the other snooty princess.

"I'm Tylak, but you already know that." He reached under the table and pulled on his boots. It seemed the luxuries of a night in a bed would have to wait. He laced up the sturdy leather and remained intent on ignoring her.

"You should leave here."

He brought his gaze up to meet hers and uncrossed his legs, but he didn't rise from his place on the bed. "Well, I won't argue that point. You speak differently than everyone else. Where's the accent? Your Jangba is nearly perfect."

She smiled, her face and expression an echo of her sister's from earlier. "As I said, I am the heir apparent. It is my duty to my country to hold such political skills." Her smile deepened into a wicked grin. "And to keep my country safe. Even from a handsome Shadow Dancer like you."

Tylak stood up, acutely aware he was on his bed, alone in his room with a princess. This couldn't end well. Women in positions of power tended to get Tylak into some sort of trouble.

"You've come to escort me out then? As your duty as princess? Has the queen changed her mind?" He started for the door but stopped as a familiar whistle sang by his ear. The dagger embedded itself deep into his wooden door. *His* dagger. He whirled around, finding Daciana held two more in either hand, one of them poised in her right hand.

"To kill me then? To warn me away?"

"Ach, you ask many questions." There was just the slightest edge of annoyance to her tone.

Tylak bit back a grin and resisted pushing her further. He took his time retrieving his dagger from the doorway before he said something he'd later regret.

"I am going to escort you out of the palace. But first I have to show you something."

"And Peppik too." Tylak grunted as he sheathed his dagger. He held out an open palm, silently pleading for his other.

She threw it at him and he caught it, snatching it out of the air and slipping it into its sheath in one fluid motion.

"No, Peppik remains. He has a debt to my mother." She replaced her own dagger, sliding it in place with another wicked grin.

"Peppik, or no deal."

She pressed her lips together, the golden chain jingling against her cheek with the gesture. "Mother will not be pleased."

"Your sister seemed to think the queen had plans for me. I

can't imagine she'll be pleased either way by my disappearance. Why not allow me Peppik too? It only makes it more believable. Besides, I'm guessing whatever you're about to show me is important enough to risk the anger of the monarchy." He opened the door wide and stepped back, gesturing for her to take the lead.

She sighed. "Fine. But we must hurry. We can't risk being caught." She poked her head out of the doorway and gave the hallway a cursory glance before nodding for him to follow.

He hadn't made himself invisible, and his desert darks were still a far cry from his shadow blacks, but despite proper clothing, it was easy to fall into the silent steps of a Shadow Dancer. Joining the guild was more than just the ability to bend light and heat; it was hiding in plain sight. It was melting into the background and becoming one with the shadows.

They crept along silently for some time, Tylak falling into step to the pattern of the steady breathing of the woman beside him. Tylak took careful note of the various tapestries covering the wall, at the measured presence of overhead light sources. He opened his mouth to ask about such trickery when Daci suddenly gasped and grabbed his bicep.

"The guard approaches!" She shoved him at the nearest door, and he fumbled for the doorknob, cursing silently to find it locked. He still hadn't heard them, but there was a wild desperation to her eyes, so Tylak did the only thing he could think to do. He threw his arms around her and willed their image to disappear.

Seconds later the guards shuffled past them. Tylak was lightheaded from the effort. He'd grown too reliant on the boost he'd received from the Everflame. It was harder to draw power from these strange magical lights. That's what he told himself. It wasn't that he was losing his powers. It had nothing to do with the fact that he gave away his stone.

"The rumors are true," Daci whispered.

Tylak released her, cringing at the look of wonder on her face. "We better hurry before they come back around." He let out an exaggerated sigh, meaning it. "I'm not sure I have many more of those left in me."

Moments later they had reached another door. Unlike every other door they'd passed, this door was made of a polished and gleaming silver. Tylak frowned at their reflection as Daciana pulled a key from around her neck.

Tylak reached for his daggers, suddenly aware of the possible dangers lurking just beyond such a door.

She smirked at him, reminding him once again of her sister. "You needn't fear anything, Shadow Dancer. The precaution is to keep him from getting out. You needn't worry for your safety." The door unlocked with an audible click. "And if I wanted to kill you, I wouldn't have returned your weapons."

She pushed, and the door swung open with a near-silent whoosh. It was incredibly dark in the room, and Tylak blinked, struggling to bring any image to focus.

"It's okay." Her voice drifted up to him as they entered the dark room. "I'm right behind you." She gave him a gentle push forward, and seconds later, he heard the door snap shut behind them.

Tylak's tension rose, every sense he held telling him to turn around and run away. But he held steadfast and continued forward, even if he did keep his hands ready on his daggers.

"Just a moment." Daciana's voice sounded so far away that Tylak couldn't resist reaching out in front of him and moving in a slow circle.

They appeared to be in a big, open room. He could barely make out something in the center. The shadow of something large, perhaps hanging from the ceiling. Light flooded the room, followed by the muted squeal of delight from his right.

"You had to see this before you go. They'll lie to you. I know they will. And you had to know the truth."

What was she talking about? Tylak blinked rapidly, struggling to regain focus in the onslaught of light.

There. In the center of the room. Not hanging from the ceiling but suspended just the same. A broken figure shackled on either side by each wrist, his arms stretched out wide as if waiting for a hug, pulled back toward either wall by thick chains. Massive wings stretched out behind, steel rings pierced through their center, anchoring them to the floor.

It was what he had been searching for, and yet it was so very wrong.

He'd found one of them. The aliferous.

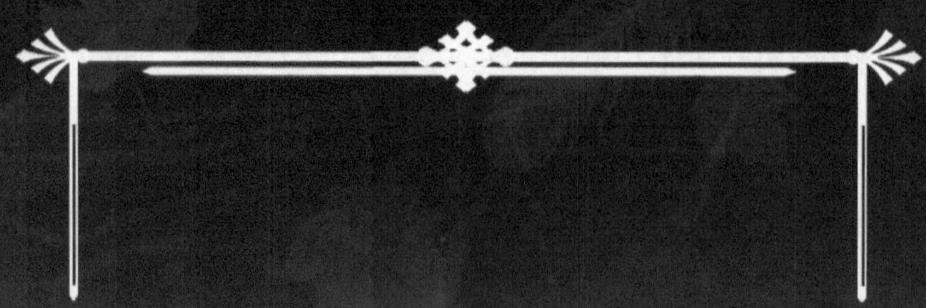

TYLAK

CHAPTER THIRTY-THREE

If it wasn't for the somber rise and fall of the chest, Tylak would wonder if the poor individual even remained alive. As it were, they appeared scarcely conscious. Their head lolled slightly from side to side, and their eyes fluttered slowly. Their clothing hung in ragged strips about their narrow frame. Their skin was gray, the wings so pale a silver that they were nearly white . . . that was except for the places they were pierced through, blood seeping through the manacles.

"Pitiful-looking creature, I know," Daci murmured. Tylak was disgusted, but there seemed to be genuine compassion in her expression as the princess continued. "He was a leader of his people, we think. A sort of religious prophet. It isn't right what we've done to him . . . That is why he will be the last of his kind."

"The last of his kind? No, that can't be. Jura was taken. I saw it—"

"You misunderstand." Daci made desperate shushing noises, casting a worried look in the direction of the closed door. "Please, allow me to explain. I know nothing of those who took your friend.

That is true. What I meant is that he will be the last of his kind who suffer so at the hands of the kingdom of Friis. I've long wanted to change this. I think we all have, and you—" She took a deep breath and began again in a softer tone. "You have the abilities to help me. To help him. To help an entire kingdom."

A small sense of dread lodged itself in his gut. This couldn't be good. He sighed, giving his head a terse shake before asking a question he knew he would regret.

"And what can I do to accomplish all that?"

"I'm sure you have noticed our lighting system? Perhaps our moving stair mechanisms or our refrigeration system for our goods? You may have wondered how we have such access to electricity while you new worlders remain without?"

Tylak's mind stumbled at the unfamiliar words, desperate to make sense of his role in it all. "Electricity?"

"Power. Power in the form of something called a battery. The ability to store energy and use it for later. *Their* energy, wind energy . . . It has so much potential. My mother was young when she came to the throne, but even at such a tender age, she knew of its worth and what she could create. This power . . . *his* power . . . it's enough to change a world."

"But you said he's to be the last of his kind? You mean to free him, then? This is no way to live." Tylak stepped forward but was stayed by Daci's gentle yet firm grip.

"There is more. Please," she continued when the aliferous let out a low moan.

Tylak glared at her, his patience waning.

"We mean to free him, of course. Soon. We almost have enough batteries stored to power the country for the next decade. And by then, Mother hopes to have—" She rubbed her arms as though to ward off a sudden chill and turned away from him. "It doesn't matter, and that's the truth of it. We have to help him. *You* were meant to help my country. There's something the queen will ask of you, and you must do it. Do it and succeed, or she will force you to suffer the consequences of her displeasure. Or leave. Now. If you disappear before dawn, you can be miles outside the city gates before midday."

"So . . . that's it?" Tylak asked, incredulous. "Why did you show me here if not to help free this poor soul?"

"I showed you so that you would see how serious the queen is. She will stop at nothing to get what she wants."

"And what does she want? What is this thing your mother will ask of me?"

"It is forbidden to speak of." Daci seemed earnest, but he noticed she remained light on her feet, shifting her weight in a light warrior's dance.

"And if I refuse?"

She snorted. "No one refuses the queen." She jerked her head back toward the door. "Come, I'll see you out now."

Tylak moved toward the chained aliferous, but Daci grabbed his hand and pulled him back toward her. "Don't. His chains are alarmed. If you tamper with them, the Queen's Guard will be notified."

"I'm not leaving them like this."

"You don't have a choice if you want to make it out of here." She pulled at him before finally shoving his hand away with a sigh. "I vow to you not to leave him like this. It's what *I* want too." The intensity in her eyes was so ferocious that he was forced to meet her gaze. "I promise. But now is not the time. We need to get you out of the palace . . . now."

He held her gaze for a beat before he sighed in acceptance.

Relief flooded her face, and she ushered him back out the steel door. "This way," she hissed when he turned to move back down the hall toward his and Peppik's rooms.

"What about Peppik? I have..." Tylak trailed off as the realization set in. "You never intended for him to leave with me." He reached for his daggers, sliding the smooth hilts into either palm.

A small flash of irritation lit her eyes before she smoothed her expression. "I told you. The queen wouldn't like it. Now we need to go before the patrol sees you in the halls."

"And *I* told *you*, I'm not going anywhere without him. I've agreed to play along with your little games, but I refuse to go anywhere without my friend. Now you can either help me or lose a finger. The choice is yours, but you're getting out of my way."

Daci narrowed her eyes, but any response was cut off by a delighted cackle. The old crone's expression was gleeful as the woman grabbed Tylak's elbow.

"Now, Tylak, I hope you weren't planning on leaving so early? And without even saying goodbye to the ruling monarch. Why, I would expect even an uncivilized Shadow Dancer to know that's simply not in good taste." Queen Vaneera turned toward her daughter, and while her expression remained light, her tone grew menacing. "Daughter. Not a very auspicious start to your morning, I gather."

"Your Majesty, I—"

"Ach." The queen waved her hand in a dismissive gesture. "We will discuss this later. You may go."

Daci hesitated before lifting her right foot off the ground and pointing her toes just above her left kneecap. She held the pose for several moments before gracefully lowering her leg and turning to depart in a motion that Tylak could only assume was akin to a bow.

She did not meet his gaze.

Tylak became aware of the queen watching him, and he turned to give the royal his full attention. "Your Majesty, I apologize for the confusion. I was merely searching out the kitchens. The princess mistook my intentions, as do you."

The queen's gaze raked over him, no doubt taking in the details of his knotted boots and palmed daggers. She was astute—that much was obvious—but she seemed content to let him rest with his lies.

"Allow me to escort you then. These old bones enjoy a bit of warmed cider in the early mornings. Come." She doddered forward, and Tylak felt he had no choice but to sheath his daggers and follow.

They were escorted by two guards who posted themselves against the wall on the far side of the kitchen. A harried cook appeared within moments—no doubt roused from sleep just seconds before. The queen snapped out orders before motioning for Tylak to follow her into an adjoining room.

"We'll take our refreshments in the small dining room rather than the large hall. A more intimate setting, mmm?" She waggled thin white eyebrows, and Tylak forced himself to nod in response.

She took her seat in one of the twelve plush cushioned chairs at the table and gestured for Tylak to do the same. He noticed her breathing was slightly labored, the small efforts of the past few moments weighing on her. And it was no wonder. She had to be close to one hundred years old.

If Jura were here, she would probably know her exact birth. She'd mentioned once that the Friisan ruler had the longest tenure of any other nation. But she had never mentioned anything about captured aliferous or electricity, and Tylak doubted either was mentioned in any of her books.

Queen Vaneera regarded him with an amused expression, almost as if she knew his line of thought. He frowned at the table, wondering if he was supposed to sit across or beside the queen, or if both were a breach in decorum. He opted for a seat in the middle and was just settling into the high-backed chair when the queen spoke again.

"I have heard of many organizations over the years. You new worlders are fond of your religions and your rulers. It must be maddening. But the Shadow Dancers...even I find myself enchanted by the tales. Tell me, is it true you can turn yourself to smoke?"

Tylak was saved a response by the reappearance of the cook who served the queen and then Tylak some warmed cider. The rich aroma of fermented fruit and spices assailed his nose. The queen watched him, her expression calculating. He didn't dare take a sip first, despite the intoxicating aroma.

The queen smiled—or bared her teeth would be a more accurate description—before taking a delicate sip from her own glass. "Mm, delicious." She gestured for him to try his own. "It isn't poisoned. Cook wouldn't dare. She's far too loyal. All my subjects are." She leaned forward, eyes gleaming over her cup. "Seventy-seven years I've held this monarch, and in all that time, not a single assassination attempt. Now, what does that tell you?"

"That you are a ruler beloved by her people."

"Wrong. My people fear me. And, worse than me, people fear change. Go on." She gestured with her hands. "Try it."

Tylak took a tiny sip, barely allowing the heated liquid to hit his tongue. There was an explosion of flavor all at once. It was delicious. He took a larger sip, his taste buds eager to work out the complex notes of flavor. Sharp and bitter, light and sweet all together in a rich, spicy liquid that nearly burned on its way down. He swallowed the urge to hack the liquid back up and then took another, much smaller, sip again to ease his racing heart. What in the flames was this stuff?

"The drink is but one of the many beautiful things enjoyed in Friis. I need you to steal something for me. Bring this item to me, and I will gift you anything in my power. Indemnity. The means to start an entire new life. Anything."

"Peppik. He's free to go with me."

The queen frowned. She tapped one of her long nails against the polished table. The soft clicking sound was distracting. "I'm afraid that's not possible. Peppik has much to answer for."

"Peppik," he repeated with a meaningful stare. "Or you can forget me stealing anything." Tylak leaned back in his chair and took another heady sip of the delightful liquid. The queen watched him. Long gone was any attempt at hiding her displeasure.

"I see." The clicking nail stopped. Queen Vaneera set her mug down on the table beside it. "And how do I even know that you can steal what I'm asking?"

Tylak swallowed. The uneasy feeling in his gut returned and grew. He forced another swallow. "I can steal anything." Almost anything. He wouldn't steal a person, no matter the cost. The queen slid a small envelope toward him.

"We do not speak of it . . . I'm assuming you can read?"

He nodded. So earlier with Daci, that hadn't been just some rule imposed by the queen then? What sort of item was so dangerous that it was taboo to say its name? Tylak set his mug beside the queen's and reached for the folded paper, scarce taking note of the wax seal before thumbing the letter open. The paper was crisp and fresh. He smoothed it out before reading the three words scrawled one above the other.

Ignacius

Nork

Windstone

"The first a name. Someone who might assist you in your search. The second a destination, and the last . . . bring it to me."

"This—"

"We do not speak of it!" the queen repeated. Her voice was shrill, her eyes opened wide and desperate. "Take the day. Consider your options. And tomorrow morning you will be escorted outside the gates and given all the amenities one could ask for in their travels. I'll grant you my best—"

"Me and Peppik, you mean to say." Tylak framed a stern expression.

"Yes, of course. You and Peppik. Go. Rest and consider your options. I'm sure you'll see my way." The queen once again gave her attention to her mug of heated ambrosia, and Tylak knew he was dismissed. He ambled back toward his rooms, watchful of the guard who seemed to linger behind him until he was safely tucked back in his hall.

He went to his room but after a few moments poked his head out to check his surroundings. The hallway remained empty, so he darted down its length to Peppik's room. His friend didn't answer Tylak's knock, and he'd had the good sense to lock his doors, so he was no doubt sleeping blissfully. Just as he himself should be. So, for the second time that evening, Tylak removed his boots and fell back on the bed with a blissful moan. The sun was barely making its appearance as he finally drifted to sleep.

He was groggy the following morning. His back ached despite the fact that he'd slept on that heavenly bed. He had spent the evening plagued by dreams of darkness and desperation. He dreamed of times he thought he'd left long behind. Of days of physical suffering and unquenchable thirst. And loss. He remembered so much loss. Days he never wanted to remember again.

After relieving himself and splashing an abundant amount of cool water on his face and privates, he once again left his room and headed toward Peppik. This time, the hallway was staffed by guards who snapped to attention as he exited his room.

"Ach, good morning to you." The familiar voice had Tylak rolling his eyes. Just his luck. The same guard again. The sea princess was the only woman he'd ever met who was as snarky.

"If we can call it that," Tylak answered. He rubbed at his neck. "What's your name?"

"Why do you want it? You haven't gone and developed a little crush on me, have you? I'm a happily partnered woman, but my man can be talked into a bit of fun if the game is right." She made a move to pinch his bottom, and he skipped past her until he was just out of reach. This entire kingdom was mad.

He hurried to Peppik's door and reached it without incident. Once again, the door was locked, but this time Tylak refused to budge without speaking to his friend. He was beginning to suspect that Peppik might not actually be in there at all until the door burst open to reveal his friend's familiar scowl.

"Oh. It's you." He stepped aside and gestured for Tylak to follow. He had barely made it inside before Peppik slammed the door shut behind him. Peppik locked the door and gave Tylak a thorough once-over. "Well?" He crossed his arms over his chest and raised his eyebrows. "What did she want then? What sort of deal did she offer you?"

Tylak handed him the note. Peppik read it quickly, his face paling at its contents. "No. This is a bad idea. You can't."

"I have to."

"Why? It won't help you get back to her."

"This isn't about her. It's about you!"

Peppik's eyes widened, and his mouth dropped open slightly. "I knew it. I knew she would never forget. Not even after all this time." He sighed, shoulders sagging. He shuffled to his bed and sat heavily, shaking his head sadly. "The mistakes of your past will always come back to haunt you."

"Peppik," Tylak started, unsure of what to ask. "Why does the queen have such a vendetta with you?"

"The queen has a vendetta against anyone who would go against what the queen wants. That's why it's so dangerous to strike a bargain with her. She'll promise you the world and then ask you to do terrible things. And when you refuse, that's when she makes you pay. That's why you can't accept this deal she offers you. You can't trust her. She won't release her hold on you after, not after you prove you can be valuable. And you are valuable, Tylak. That's why you have to leave as soon as possible, no matter what. Even if it means leaving me behind."

"What did she ask you to do?" The silence seemed to stretch forever. "Peppik?"

"She asked me to dispose of the twins. She thought it would be easier that way, rather than deal with an eventual dispute on succession." He glared at the doorway, the words leaking through clenched teeth. "She asked me to murder my infant siblings while they slept to make her life easier." Peppik clenched and unclenched his fist, his vision glazed and unfocused. Tylak doubted that he even noticed Tylak had come to sit beside him.

"When I refused, my mother saw to make my life miserable.

There are many things worse than death." His eyes had taken on a haunted look. He paused, throat working up and down. "I disappeared into the Republic. And I never looked back. That's why you can't take this deal. Leave, and carry on to the Edge. Maybe some traveler has heard some tale. Maybe someone along the way will have some knowledge of your aliferous."

"That's something else you should know," Tylak began. He told Peppik everything about last night's encounter. Starting with Ulfa's questions, when Peppik was moping behind them, and Daci's revelations and finishing up with the queen's interruption and request.

"I need to get back into that room. I need to question the aliferous. Perhaps they can shed some light on the importance of this wind—"

"Don't say it!" Peppik warned.

"You too? What's so forbidden about this word? It seems harmless enough."

"It is forbidden to speak of. A curse of sorts. It's said that uttering the word will bring ruin to our people."

Tylak frowned, finding it hard to believe that there was such power in mere words alone. "And everyone believes this?"

"This aliferous. You intend to free him, no?" Peppik asked, completely ignoring Tylak's question.

Tylak thought of Daciana and the vow the princess had made to him. Did she really intend to keep her promise? Somehow, he wasn't sure. He needed to figure a way back over to that steel door. He needed a way to break into that room, and he needed to do it quickly. He rose to his feet, ready to take action.

"I'll be back as soon as I can. Keep your door locked and remain alert. One way or another, I intend to get some answers."

JURA

CHAPTER THIRTY-FOUR

It was much later that afternoon when Jura was finally escorted to her room. The door swung open with its usual melody to reveal Markhim waiting inside. He offered her a sheepish grin, leaping to his feet. Jura felt the heat rush to her cheeks despite the fact that this room was more prison than private sanctuary. It somehow felt like an invasion of her privacy to find him waiting there.

She was beyond exhausted, she told herself. That was why she wasn't happy to see him.

Her nameless guard drifted away without so much as a backward glance. Jura missed Matteus. At least he had offered reading material. She watched the guard leave and the door shut behind him in a gentle swoosh of song. She glimpsed the closed door before finally meeting Markhim's eye.

"Things are strange between us." He studied her expression, his eyes dark and searching.

Jura shivered despite the warm breeze stirring the stale air of her room. "No, they're not." The denial sounded forced, even to her. She didn't want things to be strange. She closed the distance between them, stopping at the head of her bed. She maintained careful eye contact as she drew out the book from under her pillow.

"The other day, during my test, I had that strange waking dream."

Markhim nodded, prompting her to go on.

"And last night. Again, I dreamed of a woman I have never met before, and yet her face was familiar to me. I knew her thoughts as though they were my own." Jura wasn't sure when her eyes had fallen from his stare, but she was suddenly aware of just how much dirt she had accumulated under her fingernails. She dragged her gaze back up to him.

His eyes were compassionate, but his lips turned down in a slight frown. "Do you think it's your sister?"

"I don't know," she whispered. How had he known to ask her fear manifested?

"Do you . . . what do you want me to do?" He sat on her bed with a sigh.

"I think this book is more important than we know." Jura frowned before placing it into his outstretched hand and filled him in on everything she'd learned.

Markhim turned the book over in his hands, flipping through its pages and frowning at its contents. "All right, I'll bite. What do you think it means?"

"If I knew that, we wouldn't be having this conversation." Jura fell back across the width of her bed with a dramatic flail from her arms. Markhim caught her hand, and she opened her eyes to find his face inches from hers.

"It's going to be okay." His head was propped up by his fist, his elbow bent and holding his weight as he stretched out beside her.

She drew in a shaky breath, suddenly shy and unsure of what

to do next. Her arms were pinned above her head, and she didn't know whether she wanted to wrench free from his grasp or pull him closer.

His head remained over hers, eyes searching for some answer to a silent question.

The familiar melody from her door had Markhim rolling away with a groan.

"I, ah—" Pri made an odd strangling noise that could be mistaken for either coughing or laughter and cast his eyes toward the ground. "Pardon the interruption."

Jura sprang upright, shoving the book back under her pillow. "Nonsense. The arrival of a friend is never an interruption." She forced a smile and a quick glance at Markhim's scowl. All right, maybe some people saw it as a type of interruption.

Pri noticed the exchange. "My humblest apologies. But Jura, if I might steal you away, there is that delicate matter to discuss."

Understanding dawned on her. Of course, he wanted to talk to her about leaving. She met Markhim's gaze, searching for the right words of dismissal without hurting his feelings.

"No need," Markhim said through clenched teeth. "I'll take my leave." He inclined his head toward Jura. There was no warmth in his eyes as he mumbled, "Good evening, my lady First."

Jura bit back a sigh and caught her bottom lip between her teeth as she watched him go. He stopped at the locked door, pulling forcefully and even going so far as to give it a tiny kick before turning back toward them.

"Will you open this flaming door?" he demanded with a grunt.

"Of course. My apologies, warrior of the new world!" Pri rushed forward, although the door responded to a mere flick from his wrist.

Markhim pushed the door open the rest of the way, the melody finishing in a rushed crescendo as it snapped shut behind him.

"I don't think he likes me very much," Pri admitted with a nervous twitch.

Jura snorted in an effort to hold back an unrestrained shout of laughter. "Please, don't take it personally. Markhim has gone through a lot, and he carries much on his mind." Jura forced another tight-lipped smile. "As do we all." She gestured to her bed for seating, but Pri shook his head aggressively and instead walked to the open wall.

He sat down there, allowing his legs to dangle off the edge. Jura approached him warily, keeping a careful distance from the gaping opening. The fresh air was always welcome, the breeze constant but never too cool or too hot. She made a move to voice the thought out loud, musing that perhaps the aliferous controlled the winds, too, but something stopped her. Pri's head was cocked just to the side as though listening to some secret whispered from miles away. Perhaps he was. The breeze quickened for just a moment, stirring the tiny hairs around her face and tickling her nose. She closed her eyes and inhaled deeply, smelling a strange mix of smoke and pine.

"Dragon."

She opened her eyes to find Pri staring at her. He remained seated on the ledge but leaned back on his hands, eyeing her from over his shoulders and bare back. It struck her this was a move many of his brethren couldn't do.

Wait, dragon?

"That smell. Drifts in from the Wilds. They're migrating again."

"Migrating? Do they live in herds then?" She moved closer, aware of the distance between herself and the edge. She fought the urge to peer on her toes, as if she could see through the night sky beyond the mountains and into the Wilds.

"Herds? I suppose as much as any creature does." He shrugged. "It's harder to build cities when all the other men want to tear them down."

"Dragon cities?" Jura murmured. It went against everything she had ever been taught. Dragons were wild creatures incapable of building civilizations . . . right?

"Mmm, yes. The old world had many cities."

"Before the Everflame," Jura said flatly.

Pri's silence was admission enough.

"Are my people truly at fault then? Did we release an entity of fire and destruction only to capture it and name it our god?" There. The question had burned with uncertainty within her soul since Danos had first broached the idea. Was her entire faith based on a lie?

"Yes, but also no."

She snorted. "Do all your people speak in contradictions? Is this something you are taught as children?"

"There are no children here."

The simple statement sent chills down her spine. It explained so much. The silence from the guards, the emptiness of the halls. "But why? Where are the children?"

"We are the last children of the aliferous. Myself and the Dreamer." He sighed. "I'm going too fast. It is difficult to explain. Please, you know how children are born?"

Jura blushed. "I understand the basic workings of human and animal anatomy."

"Yes, of course." Pri waved her answer away and pushed himself to his feet. "I mean to say, you know how children are just one bit of one's life cycle through adulthood and eventually death. Such is the process of the aliferous. From a dream to reality. From child to teen. From me to aliferous." He looked down, somewhat embarrassed. "Until the Everflame and our role in its creation.

"Let me explain," he hurried on when Jura made to interrupt. He paced the length of the open wall, balancing effortlessly along its edge. "When my people were contacted with the idea of the flame's creation, we saw the various paths before us. The Dreams have always given us access to see the various paths. We knew that the flame could grow out of hand and the destruction it was capable of causing. But we also saw the path that could have led our people to greatness. A gamble for more. When we saw the paths align to one of suffering, we turned our back on the stone wielders and forbade the use of blood magic again."

"Because blood magic is so dangerous? Was that what made the Everflame so destructive? Blood magic was responsible for scorching the earth?"

"No," Pri said forcefully. "Greed and ill intentions brought about the scorching of the old world. Blood magic, *your* magic, is not directly responsible. The Dreamer knew the dangers of the various paths, and yet they made their decisions boldly. We must all suffer the consequences of the past. You are not wrong to place your faith in something you see as bigger, grander than yourself and the world around you. But do so with the knowledge that faith is not simply good or evil. It simply is." He shook his head sadly. "For every grand act of magic, there is always a price to pay. The Dreamer saw the potential of this path and still they did not stray. The Everflame was set to destroy our city, the mountain keeps, the Eerie, our home—so they did what they felt was necessary. They summoned a great wind and turned the Everflame away, altering its course and the destiny of your ancestors. The Dreamer summoned the great magic—"

"Wait a moment. The Dreamer . . . Don't tell me you mean the same person? Surely they're not that old?"

"Please." Pri gave a sharp shake to his head, eyebrow feathers fluttering. "Allow me to finish and you will understand. The Dreamer summoned a great wind magic, and for a time the aliferous rejoiced, even while thousands of people south of us suffered. We turned a blind eye to the screams of the hundreds trapped within the flames so that we could ensure the safety of our ancient cities and great libraries. Eventually, the flame was captured, and the world began to rebuild, a new world sprawling over a desert landscape. It wasn't until all of this that we began to see the true price paid by our Dreamer.

"Jura, we stopped aging. We have always been a slow-aging race, but now it is as though we are frozen in time. The years pass, and each of us remains the same. Unable to bear children, unable to age. Unable to finish our life cycle." He jerked his shoulders upward. "I'll never grow wings. Never age more than I am now. That's why you have to take me with you. I think you are the solution to the suffering of my people and that you can help restore the balance we lost. You can help me get my wings."

"Oh." Jura leaned against the wall for support, willing the room to stop spinning. She took a desperate breath, forcing herself to focus on the simple act rather than the many implications thrust upon her by Pri's monologue. "I can't . . . you can't think that I—Pri, why are you telling me all this? What makes you think I'm capable of any of that?"

"Why do you continue to insist you are less than you are?" He stepped forward, splaying his hands before him. "I have been waiting for this moment for the last thousand years. We've been waiting for you . . . and your sister."

She blinked at him. "But why? Is blood magic so rare?"

Pri hesitated, glancing about the room and peering back over the ledge for good measure. "It's because of the prophecy and your role in it. But most importantly, it's because of the stones."

"What stones? Tell me," she urged. "This isn't the first time these stones have been mentioned. I know about the prophecy. They told me when I went to meet the Dreamer. It mentions exhuming stones. I'm assuming these are the stones everyone is so worried about."

She looked up to find his gaze focused on her chest, to the amber stone hanging from a simple golden chain. "My birthstone? What about it?" Jura reached for the stone, pressing the smooth lines between two fingers.

"It's part of the bloodstone. A once great stone that was shattered during the creation of the Everflame."

"It doesn't look like it was broken." She was surprised to find her voice laced with skepticism. The stone was polished smooth. The warm amber reflected light and was pretty around her neck. A family heirloom, nothing more. Or so she'd thought.

Pri shook his head. "It was, and I would warrant your sister has a piece of her own. I believe your companion, the Shadow Dancer, has the flamestone."

She stiffened at the mention of her "companion." She'd been doing so well not thinking of him. "Why am I just now hearing about this? Is there a stone for every element of magic? What do they do?"

"The stones are meant to be an embodiment of the magic they represent. A tangible object of pure power. Together, capable of breaking worlds."

"She needs them," Jura realized. It was both terrifying and strangely exhilarating to say the words out loud. "My sister. She needs the stones for her plan. So why didn't anyone tell me this before? What else are the aliferous keeping from me?"

"I believe it is their intention to train you in your powers so you are entirely prepared to stop your sister. Then you can use the stones to eliminate the Everflame and undo the mistakes of our transgressions. You can restore the aliferous to what we once were."

"But that still doesn't explain why *you're* the one telling me all this."

"You find me untrustworthy?" Pri stepped back as though her words had been a physical slap.

"No, it's not that. But, why would I be brought here to 'train' only not to be told all the relevant information? Shouldn't we be out there collecting the stones before she does?"

"It's because of the prophecy. Of the Mistress bending the knee. They are unsure of where your alliances might lie." Pri sighed. "I have no doubt the Dreamer is aware of the locations of all the stones. All but the one that matters. The windstone. It's been missing from my people since the creation of the Everflame."

"But . . . how? How is it possible to know the location of all the stones but your own?"

"Its true location has not been spoken to the winds, not for many years."

Understanding dawned on her. "And if no one has spoken its true location, no one can use the winds to track it."

"Precisely."

She sighed wistfully. "It must be nice knowing everything the wind knows." What she wouldn't give to reach out to Amira and know that she was okay. To check on Tylak and his quest to meet her here. She said the last bit out loud.

Pri turned to her, his expression hesitant. "There might be a way." He gave the room a cursory glance, as though someone might have managed to sneak in on them while they conversed. "There's a reason blood magic was forbidden from further research, and not just because of what it was used for, but for all that it might be capable of. Scholars still aren't sure of all its properties, and there are a surprising lack of notes on the subject, perhaps becau—"

"Pri." Jura's tone had taken on a desperate note.

"My apologies. I do tend to ramble on. All that to say is there is still much we do not know about Blood Makers, but one secret I have been able to glean is that their magic, or more importantly, their *blood* can serve as a type of amplifier for other magic."

Jura widened her eyes. "How?"

"Well, I'm not exactly sure. But I'm willing to try something out . . . if you are?"

She wanted to learn more about her magic—of course she did—but the idea of trying out something new and possibly forbidden sent more than just a cautious thrill down her spine. *You've come here to train and get answers. This is how you get some answers.*

Jura twisted her torso so that she faced Pri directly.

"All right, I'm ready."

JURA

Chapter Thirty-Five

J*ura pushed away any lingering* doubts and tried to find that hidden well deep inside her core. Last time she had brought it on with thoughts of her and Tylak's first kiss, but her early attempts at recreating that experience and the memory only had her blushing.

No, focus.

Jura tried to take a deep breath to calm her jittering nerves when Pri brandished a knife from his side. She let out a choked gasp and scrambled to her feet.

"It's okay. Please, shh." Pri placed the knife on the stone floor beside him with the blade's handle pushed toward her. "There, it's for you. Go on, take it," he coaxed when she only regarded it with suspicion. "Remember, it's your blood that is the amplifier."

"Oh, right." Feeling silly, she snatched up the blade's handle and pressed the blade against the palm of her opposite hand, prepared to slice open the meaty flesh.

"Stop!" Pri cried out, smothering her hand with his.

Jura started at the feeling of his warm skin. She stared down at their hands, his covering her left palm, the blade buried between.

"What is it?"

"So much harm to oneself is not necessary." Priamos tsked, the pad of his thumb barely grazing her palm. "Just a drop of your blood should suffice." He directed the knife so just the tip poked her little finger. He released his hold on the knife, placing his palms on his lap before humming softly to himself. A slight breeze blew into the room, chilling her bones.

"Your power," he reminded her. "Harness your power and focus on who you wish the winds to speak of. Then, prick your finger and take my hand."

Jura thought of Tylak and Amira, battling with which one she wanted to speak to first.

"Will I be able to ask them anything?" she asked.

Pri continued his hum but turned his eyes toward her before lifting his arms in a shrug. Right. There wasn't much research done on Blood Makers. She tried to remember how it had felt to draw on her powers before. She wanted to recapture everything she'd been feeling in that moment, the memories that had been brought on with that kiss.

She stuck the knife into her finger, flinching at the pain. Immediately the air in the room felt warmer, thicker. The fading light in the sky intensified, shining as brightly as the Everflame.

Pri gasped, his humming cut short. "Your eyes." He shook his head. "They're glowing. Here, take my hand."

Jura grabbed his outstretched arm, and the floor dropped away from them. The sensation was like falling, only somewhere in the back of Jura's mind, she was aware that she hadn't actually left her room. Her skin was warm, as though heated through by an intense day in the sun. Despite this it prickled, hairs rising against an unknown chill. There was a moment of deafening silence and then, all at once, she heard them. The terrible choir of voices clambering to be heard over one another, the frantic whispers spoken on every wind in the world. She could spend forever trying to sort through those voices. She should cover her ears to escape the sound. No. She stared at her pinky, at the tiny drop of blood still pulsating.

Focus.

Think of home. Think of Tylak. The voices settled around her until there was only one. *His* voice. Jura wanted to wrap his voice around her like a security blanket.

"I'd rather not get into this with you."

What did he mean? Jura cocked her head to the side, straining to listen.

"No, she didn't run off with him. She was—never mind. You said a few moments, huh? What was that about? How long has he been captive?"

Jura frowned, trying to make sense of what was being said. Tylak seemed to be in conversation with someone.

Her suspicions were confirmed when she heard him snap, "She's not my lost love. She's just some girl I know who's helping me."

Jura wheeled back, breaking whatever connection she had held to Tylak and this moment. She blinked in confusion, meeting Pri's knowing eyes. He'd heard everything she had. The voices began buzzing again. Fractured whispers that could break into that terrible song. Jura pushed to her feet, severing the connection completely. The voices stopped just as she'd hoped.

Pri struggled to his feet. He appeared exhausted even though they hadn't done anything too taxing. Jura didn't feel strained at all. If anything, she felt strangely rejuvenated by the entire process.

"Thank you." He smiled at her, his canines gleaming.

"For what? You're the one with the wind magic."

"I've never heard them before. In all my life . . . all I've ever wanted was to hear them. The path of Dreams . . . it was beautiful." He regarded her with some reverence and she shrugged, uncomfortable with the credit.

"This friend of yours, Tylak, is he . . ." Priamos trailed off, allowing the unasked question to hang in the air.

Jura was unsure what he was even asking. Was Tylak what? A good friend? Still traveling toward them? She'd gained nothing useful from the experience, nothing save for the information that he didn't see her as anything more than a tool to retrieve his brother.

She felt a brief stab of guilt at the thought. Tylak had done more than his fair share in aiding her on her quest, and after all, he owed her nothing. Perhaps Tylak wished nothing more than to see her off so he could get back to searching for his brother. And what had Jura done to aid him in that request? Nothing except get Tylak into further trouble with the Queen of Shadows. She sighed. No wonder Tylak didn't consider her his great love. She'd brought him nothing but trouble since she came into his life.

"Please, do not let those words spoil what we have just accomplished. You and I have just done something that I never would have thought possible."

It was hard to argue with Pri's earnest expression. Jura tried to smile back at him, but as exhilarating as the moment had been, the magic had left a sour taste in her mouth.

"I'm happy I could help. I truly am."

"And you are capable of so much more. Again, the voices were everything I hoped they would be."

Jura wasn't so sure she felt the same way. She looked back down at her pinky, thinking to wipe the blood away before it stained anything, but it had already stopped bleeding. Was that the normal time for such a tiny prick to stop bleeding or did her magic have a way of speeding that process up? She struggled to remember previous cuts and scrapes, but she was having a difficult time remembering any.

"You must be exhausted," Pri said. He placed a hand on either of her shoulders and gently pushed her toward the bed. "You should rest now. I'm sure the Speaker has a busy day planned for you tomorrow."

TYLAK

CHAPTER THIRTY-SIX

It was a while before Tylak was able to leave his rooms and head back in the direction of the captive aliferous. He still didn't feel rested, and the pain in his neck was only getting worse. Also, his shoulders hurt, but that probably had something to do with his decision to bring Jura's books. The satchel of books had been waiting for him in his room after his cider with the queen, and Tylak couldn't stand the thought of leaving them here.

After some fumbling, he managed to bend the light around him. He reminded himself that he was simply tired, and this had nothing to do with the loss of his birthstone or the disappearance of his god. Besides, he'd gone without his birthstone before.

There weren't many guards in the hallway. Payce and two others. Tylak navigated around them easily. His pace was quick, measured. Each step careful not to find loose carpet or uneven stones. Hands loose at his sides, ready to swing, ready to punch, to slice. He found the door without issue, but the next step was more difficult.

Try as he might, Tylak was unable to pick the lock open. He had just given up and was about to seek out the local locksmith in search of more tools when the sound of distant footsteps called out a warning. He pressed himself flush against the door, straining to distinguish the sound. Just one person, so not the patrol guard. He palmed a dagger and widened his stance.

Daciana. Or perhaps Ulfa. It was honestly impossible to say which stomped into view.

"Shadow Dancer? Are you here?"

Daci then. Tylak sighed and allowed his power to dispel in a relieved rush. Burn it all, but he needed a good night of sleep. "Princess," he said by way of greeting.

"Come to see if I hold my end of the bargain?" She snorted, the sound almost a laugh. "Not that there is a bargain, seeing as how you allowed yourself to fall into the queen's clutches anyway."

"I wouldn't say I am in anyone's clutches just yet."

She shrugged. "If you say so."

"Will you let me back in?" Tylak asked. He figured it was best to be direct. The princess seemed like someone who would respect that.

"Hmm. And why should I do that? What do you hope to gain?"

"Answers."

"Answers? From him?" She did laugh then, but the sound wasn't pretty, and Tylak found he much preferred the snort. "You'll get no answers from him."

"Please." Tylak resisted the urge to grab her hand. "I have to try."

Her eyes narrowed. "Why? What's so important then? What do you think he knows?"

"Nothing." Nothing that he wished to say to her.

The princess tossed her head in a dismissive gesture. "Do as you wish, Shadow Dancer." She removed the chain from around her neck and shoved the door open.

This time there were less theatrics, and Tylak was nearly blinded by the brilliant light as soon as he entered the room. The aliferous was as before: a broken figure hanging in the center of the room, massive wings spread out and chained on either side. Tylak swallowed at the sight before walking forward.

"I'm not here to hurt you. I just need to ask some questions." Tylak continued his slow advance, surprised by his immediate response.

The disembodied voice seemed to come from everywhere at once. The lovely tenor filled the room despite the whispered request.

"Water. They need water." Tylak met Daci's gaze and she raised a delicate brow. Right. A princess. She had probably never fetched water for someone else in her life. He looked around the room, and his eyes fell on a pitcher left by the doorway. He snatched it up and gave it a cautious whiff. Thankfully the pitcher smelled clear and full of water, so he brought the pitcher back and thrust it toward the lips of the aliferous. He drank greedily. Tylak didn't fault him—he had known such thirst. After several moments the man pulled back with a strangled gasp.

"Who are you?" The man eyed him warily. Despite the fact that it was laced with utter exhaustion, it was still the most beautiful voice Tylak had ever heard. He had the thought to beg for a song, but he pushed the mad idea away, reminding himself that he was on limited time and this was not the time to ask for such a stupid thing.

"My name is Tylak. I'm hoping we can help each other."

"You can't." The man closed his eyes, for all appearances falling asleep.

Daci made a tsking sound and crossed her arms over her chest. Tylak shifted position so that his back was to her and gave his entire focus to the man in chains. "I told you this was a waste of time. The pitiful thing is drained. What do you think to ask of him anyway? More information on this other friend of yours?"

Tylak turned back to Daci and sighed. "Release him, now."

Daci scowled, considering. "You don't know what you're asking," she said softly.

"Do it."

She stared at him for a long moment before once again reaching for the skeleton key dangling from her neck. She tossed the set of rings to him in a lazy motion. His hand snaked out, half expecting there to still be some trick, but Daci simply watched him from her place several paces away.

Tylak hurried to unchain the aliferous. First the wings, the massive things each spanning longer than his height, their fall to the ground creating a slight breeze. Then the arms—they fell limply to the side, wrists cuffed red and raw from an untold amount of time spent in shackles.

Not surprisingly, the man fell to his knees, bowing his head to the ground in front of him in a crumpled and exhausted heap of skin, bone, and feathers. If not for the small imperceptible movement of their chest, Tylak would wonder if he was alive at all.

Daci raised an eyebrow as though to ask what his intentions were now, but Tylak didn't even know. It was going to be difficult navigating Peppik and himself out of the citadel. It would be all the more difficult once adding a two hundred-pound semi-conscious aliferous.

"I'm going to get you out of here—get you home. Is there anything else I can immediately get you?" Tylak dropped to his knees beside the hunched figure. Long dark hair spilled over shoulders that were once probably broad and tanned but now pale, still somehow gray and hunched. "Do you want some more water?"

They turned to look at him. The face was tired, broken. "What did you say your name was?"

"Tylak."

He closed his eyes, repeating the name in his own haunting whisper. He repeated the name several times, a near song. His eyes snapped open. Thin lips pulled back to reveal canines and a small semblance of a feral smile.

"You're wrong to seek out any answers from him. All of this is wrong. Ask your questions quickly. We need to get you out of here before the patrol guards come."

"Tylak, seeker of people." The aliferous stared at him as he sang out the words.

"What is that supposed to mean?"

Daci, too, stepped closer, eager to hear the answer.

"Only truths. Tylak seeks a lost love. A brother."

Tylak stiffened. "How did you know that?" He grabbed his shoulder, but the man only slumped forward, falling unconscious.

Tylak stifled a groan. "I suppose it's too much to ask that you help me lift him back up?"

"He will awaken in a few moments. Usually, anyway." She shrugged. "So, a lost love? Is that what's brought you and my brother to Friis?" Her lips stretched into a smile. "I wish you had told me, Tylak. Searching for a lost love? Perhaps I could have helped you in this endeavor. At least, it's more interesting than your mad plot to leave Friis with my brother. Who is this lost love that has you so secretive?"

Tylak sighed, stretching back up to his full height and once again rubbing his sore neck. "I'd rather not get into this with you."

"Why because she ran off with someone else?"

"No, she didn't run off with him. She was—never mind. You said a few moments, huh? What was that about? How long has he been captive?"

"Oh no you don't. You can ask him those questions yourself when he wakes back up. I want to hear more about this girl. Is she a princess too?" Daci stepped closer, closing the distance between them and pressing her fingertip against his chest. "Do you have a type? If I were you, I would be careful expressing any more weakness toward the queen. She already knows you hold a soft spot for my brother."

Tylak paled. How far did the queen's influence reach? She already held one aliferous captive. How far would she go after he revenge? How far would she go to reclaim her missing stone? He wouldn't risk Jura's safety and resolved not to share any more details about her to any member of the royal family.

"Well go on then, tell me about your lost love," Daci prompted.

"She's not my lost love. She's just some girl I know who's helping me."

"With your lost brother?"

"Like I said, I don't want to talk about this with you."

The aliferous gasped, the desperate breath of a drowning man. Tylak dropped to his side, reaching for a clammy hand.

"What can I do? Do you need more water?"

"Jura." The whisper filled the room. Daci's eyes widened as she watched the aliferous struggle to push himself to his feet.

"Is that her name?" Daci asked.

Tylak ignored her, bending back down and offering a shoulder for the aliferous to lean against as he finally pushed himself to his feet.

"Thank you, Tylak. Seeker of people of the new world."

Tylak resisted the urge to roll his eyes. "Okay. Let's get you straightened out here." He hoped his words were audible, muffled as they were under the weight of an arm and feathers that were surprisingly heavy.

"Urso. My name is Urso."

"Okay, Urso. Nice to meet you. That was some kind of trick you did back there. Do you always know what people desire? Is that why the old queen keeps you around?"

"I know only of the truths spoken to the winds. The desire to find Jura and your brother are those that have been spoken the most. The queen . . ." Urso glanced toward Daci. "Her Majesty has many desires."

Tylak grunted.

"Perhaps you should hold your tongue before you see that we get you out of here alive."

"Did you just threaten him?"

"Of course not." She smiled, once again wearing the poised and unbothered expression of a princess. "Not a threat. We're wasting time. We have to get to my brother and get you all out of here without being seen. Are you ready? Or did you need to ask a few more questions about your missing friends, first?" She pushed past him and Urso and pulled open the steel door.

"The hallway is clear. Fire up some of the secret magic, Shadow Dancer. We can't risk being noticed by the patrol guard."

Tylak reached for a birthstone that no longer hung around his neck and frowned, feeling his power flicker within him. Flames, but he needed a nap. For a year. Maybe then he wouldn't feel so exhausted.

"Ahem, Tylak? Any time now would work in our favor." Daci looked down the hall again.

He struggled to warp the light around them, but it was difficult to find the source of its heat. "Umm, Urso, do you think you could . . ." He squeezed his elbows and fists together and forward in a gesture he hoped was delicate enough to get his point across without insulting the aliferous.

Urso groaned slightly from the effort, pulling his wings back and tucking them as close to himself as he could manage. The effort was strenuous, and Tylak was once again horrified by the implication. How long had Urso remained chained just so? His muscles were atrophied everywhere. It was a wonder the man was even standing—unlikely that he would ever fly again.

Tylak straightened his shoulders. Urso had suffered enough. He pushed aside his exhaustion, concentrating on the flow of power within him. He gritted his teeth and focused on the lights above. He noted the strange vibration from their power, how it seemed almost alive, humming in the way the flames danced. He wondered what Jura would think of his observation. His power roared to life inside him, and he bent the light to his will.

They made short work of it, all complications considered. They only ran into the patrol guard once, and they had been spotted early enough that Tylak had simply pulled Urso and Daci against the tapestry beside him. The trio stood motionless until the guard passed.

Tylak rapped on Peppik's door, a succession of short knocks in a staccato code familiar to only the two of them. The door opened immediately to reveal Peppik, dressed and brandishing what appeared to be a whittled bedpost posing as a battle staff.

"Well go on then. Make me invisible, too, and let's get out of here."

Tylak grabbed his friend's arm and pulled him close, stifling a moan from the effort. After this, he was sleeping for ten hours.

The foursome tumbled out into the hallway, and Tylak gritted his teeth from the exertion of holding them all under his umbrella of power. They had better hurry. They ran down the hall. The princess took the lead with Urso sandwiched between him and Peppik. They were basically dragging the aliferous behind them.

"This was a terrible idea," Tylak muttered.

"This was *your* idea," Peppik retorted. "Tell me you've at least got some extra weapons in that satchel of yours."

Did a stack of books count? Tylak bit back a laugh.

Like most of his wild plans, this one was bound to get him into trouble. Well, he just had to make it a bit farther, just out of this hallway, then they would be out of the citadel. He could hold out until then. The princess made a sudden stop, and Tylak grunted with the effort to keep from falling forward with Urso who had once again gone completely limp.

"What is . . ." Tylak trailed off as he saw what was blocking their way. Ulfa. The princess was dressed in full soldier regalia, and a vicious scowl twisted her beautiful features.

"Daci? Are you there?"

Tylak bit his tongue to keep from crying out and amplified his power.

She will only see an empty hall. Don't make a sound.

Urso awakened beside him, reclaiming some of his weight, and Tylak bit back a sigh of relief. They didn't dare move.

"Daci . . . I can hear you breathing. Which means you must be with the Shadow Dancer." She sniffed the air, fingers moving to grip the hilt of her machete. "And brother? Is that you too?"

Impossible.

"Guards!" Ulfa cried out, but she needn't bother. Payce and her husky companion were already jogging forward.

"Ach. Give it up, Shadow Dancer. You can't wait us out." Payce grinned.

Well, he could flaming try! He shifted Urso's weight on his shoulder so he could palm a dagger in his free hand, but he should have known Peppik, his impetuous friend, would launch into action. Peppik hurled himself at the larger guard, tackling the man to the ground from his middle. Tylak was unprepared for the sudden onslaught of weight from the aliferous and stumbled for footing. Daci gasped and called out a warning, but he was unsure if she directed it to her sister or him.

Tylak was forced to throw his dagger at Payce, but the guard sidestepped the throw easily, flashing a wicked grin.

"I do like when you men play rough." She scowled before throwing herself at him.

It was all he could do to gently settle Urso out of harm's way. He rolled to his right, narrowly missing the blunt handle Payce swept toward his head. She was still aiming to disarm and capture. She didn't wish for his death just yet. He caught her in the stomach with his boot and then rolled away, bringing up his invisibility as he did so. Payce growled in frustration, somehow spinning in time to block his next kick. Tylak dropped low to tackle her, and they fell to the ground in a tangled mass of limbs. She bit down on his forearm, and he swung his opposite arm up to hit her temple. She hit the stone floor hard enough to make her gasp out a low, wheezing breath.

Tylak rolled over her and pushed his forearm back against her throat and retained pressure until she went limp. Satisfied he hadn't had to kill her, he turned in time to see Peppik straddle the other guard and dispatch him with the tip of his sharpened staff. The twins rolled on the floor, screaming insults as they wrestled.

"Let's get out of here!" Tylak shouted. Peppik leaped to his feet to help him with Urso. They yanked the aliferous back to a standing position, and Tylak groaned from the physical effort of turning them invisible.

"Stop! Guards, seize them!" Queen Vaneera appeared before them.

The twins broke apart and scrambled to their feet at the sound of their mother's voice. Tylak's power sputtered in and out, and he struggled to keep his vision from blurring. There was a searing pain in his side, and Tylak dipped his fingers there, shocked when they came back stained red. He'd been stabbed, somehow. He blinked at Payce's still form.

Tylak tried to push back the guards, but there were simply too many of them. Too many hands rushing forward to reach him, too much blood running from his side. He was seized on either side, his arms wrenched behind him and his dagger pried from his grip.

"You fool." Queen Vaneera stopped in front of him, staring at him with her milky gray eyes. "I offered you the world. Riches, freedom. You could have had whatever you wanted. I might have even let you have Peppik, had you completed my mission. Instead, you betray me. You try to steal from me. Why couldn't you do what was asked of you?"

She smiled. "I think I'll keep you for a bit. Goliath has been in need of a new plaything. As for you . . ." She turned toward Peppik and regarded him with absolute loathing. "You have always been nothing but a thorn in my side. My firstborn, too weak to even take the lives of those who wish only to steal my crown. Nothing but a pathetic, useless *man*. Oh, such a disappointment you have been to me. You disgust me." Her smile widened, and she clapped her hands together in girlish glee. "I should think I will enjoy watching you die."

"I did it."

The whispered words were spoken with such venom that Tylak blinked at his friend, unsure he had heard what he did.

"Did what? You're incapable of doing anything that matters." The queen snapped her fingers and called for a guard to retrieve Goliath.

The giant spider. This couldn't be good. Tylak blinked. He tried to raise his arm, but it felt glued to his bloody side.

But Peppik wasn't done speaking yet. His voice was firm, strengthening and rising with every word. "All those years ago, when I finally left Friis, when I left *you*, I'm the one who did it. I'm the one who let Nork in."

Queen Vaneera lost her smile. "You did what?"

"I sent a message to our cousins in Nork. I told them the secret to our nation's power, and I let them in so they could take what they wanted. I thought they would kill you." Peppik spat out the last bit, swallowing against the sudden pressure of dual machetes applied to the soft spots of his neck.

"No," Tylak mumbled. He tried to take a drunken step toward his friend.

"Do you realize what you've done?" The queen started forward, curling her gnarled hands into claws aimed at her oldest child. "What you've cost me? I will see you suffer if it's—"

"I didn't finish," Peppik continued. He jerked out of the guard's grasp, and they appeared too startled to stop him. He strode forward to meet his mother.

"I gave them a fake." He offered his mother a chilling smile, and Tylak finally saw the family resemblance. "They don't have it either. I honestly don't know where it is now." Peppik's voice was gleeful as he shouted out the next part. "I gave Nork a replica and then I stole the windstone and sold it in Kitoi."

There was a collective gasp.

A sudden, inexplicable breeze drifted down the hall, caressing Tylak's face and lifting tapestries from the stone walls.

"No!" Queen Vaneera screamed. She snatched a fallen machete and plunged it into Peppik's stomach. Peppik fell to his knees, clutching at the handle. The queen's scream turned feral. "Ruination! You've brought ruin to us all!"

Urso rose to his feet, thrusting his wings out on either side of him and opening his mouth to erupt a single terrifying note. Tylak wanted to rush to his friend, to hold Peppik in his arms and tell him they weren't alone as they died. Tylak wanted to cover his ears, to block out that terrible sound. Was that truly still coming from Urso? He closed his eyes or maybe he was blind now. There was only noise. So much noise.

KAY

CHAPTER THIRTY-SEVEN

She was dreaming again. Kay wasn't sure how she knew it was a dream—maybe because she dreamed of memories that were not her own. Kay used to dream about going on adventures. Sometimes she would dream she was exploring a new world on a ship or visiting her animal friends who could always talk in her dreams. Sometimes, she dreamed of silly things like eating her weight in cheese. Her dreams were different now. Not nightmares exactly . . . but nothing was ever silly.

Sky peered down at her, his gray eyes solemn in their stare.

"I'm okay," she said. She could feel his concern through their connection so she pushed herself to her feet.

Her throat hurt. She must have been screaming. Again.

Lately, Kay couldn't remember her dreams. She didn't like that at all. What if the reason she couldn't remember her dreams was because they weren't hers to remember?

The fire inside her bubbled at the thought. As always, the flame was a distant roar in her ears, a constant heat in her gut. And there faintly, as if imagined, a whisper begging for release. Once again, she wondered what would happen if she did try to release the flame. Was that even possible now, or was the fire destined to forever remain a part of her?

"I'm okay," she repeated. Kay was unsure whether she was trying to convince Sky or herself.

She Breathed deeply to dry herself. The packed dirt that made up her bed somehow remained wet no matter how she tried to heat it dry. Likely they were too close to the river. Kay had no intention of leaving her tiny shelter, not now that she was finally starting to feel like she had escaped the red-robes once and for all.

The rescued dragons were still nearby—she could feel the pair just out of sight in the woods beyond her tiny outcrop. Kay wondered why they would choose to remain so close, but the dragons seemed content to keep her near. She didn't mind. It certainly made her feel safe at night knowing the dragons watched while she slept. But that safety wasn't enough to keep the nightmares away. If anything, they only grew stronger.

Memories of her life with her parents and the horrific events in the arena continued to bleed into one another. She felt as though she were two people. One, a simple little girl who had parents and dreams of a happy life. And the other, a creature of violence and death, a monster.

Release me . . .

The voice echoed, lifting in the wind and making Kay shiver against the sudden breeze.

Sky bent his nose toward her, bumping his leather snout into her shoulder. She felt his concern elevate through their contact and she shook her head.

There was no way she had imagined that. Sky had heard the voice too.

She cast out her Breath, scanning for any intruders, but there was no sign of other creatures aside from her dragons and the birds and other critters. Kay hated to admit it, but they were alone. Which meant the voice really was the Everflame, begging for its release.

Sky growled low in his throat and Kay echoed the sentiment.

Is anyone there? she whispered inside her mind. Kay felt silly doing so, but she had heard the voice. She was sure of it. There was no response, but Sky bumped her again with his nose. "Yeah, I think they're gone too. At least for now."

Sky grunted in agreement.

The sun hadn't quite made its appearance, but Kay figured there was no point in trying to go back to sleep now. Sky was as restless as she was, no doubt feeling just as spooked.

"Maybe we should go for a fly?" She stared wistfully up at the sky. The cool morning air should have been chilling and undesirable, but Kay felt it might be just what she needed. Sky grunted again, expelling twin smoke trails out his nostrils. Kay smiled at her friend and stretched her leg up and over his neck.

She didn't bother to find the other dragons and tell them her plans, but their heads rose at her and Sky's departure, and the older, larger of the two bugled a greeting as they flew overhead. Sky roared in response, Breathing out a huge flame, and Kay joined him, enjoying the moment of happiness and total freedom with her powers.

Kay was unsure how long they flew before she once again sensed the large mass of heat that indicated dragons. But this was something different. More dragons than she had ever felt, dozens maybe, just north of her. *Should we go investigate?* Kay questioned through their link.

Sky sent back a series of colors, but Kay was unsure how to translate that.

You need to learn to speak with words. She supposed that wasn't exactly fair considering Sky's mouth was enormous and his tongue was shaped funny like a snake's. Maybe that's why he couldn't speak. But then, the Everflame was just a big ball of fire, and it had managed to speak.

Although so far all it had done was scream for its release.

Kay would release it if she could. She didn't want any more memories of her time in the Republic, even if the great flame did give her incredible strength. The problem was, what would the Everflame be like upon its release? Would it go back to burning everything in its path? Because Kay couldn't have that. She had sworn not to do any more bad things.

Sky began a lazy descent toward the ground. This was definitely the farthest north they had ever flown together, but Kay wasn't worried. The only thing she could sense when she cast out her Breath was the group of dragons, and dragons wouldn't hurt her. Dragons were friendlier than people.

People were dangerous. Even if they seemed nice at first. Even Kindle, who was one of the nicest of them all. Even she had done terrible things.

But I won't, Kay repeated to herself. *I won't do anything bad. Not anymore.*

Sky landed with a gentle boom, and Kay blinked at their new surroundings. The trees were different here. Thicker together, with larger leaves, and lower to the ground. Birds always stopped singing whenever Sky was near, but after several minutes of quiet inspection, the birds once again began their song. Sky seemed content to lie on the cool, moist earth, so Kay took the opportunity to explore their surroundings.

The group of dragons was still to the north of her, and she

wondered idly if they were making their way to the Wilds. Perhaps they were the dragons she'd rescued from the arena. She liked to imagine that, to imagine them all free and happy together. Like a family.

She turned back to smile at her napping dragon. Like her and Sky. The dragons were her only family now.

The jungle was thick around them, and Kay liked how the air hung in a heavy mist, tickling her nose. It was so quiet, with only the sporadic whistle of some distant bird.

I could take a nap here, she thought before she remembered she had awoken from a nightmare. She didn't want to wake up screaming again. She frowned, trying to remember what had been so scary about the dream in the first place. There had been someone there, something telling her she didn't belong . . . but it was just a part of the dream, right? Kay wanted to believe it was, but she'd never dreamed of strange voices before. A part of her knew the answer.

It wasn't a bad dream at all but a message from the Everflame.

She dared another glance at Sky, but if anything, the dragon had only curled in on himself more. The dragon was an expert at taking naps.

"Hello?" Kay asked. "Umm, Everflame? Are you there?"

She was met with silence. *Okay, good.* Kay hadn't actually wanted the fire to start talking back to her. That would have been horrifying.

"I'm not scared," Kay said, though she knew that saying the words out loud didn't make them true. Even she didn't even believe them. Why was she asking the great fire inside her to speak to her when she wasn't ready to hear what it said?

Why was she so sure it even had something worth saying?

Kay thought of her parents, of Mama's letter and how Mama

had worked so hard to give Kay the earrings she wore now, the same earrings the councilwoman had wanted to take from her.

The earrings were important, probably just as special as she was. Daddy would never force her to do anything, but he would tell her to be brave. Mama would remind her to do some good in the world.

I can do this.

Kay Breathed deep and touched a hand to either ear.

It was different this time. Kay felt the same weightless fall, only this time there was no pile of sand to be buried under. Instead, Kay found herself floating in darkness. It wasn't scary or anything. In fact, it was nothing, almost like being asleep, except Kay was wide awake.

"Hello?" Kay called out, surprised to hear her voice echo back to her. Mama and Daddy had taken her to a cave once, a real cave—not the tiny outcrop of slanted stones Kay liked to call her home—and the experience had been incredible. Kay would have spent hours yelling into the abyss to hear it echo back to her, but Mama had made them stop and head back to camp for campfire corn. It had been a great day.

"Hello? Is anyone there?" Kay heard her own voice in response. Once again, Kay felt silly, calling out to nothing.

Release me.

Kay choked back a gasp. It was the same command from before, whispered in the same voice. It had to be the Everflame. It had to be!

"Everflame?" Kay whispered.

"Release me! Please, release me at once." The voice was louder than the Everflame, magnified and everywhere all at once. "Please, let me go!"

It sounded less and less scary and, somehow, more like the voice of a scared girl.

"Help me."

"How? What do I do?" Kay asked. She felt terrible. If the great flame was so unhappy, and it sounded like she was, how could Kay keep it locked inside of her? But even if she wanted to set it free, could she do so without hurting everyone?

"Please, help me!"

Kay tried to walk toward the voice. She wanted to help them. Even if she didn't know how. With each step she took, the ground felt more solid under her feet. In the distance was a tiny spark of light, the only illumination in the endless void. Kay continued forward, determined to make it to the light source.

Kay walked a few more steps and then the woman was just there. She sat in front of Kay, crouched on her knees, although she didn't seem to notice her. Her head was bowed and her shoulders shook with silent sobs.

"Kay."

The woman didn't look up. Her golden hair obscured her face, and she was concentrating on something on the ground. Kay strained to see what she saw, but there was only darkness and more of the void around the woman.

"Kay. You must help me. You are the key."

"What can I do?" Kay took a step forward but stopped herself, worrying whether she could trust the stranger. Was she truly the Everflame? If so, how was she speaking to her now? Through the earrings?

The woman didn't look up, but she shook her head, the motion sharp enough so her hair shimmered, somehow catching light where there was none.

"Kay, sweet child. There is *so much* you can do. But for now, you must sleep."

Kay closed her eyes and fell asleep. Without dreams.

AMIRA

CHAPTER THIRTY-EIGHT

t first, Amira wasn't sure it wasn't just part of her nightmare. Her dreams were always filled with nightmares. One dark memory collapsing over the other. During her time with Kuru, it had been impossible to feel safe. Impossible still, even now, even after she knew he was gone, killed by her own hand.

When she was awoken by the savage grip wrapping around her throat, it took her several moments to work out that she was being attacked in her bed. She brought her knee up, satisfied when her attacker responded with a muffled groan.

Sandstorms, if only she hadn't taken to keeping her knives put away, then maybe she would have access to a bedside weapon. But Amira hadn't been able to gaze upon the polished silver for another second and had tossed the weapons aside to look upon another time. A time when she had more than memories of Kuru and his knife.

And now here she was caught unawares without any weapons and with someone's hands fast closing in on her throat. She let out a strangled yell, wishing once again she'd been able to secure a new Arbe. What she wouldn't give to have a contingency of four armed guards at her beck and call. She bucked against her bed, twisting her hips to gain enough leverage to get off her back.

She and her attacker rolled off the bed and landed on the stone floor with a hollow thud. Amira grunted as her elbow and hip made contact with the ground. She scrambled to get to her feet, but she was twisted in the sheets. There wasn't a cursed flame anywhere. She couldn't see a thing.

The door to her room burst open, and her attacker was ripped off her. Kale entered moments later, holding a strange glowing shell. The soft light framed him in the doorway and illuminated the rest of the room in pale yellow. Amira finally ripped off the sheet from where it was tangled around her ankles. She climbed to her feet and placed an uneasy hand on her side table. Her fingertips brushed her stolen stone, and she snatched it up to hide it in her hand. If only nightgowns were made with pockets.

Coral was still dressed in her strange armor, the dark leather melting into the shadows around her. The light from the strange shell illuminated her fierce expression. She pinned her trishula against the Shadow Dancer's throat.

The Queen of Shadows had already sent an assassin.

"Are you truly a Shadow Dancer then?" Coral's tone was amused. "I thought your sort would be more of a challenge."

"Release me and we'll give it another go around," the Shadow Dancer responded.

"I think not. You see, I walked in on you trying to hurt my friend. And now I'm going to hurt *you*." Coral's eyes gleamed in the yellow glow.

"Wait." Amira pushed her hands behind her back and stepped forward.

Coral sent a surly glance her way, but she lowered her weapon.

"You should leave the interrogation up to me, Amira. It could get . . . messy."

Amira had a suspicion Coral was probably right. She certainly didn't need to see any more violence, but Amira's feet remain rooted to their spot. Why was the Queen of Shadows so interested in her? Surely she had lost her worth once her alttaw'am disappeared.

"No, I want answers." Amira tightened her grip on the stone and took a hesitant step forward.

Coral narrowed her eyes but responded with a terse nod. "You heard her. Answers, now. What's your name?"

The masked figure snorted, and a drop of blood peeked from underneath the tip of Coral's trishula.

"Like I would ever disclose my name to anyone who wasn't even wearing desert darks."

"And this is why I never ask nicely." Coral flicked the tip of her weapon so that it sliced the mask off his face.

The boy was remarkably young, his face round with boyish features that brought to mind the memory of Antar. He had a long, rather bulbous nose and thick eyebrows perched above eyes as dark as his clothing. Three slim lines scratched across his cheek from where Coral nicked him with her trishula.

"Hirold." The whispered name tumbled from Amira's lips.

The Shadow Dancer let out a strangled gasp.

Amira ignored him, focused so by the sudden onslaught of voices in her head. "That's your name, isn't it? Hirold? And this is your first time being assigned a dispatch. The Queen of Shadows sent you here to kill me. To kill us all. And anyone who got in your way, but mostly the queen just wants answers." Amira trembled, her knuckles aching from their grip on the stone. "She wants confirmation that you are here, working with me still," Amira said to Coral who raised both her eyebrows in response.

"How did—you can't know that!" the Shadow Dancer sputtered.

Coral sent a wary look in Amira's direction but didn't miss a beat. "All right, Hirold, now that we know you weren't here to play nice, give me one good reason I shouldn't kill you now."

"He wouldn't have stopped there. He meant to visit Denir after." The whispers were frenzied, one word tumbling after another. "The queen questions her loyalty." Amira clutched the stone as though it were the only thing keeping her from floating away. The voices swelled, yet those who spoke of Hirold remained the loudest.

Hirold stared at her, his dark eyes so wide they appeared mostly white. "H-how? Stop! I offer an Exchange of Information!"

"He's desperate. Even this offer is a ruse, a distraction, should he fail. If he fails, he was instructed to use the poisoned tab in his—"

Hirold bit down on the tab hidden between his teeth and began foaming at the mouth.

Coral jerked her trishula back, probably to avoid his poisonous vomit, and stared at his death throes in disgust.

"Bleh, fish guts." She wrinkled her nose. "How did you know all that?" she asked, facing Amira. She didn't exactly point her weapon at her, but she didn't return it to its strap across her back either. "Well?" She arched her eyebrows.

Amira shifted uneasily under Coral's and Kale's expectant stares. At least Kale hadn't moved from the doorway. Amira knew they hadn't suspected her of anything up until this point, but how could she explain herself now?

"I . . . I um . . ." Coral's trishula wasn't pointing more toward her now, was it? Had Kale moved forward? Had he always been holding that shell? And why didn't he have on a shirt?

Amira blinked, suddenly aware of how silent it was in the room. There was no longer a rush of whispers, all frantic to be heard over the other. Now there were only Coral and Kale, waiting for answers.

"Hey, take a deep breath. No one is going to hurt you." Coral's trishula clattered to the floor.

Amira wanted to believe her, but she could only stare at the sharp iron tips and feel the pressure on her chest rising.

"It's okay," Coral repeated in that same soothing voice.

Amira wanted to believe her, but she couldn't move, couldn't do anything except stare at Hirold and wonder that it wasn't her. How was she still alive when there was nothing but death all around her? What was so special about her? She didn't know when she stumbled into Coral's embrace. Only that Coral held her close, arms wrapped tight around her.

"It's okay," Coral repeated.

Amira nodded, finally feeling in control enough to take a step back. She took a deep breath and then another.

"There we go. Are you okay?"

She nodded again, still not trusting her voice.

"Okay. Just relax. We're all friends here." Coral sent a meaningful glance to Kale who remained framed by the doorway. He seemed to understand because he started forward, the light growing brighter with his approach.

Amira took a few more deep breaths. Coral was right. They were all friends here, and everything would be fine. Just as soon as she caught her breath. But then Coral said the words that made her world come crashing down.

"Amira, I need you to tell me. What's in your hand?"

CORAL

Chapter Thirty-Nine

Amira's *face paled and her* knuckles whitened with her heavy grip. Coral thought she could barely make out a flash of gray and silver in her hand. Whatever was hidden there, Amira didn't wish to share it with them.

She felt Kale move behind her, at war with how she felt about his presence. Could the man honestly not be bothered to wear a shirt? More often than not, he was hovering, but she had to admit she was grateful for his presence now.

She didn't want to push Amira too hard; anyone could see she'd gone through enough already. But it was also extremely apparent that she was lying to them, and Coral couldn't have that. She'd felt confident in dropping her trishula. She could handle herself with her bare hands if necessary, and the weapon had seemed a bit much in front of the already panicked woman.

Amira trembled a little in her arms and Coral patted her hair. She wasn't sure the gesture was comforting, but she'd witnessed people doing it in an act of sympathy before and figured it couldn't hurt. After a few moments, Amira pushed herself out of the embrace and blinked up at her with dark, glittering eyes. The two women were nearly the same height, and Amira was far from a wispy figure, yet she somehow felt small and vulnerable in her arms.

Coral dropped her hands by her side.

"I'm sorry," Amira finally said. "I . . . I honestly hoped you would never find out." She choked back an ironic laugh. "But I guess I never should have kept it a secret. Not after you told me that prophecy about the exhumed stones." Slowly, easing each knuckle, one at a time, Amira pulled back her fingers to reveal a shining stone. The color was a muted gray. The pale silver of the moon reflecting on the ocean filled her palm, the shape just slightly ovular.

Kale wrinkled his nose. "Some sort of rock?"

But Coral didn't pay him any attention. *The stones will be exhumed.* This was one of the great stones. She was sure of it. The prophecy continued, so what did that mean for her? The next step said she would bend the knee, but why would she ever do that? What would that mean for her? She swallowed, regretting the absence of her trishula. The weapon would have done her little good in the moment, but it would have been nice to have its familiar weight across her back.

Amira was still rattled, her expression distant as she remembered only the Great Mother knew what. Coral bit back a sigh. There was no reason to get mad at the woman. She had been through so much. And yet, Coral had been honest enough to share the prophecy with her, and Amira had said nothing of her possession of the stone.

More important than all of that, had Amira somehow mastered its power? Which of the great stones was it? And what did it all mean?

"Let's all take a . . . breath." That was a phrase these Breath-catchers liked, right? She glanced at Kale, but his attention remained fixed on Amira and the stone. He was impossible to read.

"Amira, where did you get that?" Coral asked. She was intently aware of her link to the Great Mother around her neck, but the steady thrum of Kale's *wei* sounded so far away.

The woman shook her head, clutching the stone and wiping away the freshly falling tears. Coral glanced at her trishula on the ground and then forced herself to look again at Amira. She was terrified, panicked at what the discovery of her with this stone meant. Coral hated that she was the cause of this.

"Was it the stone? Is that how you knew all those things?" She frowned at the fallen assassin. "Is that how you knew about him?"

Amira nodded. She didn't make a sound, but her head bobbed up and down a little. It was something.

"How long have you known the stone was capable of such power?" She shook her head and shushed Kale before he said something stupid and ruined everything. No doubt Kale wanted to ask a rush of questions. He was worried what this next step in the prophecy meant for her, what it meant for them all. Coral was frightened, too, but that didn't mean she could back away with fear.

"I . . ." Amira swallowed, clenching and unclenching her fists. "N-not long. Just today, but I know it's special. That it was worth people's lives."

"Where did it come from?"

Coral nearly jumped out of her skin. When had Kale come so close? The three of them had their heads dipped so far toward one another, one wrong move and they would all bump foreheads. She stepped back, crossing her arms across her chest and resisting the urge to send another glare at Kale.

"Was it"—Kale cleared his throat and gave her a meaningful look—"exhumed?"

Subtle.

Amira shook her head. "I stole it. I stole it from the people who stole me. I don't know its origin. I just know that today, when I held it, I knew things. Impossible things, secrets. About everyone."

Was it her imagination or did Amira give Kale a peculiar look? Coral knew he had secrets, but what if he was keeping something significant from her? Something more about her father? Or what if it was something worse, another Mano situation? She couldn't take another betrayal like that.

Amira wasn't giving him any sort of look now if she had before. Once again, the woman was studying the stone in her hand.

"May I?" Coral asked, surprising herself. She held out an expectant palm. "I'll give it right back," she promised. Amira hesitated for a moment longer before sliding the polished stone into Coral's waiting hand.

The stone was surprisingly light. Near weightless, in fact. What she had first thought to be an opaque gray was actually a prismatic display of shimmering blues, silver, and pearl. Like sunlight streaming to the sandy ocean floor. It was beautiful. The myriad of colors shimmered and dispersed over one another, like smoke. She could see why Amira found the stone so mesmerizing. She handed it back with just the smallest sigh of reluctance.

The relief was immediate across Amira's delicate features, and she gripped the stone to her chest as though reuniting with a lost love.

"Do you think he knew to look for the stone here? What else do you know about it?"

"Nothing. Nothing else, I swear it. But we both know it's from the prophecy. I should have told you." Amira's eyes finally met hers. Her expression was tormented, her dark eyes liquid pools of ink. "You've been so honest, so *nice*. I'm sorry."

Coral tried not to look away with shame. It wasn't like Coral had been completely honest with her. "Forget it, you have nothing to apologize for." Should she recite the rest of the prophecy now? Admit her role in it? She could feel Kale's eyes on her, but she ignored him and focused on Amira. She seemed unsure, still focused on the stone.

"Oh my, I'm interrupting," a somewhat familiar voice said from the doorway.

Coral dropped to the ground and snatched up her trishula. She crouched, weapon at the ready.

The Third, Denir, if memory served her correctly, stood in the doorway. She wore an amused smile, although her eyebrows wrinkled slightly and her feet were braced in a fighting stance. Coral could barely make out the curses Kale muttered under his breath.

Coral rose slowly, keeping her eyes trained on the Third's face. The woman's expression betrayed nothing, though Coral noticed the moment her eyes found the dead Shadow Dancer. Kale hadn't been creative enough. Coral shifted her footing, but there was little chance of hiding the body now.

"How did you get in?" Amira's tone was surprisingly neutral. Coral noted that her back was now ramrod straight, nothing welcoming in her expression.

Taking her cues from Amira, Coral leveled her weapon toward the newcomer. "Answer the question or I'll assume you came in with him."

Denir lifted her chin. "I knocked, but it seems your staff and your Arbe are both missing."

Coral frowned. They'd dismissed the staff earlier that day, and Amira had yet to hire replacements. She supposed it was too much to hope the councilwoman wouldn't notice the Shadow Dancer, but now that they had been outed, what should she do? She shifted her weight slightly, preparing to strike.

The woman was alone and seemingly unarmed. It would be easy to dispatch her. Coral frowned. Why was she alone? Didn't their kind tend to run around with an Arbe in tow? She had just questioned Amira for her lack of one, so why didn't she have one for herself? Was she truly so competent a fighter in her own right or was she protected by someone? Perhaps the Queen of Shadows?

"The Second has no need for a new Arbe," Kale said through clenched teeth. Coral glanced at him, noting the hard planes of his chest, his muscles tensed and ready. Like her, Kale was waiting on the signal.

"It would appear so." Denir folded her arms across her chest. "Don't worry, I know better than to share a woman's secrets . . . especially those that happen in the privacy of their bedchamber."

Amira clasped her hands behind her back, either to hide the stolen stone or as a nervous gesture. Coral wasn't sure which.

"That didn't answer my question." Amira frowned up at the glass ceiling. "It's barely dawn. Why were you sneaking into my room?"

Denir shrugged. The gesture was so flippant that Coral felt a rush of anger and tightened her grip on her trishula before she hurled the thing right into the woman's smug face.

"I didn't sneak anywhere. As I mentioned, the door was open," Denir said.

"How do we know you're not lying? That you didn't just come here to make sure your colleague finished the job?" Kale stepped forward so that he was shoulder to shoulder with Coral, blocking Amira behind them.

"She's not," Amira whispered, but Denir raised her eyebrows.

"Thank you. I'm not." Her look was appraising. "As I said, it was easy enough to walk right in. And I came here because I think we need to talk. It took me all night, but I think I've finally worked it out. I know why you're here." Denir pushed away from the doorframe and entered the room. "I know who you are. I bet you've got some questions, and I've got some of my own. We can help each other."

"I don't know what you're talking about." Coral could hear the tremor in Amira's voice.

"I think you do, but flames, I'll play my hand first. You've been gone for some time, and I want to know why you're back. I want to know your role in all of this or if the plan has seriously gone off the rails. But I suppose first, before anything else, *Amira*, I should say welcome home."

CORAL

CHAPTER FORTY

*S*he knew. *Mother below, how* did she know?

Coral leveled her trishula at Denir, widening her stance as she did so.

"I'm only going to ask you once. Leave." She felt Kale shift beside her but didn't dare break eye contact with one of the Thirteen, especially one who Coral suspected was working with the Queen of Shadows.

"Wait." Amira gently pushed past the barrier she and Kale had created with their bodies and stepped forward to meet Denir. "She's right. We should talk."

Denir smiled, the look completely changing her face. "Wonderful. Perhaps in your study?" Denir left the room, pausing just outside the door and indicating that Amira should lead the way with a slight tilt of her head.

"You don't have to do this," Kale muttered.

He was right. Coral caught Amira's hand, giving it a gentle squeeze, but her only response was a quick jerk of her chin before Coral was forced to follow.

She came shoulder to shoulder with Denir in the hallway—well, shoulder to the top of her head anyway. The woman was nearly as tiny as Jura, and Coral wondered fleetingly if many of the people of the Republic were on the shorter side and Amira was an outlier.

To Amira's credit, she led the way with long, sure steps down the hall, shoving the door to her study open with such force that, had there been any decor on the walls, it surely would have fallen. The office was scarcely decorated—Coral remembered they were just moving in—and Denir took the liberty of seating herself in the only chair. Her nose crinkled as she took in her surroundings, but she said nothing as she adjusted the layers of her dress around her.

Amira's hands were squeezed together in front of her, and Coral wondered if she'd had time to hide the stone before Denir had intruded on them. Probably not. Which meant Amira was both distracted by it and could harness its power. If only they'd had more time to talk before Denir's arrival. Then she remembered the only reason Amira had even admitted ownership to the stone was because of the failed assassination attempt.

What sort of Breathcatchers nonsense was she involved in?

"If rumors are to be true, you've made a powerful ally." Denir dipped her head in Coral's direction. "I'd heard of the mess you were involved in back in Kitoi." She tsked lightly, shaking her head. "I can't imagine what that must have been like, betrayed by your own countryman and auctioned off in the underground market. What an *adventure*."

Coral started forward, fully prepared to plant her fist in the woman's jaw, but Amira stopped her with a persistent tug of her hand. She used the opportunity to pass the stone to Coral, and once again Coral was surprised by its weight. She shoved the stone into her leather bracer and struggled to regain her composure.

"You, there." Denir snapped her finger at Kale. "Water boy, I'll take whatever wine you can find around here. Heated, if the Second still employs a Torch . . . no? My, you truly did clean house. But then, who could blame you after what you've experienced. I can only imagine the tortures. I do hope you are not so naive as to believe you've left your problems back in Kitoi. You're in a sandstorm of trouble—you all are—and you'll be lucky if this doesn't end in your deaths." She cleared her throat. "Ahem, I'm incredibly parched."

Coral felt the water before she saw it. A massive ball of water hurtled down the hallway and into the room, splashing Denir into a sputtering mess.

"Insult either of these ladies again, and I'll do more than get you wet."

Coral could only blink at Kale's threat. She hadn't needed him to come to her defense, but it didn't feel terrible. The corners of Amira's mouth lifted in a suppressed smile, and her eyes sparkled as she exchanged glances with Coral.

"Can we skip the niceties and get straight to what you want? That is, if you've been thoroughly quenched?" Amira crossed her arms in front of her chest. "You said you have information."

Denir took her time answering, making a show of squeezing the excess water from her thick hair.

"I do. For a price."

That woman needed a good slap. Coral squeezed her fingers into a tight fist. The stone pressed into her skin, digging into the tender flesh despite its smooth surface. How had Amira tapped into its power? Could she also discover Denir's secrets?

"What do you want?" Amira asked.

Coral returned her focus to Amira, noting the small tremor in her voice.

"Rank," Denir answered. "I want to be First of the Thirteen."

Of course. It was always about greed with these Breathcatchers. If memory served her right, there were only a few ways to move forward in Rank among the Thirteen. There was a monthly vote, of course, but votes were easily bought and influenced among peers. Far more common was assassination. Death made the easiest path for the successor.

"Justir will never step down."

"Justir is an alttaw'am." Denir rose from her chair so quickly, it tumbled backward, clattering against the stone floor.

For a moment, silence filled the room. Alttaw'am? The First? Had Amira known about this? Coral studied her face, but the woman's expression gave nothing away.

"Can you do something about this?" Denir gestured to herself and the puddle she stood in. "Please?"

Coral was inclined to give the woman another dousing, but Kale pulled the water from her and the floor and sent it back to the pool he'd collected it from. The pool wasn't that far, a few rooms away, and its presence confused her. She'd thought such water wealth was rare in the Republic, but perhaps that was not the case among the Thirteen.

"I thought he was controlled by a blood chain." Amira pressed her hands together. "Jura said he was controlled by a blood chain."

"You've spoken to Jura? That bit in the Justice Dome wasn't a ruse then." Denir raised her eyebrows. "I knew it. And has she truly made an alliance with the aliferous? Does she prepare to seize the Republic from her father? What secrets do you know about the First family?"

Coral bit the inside of her cheek to keep from laughing. Were they talking about the same person? Mother below, the girl was powerful in ways Coral had never imagined, but she certainly wasn't capable of making plans to seize an entire nation from under her father and the Queen of Shadows . . . was she?

"No. I didn't say that. But where is the First then?" Amira's voice wavered. "If an alttaw'am has taken him, then Justir is . . ." Amira trailed off, likely remembering her own capture.

This was going nowhere. Now dry, the Third looked almost smug. Calculating.

But if she used the stone? What secrets might Coral be able to recover then? She wasn't certain she could harness its power, but Amira had seemed to do so easily. She reached for her *wei*, feeling its steady hum, as familiar as her heartbeat.

Then she shoved it all toward the stone.

Light filled the room, piercing and brighter than the sun. She closed her eyes tight against the searing pain and covered her ears to stop the sudden rush of sound. It sounded like a waterfall, a gentle roar that thrummed in harmony with her heartbeat. A sound that reminded her of home.

She opened her eyes, blinking the world back into focus. She was no longer in Amira's office. She must have fainted and they brought her here. Coral frowned. Except she didn't even appear to be in the Glass Palace at all. She rose to her feet, taking in her surroundings. She was in a large ballroom or perhaps an audience hall, although she'd never imagined being in one this large and this empty.

The heavy stone walls were covered in ornate tapestries. She examined the one nearest to her. It depicted an image of two soldiers facing one another. They stood alone on a battlefield littered with bodies, but the artist had chosen to keep the images blurred. The details of the two soldiers were so precise that Coral could imagine they were standing right before her. The soldier on the left had copper skin peeking between polished armor. Her raven hair was streaked gray and coiled down her back in a thick braid. The soldier on the right had the legs and chest of a man in armor, but wings stretched from his back, and his features were those of a bird. There was something familiar about the scene, but Coral knew with certainty she'd never seen the tapestry before.

"My, aren't we the conceited one?"

Startled by the sudden proximity of the unfamiliar voice, Coral turned and reached for a trishula that wasn't there. Where was her weapon? And who was this woman?

The woman was probably in her early- or midthirties. Gentle laugh lines framed sharp brown eyes and sooty lashes. Her tone had been familiar, teasing, and her expression now was one of gentle expectancy. Like she was waiting for Coral to say something. Like she wasn't surprised to see her standing there.

The confusion must have been written all over her face because the stranger's smile softened. "I only jest. Stars above, if my likeness was woven on a tapestry, I would stare at it too. But we should leave before . . . What's wrong? Why are you staring at me like that?"

"Do we know each other?"

Confusion clouded the woman's expression and she reached for Coral, but an explosion sounded in the distance. The ground rumbled beneath them, and the women exchanged uneasy glances.

"Avyanna, there's something I sh—"

The woman's confession was cut off by piercing screams and cries for help. The woman groaned but jogged toward the sound. Coral had no choice but to follow while her mind raced to piece together what was happening. How had she gotten here, and where was she? The woman had called her Avyanna and likened her to the woman in the tapestry, but that was impossible. They ran through a set of giant doors, the wood polished and shiny. Coral blinked at them as she passed through. The hall was unfamiliar and brimming with pandemonium. Dozens of people bustled across the wide stone hall, some carrying belongings, others simply pulling loved ones behind them. Everyone was running away, evacuating. Everyone terrified.

"What's happening?" Coral demanded. She didn't have her weapons, and she was becoming increasingly alarmed that she didn't even have her own body. Why had that woman acted like she'd recognized her from the tapestry?

Who was she?

Coral could feel her connection to the Mother humming within her. She still had access to her *wei*.

The woman, her companion, cursed under her breath, pulling a long sword from her scabbard. "Here." She thrust it into Coral's right hand, and she had no choice but to take the weapon or risk being sliced.

"Why don't you have any weapons? You always—never mind. Just promise me that whatever happens next, whatever you see, you won't do anything stupid."

Coral would never be so dumb as to make a promise like that. She said as much out loud.

The woman laughed, the lines around her eyes deepening. "I mean it. I can't lose you. Now I'm going to explain everything, but we have to act fast before w—"

Whatever she had been about to say, whatever her name was, Coral would never know. The woman made a strangled gurgle as she fell to her knees. Coral could only stare at the flaming arrow sticking through the woman's neck and igniting her hair.

Do something. Put it out!

Coral screamed and thrust out for her *wei*.

AMIRA

CHAPTER FORTY-ONE

A*mira felt naked without the* stone. She had somehow grown accustomed to its presence. Now, standing in her father's office without it, even with the strength of two fully armed warriors, she still felt vulnerable.

They were a steady presence at least, even if Kale dousing Denir was the most personality he'd ever shown. It proved he would be there for her when she needed him, or at least he had the potential to. And Coral was a friend she could grow to care for . . . even if she was a bit zoned out at the moment.

Coral's green eyes were unfocused and glazed. Amira couldn't blame her; everything was happening too fast, and Denir already knew too much. The old Amira would never have dreamed up this situation, but had she been in it, she probably would have made quips about killing Denir and destroying her problems in the traditional fashion of the Thirteen. The new Amira was horrified by the idea. But if Denir was telling the truth, if she truly knew the location of Jura's father, she owed it to her friend to try to bring him home. It was what Jura had done for her.

So that meant she had to agree, right? She had to help Denir with her play for the First.

Then Coral began screaming.

Kale shoved past her, and Amira dropped to the ground, preparing an escape from their new attacker.

"What's happening? Coral, wake up!" Kale cradled the unconscious Wave Mistress in his arms. Her neck was thrust back, and she continued to emit an unearthly scream. Kale murmured something else in their native tongue, but Coral didn't seem to hear.

"Shut her up before she wakes the entire council," Denir snapped.

Kale glowered at her but said nothing. What was there to say? Her screaming *would* wake the entire council, and they would have little chance of hiding the assassin's body then. The Thirteen disapproved of messy murders—murder should be an art. And a body lurking about in daylight court hours would incite an investigation. They had to do something before Coral screamed her throat raw.

Amira crawled toward them, reaching out for Coral's hand. She wanted to ask Kale what she could do to help. She wanted to be useful in some way.

No one wants to hurt you, she told herself.

Except that nearly everyone did. She took a deep breath.

You are safe.

Not really. Amira swallowed hard and squeezed Coral's hand. She squeezed back in the welcome silence.

Amira blinked, confused by the sudden tension in their intertwined fingers.

"I'm back." Her voice was hoarse, and there was something in the expression of her eyes . . . something familiar. Something that made Amira refuse to let go. She scooted closer, drawing Coral's hand into her lap.

"Where did you go?"

"I don't know. I was . . ." She looked around the room before her gaze fell back down to their hands. "I'm not sure." She broke contact, reaching up to rub her throat.

Kale thrust a glass of water toward her, and Coral took it with a grateful smile. Amira gave only a passing thought to how he had acquired the glassware. Denir scoffed as Coral took her first sip.

"Here, take it back." The words were a whisper. Amira could almost believe she had imagined them except for the gentle press of the stone into her palm. She was relieved, but its presence was still a burden. What was she to do with the thing now?

Coral shoved herself back to her feet with a grunt and Amira followed suit. She clasped her hands together, praying Denir didn't notice. She was having new sleepwear commissioned as soon as they were out of this mess. Pockets everywhere.

It seemed a fair assumption the stone was the cause of Coral's outburst. But why? How had it affected her so differently? Amira was desperate to ask but not in front of Denir.

The Third eyed them all with scrutiny.

"Is she ill?" Denir asked.

"She's fine," Amira and Kale answered in unison.

Amira noted the protective way he curled his body around Coral's frame. She swallowed, somewhat pained by the intimacy in his expression. Would anyone ever feel that way about her? Did she even deserve that? She straightened her shoulders and pressed her palm against her abdomen, taking comfort in the slight pressure, at the slight pinch of the stone against her skin.

"What's your plan?" she asked Denir. "I'm assuming you have one."

"I have more than just a plan. I have the First."

Amira nearly dropped the stone. "You what?" She clenched her fists.

"I found the First, and Justir is currently in safe-keeping, his wounds being tended." Denir raised her eyebrows. "Do we have an agreement? Justir is released into your care, and I ascend to my place as leader of the Thirteen, fully supported by your votes. The council will agree he is unfit to rule. Many have argued his reign should have ended years ago. And you remain in Second, a position you never should have been awarded but somehow managed to maintain. Your luck will only take you so far, child, so take the deal. Now, while you still can."

Amira squeezed the stone harder, willing it to speak to her, but it remained dead at Denir's words. There were no hidden truths. Or perhaps Coral had done something to the stone, rendering its magic useless.

"You have a deal."

You shouldn't have taken that deal." Kale collapsed on the couch, the delicate wood groaning from the weight.

The trio were in the salon, Kale having just returned from disposing of the assassin. Coral had muttered the sentiment earlier before she'd begun pumping her for information on the rules of the Thirteen's politics.

They were probably right, but she could do little about it now.

The foyer bell rang, and Amira strained to see through the glass wall of her entryway.

"I'll get it," Kale said with a dramatic sigh as he pulled his shirt back over his head. Amira shook her head. Honestly that boy could never be expected to stay fully clothed. He returned seconds later.

"Here. It's a letter from Ishani. She requests permission to call on you this morning."

Coral whipped her head toward Kale, and Amira could only sigh. "I don't know that I can handle another visitor this morning."

"I'll send her away when she arrives." Kale lingered by the doorway.

"No. We may as well see what she wants," Amira decided. Good thing, too, because the councilwoman had arrived.

"My lady Second, I had to gaze upon you with my own eyes to see that it was true. You are back and settled." Her eyes flicked back and forth between Coral and Kale, but she didn't acknowledge them otherwise.

Flames, but the woman was an entitled—

"Amira, if I may be so bold," Ishani continued, interrupting Amira's train of thought. "I thought to strike up a friendship. I know that you see Denir as a mentor, but her ambition will be her downfall. You'll see."

Amira resisted the urge to press her fingertips to her temples. As if she needed further warning of Denir's ambition. But what was she to do about it? She had to help Jura and her father.

Ishani regarded her with curiosity. Amira wished the stone would speak to her—tell her what Ishani was thinking, if that was even how it worked—but she had changed earlier into a dress with pockets, and she didn't wish to make a show of digging into the fabric now. Besides, she didn't need a magical stone to tell her that Ishani wasn't trustworthy.

"You've come to offer friendship, you say?" Amira asked, stalling for time.

"And why shouldn't we be allies? We are both young, independent women, forging a new world, are we not?" Ishani dared a quick glance in Coral's direction. Coral scowled back. "Ally yourself with me, with Kitoi, before you make a mistake you can't take back."

"Is that a threat?" Coral stepped toward the councilwoman, halted by Kale's hand on her shoulder.

Ishani ignored them. "I'll see you at the next meeting, Second."

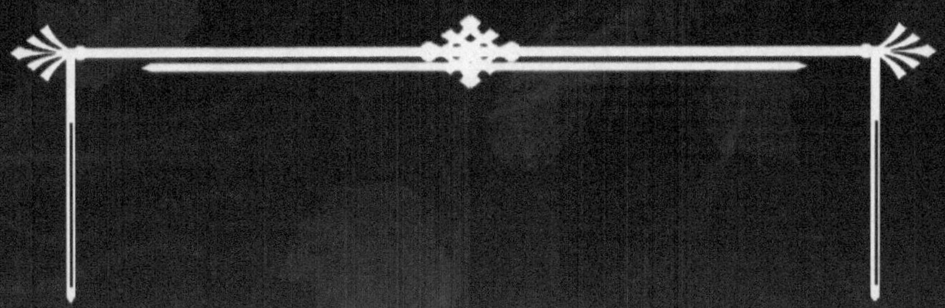

TYLAK

CHAPTER FORTY-TWO

*T*ylak *thought he'd gone both* deaf and blind. Or perhaps this was death, just an endless void of nothing. That didn't seem so bad. Perhaps now he could finally get some rest.

When Tylak opened his eyes again, it was difficult to make out any of his surroundings. *It's early morning*, he realized, barely dawn, and the sun wasn't high enough in the sky to filter any light through the canopy of trees.

He struggled to sit up, unable to stifle his groan as he did so. A searing pain in his side reminded him he'd been stabbed. He fumbled for the wound and was surprised to find it stitched up. He'd heard of such healing practices before but had never seen it in action. Most wounds in the Republic were cauterized.

He blinked, waiting for his surroundings to focus.

He was definitely out of the citadel. Far from it, he would guess. The air was once again thick and cloying with the heady perfume of flora, and Tylak suspected he was back in the jungle. It was menacingly silent, no call of birds or chittering monkeys, and the silence made him uneasy. Either Tylak hadn't been there long or he wasn't alone.

The events of the previous evening rushed back to him, and he rolled to his side to avoid choking on the sudden rush of vomit.

Peppik was gone.

Peppik with his odd thoughts and the many crinkles around his eyes. His friend, his companion for the better of the last decade, gone.

Tylak's heart hammered in his chest, and he noted it with wonder, marveling that it should beat so proudly when Peppik's would never move again.

Peppik. The name roared in his ears. Perhaps he was screaming the name. Tylak was unsure of anything but the overwhelming pain burning him up from inside.

Hours passed—when the birds began to call to one another once again—before Tylak was able to rise to his feet. He'd wiped his face, smearing dirt and tears and a mix of other bodily fluids onto his palm. His fingers were bruised, knuckles bloodied. Tylak frowned. His small finger stuck out at a horrifying angle, as though the appendage had tried to abdicate its position on his hand.

He grimaced, sniffing at the last of his tears before he grabbed his finger and twisted it back into place. Tylak gritted his teeth against the pain, taking slow, sucking breaths until the edge of his vision was once again sharp and focused.

The birds continued their call, the sound almost mournful. The long haunting notes echoed through the jungle. Tylak used the quiet moment to take stock of his surroundings. He had little on his person. His personal sack and Jura's satchel of books were gone, probably lost back in the citadel. Everything was lost back in the citadel.

He reached for the wound at his side. The stitching was neat and even, nineteen stitches stretching across his waistline and dipping toward his hip.

"I was hoping you would stay unconscious while I set your hand."

He turned toward the voice, meeting an attractive woman who appeared to be his age. She carried a basket, which she slowly set down at her feet.

"I'm not armed." She reached into her boot and pulled out a dagger. "Well, not anymore." She tossed the dagger to the ground beside her basket.

"You did this?" Tylak asked. He dropped his tattered clothing and allowed his hand to fall to his side, wincing only slightly from the pain.

"I did. I left to get a few more supplies. Make a splint for your hand. You are recovering quicker than I expected." She slowly squatted back down to her basket and pulled out twine and twigs. "May I?"

Tylak lifted his hand out for her inspection, and she tsked over it before she began wrapping it up in a makeshift splint. Tylak used their proximity to study her further. The woman had dark features, her skin likely made darker by hours spent in the sun. Her hands were slightly callused, and they moved with the certainty of one who had done the task before. She had a stunning face with an easy smile that suggested the troubles of the world couldn't find her here. Tylak wished that were true.

"My name is Izel."

"Tylak."

"I don't see many Shadow Dancers this far from the Republic."

Tylak stiffened. "I'm not—"

"Don't worry. Your business is your own. I just have to help a stranger if I see someone in need."

"That's very kind of you."

"There." She patted his hand gently after she'd finished. "Kindness always has a way of coming back to you." She pressed her lips into a thin smile. "Most of the time anyway. You're welcome to stay the evening in my home, but I—"

"How did I get here? Where are we?" Tylak bit back the urge to throw a dozen more questions at her.

"You're just at the border. Not far from River's Edge."

"Rivers?"

"It isn't much of a city. Just a simple town, mainly with families of the soldiers supporting the border."

Tylak's head was already pounding, and he could do without the onslaught of new information. He knew what a river was, but he didn't think he would ever see one. Had never imagined traveling so far away from the Republic. "The border?"

"To the Wilds. The border between the province of Friis and the last of the civilized world."

She must have read the exhaustion on his face because she shook her head. "None of that matters. You're safe, I promise you. We'll get you all healed up in no time. But first, there is something else." She hesitated. "Perhaps you want to see to your companion first?"

Tylak's thoughts went immediately to Peppik, but Peppik was dead. Urso. Of course, he had brought them here. Tylak struggled to remember, but the events from the last day and a half were all jumbled together in his brain. Burn it all, he just wanted to go back to sleep.

She walked back in the direction she'd come, stooping down to collect her dagger.

"Follow me."

Tylak hobbled after her. There was a pain around his ankle he hadn't noticed before. Between that, his hand, and his stab wound and rising headache . . . he was a mess. He couldn't imagine how Urso had managed to fly them out of the citadel. The poor man had barely been able to lift his wings much less maintain flight with cargo. But there had been a sound, hadn't there?

Nothing made sense. Moments later Tylak discovered he would never receive any answers on the matter.

Urso was dead.

The aliferous lay stretched on the jungle floor, his neck twisted at an unnatural angle and his limbs bent and broken around him.

Tylak hadn't known the man long. He had barely gotten more than a name from him, and now he was gone. Gone before Tylak could even thank him for saving his life. His family, his mother, and Sykk. Peppik and Urso. All gone.

He stared down at the broken figure, his heart full of pity that the man would never get to tell his story.

"I'm sorry."

Tylak had been so lost in his thoughts that he hadn't noticed Izel had come to stand right beside him.

"Were you two close?"

Not in the slightest. But how could he tell this stranger that it made it somehow worse? He sat beside the fallen figure, noting the pale skin and yellowed feathers. His eyes had been blue, Tylak remembered. Blue like the ocean. Blue like his birthstone, also lost to him.

The ground was moist beneath him, the jungle floor teeming with life. Already a crew of tiny insects marched toward Urso's torso. Tylak looked away before they began their feast.

"You were caught in that branch." Izel indicated a broken limb just above them.

Jura's satchel hung from the piece still attached to the massive tree. Tylak doubted he had the energy to climb for it, but he debated with the idea all the same.

"Don't." Izel's voice held a warning. She must have noticed the expression on his face. "You were suspended from your ankle, caught in that satchel. I could just reach your arms enough to pull you down. The satchel and the branch broke with the effort, but most of its contents fell to the ground when you did." She pointed to the books scattered along the base of the trunk.

"Thank you." He looked at the books along the jungle floor. So out of place. Likely already getting ruined by the moisture in the air. He had been ridiculous to bring them. What was the purpose of books in a world filled with such darkness and death? "He deserves a proper burning or . . . sandstorms. What do the aliferous do with their dead?"

"I don't know," Izel answered.

Tylak hadn't even realized he'd spoken his thoughts out loud. "Thank you," he repeated. "For everything. I would have bled out if you hadn't found me, and I have people who are relying on me."

"Jura."

"What?"

She offered him another tight-lipped smile that didn't quite reach her brown eyes. "You talked in your sleep. You mumbled her name a few times. Her and Peppik. I'm assuming that's him?" She jerked her chin in the direction of Urso's body.

"No, Peppik is . . . was." He swallowed. "Peppik isn't here. This was Urso, and I didn't know him very well, but he was a friend and he deserves a proper goodbye. He doesn't deserve to be left out here for bugs to eat. He doesn't deserve to rot away, alone and forgotten."

"He won't be." Izel took his unbroken hand and pressed it firmly within her own. "He won't be."

JURA

J*ura didn't have to wait* long before Danos opened her door. He gave her his usual once-over, his eyes tired.

"Blood Maker." He inclined his head in greeting. "It seems you are eager to continue your training this morning."

"More like I'm eager to receive some answers. I'd like to speak to the Dreamer again, today if possible." Jura couldn't shake the idea that if she could just speak to the Dreamer again, if she could just talk to them, then maybe she could discover her true role in the prophecy.

Danos gave her a tight-lipped smile. "And answers you deserve, Blood Maker, but I'm afraid that a meeting with the Dreamer is impossible today. They are indisposed."

"They're ill?"

"Unfit for your visitation in any case. I am afraid, at least for the time being, you will have to make do with me."

Jura wondered what could keep the Dreamer from wishing to see her but decided there was no sense in wasting energy on the concern. She offered Danos her best smile instead.

"Well, I suppose I wouldn't mind some assistance navigating

your library, maybe after we—"

"The library? What do you need from there?"

"Information, books . . . Is there some reason you don't want me to go?" Jura frowned, remembering that it was Markhim who had shown her the cavern library and not Danos. In fact, the Speaker had only ever mentioned the library in passing. "What are you keeping from me?" Was there something hidden in the library? Something other than the *Five Elements*? Or was Danos simply worried she would find that very book that, now, hid under her pillow.

"Ah, I thought you and I had transcended the suspicious nature of the Thirteen, but I suppose it must still come naturally to you. Do not fear, child of the new world. I will not fault you in this. But it does pain me to know you feel this way." His silver feathers ruffled behind his shoulder blades.

Jura didn't believe it for a moment. He was deflecting, not that she understood why. What could the aliferous possibly be hiding in their libraries? Danos was right about one thing though. Jura was one of the Thirteen, and she knew the value of secrets.

Despite Danos spending much of the lesson distracted, Jura finished the session feeling stronger rather than depleted. He left her outside her door and hurried down the hall and out of sight. He was acting more than just a bit suspicious. He'd been in such a hurry, he hadn't even bothered to open her door. Jura frowned with the slow realization that she was locked out of her room.

Now what? She caught her bottom lip in her mouth, worrying over her next action. She supposed she could find her way back to the library. And perhaps along the way she would find Markhim or, at the very least, someone who could open her door.

She began walking down the hall toward the library, swinging her arms in stride. She was growing strong, stronger than ever before. The thought had persisted in the back of her mind since her morning training session. Her well of power came more easily to her now. She could feel it rumbling within her. She wasn't entirely sure how she felt about that. Especially since she was still learning everything the unknown power was capable of. It didn't seem to have any obvious features. Fire Dancers and Torches had their abilities with fire, and Coral and her companions had mastery over water—those gifts all followed logic. They made sense. What was she to do with the knowledge that she was a Blood Maker? Force back every monthly cycle? Jura smiled wryly at the thought. Well, that part of her magic might not be too bad, if she could ever figure that out. And just how was she to be properly trained by someone whose power came from the wind?

She sighed. She supposed it wasn't fair to be so hostile toward her instructor, although, she could argue Danos deserved a bit of animosity. There was no reason for his mood swings. He was either disinterested or downright rude in his interactions with her. Jura felt almost certain it was personal, but she couldn't think of anything she could have done to him to make him feel so slighted. And now he had taken to locking her out of her room.

Perhaps she should just be blunt and ask him. If he evaded the question altogether, then she would at least know. She turned down the hallway with the near-hidden staircase. As usual, there was a distinct lack of other aliferous. It occurred to her this was the first time she'd been left completely unescorted since her arrival.

She had no way of knowing where Markhim's room was, and the idea of having some alone time in the library was too good to pass up anyway. She remembered the way easily enough and, within moments, found her way back to the cavern filled with books.

As always, she gave a reverent pause and inhaled deeply at the doorway. What was it about the smell of books? How was it that they could both instantly excite her and soothe her?

The cavern library was a far cry from the great library of Kitoi but still hosted hundreds of volumes on the shelves. It would take quite some time to sort through the contents of the various titles. Especially given the fact that the book she was looking for didn't have a title. Who had stolen that page? And how could she possibly hope to find the book with so little information? No author, no title, merely vague descriptions of its contents . . . it was every librarian's worst nightmare.

No matter. For the moment, anyway, Jura had nothing but time. She reached for the nearest book on the shelf.

One hour later, Jura found herself squinting at the pages before her. Odd, she hadn't needed her glasses in quite some time. She must be exhausted from all the reading. Deep within her, her power stirred. Jura reached for it, hesitating for a moment before giving in to the deepest part of her. Instantly, her vision cleared and she felt her energy restored.

Well, that was a nice trick.

She sighed as she placed the book back on its shelf. Dozens of books later, and she was no closer to finding answers. What good was unlimited energy and perfect vision if these powers couldn't help her locate the book mentioned on that ripped page? It had said it would heed the call of the Blood Maker but how?

"I thought I would find you here."

"Markhim." She turned around and offered him a quick smile. "Am I so predictable?"

"Just a bit." He winked at her, and her stomach did a tiny flip.

"I can't find it. Not yet, anyway, and I'm worried I won't locate it before we return to the Republic." She gestured widely, indicating the hundreds of other books. "It seems impossible, but the book said we were connected so I thought—"

"Have you considered this book no longer exists? Jura, you said yourself it should be impossible. The book would be a thousand years old."

"It exists. I know it does."

Markhim sighed but he didn't argue. "All right then." He began to roll back the sleeves of his tattered shirt. Jura was fairly certain the aliferous had provided him with ample changes of clothing, but he seemed to prefer his own garments. "What books have you sorted through already?"

Jura rose to her toes to kiss his cheek. "Thank you. I've gone through all of these here." She indicated with a wave of her hand before picking two more books from the shelf. "Here." She handed one to him. "Look through this one."

"What are we looking for?"

Jura wasn't entirely sure, but she felt certain she would know it when she saw it. She had to. The book had promised they were connected.

They fell into a silent routine, each picking up a book and skimming through its contents before replacing it on the shelf with a soft sigh.

After some time, Markhim cleared his throat. "It's nice here, isn't it?"

"Hmm? The library?"

"No. I mean, yes, here too. But I meant up here, on the Edge. Life with the aliferous has so much to offer."

Jura slanted a glance in his direction before sliding her gaze back to the open page. "Says the man who refuses to wear their clothing."

"But I'm not resistant to change. Jura, we could stay here."

She placed the book back on the shelf, giving him her full attention. His dark eyes pleaded with hers.

"We're safe here. Away from the Thirteen, the Queen of Shadows, everything. Nothing can reach us here. Let's stay. You and me together. Stay here with me. Build a life *here* with *me*."

He reached for her hand, but Jura stepped back. "Stay? Markhim, you can't be serious. Stay hidden away here while my father is captured by blood chains? While the entire ocean and half of the colonies threaten to wage war on the Republic? Stay? And what, abandon our people? My friends?"

"You mean Tylak."

"Tylak? What does he have to do with this?"

Markhim laughed, the sound bitter. "Right. What doesn't he have to do with this? We were all but betrothed, Jura. And then I come back and find you panting after a Shadow Dancer!" His face paled. "Jura, I didn't mean that. I'm sorry, just please—I want us to be together. I love you."

She didn't think she could have been more stunned by his actions and then he threw those words at her. What in the flaming sands was she supposed to do with this? She shook her head quickly as if she could deny he'd said anything, as if she could deny everything that had happened in the last few moments.

"Say something. Please." Markhim reached for her again, and she allowed him to take her hand in his, her fingers limp as he gave her a gentle squeeze.

"Ahem. My apologies for interrupting."

Markhim stiffened, his grip on her fingers tightening. "See, you said that the last time and yet, here you are again."

"Markhim! Perhaps the day has exhausted you. You should return to your chambers, wherever they are, and see if you can find your manners while you're there." She tried not to flinch as he snatched his hands from under hers.

"We aren't done here. Can I see you later? Please?"

She nodded in response. Some of the tension seemed to leave his expression.

"I'll see you this evening. Forgive me." He reached for her but seemed to think better of it, his hand falling back to his side before he turned and left.

Jura offered Priamos a weak smile. "I'm sorry. Things had just gotten a bit tense between us. He didn't mean it."

"Please, do not apologize for him." Pri waved the air between them. "It is nothing. Unless, you wish to speak of it?"

"He suggested we stay here. Build a life together here, he said."

"But you can't! You must fulfill your destiny."

"Of course I can't. I need to get back to the Republic. It's what I've been trying to do since I was brought here. My power is growing. I'm getting stronger every day. It won't be long before Danos deems me ready to face my sister. That's why it's so important I find this book. I just know it holds the key to everything, if only I can find it."

"And you think this book is here in our library?" Priamos's eyebrow feathers ruffled in concern. "I do not know if there exists such a book of power, but if it did, surely it would be in our royal library and not in one of our archive caverns?"

Jura's skin chilled, as if her very blood had turned ice. The archive caverns?

No. And yet it made too much sense. "What did you say? About the library? The aliferous have a royal library?"

Priamos straightened his shoulders, pride shining on his face. "Do we have a library? Only the greatest that this world has ever known. Would you like me to take you there now?"

JURA

CHAPTER FORTY-FOUR

J ura trembled with rage, though none of it was directed at Pri, who stared at her expectantly. Why? Why had Danos kept the library from her? Her thoughts swirled with various reasons. Why would he train her in her power yet deny her access to the one thing capable of assisting her in her so-called destiny?

"Yes, please. I would very much like to visit this library."

She followed Pri out of the cavern and back into the twisting halls built into the mountain. They walked in silence, Pri casting quick glances over his shoulder as if expecting to find someone following them. Jura could tell they were climbing the mountain—the burning in her thighs was indication enough—but that was her only way of knowing as the halls were completely enclosed.

"How does the hall remain lit? I've never heard of such magic." Not that she knew much, or really anything, about wind magic. She chose not to bring that part up.

"We prefer the open sun, of course, but so deep within the mountain, that is impossible. But there is great power in the wind. It is what has carved our path in the stone, and its energy is what powers our lighting system. But there is even more."

They came to the end of the hall, and Pri indicated the large imposing door with a grand flourish of his hands. "Best brace yourself, my lady. The winds are barely tamed up here."

He shoved open the door, and they were greeted by a wind that howled down the hall and caused Jura's hair to whip about her face.

"Follow me. Careful, now."

Jura followed Pri out the door and onto a wide platform. The spacious alcove gave her no relief as she realized they had nearly reached the top of the mountain. The ground was so far below, it melted into the clouds, and Jura found herself shivering against the steady gales of wind.

"Where are we?" she shouted, her words fighting to be heard against the roar of wind.

"The Eerie. It's the only means of travel for . . . people like us." He offered her a weak smile.

People without wings.

"Oh." She looked around. There was nothing around them save for a chest. "How?"

Pri smiled, canines gleaming. "A bit of wind manipulation." He walked over to the chest and pulled out a thick length of canvas. "You'll attach yourself to this," he said, indicating a short length of corded rope with buckles. "And then I will funnel the winds under the fabric, and we will ride the wind currents across."

Right. Leaping across an intensely high chasm with nothing but a tarp and a prayer to the Everflame. She gave Pri a skeptical frown.

"Don't be frightened. It's usually very safe," Pri said.

His ominous warning did little to quell the uneasiness in her belly.

Moments later, Jura had the rope twisted around her waist and thighs, all securely buckled at her midriff.

"Hang on to me." Pri pulled her close and stepped off the ledge.

For one terrifying moment, they were falling, and Jura's grip on Pri's shoulders tightened. Just as suddenly, they were hanging in the air. It seemed less windy somehow, as if all the wind was directed above them, only there to hold them aloft.

All too soon they alighted on the opposite mountain peak, on a platform similar to the one they had left. Pri returned the air balloon to the matching chest on this side and gave her a grin.

Jura returned the smile. "That was amazing."

"I hoped you might like it. It's the closest I've ever been to flying and—" He cut himself off, giving her a hapless shrug. "It is nice to share such simple pleasures with a friend."

"We are friends, right Pri? So can't you help me? I need to get another message to my friends. I'm going to retrieve this book and then I'm leaving for the base of the mountain. I have to get back to the Republic. Come with me if you still wish. Take me home. "

"Jura, you are my friend. And of course I will help you reach out to your friends, but I can't take you off the Edge. Not even if I wanted to. They would only bring you back."

"Who?" She leaned toward him, though they were alone on the steep cliffside. "Danos?" The name was barely a whisper over the wind. "Or the Dreamer?"

Pri gave an emphatic shake to his head. "No, please. I shouldn't have said anything. Come, let's get you to your library."

Pri indicated the door carved into the stone cliff. It boasted the same design from her bedroom and swung open easily at Pri's breathy song.

Jura was not prepared for what awaited them on the other side. She had assumed she would be greeted by another closed-off hallway, but instead the door opened to reveal an enormous cavern. Light streamed in from various windows carved into the rock and stone, and dozens, no, hundreds of buildings sprawled out before her.

Jura gasped in wonder. This entire mountain was hollow, and inside was the greatest view of a city Jura had ever seen.

She turned to Pri and he laughed. "You didn't truly think all of the aliferous resided within the great hall, did you?"

Honestly, she had. Jura knew the aliferous had stopped their evolution—they were frozen in time, Pri had said. The halls had been sparsely populated, sure, but then Jura had been forced to keep to her rooms, so she had merely assumed the inhabitants all resided in an area she had yet to explore. She had pictured nothing like this.

"It's beautiful."

Pri offered a small smile, but his eyes remained haunted. "The city no longer sings. Come, I will take you to the library."

The library was the tallest building she had ever seen. It was a twisting spire at the center. Unlike many of the rock and stone structures in the city, this building was made of deep bronze metal with windows placed up its height in a seemingly haphazard fashion.

"This is the library?" She couldn't keep the skepticism from her voice. It was by far the tallest building.

They entered through the tall imposing doors, and Jura sucked in a sharp breath. It was the most wondrous thing she'd ever seen. The walls were rounded and lined with shelves curling about the room in a circular pattern, similar to the design of the cavern archive. However that was where all the differences lie. Shelves also floated in mid-air. Some sailed from one point to another, on an unknown quest to meet someone's reading needs. Loose papers trailed about like a flock of migrating doovers.

Despite the sheer wonder of the library, she was immediately comforted by the smell and the familiarity of being greeted by an untold number of books.

"Oh, Pri. This is . . ."

"Isn't it? My mother said that in its day there were almost none that compared. We've every volume ever written. And scribes! Air scribes who transcribe what the winds whisper to us."

"It's incredible." Jura gravitated to the nearest shelf and reached for a book at random. The textured leather and smooth edges were instantly calming. She skimmed the pages; it was a book of various farming practices by region. Some of the land maps were unrecognizable, no doubt changed by the Everflame. She felt the familiar tug of loss and reached for another book. She had just decided she was ready to move on to the next shelf when Pri gently tapped her shoulder.

"Of course, I am happy to escort you back at any time, but if you think you will be entertained here for a while, I do have business that I can see to."

She waved him off with a quick flourish of her hand. Would she be here awhile? If Jura was honest with herself, she never wanted to leave. Why was it that the last two times she'd traveled to stunning new libraries, she had more pressing things to attend? Pri left and she walked to the next shelf.

At least this time, Jura could think of no better use for her time. Train in her powers, find the book. Even if her captivity here didn't hold such a purpose, it might still be worth it if only to experience the wonder of this collection of books. She walked deeper into the library, heading for the next shelf.

Jura was unsure how much time passed—surely no more than an hour—when she first felt it. It was a soft rumble in her chest, a tug at her source of magic. She felt inexplicably drawn toward some gravitational force.

An enormous spiraling staircase dominated the center of the library. At least, Jura suspected it was one. The monstrosity was a mix of stone and gravel stretched so high that she couldn't see the top. She gently placed the miniature mountain of books she'd collected on a nearby cart and reached for the handrail.

A woman with red-and-blue wings and dark eyes frowned at her, but other than that no one seemed to pay her any mind. She took a step up and felt the invisible string tighten between her magic and whatever called to her.

It was the book; it had to be. Jura resisted the urge to run up the stairs and instead began her slow ascent, placing one careful step after the other. She kept a watchful eye out for anyone who would try to stop her, but aside from the few souls she'd spotted down by the entry room, she was alone.

Just her and this irresistible call.

At the next landing she paused. The tug on her magic was still there, but now there was something else. The landing was like the other ones she'd passed, a narrow shaft of space with more shelves seemingly floating in mid-air. They must remain in place with more wind magic, Jura supposed, although none of the pages rustled. It was wondrous and beautiful at the same time. She stood on its edge, reaching out into the air and closing her eyes.

What if she were to jump, right now? Would she be caught in the magic air and lifted away? Or would she plummet to her death, dooming everything she ever cared about?

Jura shook her head to clear away such dark thoughts. And there were so many of them. Every passing moment the weight of her destiny crushed her. The responsibility of changing the world was more than any one person should bear. The self-doubt always crept back in. That the prophecy was wrong about her, wrong about everything.

Markhim had mentioned they worried where her alliances might lie—what it would mean for the Mistress to bend the knee. Did that mean she made an alliance with the aliferous? With Kitoi? And how could they even be sure this magic they had awakened in her could be controlled? The meanings of prophecies could be misinterpreted all the time. There were a dozen different ways a phrase could give meaning. Why, even the term *mistress* was more likely to refer to Coral.

The invisible truth was as damaging as a wound to the gut. Jura might be the Blood Maker the prophecy referenced, but she knew with sudden clarity that the prophecy's greatest action had never centered on her but on Coral, the Wave Mistress and Commander of the Three Oceans.

Sandstorms, but what did it all mean? She wanted to scream in frustration and bit her bottom lip to keep an unladylike growl from escaping, though there was no one around to hear it.

She wasn't offended that the prophecy wasn't all about her . . . was she?

Don't be ridiculous. That's how a child behaves, she chastised herself. But hadn't it felt nice to be the important one for once? And here she thought the discovery of the book and her awakened powers had all been building toward something. She had felt important, irreplaceable. Instead, she was still a pawn. And not even a good one at that. She still had to find the book.

Jura was tired of waiting.

She ripped a hair pin from her twisted braid and jabbed it into her finger.

Please work. Jura grunted in satisfaction as the tiny drop of red welled up on the pad of her pointer finger. She splayed her hand wide, reaching into the space around her.

"I am the Blood Maker," Jura whispered.

At her words, the well of power within her roiled, a serpent ready to strike. "If this book is meant to heed my call . . ." She paused, looking around.

The rising wind tousled her hair and clothing, its soft howl rifling the dozens of pages floating in the air before her. She stared at the drop of blood pulsing on her finger and gave in to her power.

"I command you to come to me."

JURA

CHAPTER FORTY-FIVE

Jura thrust out all of her power, aching with the need to claim the book. The wind tore around her, ripping pages and tossing books into the abyss, and for one desperate moment, Jura worried she would be swept away along with them.

An unremarkable brown leather book hit her in the chest with enough force to knock her backward. She fell on her bottom, legs splayed before her. Instantly the roaring winds ceased. Jura peered down the landing, but no one seemed aware of what had transpired.

She studied the book, not even bothering to rise from the smooth stone ledge. The book was small, its pages frayed, likely because it was missing the second half and had no back cover for protection. Who would dare to rip a book in half!

Jura was growing increasingly annoyed about the level of disrespect someone had shown these books. Especially ones so important—or *because* this one was so important, so dangerous, someone decided it was safer if it was torn in half. Of course.

But what had happened to the rest? Was it truly hidden away somewhere safe or was it destroyed and lost forever? She tucked the book against her abdomen, adjusting the length of fabric so it hid the book from sight.

In the distance, alarms sounded.

Jura froze, straining to listen. A note filled her ears, vibrating her body with its hum and trembling beneath her feet. Jura realized the sound was coming from the library itself, likely from the force of winds flowing through the windows. Perhaps it wouldn't have been so loud if she hadn't been high up.

Another note, this one closer, made the ground tremble again. Jura clung to the archway for support.

The sound was so clear, so deafening, that for a moment, her eardrums still hummed despite its absence. Perhaps that was why she didn't understand at first, why it took her so long to hear the words of an achingly familiar voice.

"Jura was less favorable toward the idea than I had imagined, but I doubt she has somehow discovered your plans," Markhim said.

Jura clamped her hand over her mouth to prevent a startled squeak from escaping. She dared a quick glance through the archway and pulled back as Markhim and Danos climbed the stairs past her alcove.

"The Blood Maker's destiny is among her people," Danos returned, his tone bland. "But, if she suspects we have forced her hand? Or if she truly has found the book?"

"No, she would have told me. But I don't like lying to her. Jura needs . . ." Markhim's voice trailed off with distance.

No, I need to know what he says! Jura peered at the staircase, squinting at Markhim's and Danos's retreating forms. If only she were a Shadow Dancer and could melt into the shadows and chase after them. If only she could control the winds and force their whispered words back to her.

And why can't I? Hadn't she done so before with Pri's supervision? The book grew warm against her skin at the thought, as if it, too, were eager to test her new powers. She remembered the feeling with Pri, the weightlessness, the choir of voices. She focused on Markhim.

"—if the winds are wrong? What if none of this has anything to do with Jura?"

He sounded so close, it was almost like he was standing there beside her.

Danos's response was hesitant. "The winds are rarely wrong. But it is not impossible. That's why it's so urgent the young Blood Maker be trained in her skills, however strong they may be. I sense great power in her. The winds were not wrong about that."

"And you think the Mistress will bend the knee soon?"

"Yes," Danos replied. "The patterns have been quite clear. Likely today. But if Jura has discovered the book before—"

"She won't." Markhim's response was so emphatic that she reeled back as if she'd been slapped.

None of this was making any sense. Why would Markhim keep this from her? Whatever this was.

"Honestly, I think we're both still accepting her role in all this. The Jura I know is scarcely capable of managing her own emotions much less reshaping an entire world. In fact, I wouldn't be surprised if we find out the wind's translations were confused, and it's her sister or maybe even Amira who is meant to change everything. Now that's a—"

She broke the connection, flinching at his harsh words. How could he? How could he promise to have her best interest at heart and then prove otherwise? The betrayal somehow stung worse that it was an attack on her character. That Markhim would paint her as some weak hapless female unable to do anything.

But she was so much more than that.

She raced down the stairs, grateful for her pants and new sturdy boots—gifted from Danos just that morning—which prevented her from any misstep down the many flights. The few inhabitants of the library all huddled near its doors, and she caught Pri there, anxiously wringing his hands.

"There you are." His shoulders sagged in relief before he threw a colorful cloak over her shoulders. The light blue color shimmered and deepened in intensity to a royal purple where it grazed the floor in a mass of feathers.

"I'm guessing the alarm was caused by me?" Jura asked as she adjusted the cloak to cover her head. "I had hoped to return to my rooms without any suspicion." Another terrible gong reverberated throughout the building. Someone screamed, and the library patrons pressed toward the doors.

"What did you do?" Pri hissed.

"I told you, I needed to find a book." Someone shoved past her in their effort to leave the library. The remaining aliferous panicked, everyone flying toward the doors as another note rattled the ground.

"The library hasn't sung of creation in over a thousand years. Whatever you did, I don't want to know. Why, for the library to even remember such a song suggests . . ." Pri's face paled. "You didn't. Come, we have to get you out of here."

He pulled her hand toward the library door, and they were waved by a librarian who had more on their mind than whether or not someone left without properly checking out their books. And certainly not one who gave thought to the stolen book pressed tightly against Jura's rib cage.

The city inhabitants were more confused than worried. Several peered up toward the entry and still others took flight.

"We should hurry." Pri looked around, straining to find something or someone. His head tilted, and Jura realized he was listening to the wind.

"What is it? What's happening?"

He turned to her, eyes wide as he vigorously shook his head. "Don't say another word." He grabbed her arm and pulled her behind him.

Jura wanted to demand answers, but Pri's frantic expression stopped her from taking further action. He pulled her down a side street, away from the crowd. The two of them pressed their backs against the smooth stone alley. Pri held up a finger, indicating for her to wait for him, and then he disappeared back into the busy street.

Jura frowned after him. The alarms had stopped ringing, but she knew she had likely tripped them when she summoned the book to her. Oh.

And then there was the fact that she had verbally commanded the winds to bring her the book. She'd spoken directly to the wind. And the winds told them everything.

Sandstorms . . . they *knew* she had it.

Jura pulled the feathered cloak tighter around her, knowing that if it truly came down to Pri rescuing her, she didn't stand a chance. The book no longer felt warm but still felt light as air. Even dormant as it was, she could feel the power radiating from it. What did it mean for the words written inside? How powerful was the knowledge on its pages?

She was beginning to worry Pri had been gone longer than necessary when she felt a hand grasp her shoulder.

She whirled around, clutching her throat as she made eye contact with Markhim. Danos joined them from the opposite end of the alley.

"Jura. We've found you."

AMIRA

Chapter Forty-Six

*A*mira *wished to be doing* anything else at the moment. To her credit, Coral appeared just as uncomfortable, her cheeks flushed a deep red.

"I'm sorry," Amira apologized again. "I do plan to hire a new staff." With everything else going on, it hadn't been a priority.

"I just don't understand all the laces." Coral pulled tight and knotted the loose string together in a pattern that looked suspiciously like fishing net. She was a far cry from a handmaid.

Amira sighed. It didn't matter. The ill-fitting dress would be mostly covered by her traditional robes anyway.

There was a quiet knock at her door, and Coral gave her a questioning look. Amira offered a quick nod in response, and moments later, Kale filled the doorframe.

"Oh, I'm sorry." His eyes grew wide as he caught her in the action of settling the thick traditional cloths over her shoulders. Amira wanted to laugh. It was surprising the two could be so modest when she'd seen Kale with his shirt off more often than not.

"It's fine. I'm just about ready." At the very least she was near ready to fake it. She had survived one council meeting before. Everflame willing, this one would be an improvement. "Are you certain we can't go with you?"

Amira was surprised at the genuine concern in Coral's expression. The Wave Mistress was usually so stoic. Perhaps she was sleep-deprived too. It had been a long night for all of them.

"No. Council rules strictly forbid it. No one but the Thirteen. Well, what's left of it anyway."

That's what the meeting was about, filling the empty holes in the council. That and the discussion of the Everflame's disappearance.

"But what if something happens? I don't trust those women, either of them." She cleared her throat. "I don't like it."

"I'll be fine," Amira said with more confidence than she felt. "In any case, the plan is to deflate the threat of war between our people, not strengthen it. If something were to happen and you strike out, trishula swinging and water magic . . . no. We need the council to see you as a diplomat, a powerful ally, not a dangerous threat." Amira narrowed her eyes, a thought coming to her. "You know, perhaps you could borrow a dress?"

"Absolutely not." Coral gave her head an emphatic shake. "I'll wait outside the council hall, and that's the most you're getting from me."

Amira bit back a quick smile. It was a wonder that she could find any joy in such a small moment. The thought gave her hope. She went to check her appearance but then remembered that she had destroyed her mirror, so she smoothed her hair as best she could and straightened her shoulders.

"I'm ready."

It was still unsettling that Amira was expected to call the meeting to order. Even more so that she still hadn't learned the names of the new members of the Thirteen. She studied their faces now, each listening to Justir with rapt attention.

Like she should be doing. She focused on Justir's words. It was hard because she could feel Denir's eyes on her. The Third's watchful gaze likely intended to remind Amira of her promise to step down once she revealed the alttaw'am for what he was. Amira swallowed as she clasped her hands together to prevent them from shaking. There was nothing to be nervous about.

She had purposefully selected the rare dress with pockets and the stone was secure, a slight pressure if not an actual weight against her thigh. She wished she could hold it, if only for a moment, but she didn't want to raise suspicions while Denir watched her.

"Now, shall we open the forum for current events? Amira?"

Amira jerked her back straight and met Justir's placid expression.

"Greatness?"

"As Second, it is your privilege to begin the forum." The First sneered from his raised dais.

Amira willed her toes to remain firmly in place. Any fidgeting now would display weakness. It was becoming increasingly difficult to ignore Denir's stare. She made a great show of looking instead at the remaining Thirteen. Most wore an expression of concern or unease, though Ishani appeared to be doodling on a piece of papyrus.

Amira took a deep breath before shaking her head. "No, Greatness. Perhaps someone else in the council wishes to speak."

Denir made a somewhat strangled sound in the back of her throat.

After a small stretch of silence, Geedar rose from his chair. The wooden legs scraped terribly against the stone floor and Amira winced from the sound.

"It's appalling to me we have yet to discover a solution for the Everflame."

"What about it?" Ishani met Amira's eyes with a slow wink before turning to stare down the length of the table at Geedar.

"Well, it's missing," Geedar said, his voice uneven. "The people . . . It—it's even worse outside the palace gates. All of Elek and Nutir are in uproar. And the people of Toik turn away to the Unburdened and—"

"And is there something wrong with my faith?" Ishani crossed her forearms and leaned over the table. "Or the faith of my uncle Cabochon Azaha?"

Amira shivered.

"No, of course not! It's just that the Everflame has gone missing, and we've still not even come up with a course of action!" Geedar looked around him, his eyes desperate to find purchase. "Tamir?"

The Seventh shook his head. "Sorry, Geedar, but what would you have us do? We cannot control the whims of a god, especially one who would so easily abandon its people."

"But the common people need faith. With the change of season, water is now more valuable than ever. We must focus on the future."

Ishani rolled her eyes at Denir's words. "The future of our water supply. Has the First given more thought to my nation's proposed alliance? A union between Jura and my uncle not only solidifies the strength of our countries' armies, it grants the Republic access to our oasis."

Denir snorted. "That puddle of water will be gone in less than a decade. Your country can barely sustain it now with the constant flow of new water wielders."

Amira's chest tightened at those words. Coral had warned her. Flames, Amira had witnessed it firsthand, but it still stung to hear.

Maybe she had once believed in a world with Torches and Wielders, but that world was gone, needed to be gone. Maybe it was a blessing the Everflame had abandoned them.

"The Third is right," Amira said. She frowned as she realized she took a step forward, drawing more attention to herself. She cleared her throat. "That is, we must find a long-term solution for water. A solution of our own."

"My dear girl, that's exactly what we've been saying." Ishani tilted her head and smoothed her expression into one of mock concern. "She's so young. Perhaps it's also time to analyze the reasons that led us to vote a child as Second of the Sand Sea?"

Amira clenched her jaw and pressed her lips into a thin line, determined to keep her tongue. She reached toward the stone, comforted by its smooth familiar surface. Amira reminded herself this situation was temporary; Kale and Coral were just outside the doors. But how could she remain calm when the world kept crashing around her? She hadn't realized how hard she squeezed the stone until her vision clouded and the voices swarmed in. This time, though, it was different. This time it was only one voice, over and over again.

Coral's.

Coral asking her father to show her the best place to stab a shark. Coral, as a child, laughing as she explained red was her favorite color. Coral begging for her parents to come back, for Jura not to stand in her way. And then, the most damning words of all: *My father was a good man, a good leader. He tried to help the Republic, offered to double our water shipments or send a team to try to create an oasis, like we did for Kitoi. Your father refused.*

Amira released the stone. She didn't want to believe it possible. Amira had never believed the First to be a doting or overly caring father, but she had never imagined him capable of anything so evil.

She turned to Justir. She wasn't thinking, couldn't have been thinking clearly, or she never would have gone through with the accusation.

"This is all your fault." She threw an accusing finger at the alttaw'am. "You could have changed the agreement with the sea king and assured the Republic access to fresh water. You kept it from us to remain in control!" Amira didn't care that the being before her wasn't the actual First. None of that mattered now. Nothing mattered, nothing but releasing the truth from the stone.

"We can't trust the First. He is a puppet of the Queen of Shadows. So is Ishani."

Amira turned toward the accusation, stunned by Denir's bold claim.

"I am no puppet!" the First yelled with such force that even Amira believed him, flinching from his harsh tone.

"Lies!" Denir pushed back from the table. "You are an alttaw'am, and the Thirteen will follow you no more."

Amira didn't know where the knife came from. Denir threw it so fast, it was simply a flash of silver in the air.

And then it was nothing but a silver hilt embedded in the First's chest.

AMIRA

Chapter Forty-Six

*S*he *screamed. Justir rose from* the chair, clawing at the dagger embedded in his chest. His strong brown hands, usually so capable, snapped and popped as bones cracked and joints shrank. His skin turned a muted gray as it stretched over unnaturally long arms.

His mouth yawned open, and he emitted a single inhuman screech before falling forward.

No one rushed forward to catch the First as he lay in his final death throes.

It's so dark, Amira thought, staring at the deep rust color of his blood pooling around him.

"There."

Amira jerked toward the sound. She hadn't realized Denir had come to stand beside her.

The Third pointed at the bloodied corpse on the ground. "Undeniable proof the First was not himself. He was an alttaw'am."

Pandemonium broke out as each of the remaining Thirteen clamored to be heard over one another.

"How is such a thing possible?"

"—madness is this?"

"Alttaw'am."

"He was an alttaw'am."

Amira stared at the corpse and willed herself to remember the creature in Justir's form, as he had appeared just moments before. He had looked exactly like him, when in truth this creature hid beneath the facade all along. This alttaw'am who drank the blood of others to hold their form. The same sort of monster who had attacked her and masqueraded around as her for months. Amira touched her shoulder, feeling the contact on her scarred flesh despite the layers of fabric. The Thirteen still buzzed around her, but they weren't saying words, not any that meant anything.

"Where is the First?"

"Missing for weeks."

"Move aside, child." Denir shoved past Amira and stepped onto the abandoned dais of the First. "Council members, please, be at ease. Ask your Arbe to stand down." Denir's voice echoed in the Justice Dome. "We have been attacked from within, a threat to our fine Republic, and we have been lied to by our leaders. But no more. The line of the First has been corrupted, and his house will rule no more."

The council members fell silent.

Coral grabbed her shoulder, helping Amira to her feet. She had been kneeling beside the corpse and hadn't even realized it. Hadn't even realized Coral, Kale, and most of the Arbe who had waited outside the Justice Dome were now inside.

"I will need to write to my uncle." Ishani cleared her throat. "I'm happy to continue the betrothal negotiations in his stead until Justir can be found."

Her words started an immediate reaction from the Thirteen, and they fell to muttering among each other.

"There's no need. He was found this morning by some of my men. Or rather, his body was found. Poor soul was nearly drained dry. It's how I knew of the impostor. It was only a matter of time before he would have been forced to claim a new victim."

Amira trembled at Denir's lie. Or perhaps now she was finally telling the truth? None of that mattered now. She had led Amira to believe she could save the First but she had failed. Now Jura was an orphan just as she was. Worse, she was an orphan without Rank.

Denir slanted a look over at Amira before continuing. As if she read Amira's thoughts plainly from her expression. "Justir the First of the Thirteen is dead, and his heir is not only a minor, she is missing. There will be no more talk of this betrothal until she is found. For now, I propose we focus on our present situation. It is a voting day. Let's vote. I nominate myself as First."

"Of course. You reject my uncle's proposal for your own gain. Surely the council sees beyond your plan." Ishani crossed the length of the room and stood next to the trio, pointing at Amira. "Second, what are your thoughts?"

Amira blinked. Her tongue suddenly felt too large for her mouth, and she was desperate for a glass of water.

"We must regain order in this council. The chaos of today is unprecedented. Perhaps we should pause and reconvene after everyone has had a moment to reflect," Geedar said.

"You mean until you get a chance to buy enough votes. You're as bad as former councilman Beshar," Nasir said, voice laced with venom.

Amira could not get air into her lungs fast enough. Was the First really dead? Jura's father dead? The Everflame was still missing, and the remaining Thirteen bickered over votes?

"Are you okay?" Coral asked, still at her side. What was she doing in here witnessing a vote? Arbe were forbidden after an incident with a mis-vote caused the massacre of over half of the Thirteen and dozens of men back in the days of her grandfather.

The entire thing was a mess.

Amira wanted to cover her ears. Instead, she plunged her hand into her pocket, desperate to feel the smooth comfort of the stone. She felt instant relief and relished in the moment, however fleeting it would be. She knew if she held the stone for too long, the voices would start again, and she didn't want that. Not yet anyway.

"Jura, I'm sorry. I'm so sorry. I made a mess of things, of everything. I tried to rescue your father, but now I've ruined everything. I don't deserve to be here right now."

Amira, you are stronger than you think.

Jura's tender words were everywhere, filling her mind, echoing in her ears, and filling her soul. She didn't know how it was possible, but she didn't dare release her hold on the stone, suspecting it was somehow connected.

"Jura? Is it really you?" Amira felt silly whispering the words to her pocket, but her friend had responded to her fervent prayer. She didn't know how, but she had. "Jura, if you can hear me, we need you here. I need you. I don't know what to do."

Use your strengths and reach out to your new alliances.

Amira's heart sang as the response filled her head. She looked around, but no one seemed to hear her.

There's a prophecy—

"I know of the prophecy. I have a stone. Is there—" She stopped short, unsure of what she wanted to ask. "Jura, what do I do?"

Amira wondered if she should tell her friend about her father, but to do so over such a strange connection felt wrong. Jura didn't need empty words and condolences; she needed a friend waiting for her in the Republic.

Amira, I'm on my way. The Mistress will bend the knee soon. Be ready.

Amira released the stone. For once, she knew exactly what she had to do.

CORAL

CHAPTER FORTY-SEVEN

Coral didn't care for how quickly the situation had escalated. She didn't care for how pale Amira was, or the fact that she trembled and her eyes held a vacant expression. Coral also didn't like the fact that so many armed men crowded the domed room, each looking more dangerous than the last. And Coral hated the fact that some misshapen man with gray skin lay dead on the floor, yet the Thirteen would rather argue over the number of votes each held.

Breathcatchers. They were a sodden mess.

Poor Amira seemed to be taking the commotion especially bad. She had taken to mumbling a fervent prayer under her breath. It sounded like she prayed for Jura's forgiveness, though it was difficult to hear over the madness.

Was this poor dead man Jura's father? And was everyone just going to leave him in the center of the room?

She caught Kale's eye and wondered if his thoughts mirrored her own. She was about to ask him to help her move the body when Amira abruptly stepped away from Coral's side and came to stand beside Denir on the dais.

Coral cocked her head to the side as Amira clapped her hands once and called for silence. What had gotten into her?

"Denir's claim to First is her right proven through her tenure, her great longevity on this council. A solid choice."

"Thank you for the endorsement, my lady Second. Now if we could just—"

"I wasn't finished," Amira interrupted. "However sound the Third's claim may be, the fact remains that she is currently the Third, and therefore, her Rank is below mine."

"I don't understand," Denir said.

If she and Kale hadn't stood so closely, Coral might not have even heard the murmured words, but Amira's response rang clear and true.

"I think you do. As Second, it is my right to claim First as my own. I also nominate myself as First."

"But you can't! The First is meant to be mine. I won't have it." Denir's tone had taken on a tense edge, and Coral shifted positions to accommodate the potential threat.

"It isn't up to you. It's up to the members of the voting council, and as Second, I hold three votes." Amira smiled brilliantly, the expression changing her face. She was glorious.

"Votes are irrelevant. You are a child, and we are at war. What do you know of feeding an army? Or preparing an entire Republic for a siege?"

Coral heard a few of the Thirteen mumble in agreement.

"There doesn't have to be a war." Amira pointed at the corpse. "We have no way of knowing how long the alttaw'am has posed as our leader. I speak truthfully when I tell you the sea people do not wish a war against us—they merely wish for justice against misdoings brought to their people. Likely not even from citizens of the Republic." Amira said that last part with an emphatic look in Ishani's direction.

"Y-you can't know that," Ishani sputtered. "Kitoi has sent me here in good faith, and I have represented both of our countries fairly. I hope only to strengthen a union between our nations. Through the bonds of a marriage—"

"Sandstorms, give up on the flaming betrothal, Ishani," a man in brightly colored cloth snapped. "We're worried about water, and my vote goes to whoever can promise the Republic doesn't die of thirst."

"I have a plan," Amira began, but she was cut off by Denir, and seconds later they were all screaming over one another.

Fish guts. Someone needed to deescalate the situation before more blood was spilled. Why was it always about power? Greed? If Mano hadn't coveted her father's position, her people would never have been massacred. The Queen of Shadows wanted control of the entire Sand Sea, and her people were ripped from their homes and enslaved to Kitoi, and still, the Thirteen argued.

Over water. Always it came down to water.

Coral reached to the tiny current of water twisting around her neck. Her connection to the Mother was constant, her *wei* beating fiercely in time with her heart, in time with the waves of the ocean, of the very breath of the Mother herself.

Coral dropped down to her knees and thrust her hands into the stone, keening with the effort.

It parted like water.

A deep rumble shook the earth, and the heated argument of the Thirteen dissolved into chaotic screams as people scrambled to find stable footing on a stone floor that opened beneath them. A fissure widened to the size of a small boat, and panic created a new madness, but Coral didn't move as the crevasse opened in front of her.

The ground finally stopped shaking and Coral remained kneeling beside it, panting heavily. Kale dropped down beside her.

"What did you do?" he asked. But she knew he could feel the answer.

Water gushed out from the fissure, slow and brown from the minerals at first, but it kept coming, more and more of the precious liquid, until the water began to pool at their feet.

"It's fresh. It's pure water."

"It's real. Real water. A fortune of it."

Coral took a deep breath, trembling from the incredible effort of what she had done. She struggled to climb to her feet, but her legs refused to work, as useless as a lifeless jellyfish, so she made do by dragging one foot to the ground and resting either elbow on her raised knee.

"Amira might be young, but so am I. But I am still the leader of my people. I'm Coralynn Cur'en, Grand Wave Mistress and Commander of the Three Oceans, and I pledge allegiance to the Republic of the Sand Sea under the leader of Amira the First. Deny Amira her claim, by not only her birthright but by *my might*, and I will see to it that the wrath of all three oceans is upon you."

JURA

Chapter Forty-Seven

J*ura supposed the alarms should* have been a larger indication that she'd done something wrong. Now she was back in her room, secure behind her wind-magicked door. She sighed. She needed to stop pacing. At this rate, she'd wear a hole in her new shoes before she ever escaped, and she couldn't have that.

Besides, she needed to hurry and develop a plan. It was only a matter of time before they came back with more questions.

She had refused to say anything earlier, despite Markhim's reasoning and much to Danos's grave disappointment. Jura took small pleasure in the fact that while they knew she had the famed book, they couldn't prove she hadn't stashed it somewhere. Most likely, they thought the book missing and in the hands of Pri. Markhim had alluded to as much before they locked her back in her room. She hadn't given Markhim much attention and she certainly hadn't wanted to hear his excuses.

His betrayal still stung, and Jura forced thoughts of him aside. She had to focus on her present situation. She had to figure out how she and the book were going to get back to the Republic. She finally pulled the book from under her wrap and gave it a thorough inspection. It was still astonishing how unremarkable the book appeared. And yet Jura could feel the power radiating from it, calling to her own.

She ran her fingers along the length of the torn spine and sighed. How was she supposed to discover how to use the book when she couldn't even read what was inside?

She had never felt lonelier in her life than here, locked away in her room with only her books for company. Was Tylak still on his way to her? Was Amira safe? And what had become of Coral? If Pri were here, he could help her reach out to them, send a message directly to them through the winds. If only that were a trick she could do on her own . . . but then, wasn't it? Hadn't she accessed wind magic before through the book? Could she do it again?

Perhaps the book didn't hold answers for her friends' current predicaments, but it was capable of altering their future. She reached for her power and thought of her friends.

Tylak first. A distant pull followed with such an intense feeling of loss and torment, Jura nearly fell to her knees, gasping from the pain of it. He needed her. She increased her draw on her power, begging the winds to heed her call.

Jura! Not Tylak, but a voice just as familiar, just as dear.

Jura, I'm sorry. I'm so sorry. I made a mess of things, of everything. I tried to rescue your father, but now I've ruined everything. I don't deserve to be here right now.

Impossible. And yet, Jura would know that voice anywhere. The book grew hot in her grasp. "Amira, you are stronger than you think."

Why had she doubted it for so long? Why had she dared to believe the prophecy was anything less than its truth? She saw things clearly now. It was time to go back home.

Her chat with Amira brought clarity and peace. Jura chose to rest in the moments afterward, stretching out in her comfortable bed and appreciating what was sure to be one of her last few moments of untroubled sleep.

It was no wonder she didn't hear the knock at her door. Not at first anyway. The knock returned, just as soft but more persistent.

"Jura?"

She ran to the door, touching its intricate pattern.

"Pr—come in!" She didn't dare use his name, just in case the winds listened to them now. Her door began its musical whistle, and moments later, Pri scuttled inside.

"Markhim! Visiting at this hour? Why, my father would take your head!" Pri seemed to understand the purpose of her words as she waved him inside. She gave the hall a careful survey before she allowed the doors to close. If only they had glass halls, perhaps then she could feel a measure of safety.

"Do you still . . ." Pri trailed off, his feathered eyebrows wriggling in question.

Jura nodded, holding the book out for his inspection, but Pri backed away from it, shaking his head and thrusting his hands out before him.

Jura frowned but returned the book to its hiding place under her wrap.

"What can I do to help?" Pri asked.

"I need to leave. Please, I need to get off this—"

Pri nodded emphatically. "Shh, say nothing else." He waved at her door and it whistled open.

Jura held her breath, half expecting Markhim, Danos, or even

Matteus waiting in the hall for them, but it was blessedly empty.

Pri gestured for Jura to follow him, and he hurried into the hall, heading back in the direction of the Eerie. Jura was eager to leave the mountain and find her way to the Republic, but it occurred to her that once she left on such terms, she would not be welcome to return. This was her last chance to speak with the Dreamer. Her last chance at any new answers.

"Wait." She grabbed Pri's shoulder.

His eyes widened when he realized her intention. She pointed at the hall that led toward the Dreamer's atrium. Pri shook his head, eyes desperate. Jura ignored him and turned down the path that led to answers.

The Dreamer waited for them, their hands clasped neatly in their lap, wings slightly expanded and brushing against the stone floor.

"You have something that belongs to the aliferous," the Dreamer said by way of greeting.

Jura shook her head. It took everything in her not to reach for the book hidden in her wrap.

"Do not try to deny it. I have seen this path many times." The Dreamer sighed, their voice a sad ballad. "And now? What is it that you seek, Blood Maker?"

"Answers! It's all I've ever wanted."

"Ask your questions. But be warned, you do not have much time."

Jura's questions caught in her throat as the weight of the moment crushed her. What was she to ask? What would be most beneficial to know now in her limited time?

"Where is the other half of the book?"

The Dreamer's eyes darkened. New colors splattered across the bare skin of their arms and chest. One image after another, colors swirled in rapid succession. The Dreamer wailed.

"Its power too great. You've seen what it was capable of." The voice that came from the Dreamer was not their own.

"That was before. We can try again. This time we'll use the proper—" A second voice, this one a deep baritone.

"No. I won't do it. It should be destroyed."

"No!" a choir of voices shouted at once.

"What if it was broken into pieces. We can keep it safer that way. I'll take half back with me, and you can return to Shrivo with your piece. It will be safest . . ."

The other half of the book was in Shrivo, the coastal country that bordered Kitoi.

"Those voices, it was a memory, right? Of words previously spoken and captured by the wind? Can you tell me who said them?"

"Please, I can bear no more." The Dreamer shuddered.

"But who is—"

"They approach." The Dreamer blinked at her. "I'm sorry, but you've run out of time."

"No, please wait. Tell me what my sister plans to do with all the stones. Tell me who took the book to Shrivo!"

The Dreamer lifted their shoulder, feathers ruffling in the movement.

"I see all your paths." They smiled. "Give me your hand."

"Jura, wait."

Jura heard the clear warning in Pri's voice but she ignored him, thrusting her hand out toward the Dreamer. She was greeted by the voices, the invisible choir singing in raucous harmony. It was beautiful, and it was excruciating. Jura shuddered at the shared pain.

I can grant you one last boon. Information, knowledge of a skill that is open to you.

One of the voices rose from the others, a clear soprano note that gave Jura the chills. For one spectacular moment, the note was all she could hear.

It told her everything.

"Let them go." Danos grabbed Jura's shoulder and pulled her back, severing her connection with the Dreamer.

Little did he know, he was too late.

"I'm not letting you leave anywhere. We know Amira has the windstone. And the Mistress has just bent the knee. Stay here and see that the world is never made new in blood. Stay and see that you don't repeat the mistakes of your ancestors. *Stay.*" Danos drew out a dagger, waving its point at her chest.

Jura had never seen the aliferous wield a weapon, despite his soldier's physique, but she noticed the practiced way he held it. He would make good on his threat if he had to. He loved his child.

It was why he had built such resentment toward Jura, because the Dreamer had seen the various paths and known the choices Jura was likely to make.

The Dreamer had granted Jura one final boon. The connection between them, that final song, provided Jura with a new wealth of knowledge. It was heartbreaking in its simplicity because for all they had spoken of Jura's various paths, there was only one choice left for her to make.

"Speaker, please. The paths are clear. They've always been clear." The Dreamer's voice was gentle, their tone a soft lament.

"No!" Danos shouted. He stepped closer, pressing the dagger toward Jura. "No, I won't allow it. I'm not letting her leave. It doesn't have to be this way."

Danos thrust the dagger down into Jura's chest.

Jura caught the blade before Danos could shove it to the hilt but screamed as the hot, searing pain of the icy steel ignited her flesh.

Markhim tackled Danos to the ground, Pri jumping in to assist when Danos proved he didn't want to stay down. Jura yanked the dagger from her chest, staring at the thick blood oozing from the wound.

She reached for her power, commanding the blood within her to cease leaving her body. The wound began to stitch itself up. She wanted to hate Danos for what he had done, and part of her always would, but another part of her understood his pain.

"I'm sorry," she said to him and to the Dreamer. Jura held her hand out once again. "Are you ready?"

The Dreamer nodded. "I have lived with the voices for so long, I should think I will like a bit of quiet."

"What's happening?" Markhim demanded. "Jura, please just talk to me."

"The Dreamer knew this would happen. They all did." Jura took a deep breath, drawing more of her power, more than she had ever dared to tap before. "It really was the only path left for me to take," she murmured. Jura reached her bloodstained hands into the wrap, pulling out the book. If she was right, and Jura had no reason to believe the information from the Dreamer was wrong, then she was about to do something outrageous. Something she would probably regret. But it was the only way.

She opened the book to the first page and began to read the unfamiliar language, her tongue somehow knowing the proper way to form each of the words.

"Jura, what are you doing?" Pri asked. He was sitting on Danos's chest while the aliferous howled in anger.

Jura recited the last word on the first page and sliced her palm open so fresh blood dripped from the wound.

"I'm going home."

KAY

CHAPTER FORTY-EIGHT

ay woke up with pieces of dirt and rock stuck to her skin. She missed her pillow and her bed back home. Even her cot in the Republic had been better than this.

Sky watched her, and when she sat up, he sent a rush of images and sounds to her.

Her sleeping, rabbits sleeping in a nest, a large furry creature that resembled a bear but snored louder than Daddy and the moon, moving in the night sky.

I do not sound like that! she replied with a giggle, but she was a little worried. Sky seemed to think she had been sleeping for days. Had she truly been sleeping for so long?

Kay's belly interrupted with a loud growl, and she decided that it didn't matter if she'd been asleep for days. She was starving. It occurred to her that she was still far away from her rocky enclosure and that she would need to fly back home before she could check her fishing line and quench her thirst. She would have to either wait or beg Sky for some food. That didn't sound bad as even another burned rabbit sounded delicious at this point. But first, more than anything, she needed to use the bathroom.

Kay shushed Sky and ignored his worries so she could hide behind a tree to relieve herself.

"Kay." It was barely a whisper above the wind in the treetops.

"Everflame?" Kay cocked her head to the side, straining to hear.

"Kay. It's time."

Kay ran back to Sky, not caring that she made a terrible racket as she crashed through the jungle.

Sky waited for her, snorting out small bursts of smoke.

"I'm sorry, I had to go! But she's back. The Everflame, I think." Kay swallowed. "She's talking to me."

Sky sent her images of the arena and the scary woman from there, Denir. Another of a lizard in a trap. A dragon in chains.

"I don't think it's a trap. But I don't know. I'm scared too." She rubbed his nose.

"Hurry, Kay, go to Izel. Go, now. Save me."

Izel? The lady she'd found by the river? Kay frowned. Why would the Everflame want her to go there? Even if Kay did find her house, how was she supposed to help Kay and the flame? It didn't make sense.

"Go, Kay. You must go, now!"

"We gotta go." Kay gave Sky a meaningful look.

Sky didn't want to visit Izel. He pawed at the ground, digging tiny furrows in the dirt with his claws, and sent images of a mother lecturing a young boy.

"It's not safe to run wild in the streets, talking to strangers." The woman's voice was stern, but her expression was familiar, that of a loving mother who only worried for her child.

The memories, if that was truly what they were, had grown more frequent, more real lately. Sometimes, Kay felt like she was actually living in that moment. She gave Sky another reassuring pat on his snout. His forked tongue darted out, flicking at the air in perfect time to his impatient tail, which tapped the ground beside her.

"Even if she did make me sleep for a while, I have to try and help her. I have to try to do good in the world. It's what Mama would have wanted me to do," Kay told him.

Sky grunted, twin lines of smoke trailing up from his nostrils.

"Well, I'm gonna try anyway." She clambered on top of his neck before he had a chance to argue the point any further, and moments later they were taking flight and traveling toward Izel.

When Kay arrived at Izel's home, she could instantly feel something was wrong. Kay Breathed, searching for Izel's presence. She felt another fire, but this one was larger than Izel. Somehow Kay knew she faced an intruder.

"You need to stay here," Kay whispered to Sky. "No, stop," she continued, ignoring the worry he sent through their connection. "You have to stay here. I'm just going to take a quick look around."

Kay crept up to the house, determined to peek in the window and nothing more. The slatted wood door offered plenty of opportunity for Kay to spy through a crack if she was quick enough. Kay ducked close and looked through the narrow strips.

Izel was missing, and in her place was some sneaky man from the Republic. Kay recognized the cut of his dark clothing.

She stifled a gasp, determined not to make a sound that would give her away. Was this a rescue mission? Did this guy have Izel captured somewhere? Had he hurt her? Did he know anything about the Everflame? How were the two connected?

Kay Breathed.

She didn't know what she was going to do to him. She just knew she had to do something, anything to stop his plans. She wouldn't let him hurt Izel. And she wouldn't let him take her away. She wasn't the same girl who had allowed herself to get stolen away from her home. She would never be that girl again, and she was never going back.

TYLAK

CHAPTER FORTY-NINE

Tylak woke up alone despite the early hour. He had slept fitfully, in turns either shivering under his blankets or throwing them off in a sweat. Thin beams of morning light shone through the narrow planks of the tiny cottage.

The one-bedroom home was sparsely decorated with a large hearth oven and several dried herbs hanging from a beam on the ceiling. Aside from a table and three chairs, there were only a few stacks of books haphazardly placed in tiny piles around the room. Tylak had slept on the floor close to the hearth. The fire had been a roaring entity last night but now smoldered in tiny embers. Tylak frowned at it, wondering if he should feed it any timber, but the decision was taken from him when he realized there was nothing around.

He clambered to his feet with an unsteady groan, searching for the source of pain at his side. He still wasn't sure which ached more, his stab wound or his broken hand. He hobbled toward the hearth and whatever the delicious smell was, intent on breaking his fast.

Izel hadn't left a note, but if that smell was any indication, she would be back shortly; perhaps she'd gone to forage for more supplies. She had mentioned taking him to town once he was capable of travel. Tylak hoped to barter for more supplies and perhaps a guide who could lead him to the Edge.

A distant rumble caught his attention, and he cocked his head to the side, listening for the sound. What was that? It sounded like soldiers, dozens, maybe hundreds marching through the jungle. Tylak tensed, searching the room for weapons. He had a single dagger and waning strength, not enough to make a dent in an army this size. He needed to hide then. The cottage didn't offer much. He was too large to fit under the bed or in a cupboard, so he would have to rely on his invisibility. His body groaned at the thought. Flames, he hadn't had enough time to recover.

The grounds had grown eerily quiet until only the distant call of singing birds was heard. Had they veered so far from his course that they were now out of his range of hearing? It seemed unlikely that would happen so quickly, but he could think of no other reason for the sudden silence. Unless the army lay in wait just outside?

Tylak hobbled toward the door and dared to wedge it open the tiniest crack. He peeked through the narrow slats of wood but found nothing.

What had happened? With that much noise, such a large force of people couldn't have disappeared into thin air. Unless . . . the Queen of Shadows had mobilized the league, and they had come after Jura just as he had. His chest tightened at the thought. No. He shook his head. She couldn't have found her way here so quickly. Even accounting for the time spent in Friis, it was unlikely the Queen of Shadows had found her way there. Perhaps the Friisan army searched for vengeance? Or perhaps he'd been wrong, and Tylak heard a phantom army, the drums of war forever tattooed on his heart.

He shut the door and took a seat at the square table meant for dining. In a moment he would get back up and finally break his fast. In a moment he would be full, and for now he was safe. He reminded himself a few more times before he actually began to believe it.

Finally, Tylak pushed himself to his feet and reached for the simmering pot. The smell truly was intoxicating. A mix of herbs and vegetables bubbled in a sweet-smelling sauce that was slightly orange in color. Whatever it was, Tylak was about to enjoy it.

He finally found a small stack of firewood tucked in a corner and brought it to the hearth, feeding a few logs to the fire. It was odd, a fire unattached to the Everflame. For all the warmth it provided, it was a dim comparison to the magnitude of the missing flame.

Tylak hated that they still didn't know the source of its disappearance. Even worse was the lingering doubt that perhaps he had something to do with it. Was it truly gone forever?

The fire popped back in response, and Tylak grunted before shoving one final log on top.

Another noise sounded just outside the door. Maybe Izel waited outside, likely returning from her morning errand. But Tylak drew his dagger just in case, tensed and ready. Moments passed and no one entered, and Tylak scowled at the door. He truly was hearing things then.

He turned back to the hearth and was shocked to see the fire had gone out. It had been burning happily just moments ago. The logs were still hot to the touch, and yet, the fire was gone. Burn it all, how was he supposed to get the flaming thing going again without a Torch?

He heaved himself to his feet and nearly dropped his dagger when the door opened to reveal a young girl. She was wild in appearance, her clothing in tatters and covered in dirt or ash or both. She was a tiny thing. Tylak wasn't good with ages, but he would guess maybe five or six years, certainly not the age to be left in the jungle unattended and in such a state. Her eyes, already impossibly large and as blue as his birthstone, widened as they met his.

Then she threw a fireball at him.

Tylak dropped to the floor, instinct turning him invisible as he did so.

"Where's Izel?" the girl asked. She spun around in a tight circle, eyes surveying everything. Fire snaked up her arms, the flames licking at her skin, but she did not burn.

Tylak blinked. If he didn't know better, he would say the girl was a Fire Dancer. And one who had just taken a defensive stance.

His last intention was to threaten a child. He shoved himself back up. He released his hold on the bent heat and light and put the dagger on the table. He held up his hands, despite the pain it brought to his side.

"She isn't here. Sh—"

"What did you do to her?" The girl threw a tiny ball of fire at his head.

He ducked, cursing before he made himself invisible once more. Burn it all, he didn't have the energy for this.

"I'm not going back to the Republic. You can't make me!" The flames surrounding the girl intensified, bellowing out with each of her heaving breaths. "Sky!"

The girl was in a frenzy, the flames growing stronger, and yet the fire didn't consume her. Tylak had no idea how such a thing was possible. Even Fire Dancers could get burned, couldn't they? He never should have underestimated this girl. Now he was weaponless, with this flaming child between him and his only escape. She was going to burn him and this entire cottage down, and there was nothing he could do about it.

"Stop it. I don't want to take you to the Republic. I don't even know who you are!"

The girl turned on her heel and flipped sideways toward his voice. The movement was as fluid as any Fire Dancer's, better than the great Ash himself. Then she threw another fireball.

None of this made sense. Tylak would have spent another few moments trying to puzzle her out, but he was too busy concentrating on holding his invisibility. It seemed to be the only thing keeping him alive.

She missed again, but the flame caught on the dining table, and it filled the room with dark smoke.

He had to get out of here. Tylak gave one final look toward his dagger, now encased in flames on the burning table, and made a run for the front door.

The girl gave chase, throwing another fireball. Tylak ducked, but the swift motion caused him to lose his footing and he tumbled forward, losing the last clutch of his invisibility as he did so. He was barely able to throw his hands out to catch himself, and he felt an intense burning pain on his side. Warm, fresh blood seeped from his wound.

He crawled as far as he could, rolling onto his back and praying to the Everflame for guidance. It wasn't supposed to end this way. He couldn't be brought down by a mere child. But this was unlike any child he had ever seen.

The earth shook beneath him, as though there were a tiny explosion in the distance. And then, once more, the sound of hundreds of people marching through the jungle. The army was back, and they'd heard them. Tylak struggled to sit up, clutching at his side.

The girl approached him. She still held the same wild look in her wide-set eyes.

"I'm not going back." She stomped her tiny foot, seemingly on the verge of a tantrum, but Tylak had never seen a child with outbursts that involved fireballs.

"Please." Tylak held up a hand, trying one last time to reason with her. "I meant no harm. But the army is approaching, and neither of us should be here when it arrives."

"Army?" The girl paused, the flames around her weakening slightly, although, her skin still glowed with a brightness that would rival the sun.

"Yes, the soldiers approaching. Can't you hear them marching?" He had another dagger in his boot. A tiny thing, more often used for skinning desert lizards than anything else, but if he could just reach it, then maybe he would stand a chance at survival. He just had to keep the tiny psychopath talking. "Yes, an army." He coughed. "Who are you? I only just met Izel. I have no intention of hurting her. Or you. Or any intention of taking you anywhere. Look at me." He gestured toward himself, at the dark stain growing on the tunic Izel had lent him. "But that army is coming. And you—" He broke into another fit of coughing. "You burned down her home."

The girl's cheeks grew red, and she turned back to survey the damage she'd done to the house. Tylak used the opportunity to fish in his boot and pull out the dagger. He nearly dropped it in surprise when the girl sucked up the fire.

There was no other way to describe it. One moment the inside of the cottage smoldered, and the next the fire was gone, the only evidence the charred wood and gasping child.

A small smile played on her lips as she turned back toward him, one that she lost once she noticed the dagger in his hand.

"You're a liar! You were just trying to trick me!" The girl began to glow brighter as flames once more licked down the length of her arms.

"No." Tylak tried to scramble to his feet, to pull his invisibility, but he was exhausted and could barely move. "No, I just—"

"You're a bad man. A bad man! You're like Udo and the red-robes, and I'm not going to let you trick anyone anymore. Never again." The flames around her grew, glowing brighter and brighter until Tylak had to look away from the sight. "Sky, I need you!"

He thought of his mother and his brother, Sykk. He thought of Jura.

The sound was deafening. A roar that shook trees and sent tremors in the ground. A roar that rattled his bones.

The soldiers rushed forward in their charge. No, not soldiers, but a single blue dragon barreling toward them. Tylak's jaw went slack, and he had the fleeting thought that he had never seen a dragon so close before.

The creature bugled out another roar, and Tylak glimpsed its ferocious maw. Teeth the length of swords and twice as sharp. He was terrified, and when he met the gaze of the small girl, her eyes were triumphant.

This was no child fearful of dragons. This was the great goddess of the dragons themselves, and they had come to see to his end.

So be it.

The dragon came to a stop before him, tilted its magnificent snout down, and touched it to his forehead. Then the creature turned back toward the girl and once again roared.

The girl's flames sputtered out.

"What?" Her face paled, and she turned disbelieving eyes to him. "Tylak?" she asked.

He felt his blood run cold. How did she know his name? Was she truly the goddess of death? Was this how he would meet his end?

"Tylak, he says he's your brother."

KAY

CHAPTER FIFTY

Sky jumped in front of her, blocking the path of her Breath and shoving dozens of memories at her as he did so.

Two boys, one about her age and the other on the verge of becoming a man, holding one another as a woman said goodbye. One boy's hand reached for another, helping him up, feeding him bread, poking his arm.

I don't understand, Kay thought.

Another rush of images. Two boys playing in the desert sand. Two boys listening to their mother tell them stories. The arena. So much darkness at the arena. Stones and red-robes chanting.

A man, this man, though he was years younger and his face was missing that terrifying scar . . . this man, crying and reaching out for a boy, Sykk, screaming for his brother.

"What?" she said, looking at the man.

Tylak.

The name wasn't spoken, not exactly, but Kay was sure of it all the same. "Tylak?" She didn't know how it was possible, but somehow, this man was Sky's brother.

Sky's eyes were wild and full of fear. Through the link she could feel Sky's confusion. She could tell he was excited—so happy, as happy as she would be if she could see Mama and hear Daddy's laugh again.

But beneath all the joy was a great and terrible sadness. And shame. Sky was worried he wouldn't accept him.

"Don't worry," Kay whispered. She was so quiet, it was unlikely Sky could hear her, but she knew he felt the rush of love she sent toward him through their bond.

If Sky believed this man was his brother, then Kay believed it too. She didn't know how that could be possible or what that meant for them, but she knew they would figure it out.

"Yes." The Everflame roiled in response.

Kay smiled. Yes. They would figure it out, the three of them, together.

"Tylak, he says he's your brother."

Sky's brother looked at the dragon. His face paled as he stared at Sky's body, his eyes roving over the sharp talons and the length of his curled tail.

"Sykk?" he asked.

"He goes by Sky now."

Tylak's eyes rolled up and disappeared. Then he fell back against the grass.

Kay blinked at the unconscious man. "I guess he needed a nap."

JURA

Chapter Fifty-One

anos let out a final keening wail as Jura plunged the dagger into the Dreamer's heart.

"Thank you." The Dreamer grasped Jura's shoulder with either arm, staring deep into her eyes as the blade sank into their flesh.

The Dreamer disappeared, exploding in a mess of feathers and colored dust. Suddenly the atrium filled with sound, the terrible cacophony of a familiar choir.

"The winds, the winds will destroy us if left untamed!" Pri shouted at her.

Markhim stared at her with a haunted expression. He still held back Danos, although the fight had left the man and he sat on the floor, sobbing over hunched shoulders.

"Then tame them!" Jura shouted back. "You can do this, Pri. The Dreamer believed you would walk this path."

Pri blinked at her, the realization slowly spreading across his face. He looked at her, questioning.

"Do you want this?" Jura asked softly.

Pri nodded. She gave his shoulder a gentle squeeze, releasing some of her magic as she did so.

The roaring winds ceased. Pri looked up at her, his expression one of pure wonder. "The choir, I hear them." A myriad of colors exploded against his skin.

Jura smiled.

She tucked the book back into her wrap, frowning down at her hands. They were still a mess. She willed the blood to disappear, and it faded as though it had never been.

Danos clambered to his feet. "What have you done? I would have given you anything. You could have been happy here."

"No." Jura shook her head. "I know the truth now. You are a long-lived race, yes, but that should not be the case for your Dreamer. The Dreamer walks the path of Dreams, and to do so daily means they must battle against the forces of the winds. For over a century, the Dreamer had pleaded with you to release them from the burdens of this world, knowing that only you, the Speaker, had the power to release them from their bond. They knew my arrival would grant them the means for their freedom. They knew, just as you did. This was the path they chose.

"I could never be happy here, not truly." She turned to Markhim. "You should have never plotted against me. I thought we were friends."

"Jura, I only did it because I love you. We can be happy together. We—"

"I'm sorry, Markhim. Maybe, once upon a time, I could have done what you wanted. But I'm not that girl anymore. The Republic needs me. This world grows more dangerous every day, my sister grows more powerful, but the prophecy says that I am meant to stop her. I don't want to leave you behind, Markhim, but I will."

She walked to the atrium ledge, staring out at the range of mountains, at the ground so far below.

"You're not ready to face your sister. She's been training with her magic years longer than you."

Jura smiled. "You're wrong. I am the Blood Maker, and I am so much more capable than you believe me to be."

Jura reached into her reserve of power, remembering the last words of wisdom she'd received from the Dreamer.

Sing with your diaphragm.

Jura opened her mouth and sang out a single soprano note. The sound was all-encompassing, its clear, crisp tone echoing throughout the small atrium. It was all she could hear. The note filled her up and touched her soul, feeding upon her magic until it posed an inaudible question:

Where would you like me to take you?

Home, Jura commanded the wind and stepped off the ledge.

END OF BOOK THREE

BESHAR

EPILOGUE

The lizard had chosen to hitch a ride. Intelligent move for a creature with such a small brain, Beshar thought.

The desert sands were unbearably hot any time of the year but seemed all the more so now. Perhaps that had something to do with the fact that Beshar now rationed drinking water, something he hadn't had to do in nearly thirty years.

Likely the lizard was only looking for a way to cool off. Beshar couldn't blame him for that. The lizard was the only wildlife he'd seen for the last two days. On second thought, the lizard had better remain in his hiding place before Kenjiro or one of the other men chose to make him their dinner.

Beshar's stomach growled at the thought. Flames, but it had been weeks since he'd last enjoyed a meal. So distant was the memory that Beshar doubted he could even remember what he'd had. Roasted doover bird on a bed of root vegetables with olive oil. His mouth watered at the thought.

He was starting to question his decision to grant the lizard sanctuary when Kenjiro called their small party to a stop.

Beshar reined in his Bactrian awkwardly, still an incompetent rider despite the near month he'd spent bonding with the big dumb beast. The camel grunted its displeasure at the sudden stop.

Beshar had to agree with his Bactrian. They had stopped in the middle of nowhere, nothing visible but rolling dunes of sand. A terrible place to make camp, in his opinion, not that anyone ever bothered to ask his opinion these days.

"What is it? Why are we stopping?" Beshar asked as he climbed down. His legs dangled, desperate to find purchase in the soft sand. Even lowered to its knees, the giant camel was still nearly eight feet tall.

Beshar landed, flinching as his ankle turned. Awkward landing.

"We are here." Kenjiro frowned, noticing Beshar's limp. "Please, stop. Are you injured?" There was no denying the flash of concern in his dark eyes.

"Fine, just a turned ankle. Where are we?"

Kenjiro peered down at his ankle, but he seemed satisfied when he didn't notice any instant swelling. "We have made it to my ancestral home."

Beshar blinked at the empty desert, and Kenjiro grinned in response.

"Watch. You will see." He waved to the rest of his men, and they fell in formation behind him. Kenjiro pressed his palms together and held them over his chest, muttering in his language. Soon, all the men had taken up the chant.

Over and over again the words crashed over one another in a tapping staccato beat. Beshar thought they had taken to stomping the ground as well but then realized they remained immobile save for their chanting.

No, the rumbling came from the ground itself.

Ahead, the dunes began to vibrate, sporadic grains of sand flying up like overcooked corn. Soon the dunes were roiling waves, and the sand was everywhere. It took Beshar a moment to realize that the larger pieces of sand weren't sand or even dirt but some sort of structure rising out of the ground.

The earth trembled violently, and Beshar fell to his knees before he had more than a wounded ankle to worry about. He had no idea what sort of earthen magic was at work, but he didn't dare turn his eyes away.

The chanting continued, louder than should be possible coming from just five men, and the desert roared in response. Another piece of the building ripped itself from the clutches of the earth.

When the dust settled, Beshar could only blink in wonder at what he saw.

ACKNOWLEDGMENTS

The first person I have to say thank you to is my beloved partner, Robert. He is the absolute best hubby a girl could ask for and has always been so supportive of me following my passion. Next, I have to say thanks to my sister and alpha reader, Courtney Landers. Yes, I'll get you the hat! Thanks for the many hours of dissecting plot holes and fun times with accents. Heather, thank-you for keeping it honest! To my parents for always showing they care (my dad has cosplayed Ash, y'all) and the endless support from the rest of my family, thank-you!

Next, a huge huge thank-you to the team at Kingsman Editing. Cayce, you are an amazing CP, a better editor and I'm fortunate enough to also call you my friend. Thanks for all your incredible work on bringing Windswept to its conclusion, it wouldn't be where it is without you! (Bloodstained coming soon??) Crystal, my love! Thanks for all the pretties and for keeping up with my insane deadlines.

To my writing group, The Creative Collaboration, you CPs are amazing and I am humbled by the acceptance, joy, and education I've received from this group. Dyan, Stacy and Steph I would be lost without you!

More big thanks to authors Melody Greene and Cari Jehlik for always giving me a listening ear and a launch pads for my crazy ideas (or for talking me down from insanity.)

Another huge thank-you to the online communities I feel blessed to be a part of: The Author's Tale Writing Community and Fantasy Romance Writers on Facebook as well as the incredible Indie authors and supportive readers on Booktok. Thank you, everyone!!

Lastly, but perhaps most importantly, thank you to all my readers, old and new. There are so many wonderful stories in the world, all begging to be told and I'm so honored you chose to take a chance on this one. Thank you all for allowing me to pursue my dreams and chase my passion in this world.

Thank you!!

XOXO
A. M. Deese
aka Lexi

About the Author

Alexis Marrero Deese is an avid reader of young adult and fantasy. Her favorite authors include Brandon Sanderson and Jaqueline Carey. She graduated from the University of South Florida with a Bachelor's Degree in Creative Writing and a sun tan she misses dearly since her move to north Georgia. She has a passion for cooking, spends entirely too much time on Pinterest, and is a self-proclaimed dog training expert for her family's legion of dogs. For more information, visit www.amdeese.com or follow her on Instagram at Instagram.com/authoramdeese.

The World of Jangbahar

●

The Thirteen

Recent events (including the tragedy at the arena) has left the Thirteen in shambles. There are currently only eight members until council members can be voted in replacement.

Justir

Amira

Denir

Geedar

Kader

Nasir

Tamir

Ishani

WINDSWEPT

DANCE OF THE ELEMENTS
BOOK III

Learn more about A.M. Deese
and explore her other titles at
www.amdeese.com

www.ingramcontent.com/pod-product-compliance
Lightning Source LLC
Chambersburg PA
CBHW030705190726
48286CB00001B/180